Have Mercy on Us All

ALSO BY FRED VARGAS
FROM CLIPPER LARGE PRINT

Seeking Whom He May Devour

Have Mercy on Us All

Fred Vargas

Translated from the French by David Bellos

W F HOWES LTD

This large print edition published in 2006 by
W F Howes Ltd
Unit 4, Rearsby Business Park, Gaddesby Lane,
Rearsby, Leicester LE7 4YH

1 3 5 7 9 10 8 6 4 2

First published in the United Kingdom in 2003
by The Harvill Press

A CIP catalogue record for this book is available
from the British Library

ISBN 1 84632 446 7

Typeset by Palimpsest Book Production Limited,
Polmont, Stirlingshire
Printed and bound in Great Britain
by Antony Rowe Ltd, Chippenham, Wilts.

Fred Vargas – an academic archaeologist by another name – wrote this novel in the course of the year 2000, when French francs were still legal tender and no-one had dreamed that a deadly disease might be mailed to its victims through the US post. *Have Mercy on Us All* was first published in French in mid-October 2001.

FRANCE

THE CHANNEL

NORMANDY

CHAMPAGNE

PARIS

Troyes

Brest
Quimper
BRITTANY
Vannes

⊙ Romorantin

⊙ Châtellerault

ATLANTIC
OCEAN

⊙ Clermont-Ferrand

⊙ Périgueux

⊙ Bordeaux

PROVENCE
Marseille

THE PYRENEES

MEDITERRANEAN

0   200   Kms

XIVth

PARIS

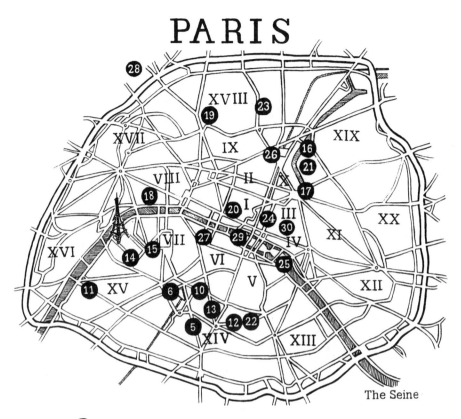

CHAPTER 1

When manie woormes breede of putrefaction of the earth: toade stooles and rotten herbes abound: The fruites and beastes of the earth are unsavoury: The wine becomes muddie: manie birds and beastes flye from that place

CHAPTER 2

Joss's settled view was that folk walk faster in Paris than they do in le Guilvenec, the fishing village where he'd grown up. They would steam down Avenue du Maine every day at three knots. This Monday morning, though, Joss himself was doing almost three and a half, trying to make up the twenty minutes he'd lost because of that blasted coffee.

It hadn't surprised him one bit. Joss had always known that objects large and small have secret, vicious lives of their own. He could perhaps make an exception for pieces of fishing tackle that had never taken him on in the living memory of the Brittany fleet; but otherwise the world of things was manifestly focused on making man's life sheer misery. The merest slip of a hand can give a supposedly inanimate object enough freedom of movement to set off a chain of catastrophes which may peak at any point on the Murphy Scale, from 'Damn Nuisance' to 'Bloody Tragedy'. Corks provide a simple illustration of the basic pattern, viz. a wine cork dropped from the table never rolls back to nestle at the boot of whoever let it slip.

Oh no, its evil mind always elects to reside behind the stove, like a spider looking for inaccessible sanctuary. The errant cork thus plunges its hereditary hunter, Humankind, into a trial of strength. He has to move the stove and the gas connection out of the wall; he bends down to seize the miscreant bung and a pot falls off the hob and scalds his head. But this morning's case arose from a more complex concatenation. It had begun with the tiniest error in Joss's calculation of the trajectory required to shift a used coffee filter paper to the bin. It landed just off target; the flip-top lurched sideways then swung back and scattered wet ground coffee all around the kitchen floor. Thus do Things transform justified resentment of their human slavemasters into outright revolt; thus do they force men, women and children, in brief but acutely significant bursts, to squirm and scamper like dogs. Joss didn't trust inanimates, not one bit; but he didn't trust men either, nor did he trust the sea. The first could drive you crazy; the second could steal your soul; and the last could take your life.

Joss was an old and seasoned hand who knew when to yield, so he got down on all fours and cleaned up the coffee mess, grain by tiny grain. Since he did his penance without complaint, the thing-force receded behind its usual sandbank. The breakfast incident was quite negligible in itself, just a nuisance, but Joss wasn't fooled. It was a clear reminder that the war between men and things was far from over, and that men were not always the victors, far from it. A reminder of tragedies past, of ships unmasted, of trawlers smashed, and of his boat, the *Nor'easter*, that had started taking water at 0300 on August 23, in the Irish Sea, with eight crew on board. Yet Joss had always indulged his old trawler's most hysterical demands; man and boat had always treated each other with kindness and consideration far beyond the call of duty. Until that infernal storm when Joss had suddenly got angry and pounded the gunwale with his fist. The *Nor'easter*, which was already listing heavily to starboard, started shipping water at the stern. The engine flooded, and the boat drifted all night long, with the crew baling non-stop, until it came to a grinding halt on a reef at dawn, with two men lost overboard. Fourteen years had gone by since that sad day. Fourteen years since Joss had beaten a lesson into the shipowner's thick skull. Fourteen years since he'd left Le Guilvenec after doing nine months for GBH and attempted manslaughter. Fourteen years since almost his entire life had gone down that unplugged hole in the hull.

Joss gritted his teeth as he made good speed along Rue de la Gaîté, choking back the anger that surged up inside him every time the *Nor'easter*, Lost at Sea, breasted a wave of his thoughts. But it wasn't really the *Nor'easter* he was angry with. That good old ship had only reacted to the punch he had given it by shifting its aged and rotting timbers. He was sure the ship hadn't realised what

4

the consequences of her brief rebellion would be, because she had had no idea just how old and run-down she really was, nor had she grasped how heavy the sea was that night. The trawler certainly hadn't meant to kill the two sailors; she was surely full of remorse as she lay like an idiot at the bottom of the Irish Sea. Joss often talked to her, mumbling words of comfort and forgiveness. He reckoned the old girl must have found peace by now and made a new life for herself at full fathom five, just as he had up here, in Paris.

Making peace with the owner, on the other hand, was out of the question.

'Come off it, Cap'n Le Guern,' he used to say with a hearty clap on Joss's shoulder, 'you can keep the old girl going for another ten years, no doubt about it. She's a sturdy ship and you're her master.'

'The *Nor'easter*'s no longer safe,' Joss kept on telling him. 'The hull's out of true and the boards are warping. The flooring of the hold has worked loose. I'll not answer for what she might do in a gale. And the lifeboats wouldn't pass inspection.'

'I know my ships, Cap'n,' rasped the owner. 'If you're afraid of the *Nor'easter*, that's fine by me. I've got ten others who'd take your cap at a moment's notice. Men made of sterner stuff who don't grouse about safety regulations like those wimps at the inspectorate.'

'I've got seven lads on board.'

The owner brought his fleshy, glowering face right close up to Joss's.

5

'If you so much as whisper what's on your mind to the harbour master, Joss Le Guern, you'll be out on your ear as fast as you can say sea shells. Right round the coast, from Brest to Saint-Nazaire, it'll be "Sorry, nothing doing". So if you want my advice – think again.'

Yes, Joss was really sorry he hadn't done him in right and proper the day after the shipwreck, instead of only breaking one of his legs and fracturing his sternum. But his crewmen – it took four of them – pulled Joss off his prey. Don't ruin your own life, Joss, they said. They blocked him and then held him down. Later, they stopped him slaughtering the owner and all his henchmen, who'd blacklisted him when he came out of prison. Joss bawled the fact that the port authority fat cats were on the owners' payrolls in so many bars that he made being taken back into the merchant navy simply impossible. Blackballed in one port after another, Joss jumped on the Paris express one Tuesday morning and landed – like so many Bretons before him – on the forecourt of Gare Montparnasse, leaving behind a wife who'd already taken her leave, and nine men to slay.

As the Edgar-Quinet crossing hove into view, Joss stuffed his ancient hard feelings into a mental back pocket, and clapped on full steam. He was running late, as the business with the coffee slops and the wars of the things had wasted at least fifteen minutes. Punctuality was a key part of his work, and it mattered very much that the first

6

edition of his newscast should take place every day at 0830 sharp, with the second edition on the dot of 1235 and the late final at 1810. That's when the street was at its busiest, and in this town people were in too much of a hurry to put up with the slightest delay.

Joss took the urn down from the tree where he strung it up overnight with a double bowline and two bike locks to secure it. This morning there wasn't a lot inside, so it wouldn't take too long to sort. He smiled to himself as he took the urn into the back room that Damascus let him use in his shop. There were still a few decent fellows left, he thought, people like Damascus who would let you have a key and a bit of table space, without worrying about you running off with the till. Talk about a stupid name, though! Damascus was the manager of Rolaride, the skate shop on the square, and he let Joss use the place to prepare his newscasts out of the rain. Rolaride – that's another ludicrous moniker, if you ask me.

Joss took the padlocks off the urn. It was a big wooden lap-jointed box that he'd made with his own fair hand, and dubbed *Nor'easter II* in memory of his dearly departed. A great fishing vessel of the deep-sea fleet might not have thought it an honour to have her name perpetuated by a modest letter box, but *Nor'easter II* was no ordinary mail drop. It was a very clever seven-year-old indeed, born of a brilliant idea that had allowed Joss to pull himself up the ladder again after two years' unemployment, six months spinning cables and three years in a cannery. It was on a gloomy December night in a Paris café that Joss had been struck by sheer genius. The place was full of nostalgic Breton exiles droning on about their families and home ports, about when the fishing was good and the onions too. Some boozed-up old sailor mentioned the village of Pont l'Abbé, and all of a sudden Joss's great-great-grandfather, born at Locmaria in 1832, sprang out of his head, propped himself up at the bar, and said good evening.

'Good evening to you,' said Joss, tightening his grip on his glass.

'You do remember me, don't you?'

'Sort of . . .' Joss mumbled. 'You died before I was born. I didn't shed no tears.'

'C'mon, Joss Le Guern, I don't drop in very often, so cut out the insults for once. How far have you got?'

'Fifty.'

'You've taken it hard. You look older.'

'You can keep your views to yourself, thanks very much. I didn't ask you to drop in. Anyway, you were no oil painting yourself.'

'Watch your tongue, young man. You know what happens when I get excited.'

'Sure I do, like everyone else. Specially your wife, who got thrashed all her life long.'

'Sure, sure,' the forefather scowled. 'But you have to put that in context. In its appropriate cultural-historical circs.'

'Circs my arse. You liked bashing her up, that's all there is to it. And you blinded her in one eye.'

'Belt up, will you? Or are we going to go on about that eye for another two hundred years?'

'Sure we are. It's symbolic.'

'Joss Le Guern wants to teach his great-great-grandfather a lesson, does he? The same Joss who nearly kicked the guts out of a man on the dock at Le Guilvenec? Or have I got the wrong address?'

'He wasn't a woman, in the first place, and in the second place he was hardly a man. He was a bloodsucking money-grubber who didn't give a fart if men died as long as he made a pile.'

'Yeah, I know. I can't really fault you on that one. But that's not all of it, lad. Why did you call me down?'

'I told you, I didn't.'

'You're an obstinate bastard. You're lucky you've got my eyes otherwise I would have given you a black'un. Can you get it into your head that if I'm here it's because you rang, and that's that. Anyway I'm not a regular in this bar, I don't like piped music.'

'OK,' Joss conceded. 'Can I get you a drink?'

'If you can still raise your arm. Because I'll be so bold as to tell you you've had one too many already.'

'That's none of your business, old man.'

The forebear shrugged. He'd seen a lot in his time and he wasn't going to rise to this tiddler's bait. This young Joss was a fine specimen of the tribe, no question about it.

'So,' the oldster said after he'd downed his pint, 'no woman and no dough?'

'You've put your finger on it first go,' Joss answered. 'You weren't so canny in your own time, I've heard tell.'

'Comes from being a ghost. When you're dead you know things you never knew before.'

'Are you kidding?' said Joss as he made a feeble gesture towards the barman.

'As far as women are concerned, there was no point calling me down, it's not my strong suit.'

'Could have guessed that.'

'But work isn't a hard nut to crack. Just follow in your family footsteps. You weren't right in cable-spinning, that was a big mistake. And you know, things aren't to be trusted. Ropes are OK, at a pinch, but as for cables, wires, let alone corks, well, it's best to give them a wide berth.'

'I know,' said Joss.

'You have to make do with your inheritance. Copy your family.'

'But I can't be a sailor no more.' Joss was getting ratty. 'I'm *persona non grata* in the whole bloody fleet.'

'Who said sailor? If fish were the only thing, God knows where we'd be. Was I a sailor, then?'

Joss drained his glass and pondered the point.

'No,' he said after a pause for thought. 'You were a crier. From Concarneau to Quimper, you were the itinerant town crier.'

'That's right, my boy, and I'm proud of it. *Ar*

Bannour was what I was, the "Crier". And the best on the whole south coast of Breizh. Every day that God gave, *Ar Bannour* strode into another village and on the stroke of half past noon he shouted out the news. And I can tell you, there was folk there who'd been waiting since dawn. I had thirty-seven villages on my round – that was quite something, eh? That made a whole lot of folk, didn't it? Folk living in the world, thanks to what? Thanks to news! And thanks to whom? To me, my lad, to *Ar Bannour*, the best barker in Finisterre. My voice carried from the church steps to the wash house, and I knew all my words. Everyone raised their heads to listen. My voice brought the whole world to them, and believe you me, it was worth a lot more than fish.'

'Yeah, yeah,' said Joss as he took a swig straight out of the bottle on the bar.

'Ever heard of the Crimean War? I covered that one. I went to Nantes to get the news and brought it straight back in the saddle, fresh as the new tide. The Third Republic, heard of that? That was me again. I shouted it on all the foreshores, you should have seen the commotion. Not to mention all the local stuff – marriages, deaths, quarrels, lost and found, stray children, horses needing re-shoeing, I lugged it all around. From one village to the next people gave me news to cry. The love of a girl in Penmarch for a boy in Sainte-Marine, that's one I still remember. A hell of a scandal, that was. It ended in murder.'

11

'You could have been more discreet.'

'Hang on, lad. I was paid to read out the news. I was only doing my job. Not to read it out would have been robbing the customer. You know, Le Guerns may be rough customers but we never stole a penny. Fisherfolk's affairs and squabbles were none of my business – I had enough of that in my own family. I dropped in on the village once a month to see the kids, go to Mass, and bed the wife.'

Joss sighed into his mug.

'And to leave her some money,' the ancestor added, with emphasis. 'A wife and eight kids needs a lot of bread. But believe you me, *Ar Bannour* never left them short.'

'Of a thrashing?'

'Of money, you nitwit.'

'You earned as much as that?'

'Loads of money. News is the one line of goods that never runs short on this planet, it's the one tipple people never get too much of. When you're a crier, it's like you're giving the breast to the whole of humanity. You never run out of milk or of suckling babes. – Hey, lad, if you go on lifting your elbow like that, you'll never make a crier. It's a job that calls for a clear head.'

'I don't want to depress you, old forebear,' said Joss as he shook his head, 'but there aren't any criers any more. Nobody even knows what the word means these days. "Cobbler", well, just maybe, but 'crier', that's not even in the dictionary. I don't

12

know if you've kept up since you died, but down here things have moved on a bit. Who needs to have the news shouted down his lughole in the church square? Everyone's got the newspapers, radio and TV. You can log on at Loctudy and see who's having a piss in Pondicherry. That's the way it is.'

'You really think I'm an old idiot?'

'I'm telling you the way it is, that's all. My turn now.'

'You're losing it, my poor Joss. Pull yourself together. You've not understood much of what I've been telling you.'

Joss stared vacantly at the stately silhouette of his great-great-grandfather as he slid off his bar stool with considerable style. *Ar Bannour* had been a big man by the standards of his day. It's true Joss was quite like the brute.

'The Crier,' the forebear declared firmly as he brought the flat of his hand down on to the bar to underscore the point, 'is Life itself. Don't tell me that nobody knows what it means any more or that it's disappeared from the dictionary, or else the Le Guerns really have gone to wrack and ruin and no longer deserve to cry it out loud. Life!'

'What a pathetic old fool!' Joss mumbled as watched the old man depart. 'What a load of balls.'

He put his glass back down on the bar and bawled out after him: 'In any case, I did not call you down!'

'That'll do, now,' said the barman as he took

Joss by the arm. 'Go easy, friend, you're disturbing the customers as it is.'

'Bugger your bloody customers!' Joss yelled as he held tight on to the bar.

He later recalled that two guys much smaller than he was ejected him from the Mizzen and sent him rolling along the road for almost a hundred yards. He woke up nine hours later in a doorway at least ten metro stations away. Around noon he dragged himself back to his room, using both hands to hold up his splitting head, and went back to sleep until six the next evening. When he finally opened his sore eyes he stared at the filthy ceiling of his flat and said out loud, unrepentantly, 'What a load of balls!'

So seven years had now passed since Joss had taken up the outmoded calling of Town Crier. It had been a slow start. It took time to find the right tone of voice, to learn to project it, to find the best site, devise the headings, acquire a clientele, and set the rates. But he'd done it and there he was, *Ar Bannour*. He'd taken his urn to various spots within a radius of half a mile of Gare Montparnasse (he didn't like to stray too far from the main line to Brittany – just in case, as he said) and about two years ago he'd settled for a pitch on the square where Boulevard Edgar-Quinet crosses Rue Delambre. That location allowed him to tap the local residents who shopped at the market stalls as well as office workers and the well-camouflaged regulars of the local red-light streets; and he could also fish among the crowds pouring out of Gare Montparnasse on their way to work. Dense knots of people crowded round him to hear him bark the news. Maybe not as many as mobbed his great-great-grandfather Le Guern in his day, but against that you had to reckon that Joss gave three performances a day, seven days a week, on the same spot.

What he got a really large number of, though, were messages – on average, about three score were dropped in the urn each day. There were always more in the morning than the evening, as night-time seemed more conducive to people slipping things in without being seen. The routine was that messages had to be sealed in envelopes weighted down with a five-franc coin. Five francs wasn't an exorbitant amount for hearing your own thought, your own announcement or quest cast into the Paris air. In the early days Joss had tried rock-bottom pricing, but people didn't like to see their sentences valued as low as one franc. It cheapened what they had given. So the five-franc rate suited the crier and his customers equally well, and Joss grossed about nine thousand francs a month for his seven-day job.

Old *Ar Bannour* was right, there was never any shortage of material. Joss had to give the old man his due when he saw him again one drunken night at the Mizzen. 'They're packed full of things to say, people are, just like I told you,' the old man said, delighted to see his descendant getting the

15

business back on its feet. 'Packed as tight as horse-hair in a mattress. Packed to the edges with things to say and things not to say. You're doing them a good turn, and you clean up at the same time. You're their outlet pipe. But watch it, lad, it's not always a piece of cake. Flushing through pipework brings out the shit as well as the water. So keep an eye out for trouble. There's loads of muck in men's heads.'

Old *Ar Bannour* was right about that too. In his urn Joss found things he could say, and things he had better not. 'Things better left unsaid' was how the bookworm who ran a kind of lodging house next door to Rolaride put it. When he picked up his envelopes, Joss always began by sorting them into two piles, the 'can dos' and the 'better nots'. The 'can dos' were the sort of things usually dealt with naturally by human speech organs, in normal trickles or in howling waves, a process which prevents the build-up of words from reaching suffi-cient pressure to cause an explosion. Because people were not like mattresses, in the sense that they packed more and more words in every day, and that made evacuation an absolutely vital issue. A trivial portion of the 'can do' material came to the urn under the headings of 'For Sale,' 'Wanted,' 'Lonely Hearts,' 'Miscellaneous' and 'Technical'. Joss put a quota on that last category and also charged a one-franc premium because 'Technicals' were such buggers to read aloud.

What struck the crier most was the unforeseen

quantity of 'better nots'. They piled up because there was no other drain for getting this kind of verbal matter out. 'Better nots' were either way beyond acceptable bounds of violence or outspokenness, or else weren't within striking distance of the level of interest that would justify their existence. Whether they were over the top or short of the mark, these 'better nots' were thus condemned to a shadowy, silent and shameful life in the darker recesses of the mattress. All the same, as Joss had learned from his seven years on the job, those messages didn't just wither away. They built up into piles over the years, they clambered on top of each other, getting ever more sour at their mole-like existence as they angrily watched the infuriating comings and goings of authorised and thus more mobile messages. The thin six-inch slit in the crier's urn offered a breach to which these prisoners flew like a plague of grasshoppers. Not a morning passed without him finding a crop of 'better nots' at the bottom of his letter box – harangues, insults, expressions of despair, calumnies, denunciations, threats, ravings and rantings. Some of the 'better nots' were so feeble, so desperately mindless, that they were hard to read right through; some so convoluted that their meaning was all but lost; some so creepy as to make you drop the sheet of paper to the ground; and some so vindictive and so destructive that the crier got rid of them.

For Joss did not leave his news unfiltered.

Though he was a dutiful man aware of his

responsibility to save the mind's least wanted waste products from total oblivion, in pursuance of his ancestor's work of salvation, Joss assumed the right to exclude anything he could not utter with his own tongue. Unread messages could be taken back together with the five-franc fee, since the Le Guerns, as the forebear had emphasised, may be rough customers but they never stole a penny. So at every newscast Joss laid out the day's rejects on the orange box he used as a stand. There always were rejects. He never read messages promising to reduce women to pulp, or to send blacks or wogs or Chinks or queers to hell. Joss guessed intuitively that he could easily have been born female or black or queer, so he exercised censorship not out of moral principle but from an instinct for self-preservation.

Once a year, during the low tide of the mid-August holidays, Joss would put the urn in dry dock: he would sand it down, repaint it bright blue above the Plimsoll line and ultramarine below it, with *Nor'Easter II* in copperplate black lettering on the bow, *Timetables* on the port side, and *Rates, Conditions and Terms After the Fact* to starboard. He'd heard 'after the fact' many times during his arrest and trial, and had hung on to the formula as a souvenir. Joss felt that 'after the fact' gave a touch of class to his newscasting, even if the lodging-house scholar seemed to think there was something wrong with the word. He didn't quite know what to make of the scholar, actually. He was called Hervé Decambrais, was certainly an aristocrat – he had a very grand manner – but he was so broke that he had to sublet the four bedrooms on his first floor, sell off the table linen and take fees for giving perfectly useless counselling sessions. He camped in two ground-floor rooms mostly occupied by piles of books. Even if Hervé Decambrais had ingested millions of words from his books, Joss wasn't worried about his choking on them because the toff talked his head off all the time. He took words in and spewed them out all day long, sometimes with complicated parts which Joss did not always understand. Damascus didn't get all of it either, which was reassuring in a way; but then, Damascus wasn't a rocket scientist either.

As he emptied his urn on to the table in Rolaride and then began to sort the messages into 'can dos' and 'better nots,' Joss lighted upon a particularly wide envelope in thick, off-white paper. For the first time it occurred to him that maybe the bookworm was the source of these fancy envelopes he'd been getting for the last three weeks, weighted with no less than twenty francs apiece. They contained the most disagreeable messages he'd had to read in all his seven years as crier. As he opened this missive Joss could hear his forebear leaning over his shoulder and whispering, 'Keep an eye out for trouble, Joss my lad, there's lots of muck in people's heads.'

'Shut up,' Joss said out loud.

He unfolded the sheet of bond and softly read out the following message:

When manie woormes breede of putrefaction of the earth: toade stooles and rotten herbes abound: The fruites and beastes of the earth are unsavoury: The wine becomes muddie: manie birds and beastes flye from that place

Joss turned the page over for the rest of the sentence, but the verso was blank. He shook his head. He'd drained off plenty of weird language, but this really took the biscuit.

'A nutcase,' he mumbled. 'This one may be loaded, but he's a nutcase.'

He put the sheet aside and got on with opening the rest of the day's haul.

CHAPTER 3

Hervé Decambrais emerged from his front
door a few minutes before the start of
the eight-thirty news, leaned back on the
door post, and waited for the crier to turn up. His
relationship with the ex-sailor was fraught with
unspoken hostility. Decambrais couldn't work out
why or remember exactly since when, but he was
inclined to make it all the fault of that weather-
beaten, rock-hewn Breton, who was quite possibly
a violent man too. With his soapbox, his eccen-
tric urn and his newscasts spewing a ton of trivia
on to the public highway three times a day, Joss
had been a disturbance to Hervé's cunningly
ordered life these past two years. At the start he
hadn't worried about it very much, since it seemed
obvious that the fellow wouldn't last more than a
couple of weeks. But the newscasting business had
done surprisingly well; the fisherman had netted
a real audience, and had a full house, so to speak,
day after day. That was what made the whole thing
a real pest.

Decambrais wouldn't have missed the newscasts
for anything, but nothing would have made him

own up to being a fan. So when he took up his position every morning to listen to the news he kept a book in his hand, slowly turning the pages, his eyes down, though he never read a word. Joss Le Guern sometimes shot a glance at him in a pause between two headings. Decambrais really didn't like being looked at by those narrow blue eyes. It felt as if the crier was checking up on him being there, as if he imagined he'd hooked him and worn him down like some lousy fish. Because all the Breton had really done was to apply his brutal fishing skills to the city: he'd cast his net along the boulevard among the shoals of pedestrians and had trawled them in just like they were cod. It occurred to Decambrais that Joss probably couldn't tell men from mullet any more, seeing the way he treated both kinds of catch, that is to say, making his money by pulling out their guts.

But Decambrais was hooked, and he had enough insight into human nature to know it. The only thing that made him slightly different from any other outdoor newscast addict was the book in his hand. But wouldn't he be less of a rat if he were simply to put it away and to assume his new identity, three times a day, as a fish on a line? For he had to confess he had been caught. Despite his education he'd failed to swim against the tide of the street.

Joss Le Guern was a bit late that morning, which was very unusual. From the corner of his lidded

22

eye Decambrais saw him arrive in a great hurry to rehang *Nor'Easter II*, as the ex-sailor had pretentiously dubbed his gaudy blue-painted box, on the trunk of the plane tree in the square. Decambrais wondered if Joss was really all there. Maybe he'd given pet names to all his personal possessions – chairs, table, and so forth. He watched Joss flip his heavy stand upright with his brawny hands and set it up on the square as easily as he would have put a parrot on a perch, then spring on to it with a single leap as if he was hopping on board. He took the messages out from inside his pea-jacket. There were about thirty people waiting for him to start reading. One of them was the ever-faithful Lizbeth, standing as she always did with her hands on her hips.

Lizbeth lived in room 3 at Decambrais's place, and instead of paying rent she saw to the running of his unofficial hotel. She was a pillar of strength. Decambrais could not possibly have managed without her, and he lived in fear of the day when someone would steal his splendid Lizbeth from him. It had to happen, one way or another. She was tall, she was stout, she was black, and she stuck out a mile. Not someone you could hide away from the peering eyes of the world. Nor was Lizbeth afflicted by timidity – she had a voice that carried, and was inclined to state her mind on anything that crossed her path. The worst of it was that Lizbeth's smile – fortunately, it was not on display terribly often – made you want to throw yourself into her capacious arms, bury yourself in her expansive bosom and settle in for the rest of life. She was thirty-two, and one day, Decambrais knew, he would lose her. But right now Lizbeth was taking it out on the newscaster.

'What's been keeping you, Joss?' she asked, arching her back and jutting her chin towards him.

'I know I'm late, Lizbeth,' the crier admitted breathlessly. 'It was those coffee grounds.'

Lizbeth had been swept from the black ghetto of Detroit at the age of twelve and flung into a brothel as soon as she hit Paris, where she'd learned the language on the street – to wit, Rue de la Gaîté. Fourteen years of immersion, until she'd been moved on again because she'd grown overweight and could no longer plausibly appear in a peepshow. She'd been sleeping rough on a bench in the square for ten days when Decambrais decided to haul her in one cold and rainy night. One of the four upstairs rooms that he rented out in his old house was vacant. He offered it to her. Lizbeth said yes, and as soon as she got into the hall she took off her clothes and lay on the carpet with her hands behind her head, staring at the ceiling and waiting for the bookworm to get on with it.

'That's not what I meant at all,' Decambrais muttered as he handed her back her clothes.

'Can't pay no other way,' said Lizbeth as she sat up on her haunches.

'Look, I can't manage here on my own any more,'

24

Decambrais went on with his eyes riveted to the carpet. 'There's the cleaning to do, the lodgers' dinner to make, there's shopping, and all the bills to see to. Give me a hand, and you can have the room for free.'

Lizbeth smiled, and Decambrais nearly swooned into her arms. But he was an old wreck and he reckoned the woman could do with a break from all that. And she certainly had taken a break – she'd been in the house for six years now, and there'd never been the slightest sign of a lover. Lizbeth was recuperating, and Hervé prayed for her convalescence to last a while longer.

The newscast had begun and the small ads were flowing thick and fast. Decambrais realised he'd not been paying attention, as Joss was already on to ad number 5. That was how it worked: you had to memorise the number of the ad that caught your ear, and go to see the crier afterwards for 'further details after the fact'. Decambrais wondered where Joss had picked up that strange charge-sheet formula.

'Five!' barked Joss.

For sale, litter of white and ginger kittens, three male, two female. Six: Could the tam-tam players making jungle noises all night long opposite number 36 please desist. Some people have to get some sleep. Seven: All types of carpentry, especially furniture restoration, perfect finish, will collect and deliver. Eight:

The gas and electric company can go jump in a lake. Nine: Pest control is a complete scam. There are just as many cockroaches as before, and they take 600 francs off you for nothing. Ten: Helen, I love you. I'll be waiting for you tonight at the Chat-qui-danse. Signed: Bernard. Eleven: Another rotten summer, and now it's September already. Twelve: For attention of the butcher on the square. Yesterday's meat was old boot leather, that makes three times this week. Thirteen: Come back, Jean-Christophe. Fourteen: cops means perverts means pigs. Fifteen: For sale, garden apples and pears, tasty and juicy.

Decambrais glanced at Lizbeth, who jotted down number 15 on her pad. Since the crier had started his newscasting you could get all sorts of first-rate supplies for a song, with consequent benefits for his lodgers' *table d'hôte*. Hervé had slipped a blank sheet between the pages of his book, and waited with pencil in hand. For the last few weeks the crier had been barking very bizarre texts that didn't seem to raise the fisherman's eyebrows any more than small ads for cars or kittens. But the morning catch now regularly included these special messages – refined, sometimes crazy, and often sinister snippets. A couple of days ago Decambrais had decided to keep a private note of them. His two-inch pencil was completely hidden by his large hand.

Joss had got to the forecast break. He would raise his eyes to the sky and give his estimate of the coming turn of the weather on Avenue du Maine, and then forecast wind, sea and visibility for Channel, Falmouth, Finisterre and Irish Sea as if this was vital information for his land-lubbing listeners. But nobody, not even Lizbeth, had ever dared tell him what to do with his shipping news. People listened with religious awe, as if they were stranded on Rockall with a radio tuned in to the BBC.

'Dull September weather,' Joss clarified, with his face to the heavens.

No clear spells before 1500 GMT, brightening around sunset. You can go out this evening if you like, but take a woolly. Wind fresh, moderating to light. Now here is the shipping forecast. General situation: anticyclone 1030 millibars off south-west Ireland, cold front strengthening south of Cornwall. Biscay, Fitzroy, Sole, east-north-east, 5 strengthening to 6; Fastnet, Lundy, Irish Sea, 6 strengthening to 7. Sea moderate, turning heavy locally in west to north-west gales.

Decambrais knew that the shipping forecast would take some time. He turned over his note-sheet to reread the ads he'd jotted down over the past two days:

Up and walked with my little boy (whom because of my wife's making him idle, I dare not leave at home) . . . to excuse my not being at home at dinner to Mrs T; who I perceive is vexed because I do not serve her in something against the great feasting for her husband's reading in helping her to some good penn'orths, but I care not.

Decambrais's forehead creased as he scoured his memory. He was sure this was a quotation from something he'd read, once upon a time, somewhere, at some point in his life. Where? When? He moved on to yesterday's puzzle-message:

Moreover if at that time there appeare any increase of such creatures as are engendered of putrefaction; when as rats, moules and other creatures accustomed to live underground do forsake their holes and habitations; it is a token of corruption of the same

The sailor had stumbled over the last phrase, pronouncing it 'correction of the sane'. Decambrais reckoned it might have been a seventeenth-century text, but he was far from sure.

Most likely they were quotations collected by a nutter, by someone with an obsession. Or by a pedant. Or by some poor blighter trying to assert his own power over people by feeding them incomprehensible scraps, so as to raise himself above the *vulgum pecus* by forcing it to admit to its own crass ignorance. In which case, he was probably present somewhere in the crowd, gloating over the blank stares in people's faces as they listened to the learned texts that the crier could barely decipher.

Decambrais tapped his pencil on the paper. Even with those assumptions, he thought, the purpose and personality of the culprit were still mysterious. While yesterday's number 14, *Up yours, you arseholes* – one of a thousand variations of the same oft-heard theme – had the virtue of expressing its author's rage in summary, crystal-clear form, the contorted, cryptic communications from the pedant were just unfathomable. He needed to enlarge the corpus before trying to decode it; he would have to listen on, day after day. And maybe that was actually all that the message-writer wanted – to have people hanging on his lips every morning.

The shipping forecast came to its abstruse conclusion, and Joss resumed his newscast in his fine deep voice that carried right to the other side of the square. He went through 'The World This Week,' a regular feature that allowed him to put his own cast on recent international news. Decambrais caught the last few sentences: *Life's still tough in China, you can get flogged for a farthing. In Africa it's not too hot either, like it always has been. Not likely to improve very soon seeing as no-one's lifting a finger to help.* Then he came back to the small ads with number 16: *For sale, electric pinball machine, first registered 1965, topless backboard, perfect condition.* Decambrais was waiting, almost impatiently, with his pencil at the ready. And when it came it was quite easy to make out among the *I love . . . I hate . . . For sale . . .* and *Wanted*. Decambrais imagined he saw a moment's hesitation on the seaman's face before he started on the message. Had the Breton identified the intruder?

'Nineteen,' barked Joss.

> Moreover if at that time there appeare any increase of such creatures as are engendered of putrefaction . . .

Decambrais jotted it down on his sheet of paper. Always the same old stories, the same ancient stories of filth, vermin, and beasties. He pondered over the complete message on his page while Joss concluded his newscast with his customary extract from *Everyman's History of France*, consisting exclusively of tales of ships lost at sea. Decambrais supposed that this Le Guern must have once been in a shipwreck. And it wasn't too hard to guess that the boat must have been called *Nor'Easter*. That must have been when the fisherman's mind sprang a leak just like his bathtub. Because just below the Plimsoll line, that apparently fit and firm-minded man was mad, clutching on to obsessions like they were lifebuoys. Just like me, really,

Decambrais thought, though I'm neither fit nor firm.

'City of Cambrai,' Joss declaimed.

> September 15, 1883. French steamer, fourteen hundred tons. Out of Dunkirk for Lorient, carrying iron rails. Ran aground at Basse Gouac'h. Boiler burst, killing one passenger. Twenty-one crew, all saved.

Joss didn't need to signal to send his listeners on their various ways, because everyone knew that the shipwreck story always marked the end of the news. It was such a famous feature of the show that people had started to lay bets on how that day's story would end – 'all saved,' 'all lost,' or half-and-half, and they settled up in the café opposite straight after, or else when they got to the office. Joss had misgivings about cashing in on tragedy, but he also realised that weeds had to grow back over wrecks on the seabed and that life had to go on – and that was no bad thing.

As he jumped off his podium he saw Decambrais putting his book away, and their eyes met. As if Joss didn't know that the old hypocrite had just listened to the newscast! The old bore couldn't bear to admit that a mere Breton fisherman could brighten his gloomy life. If Decambrais only knew what he'd found in this morning's catch: *Hervé Decambrais makes his own lace napkins. Hervé Decambrais is a queer.* Joss had a moment's temptation before

31

putting the message in the pile of 'better nots'. That made two of them – three perhaps, if you included Lizbeth – to know that Decambrais had a clandestine one-man lace-making business. In one way this made the bookworm less repulsive; for Joss had spent many a long winter evening watching his own father mending the nets.

Joss gathered up the rubbish, put his pulpit on his shoulder and, with the help of Damascus, put all his tackle away in the back room of Rolaride. Two cups of hot coffee were waiting, as they always were after the morning cast.

'I didn't get number 19 at all,' Damascus said from his perch on a tall bar stool. 'That thing about putrefaction. It wasn't even a complete sentence.'

Damascus was young, burly, quite handsome, as open as the mouth of the Loire, but just not very bright. His eyes reminded Joss of looking at windows papered over on the inside. Was it to hide an excess of feeling, or a genuine vacancy? Joss couldn't make up his mind on that. Anyway, Damascus never looked straight at anything, even when he was talking to you. His vague and woolly eyes ranged all around; his glance was as hard to pierce as a Channel fog.

'A nutter,' Joss explained. 'Give up.'

'I'm not trying,' said Damascus.

'Hey, did you listen to my weather forecast?'

'Yep.'

'Didn't you twig that summer's over? Or are you trying to catch cold?'

Damascus was wearing shorts, a denim sleeveless V-neck top, and nothing else.

'It's OK,' he said. 'I can manage.'

'What good does it do you to have your biceps on show?'

Damascus downed the rest of his coffee.

'Look, I'm not selling lace napkins here. This is Rolaride: surfboards, rollerblades, skateboards and go-karts. This,' he said, pointing to the hair on his chest, 'is what moves the stuff.'

Joss suddenly became suspicious.

'Why did you say that about lace?'

'Because that old stick insect Decambrais sells it.'

'Do you know where he gets his napkins?'

'Sure I do. From a wholesaler in Rouen. Decambrais is not a fence. He even gave me a free session.'

'You asked for one?'

'Sure. So what? "Even Keel Counselling" is what his nameplate says, doesn't it? There's nothing wrong in getting advice, is there, Joss?'

'The sign also says "Thirty minutes, 40 francs. Charges apply per quarter-hour." That's pricey for a rip-off, Damascus. What does the old fogey know about keeping an even keel? He's never even been on a boat.'

'It's not a rip-off, Joss. You want me to prove it? "Damascus," he says to me, "you're not showing off your body for the sake of your business, you're doing it for yourself. Let me give you some friendly advice: Put on a proper jacket, and trust yourself. You'll be just as good-looking and you'll look less of a twit." How about that, then, Joss?'

'That's fair enough, I grant you,' Joss agreed. 'So why don't you put on some sensible clothes?'

'Because I do what I like doing. Only Lizbeth's afraid I'll catch my death, and so is Marie-Belle. In five days' time I'll pull myself together and get dressed.'

'OK,' said Joss. 'Because there's real rough weather coming in from the west.'

'Decambrais?'

'What about Decambrais?'

'He really gets up your nose, doesn't he?'

'Not quite, my friend. It's me who gets on Decambrais's nerves.'

'That's a pity,' Damascus said as he cleared away the coffee cups. 'Because I've heard one of his rooms is free. Would have suited you down to the ground. It's right next to where you work, it's got central heating, you get your room cleaned and a square meal every evening.'

'Bugger that,' said Joss.

'Right. But you can't take the room because you can't stand the man.'

'No, I can't.'

'Really stupid, that is.'

'Extremely.'

'Then there's Lizbeth as well. That's a very big plus.'

'A huge plus.'

34

'Right. But you can't do it. Since you can't bear the guy.'

'Not quite. He can't bear me.'

'Comes to the same thing as far as the perch is concerned. You just can't do it.'

'No, I can't.'

'Things don't always work out as they should. Are you sure you can't?'

Joss tightened his jaw. 'I'm sure, Damascus. No point going on about it. End of story.'

Joss left Rolaride to saunter into the Viking, the café over the road. Now the Bretons had never got on well with the Norse, they'd even spent a few centuries barging their boats into each other's, but Joss knew full well that he could easily have been born the other side of St Malo Sound and been a Norman instead. Bertin the barman, a tall man with ginger hair, fair eyes and high cheekbones, had a supply of *calva* like no other. What it did to your insides was nobody's business, save that far from hastening your path to the grave it injected an elixir of everlasting youth. The apples from which it was made were supposed to come from Bertin's own orchard, and in those parts, apparently, the cattle lived to a hundred and were still full of beans when they died. So just think what the apples were like.

'Rough patch this morning?' Bertin asked as he poured the precious liquid.

'Not too bad, really. Just that sometimes things

don't work out as they should. Would you say that Decambrais just can't bear the sight of me?'

'No, I wouldn't,' said the Norman, with the caution characteristic of his race. 'I'd say he thinks you're a rough customer.'

'What's the difference?'

'Well, let's say it could sort itself out, given time.'

'Time, that's all you ever talk about, you northerners. One word every five years, if you're lucky. If we were all like you, things wouldn't move very fast, you know.'

'But maybe they'd move better.'

'Time! But how much time, Bertin? Tell me that.'

'Not long. Ten years, maybe.'

'Well, that's that, then.'

'So it's something urgent, is it? Are you in need of an "Even Keel" session?'

'Bugger that. I wanted his room.'

'Better get a move on, then. I hear there's already a candidate. He's stalling because the guy is crazy about Lizbeth.'

'Why should I get a move on? The old fraud thinks I'm a rough customer.'

'Have a heart, Joss. The fellow's never even been on board. Anyway, aren't you a just a bit rough really?'

'Never denied it.'

'So you see. Decambrais knows a thing or two. Say, Joss, did you understand your number 19 this morning?'

'No.'

36

'I thought it was a special. Like those other specials we've had these past few days.'

'Very special. I don't like those specials one bit.'

'So why do you read them out?'

'They've been paid for, top rate too. And though the Le Guerns may be rough customers, they've never stolen a penny.'

CHAPTER 4

'I wonder,' mused *Commissaire Principal* Adamsberg, 'whether spending all this time in the force isn't going to turn me into a *flic*.'

'You've said that before,' Danglard remarked. He was trying to set up the paperwork system for the still-empty steel cupboard. Danglard wanted to make a fresh start and keep things neat, like he'd said. Adamsberg entertained no such wish and had already laid out the files on the seats of the chairs around the conference table.

'Do you think there's a risk?'

'Well, it wouldn't be a disaster if twenty-five years in the service did make some kind of a *flic* out of you.'

Adamsberg stuck his hands into his trouser pockets, leaned back against the recently redecorated wall, and cast a nonchalant eye over the new incident room he'd been allocated just a month ago. New case, new room. The Brigade Criminelle attached to the thirteenth arrondissement of Paris. No more cat burglars, handbag-snatchers, alleyway bruisers, idiots with flick knives – on or off the catch – and all those tons of papers after the fact.

He'd heard that phrase 'after the fact' twice over in recent days. Must come from being a *flic*, he reckoned.

Not that there wouldn't be tons of paper after the fact landing on his desk here as well. But here, like everywhere else, he would find men who liked to chew through paperwork. In his early youth, just when he'd left the Pyrenees, he'd discovered that there really were people who lived on paper, and he'd quickly come to regard them with considerable awe, a degree of pity and boundless gratitude. Adamsberg mostly liked to walk, muse and act, and he knew that his tastes inspired little awe and much pity in many of his colleagues. An eloquent penpusher had once explained: 'Paperwork, that's to say drafting and then perfecting the charge sheet, is the mother of all Ideas. No Ink means no Idea! Ideas germinate in wordage like bean sprouts in blotting paper. An action not written down is a seed that can't sprout.'

In that case, he thought, he must have left many a bean high and dry in his life as a *flic*. All the same, his long walks often left him with the feeling that not entirely uninteresting notions had started to squirm inside his head. Maybe they weren't quite as straight up as bean sprouts, maybe they were more slippery and tangled, more like seaweed, but germination is germination whatever you say, and once you've got your idea it doesn't matter two hoots whether it grew on a clean piece of blotting paper or on a rubbish tip. That said, Danglard, his number two, was a paper addict. He loved the stuff in forms high and low, from incunabula to kitchen rolls, including books new and old, fly-sheets, loose sheets and pre-punched bond. He could even think while sitting down, and as long as he had a beer to sip and a pencil to chew, he could be relied upon to germinate a whole tray of sprouts at a time. A worrier like Danglard, with his slack, heavy, slightly weary physique, cultivated fully grown ideas equipped with beginnings, middles and ends, quite unlike those that Adamsberg came up with.

They'd often come into conflict over this. Danglard had no time for ideas not issuing directly from conscious thought and he looked on informal, intuitive reckoning with deep suspicion. Adamsberg didn't try to distinguish the one from the other, and in any case held no strong views. But when he was transferred to the Brigade Criminelle, Adamsberg stamped his foot until they allowed Danglard to come along, with a promotion to boot. He could not manage without that dogged mind and its carborundum edge.

Well, in the new digs they'd got, neither Danglard's trained and powerful nor Adamsberg's woolly wanderer would be switching from smashed windows to bag-snatchings. Their job had one name and one name only: murder. Murder *ad infinitum*, without a broken pane to let a healthy gust of teenage delinquency take your mind off the subject; murder *ad aeternam*, unrelieved by having to lend a handkerchief to the nice young lady who'd just lost her keys, her address book and a love letter. It would be total immersion in the nightmare of humanity, the killer species.

No, sir, no relief. Violent crimes only. Murder squad.

This unambiguous definition of their duties felt as sharp as a knife. Well, all right then, he'd got what he asked for, what with having solved a score and more mysteries through his walking, dreaming, straggly-thinking method. As a result they had put him right up on the front line. Tracking killers was something he'd been unexpectedly good at. Diabolical, in fact. That was Danglard's term, to account for the surprising results of Adamsberg's impenetrable mental meanderings.

So they there were, at the sharp end, with a squad of twenty-six men and women under their command.

'I was wondering,' Adamsberg said as he ran the flat of his hand over the damp plaster, 'whether what happens to cliffs doesn't also happen to us.'

'What happens to cliffs?' Danglard snapped.

Adamsberg had always been a slow talker, hovering around his main point and sometimes forgetting entirely where it was; Danglard found it increasingly hard to put up with.

'Well, the rock isn't, so to speak, all of a piece, on a cliff by the sea. I don't know, but let's say it's made up of hardstone and softstone.'

41

'Softstone isn't a geological term, sir.'

'That's as may be. At any rate, there are harder bits and softer bits in a cliff, like there are in all living things, like there are in you and me. So you've got a cliff, all right? And as the sea laps at it, and washes it, and splashes over it, the soft bits begin to melt.'

"Melting' is not the right word, sir.'

'That's as may be. At any rate, bits drop off and the harder bits start to stick out. And as the sea and the storms go on bashing away at the cliff, the weaker parts vanish into thin air. When it gets to be an old man, the cliff is all craggy and hollow, like a ruined castle or keep. Like a gaping jaw with a stony bite. What you've got where the soft bits were are gaps, holes and voids.'

'Yes, sir?'

'Well, I was wondering whether *flics* – and heaps of other people exposed to life's stormy seas – don't suffer erosion as well. Lose their soft bits, keep their tough bits, grow hard and craggy and hollow. Basically, fall to pieces.'

'So you think you're turning into a stone jaw?'

'I guess so. I could be turning into a *flic.*'

Danglard pondered the point.

'As far as your personal geological make-up is concerned, sir, I reckon you are not eroding normally. I'd put it this way, sir: your soft bits are quite hard and your hard bits are fairly soggy. So the result is rather unique.'

'Does that make any difference?'

42

'All the difference in the world, sir. Soft rocks that resist erosion turn things upside down.'

Danglard tried to imagine himself in the same light as he put another clip of papers into a hanging file. 'So what would happen, sir, if you had a cliff made entirely of soft rock – and let's say the cliff is a *flic* in this case.'

'He'd erode into a tiny pebble and then vanish for good.'

'How reassuring.'

'But I don't think you can get that sort of cliff arising naturally in the environment. Especially not if it's a *flic*.'

'Let's hope you're right, sir.'

A young woman stood uncertainly at the Commissariat door. The door did not actually stay 'Commissariat,' but there was 'Brigade Criminelle' in bright black lettering on a door plate affixed to the lintel. It was the only thing that was clean about this otherwise filthy and dilapidated building, where four workman with an ear-splitting power drill were still putting iron bars on the outside windows. Maryse reckoned that whatever was on the door, there had to be policemen behind it, nearer to hand than at the Commissariat down the road. She took a step towards the door, then checked herself. Paul had warned her that the police would just laugh her off. But she was worried, what with the children and all. What would it cost her? Five minutes of time, no more.

She would just say what she had to say, and then go.

'My poor Maryse,' Paul had said, 'the *flics* won't take a blind bit of notice. But if that's what you want to do, go tell them!'

A fellow emerged from the side door, went past her down the street and then turned back. Maryse stood there fiddling with her handbag strap.

'Are you all right?' he asked.

The man was short and dark, and he looked like a pig's breakfast. His hair was all tousled and he'd rolled his jacket sleeves halfway up his unshirted forearm. Looked like a guy with troubles to tell, just like she had. But he was on his way out.

'Are they nice, inside?' Maryse asked him.

The dark fellow shrugged. 'Depends on who you get.'

'Do they listen?'

'Depends on what you tell them.'

'My nephew thinks they'll make fun of me.'

The man leaned his head to one side and looked at Maryse attentively.

'So what's this all about?'

'My block, a couple of nights ago. I'm sick with worry because of the kids. If there was a nutter inside the other night, how do I know he's not going to come back? Am I right?'

Maryse was blushing and biting her lip.

'Look, this is the Brigade Criminelle here,' the man said, waving at the grimy frontage. 'It's for murders. You know, when someone gets killed.'

'Oh!' said Maryse in consternation.

'Go down to the station on the boulevard, please. It's lunchtime, they'll not be too busy, and they'll listen to you properly.'

Maryse shook her head vigorously. 'No, I can't do that. I can't because I've got to be back in the office at two and the manager is a right dragon. Can't the men here pass it all on to their boulevard branch? I mean, *flics* all work for the same firm, don't they?'

'Well, not quite,' the man answered. 'But what's happened? A burglary?'

'Oh no.'

'A fight?'

'Oh no.'

'Tell us what it was, it'll make it easier to put you on the right track.'

'OK, OK,' Maryse blurted out, beginning to quake.

The man propped his elbow on a parked car and waited patiently for Maryse to find her words.

'It's black paint,' she explained. 'Or rather, thirteen black paintings, on all the front doors of the staircase. They scare me. I'm on my own with the kids, you see.'

'Paintings? You mean pictures?'

'Oh no, not pictures. They're fours. Number 4s. Big black 4s, like they were old-fashioned or something. I wondered if it wasn't some gang doing it for a lark. Maybe the *flics* know what it is, maybe they'll understand. But maybe they won't. Paul

45

told me, "If you want to get laughed at, go tell the *flics*."'

The scruffy fellow stood up straight and took Maryse by the arm. 'Come on,' he said. 'Let's go and get that all down, and then you'll have nothing more to worry about.'

'Hey, wouldn't it be better to find a *flic* first?'

He looked at her for an instant with his eyebrows raised.

'I am a *flic*,' he said. '*Commissaire Principal* Jean-Baptiste Adamsberg, at your service.'

'Oh!' said Maryse in embarrassment. 'Excuse me!'

'No harm done, madam. Incidentally, what did you think I was?'

'I don't dare say.'

Adamsberg led the way through his new warren.

'Need a hand, sir?' asked a bleary-eyed brigadier on his way out to lunch. Adamsberg steered the woman gently towards his office and stared at the young man in an attempt to remember who he was. He still hadn't really met all the juniors in his new squad, and he had terrible trouble remembering the names. They had all realised this early on, and now made a point of giving their names every time they said so much as good morning to the boss. Adamsberg hadn't quite decided whether they meant to be kind or to take the piss – but he wasn't very bothered either way.

'*Lieutenant* Noël,' the man said. 'A hand, sir?'

'A young woman cracking up, that's all. Some

kind of silly joker in her block, or maybe just a wall artist. She just a needs a bit of support, that's all.'

'We're not supposed to be social workers, are we?'

Lieutenant Noël curtly zipped up his bomber jacket.

'And why shouldn't we be, *Lieut . . .*'

'*Lieutenant* Noël.'

'. . . *tenant* Noël,' Adamsberg finished.

He tried to register the face and the name: box-head, pale face, crew cut, and big ears add up to: *Noël*. Noël means *tired-out*, *touchy* and maybe *tough*. Big ears plus tough guy make *Noël*.

'We'll talk about that later, *Lieutenant* Noël. She's in a hurry.'

'If the lady needs supporting,' said another and equally unnameable *brigadier*, 'I'm ready and waiting, sir.' Then with a smirk he stuck his thumbs in his belt. 'I've got all it takes right here.'

Adamsberg turned slowly towards the man.

'*Brigadier* Favre, sir.'

'While you're here, *brigadier*, you are going to learn something that may surprise you,' Adamsberg said slowly. 'In this branch, women are not just little dumplings with a hole in the middle. If this comes as news to you, as I fear it might, then let me encourage you to learn a little more about them. Women have legs and feet underneath; you will also find a torso and a head when you look at their upper parts. Think about that, Brigadier

Favre. Assuming you have something to think with.'

Adamsberg went through his mental memory routine as he entered his own office. Fleshy face, bushy eyebrows, prize hooter and birdbrain all add up to: *Favre*. Favre means *hooter, brows* and *birds*.

He propped himself up against his office wall so as to face the woman who was now perching almost apologetically on the edge of a chair. 'Now tell me all about it. You've got kids, you're on your own. Where exactly do you live?' To calm Maryse down Adamsberg scribbled her name and address and other answers on a notepad.

'So these 4s were painted on the doors, have I got that right? All in one night?'

'Oh yes. Every door had a 4 yesterday morning. Really big ones, as big as this,' said Maryse as she showed Adamsberg a distance of maybe two feet between her two hands.

'No signature? No initials?'

'Oh yes, there was something. Underneath each 4 there were three really small capital letters: CTL. Sorry: CLT.'

Adamsberg wrote that down. *CLT.*

'In black like the numbers?'

'Oh yes, black.'

'Nothing else? Nothing on the front of the block, nothing in the stairwell?'

'Just the doors. Black paint, like I said.'

'The number, was it painted correctly, or was it

48

a bit different or distorted? Like a logo, for instance?'

'Oh yes. I'll draw it if you like. I'm a dab hand at drawing, you know.'

Adamsberg passed over his pad and Maryse concentrated on reproducing a large printed 4, with the downstroke splayed at the foot like a Maltese Cross, and two notches on the outer leg of the cross.

'There you are.'

'You've done it back to front,' Adamsberg said gently as he took back his notepad.

'That's because it is backwards. It's a backwards 4, with a fat foot and two little notches at the end of the crossbar. Do you know what it is? Is it a make of burglars? Are they called CLT? Or what?'

'Burglars usually leave as few signs on front doors as they can manage. What are you frightened of?'

'I think it's *Ali Baba and the Forty Thieves* that put the wind up me. The story about the murderer who marked all the doors with a big X.'

'In the story, Ali Baba only marked one door. If I'm not mistaken, it was his wife who marked all the others so as to confuse him.'

'That's true,' said Maryse, who seemed genuinely comforted.

'It's just graffiti, really,' Adamsberg said as he showed Maryse out. 'Teenagers from down the street, I should guess.'

'The point is I've never seen a 4 like that down our street.' Maryse had lowered her voice to a

49

whisper. 'Nor have I ever seen graffiti on front doors up the staircase. Because graffiti are supposed to be on the street, aren't they? For everyone to see.'

'There's all kinds, you know. Scrub your front door and forget all about it.'

Maryse left and Adamsberg tore the sheets out of his pad, screwed them up into a ball which he then aimed at the bin. Then he went back to his leaning wall so as to think while standing about how to pump the mental filth out of people like Favre. Not easy to do. There was something twisted deep down inside the man; and he would hardly be aware of it. All Adamsberg could hope was that the rest of the squad didn't have the same problem. Especially as there were four women in it.

As he always did when he let himself have a good think, Adamsberg quickly lost touch and fell into a kind of void close to sleep. Ten minutes later he came back to the surface with a start, then got the list of his team out of his desk drawer and began a memory session: reciting over and over the names of each one of the twenty-seven members he had to get into his head, with the exception of Danglard's. In the margin he entered next to the name of Noël: *Ears, Toughguy,* and next to Favre's: *Hooter, Brows, Birds.*

Then he went out to have the coffee that his encounter with Maryse had put off. The coffee-maker and snack dispenser still hadn't been delivered to the office; there were constant squabbles over chairs and writing paper; the electricians were still putting in the computer cables, and workmen had only just started barring up the ground-floor windows. What would crimes be without iron bars? Murderers would just have to control themselves until the Brigade had got itself into shape. So he might as well carry on musing in the fresh air and rescuing damsels in distress. He could have a think about Camille, too; he'd not seen her for more than two months. Unless he was mistaken, she was due back tomorrow, or maybe the day after, as he wasn't sure what day it was anyway.

CHAPTER 5

On Tuesday morning Joss handled the ground coffee with heightened care and attention. He'd not slept well. The fault surely lay with the 'room to let' sign dangling before his eyes but quite out of reach.

He looked up from his bowl of coffee, his baguette and garlic sausage, and cast an angry glance around his gloomy cabin. The plaster was all cracked, there was no proper bed, and to get to the toilet you had to go out on to the landing. He could have afforded a better place on the money he was making, but half of it went back to his mother at Le Guilvenec. The long and the short of it, he told himself, is that you can't keep warm if you know your mother's in the cold. Joss knew that the bookworm couldn't charge very much, because his rooms weren't self-contained and the rental income wasn't declared. To be fair to the man, Decambrais wasn't one of those scavengers who take an arm and a leg for a pint-sized piece of property in Paris. In fact, Lizbeth paid no rent at all, in return for doing the shopping, making the dinner, and keeping the sole bathroom clean and tidy. Decambrais did all the other chores – hoovering the hall and stairs, washing the woodwork, laying the table for breakfast. For a man of his years, he certainly wasn't taking it easy.

Joss dipped his bread in the coffee, took a bite and chewed it slowly as he waited for the shipping forecast to come up on the radio that he'd set to low. The bookworm's vacancy had everything going for it. It was a stone's throw from Gare Montparnasse, just in case. It was roomy, it had central heating, a proper bed, oak flooring and well-worn rugs. When she'd first got there Lizbeth hadn't worn shoes for days on end, for the sheer pleasure of feeling warm carpet underfoot. Then there would be hot dinners every day. Joss could grill bream, open oysters and squeeze a lemon, but that was just about all he could manage in the galley; so for seven years he'd been eating mostly out of tin cans. And last of all there would be Lizbeth in the next room. No, of course he would never try anything, never put his callused old hands on a woman who was his junior by a quarter of a century. And in fact, Decambrais had also always done the right thing by Lizbeth. She had told Joss a dreadful story about her first night, when she lay down on the carpet. Well, the toff hadn't batted an eyelid. Hats off to him, I say – that's what you call style. If the toff could cope in that quarter, well so could Captain Joss. Say what you like, the Le Guerns may be rough customers, but they never took anything that wasn't theirs.

But that was the sticking point. Decambrais thought Joss was a rough customer, and so would never let him have the room. No point dreaming about it, then. Or about Lizbeth, or hot dinners, or central heating.

But he was still thinking about it when he emptied out the urn an hour later. He saw the thick ivory envelope straight away and ripped it open with his thumb. Thirty francs inside. The rate was going up all on its own. He glanced at the text without bothering to read it all through. The incomprehensible witterings of that crackpot were getting really tiresome. Then he sorted the 'can dos' from the 'better nots' almost unconsciously. The latter pile included the following message: *Decambrais is a queer and he makes his own lace.* Same as yesterday, but the other way round. Not very original, my friend! You'll soon be repeating yourself. Just as Joss was about to put that message in the 'return to sender' pile, his hand hovered in mid-air for a little longer than it had the day before. Rent me the room or I'll put the whole bang shoot into the newscast. Blackmail, that's what it would be.

At 0828 Joss was on his orange-box stand ready to go. All the cast were in position, like members of the corps de ballet in a show that had now been running for more than two thousand performances: Decambrais on his doorstep, with his head down in his book; Lizbeth to starboard in the middle of

54

a little group; Bertin to port behind the red-and-white-striped curtains of the Viking; Damascus to the stern, leaning against the shop window of Rolaride, not far from the tenant of Decambrais's room number 4, almost hidden by a tree trunk; and finally all the regular fans standing round in a semicircle, each occupying as if by ancient tradition the same spot they had been in the previous day.

Joss launched the newscast.

> One: Looking for a fruitcake recipe that stops the raisins from all settling at the bottom. Two: There's no point in your closing your door to hide your filthy habits. God above will judge you and your little tart. Three: Helen, why didn't you come? I'm sorry for everything I've done. Signed, Bernard. Four: Lost in the square: six bowls. Five: For sale: ZR7750 1999, 8,500 km, red, alarm, windscreen and engine cowling, 3,000 francs.

Some newcomer raised a hand in the crowd to indicate his interest in the last item. Joss had to break off to growl 'Later on, at the Viking'. The arm went down in embarrassment as fast as it had shot up.

'Six,' Joss resumed.

> I don't do meat. Seven: Wanted: pizza van with wrap-around window, usable with

ordinary driver's licence, six-pizza-capacity oven. Eight: Hey, you kids with the drum set, next time I'll call the *flics*. Nine . . .

Decambrais wasn't concentrating on the regular messages since all his attention was focused on catching the Pedant's next missive. Lizbeth had jotted down some Mediterranean herbs for sale, and it was nearly time for the shipping forecast. Decambrais twiddled the pencil in his hand into note-taking position.

> . . . force 7 to 8 weakening gradually 5 to 6 then backing west 3 to 5 during the afternoon. Heavy; rain or showers, decreasing steadily.

Joss got to item 16 and Decambrais knew what it was from the first word:

> And by and by did go down by water to dot dot dot and then down further and so landed at the lower end of the town; and it being dark there did privately *entrer en la maison de la femme de* dot dot dot and there I had *sa compagnie*, though with a great deal of difficulty; *néanmoins je avais ma volonté d'elle*. And being sated therewith, I walked home.

A stunned silence followed, which Joss quickly brought to an end by launching into more comprehensible messages and then that day's chapter of *Everyman's History of France*. Decambrais scowled, because the text was too long and he couldn't get it all down. He pricked up his ears to hear the fate of *Rights of Man*, French warship, seventy-four guns, on January 14, 1797, making for home port after an unsuccessful engagement off Ireland, with 1,350 men on board.

> . . . pursued by two English vessels, *Infatigable* and *Amazon*. After a night exchanging fire, *Rights of Man* ran aground off the beach of Canté.

Joss packed his papers back into his pea-jacket.
'Hey, Joss!' someone yelled out. 'How many were saved?'
Joss jumped down from his soapbox.
'You can't always know the whole story,' he said somewhat pompously.
Before stashing his gear at Damascus's place, Joss's glance met Decambrais's. He was about to take a step towards the old man but decided to leave off until after the noon newscast. Downing a calva beforehand would strengthen his arm for what lay ahead.

At 1245 Decambrais used lots of abbreviations to scribble down the following as he heard Joss bawl it out:

Twelve: Conftables shall draw up the rules to be obferved and shall have them pofted on thoroughfares and at gathering places so that none shall know them not dot dot dot. That no swine dogs cats homing birds or conies be suffered to be kept within any part of the city, and that dogs be killed by the dogkillers expressly appointed. That every householder do cause the street to be daily prepared before his door, and that the fweepings and filth of houfes be daily carried away by the rakers. That the layf-talls be removed as far as may be out of the city and that no nightman or other be suffered to empty a vault into any garden near about the city dot dot dot

Joss was already berthed in the Viking for lunch when Decambrais made up his mind to speak to him. As he opened the door of the bar, Bertin drew a beer for him and put it on one of the mats deco-rated with the two yellow lions rampant of Normandy, specially made for the house. The call to lunch took the form of Bertin's fist hitting a large brass plate hanging over the counter. Bertin banged his gong twice a day, for lunch and for dinner, and the effect of the thunder-roll was to make all the pigeons in the square flap their wings and take off at once, while the hungry, in a parallel but inverse movement, flocked into the Viking. Bertin's gesture effectively reminded people that is was time to eat, but it was also an allusion to his own fearful ascendancy, which was supposed to be common knowledge. For Bertin's mother's maiden name was *Toutin,* which made the barman, by onomastic filiation, a direct descendant of Thor. There were those who considered the etymology rather dubious, and Decambrais was of their number; but nobody thought it sensible to cut Bertin's family tree down to size and thereby lay to waste the dreams of a man who had been soldiering away at the sink for the past thirty years.

All the same Bertin's gong and his ancestry had made the Viking famous well beyond its immediate catchment area, and the place was never less than packed.

Holding his glass of beer aloft, Decambrais cut a careful path towards the table where Joss was sitting.

'Could I possibly have a word?' he asked, still standing.

Joss didn't answer, but carried on masticating as he raised his narrow blue eyes. Who had spilled the beans? Bertin? Or Damascus? Was Decambrais going to tell him to forget about the vacant room, just so he could gloat over declaring that rough customers weren't welcome in a place with proper flooring? If Decambrais had it in mind to insult him, then Joss would let the cat right out of the bag. He gestured vaguely to the bookworm to sit down.

'Ad number 12,' said Decambrais.

'I know,' said Joss, surprised. 'It was a special one.'

So the Breton had noticed. That was going to make things easier.

'It's got brothers and sisters,' said Decambrais.

'Yep. For the last three weeks.'

'I was wondering if you had kept them.'

Joss cleaned the gravy off his plate with a piece of bread, which he popped in his mouth before folding his arms.

'And if I had?'

'I'd like to reread them. If you like,' Decambrais said to overcome the fisherman's blank expression, 'I'll buy them off you. All the ones you've got and all the ones you'll get from now on.'

'So you're telling me you didn't write them yourself?'

'Me?'

'Yep, and put them in the urn. I was wondering. It could be your kind of thing, writing old-fashioned sentences no-one can make head or tail of. But if you're offering to buy them off me, you can't have written them. That's a logical deduction, if you ask me.'

'Name your price.'

'I haven't got all of them. Only the last five.'

'The price?'

Joss pointed at his empty plate. 'An ad that's been read out is like a lamb chop after lunch. As there's nothing left on it to eat, it's not worth a sou. So I'm not selling. The Le Guerns may be rough customers, but they never stole a penny.'

Joss gave the bookworm a knowing look.

'And so?' Decambrais asked.

Joss wasn't sure what move he should now make. Could he really land a room with his five bits of gibberish?

'I've heard that one of your rooms is going to be vacant,' he mumbled.

Decambrais's face froze.

'I've got applicants already,' he replied, almost in a whisper. 'They have priority, you know.'

'OK, fine,' Joss said. 'You can keep your patter for yourself. Hervé Decambrais Esquire doesn't want a rough customer clumping muddy boots over his fine carpets. Better to say it straight out, isn't it? Only graduates get into your place, unless you're called Lizbeth, isn't that right? And I'm not likely to turn into one or the other any time soon.'

Joss drained his glass of wine and put it down rather sharply. Then he shrugged his shoulders and all of a sudden calmed down. The Le Guerns had been through much worse in their time.

'That's fine,' he said as he poured himself another glass. 'Keep your room. I can see your point of view. You're not my kind of bloke, and I'm not yours, and that's the end of it. Can't do a thing about it. You can have your bloody messages if that's what you're excited about. Meet me at Damascus's place this evening, just before the 1810 newscast.'

★   ★   ★

61

Decambrais turned up on time at Rolaride. Damascus was busy adjusting a customer's roller-blades. His sister, standing behind the till, beckoned to the bookworm.

'Monsieur Decambrais,' she whispered, 'please, could you tell him to put on a pullover. He's going to catch his death, you know. His lungs aren't that good. I know he listens to what you say, no two ways.'

'I've already spoken to him about that, Marie-Belle. It's a slow business, trying to get something into his skull.'

'I know,' said Marie-Belle, biting her lip. 'But couldn't you try just one more time?'

'All right, at the next opportunity. Cross my heart. Is the sailorman around?'

'He's out the back,' said Marie-Belle, waving towards a door.

Decambrais hunched his shoulders to get under all the bicycle wheels hanging from the ceiling and made his way through the stacks of surfboards to the workshop, itself brimful of roller skates of every size and description. One end of the workbench was occupied by Joss and his urn.

'I've laid them out for you down the end of the table,' Joss said without looking up.

Decambrais picked up the sheets and took a quick glance at them.

'And here's this evening's addition,' Joss added. 'Special preview, just for you. The nutter is picking up speed. I'm getting three a day now.'

Decambrais unfolded the latest message and read the following:

> That special care be taken that no tainted fish, or unwholesome flesh or musty corn or other corrupt fruits of what fort foever be suffered to be sold about the city, or any part of the fame.

'I don't know what forts these are,' Joss said, still poring over his evening news messages.

'Sorts, if I may be so bold.'

'Look here, Decambrais, I don't want to seem unfriendly, but would you mind your own business. The Le Guerns know how to read the alphabet, thank you. Nicolas Le Guern was town crier as far back as the Crimean War. So you're not going to teach me the difference between forts and sorts, dammit.'

'Look here, Le Guern, these are copied out from texts from long ago. Our nutter has copied them out and used special letters. At the time, people made the letter "s" almost the same way as the "f," at least in some positions in the word. So what you read out at the lunchtime newscast today wasn't about things being pofted or about houfes, and it wasn't addressed to juftices either.'

'What, you mean they were all "s"s?' Joss stood up straight at last, and his voice was getting louder.

'That's right, Le Guern, they're "s"s. *Post, house, justice.* Old-style "s"s shaped like "f"s. Look at them closely and you'll see for yourself that they're not quite the same.'

Joss grabbed the letter from Decambrais's hand, and looked closely at the script.

'All right,' he said grudgingly. 'But supposing you're right, so what?'

'It'll just make it easier for you to read. I wasn't trying to get up your nose.'

'Well, you did. Take your bloody screeds and get going. Because reading is my job, not yours. I don't poke my nose in your funny affairs, do I now.'

'What did you say?'

'Look, I know a fair bit about you, what with all these poison pen messages lying around,' said Joss, pointing to the pile of 'better nots'. 'As my great-great-grandfather Le Guern reminded me only the other evening, people have loads of muck between the ears. You're lucky that I filter out the worst of the shit.'

Decambrais went quite white and cast about for a stool to sit on.

'Good Lord,' said Joss, 'there's no need to panic.'

'Le Guern, do you still have those . . . poison pen messages?'

'Sure, I put them in with the rejects. Do they interest you?'

Joss rummaged about in his pile of 'return to senders' and picked out two messages for Decambrais.

'After all, it's always useful to know your enemies,' he said. 'Forewarned is forearmed, that's what I say.'

Joss watched Decambrais as he unfolded the sheets with trembling hands. For the first time he felt a little bit sorry for the old fellow.

'You mustn't let it affect you, really,' he said. 'They're the real dregs, the people who write that sort of muck. You wouldn't dream what filth I have to read. You should let sewage slip down the pipe and out to sea.'

Decambrais read the two messages and smiled weakly as he laid them on his lap. He seemed to be breathing more normally, Joss reckoned. What was it that had made the toff so scared?

'There's nothing wrong with lace-making. My father used to make nets. Same thing, really, isn't it, except the thread is thicker.'

'That's true,' said Decambrais. He gave the messages back to Joss, then added: 'But it's better for it not to get around. People can be very petty.'

'Indeed,' said Joss as he went back to sorting the evening newscast.

'I learned how to make lace from my mother. Why didn't you read these messages out in the usual way?'

'Because I don't like bloody idiots.'

'But you don't like me either, Joss Le Guern.'

'True. But I don't like bloody idiots either.'

Decambrais got up and started to leave. But just as he was going through the low doorway to the front shop, he turned round and said:

'The room's yours, Le Guern.'

CHAPTER 6

As he was going back through the archway into his new HQ around one o'clock, Adamsberg was intercepted by a junior he'd never seen before.

'*Lieutenant* Maurel, sir,' the young man said. 'There's a young woman waiting for you in your office and she insists on speaking to you alone. Name of Maryse Petit. She's been there for about twenty minutes. I took the liberty of shutting your door because Favre was wanting to give her a counselling session.'

Adamsberg frowned. It was the woman who'd come in yesterday about the graffiti. Good Lord, he must have been too nice to her. If she was going to drop in every day for a chat from now on, things could get very tangled.

'Have I put a foot wrong, sir?' Maurel asked.

'No, *Lieutenant* Maurel, not a bit. All my own fault.'

Maurel was made up of: tall, slim, dark, acne, prognathous jaw and solicitude. *Acne* plus *jutting* plus *solicitude* equals *Maurel*.

Adamsberg went into his office with a degree of

66

circumspection, sat down at his desk and nodded curtly.

'Oh, *commissaire*, I'm really sorry to take up more of your time,' Maryse began.

'One moment, please.' Adamsberg pulled a sheet of paper out of a drawer and pored over it with a pencil in his hand.

It was a well-worn trick used by *flics* and bosses since time immemorial to pull rank and make people on the wrong side of the desk aware of their own insignificance. Adamsberg resented having to use the ploy. You think you're a million miles from the likes of Noël and his authoritarian zipper, then all of a sudden you're behaving a lot worse than that. Maryse had stopped her chatter and lowered her head, and her reaction told Adamsberg she was used to being put in her place, by a boss or whoever. She was quite pretty and the way she was sitting gave a good view through the top of her blouse. You think you're a million miles from the likes of Favre, and when occasion arises, there you are puddling about in the same pigsty. Adamsberg wrote on his staff list, with time-wasting precision: *acne, prognathous, solicitude, Maurel.*

'Yes?' Adamsberg looked up as he spoke. 'Still frightened, are we? Maryse, you do remember, don't you, that this is the murder squad? If you are really disturbed, maybe you should see a doctor instead.'

'Oh, well, perhaps.'

67

'It's all right,' Adamsberg said as he stood up. 'Stop fussing over it. Graffiti never broke any bones.'

He opened the office door wide and smiled at Maryse to indicate that it was time for her to leave.

'Hang on a minute. I haven't told you about the other blocks.'

'What other blocks?'

'Two apartment blocks at the other end of Paris, in the eighteenth arrondissement.'

'And so?'

'Black 4s. On every door. It actually happened over a week ago, so it was before the writing on my own block.'

Adamsberg stood still for a minute, then closed the door quietly and motioned the young woman to sit down again.

'Teenage paint-sprayers, don't you think, *commissaire*, they usually do their stuff in their own streets,' Maryse suggested timidly as she sat down. 'I mean, don't they usually mark their own patch, like just a street or two? They don't go around putting their graffiti on one block and then on another one at the other end of town, do they? Am I right, do you think?'

'Unless they live at both ends of town.'

'Oh, I'd not thought of that. But don't gangs usually come from the same patch?'

Adamsberg held his counsel and got out his notepad.

'How did you know about this?'

'I'd taken my son to the therapist – he's dyslexic, you know. While he has his session I always while away the time in the café downstairs. So I was leafing through the local free sheet, you know, the one that has local news and political bits in it. There was a whole story about graffiti, on one block in rue Poulet and another in rue Caulaincourt. Black 4s, on the front doors of all the flats.'

Maryse paused.

'I brought you the cutting,' she said, and slipped a piece of old newspaper on to the table. 'So you can see I'm not telling you stories. I mean, I'm not trying to make myself interesting or anything.'

As Adamsberg ran his eye down the article, Maryse got up to go. Adamsberg glanced at his now empty waste-paper basket.

'One moment,' he said. 'Let's go over this again, from the top. Name, address, the shape of these 4s and so on.'

'But I told you all that yesterday.'

'I'd still like to go over it again. As a precaution, if you follow me.'

'Oh, all right then,' said Maryse, and she sat down again obediently.

When Maryse had left Adamsberg went for a walk, since he had just spent a whole hour at his desk, and that was as long as he could manage comfortably in a sitting position. Dining out, going to the cinema or to a concert, or spending a long evening on a soggy sofa were experiences that Adamsberg enjoyed at the start but which left him at the end in a state of physical distress. His irrepressible desire to go out and walk, or at least to stand up, would always in the end overwhelm his attention to the conversation, the movie or the music. But this personal handicap had its advantages. It allowed him to understand what other people meant when they spoke of agitation, impatience, even panic – for he never felt those emotions in any of life's circumstances, except when he had to stay sitting down for too long.

Once he was up and away on his two feet, Adamsberg's agitation subsided as quickly as it had risen, and he resumed his natural tempo – slow, steady and calm. He circled round and back towards the Brigade without having thought very much during his walk, but he had the feeling that these graffiti were not some teenagers' stunt, nor any kind of tit-for-tat. There was something unpleasant about those sets of numbers; something awkward; something vaguely sinister.

The Brigade building came into view, and Adamsberg knew that he should better not mention any of this to Danglard. Danglard hated seeing his boss's mind drift on a swell of unsubstantiated feelings, the root cause, in his view, of all the mistakes the police ever made. At best Danglard would call it all a waste of time. Adamsberg had given up trying to explain that wasting time was never a waste of time, because Danglard remained totally resistant to what he saw as an illicit mode of thought – thinking unsupported by rationality. Adamsberg's problem was that he had never known how to think any other way. He didn't have a system, in fact, or a philosophy or a persuasion or even a liking for his kind of musing. It was just the way he worked; it was the only way he could.

Danglard, looking stolid after a copious lunch, was at his desk, testing the computer network that had just been booted.

'I can't manage to download the fingerprint files from the central server,' he grumbled as Adamsberg wandered past. 'What are they playing at, I ask you? Do we have authorised access or do we not?'

'It'll download eventually,' Adamsberg said soothingly. It was easier for him to keep calm about it, as he never got too involved with computers.

Adamsberg's informatic incompetence didn't bother Danglard one bit, since he was as happy as a sandboy when playing with data bases. His capacious and well-ordered mental faculties were entirely suited to saving, sorting and merging as many megabytes as came his way.

'There's a message on your desk,' Danglard said without raising his eyes from the screen. 'Queen Matilda's girl. She's back.'

Danglard only ever called Camille 'Queen Matilda's girl'; the habit went back to the time when the Matilda in question had given him quite an upset, of an aesthetic and sentimental sort.

He worshipped Queen Matilda and his devotion spilled over on to her daughter Camille. Danglard thought Adamsberg fell far short of the level of care and attention that Camille deserved; some of Danglard's grunts and his silent reproaches made Adamsberg quite aware of the disapproval of his number two, despite the fact that the latter was generally quite careful not to meddle in other people's business. The present moment was a case in point: without saying anything directly, Danglard was making it clear that Adamsberg had been wrong not to try to get news of Camille for the past two months. And he blatantly disapproved of Adamsberg going around of an evening with another girl on his arm, no more than a week ago. On that occasion neither man had said a word to the other.

Adamsberg walked behind his deputy and looked over his shoulder at the flickering screen.

'Listen, Danglard, there's some bloke playing around at painting funny kinds of 4s on apartment doors. In three different blocks, actually. One in the thirteenth arrondissement, and two in the eighteenth. I'm wondering if I shouldn't go take a look.'

Danglard's fingers hovered over his keyboard.
'When?'

'Well, right now. As soon as we can get the photographer lined up.'

'What for?'

'Well, so as to photograph the things before

people scrub them off. Unless they've already been wiped.'

'But what for?'

'I don't like those 4s. Not one bit.'

Damn. Now he'd said it. Danglard hated him saying 'I don't like this' or 'I don't like that'. It wasn't a *flic*'s job to like or to dislike. A *flic*'s job is to get on with the job and to keep on thinking at the same time. Adamsberg went back into his office and found the note from Camille. If he was free this evening she would be too. If not, please call. Adamsberg nodded to himself. Yes, of course he would be free.

Feeling better for that, he picked up the telephone and asked to be put through to the photographer. Meanwhile, Danglard, whose face expressed perplexity and irritation, had burst into his office.

'Danglard, tell me, what does the photographer look like?' Adamsberg asked. 'And what is his name?'

'The whole team was introduced to you three weeks ago,' said Danglard, 'and you shook the hand of every man jack in the room, and every woman too. You even spoke to the photographer.'

'Well, that's as may be, Danglard. In fact, you're surely right. But all the same it does not provide an answer to my question. What does he look like and what's he called?'

'Daniel Barteneau.'

'Barteneau, Barteneau, that's a hard one. And his face?'

73

'Quite thin. Sparky, big smile, excitable.'

'Anything special?'

'Lots of little freckles, reddish hair.'

'That's handy,' said Adamsberg as he reached for the list in his drawer. 'That's very handy.'

He leaned over the desktop and wrote down: *Thin. Redhead. Photographer . . .*

'Remind me of the name . . .'

'Barteneau.' Danglard almost spat it out. 'Daniel Barteneau.'

'Thank you,' said Adamsberg as he finished writing it down in his memory-jogger. 'Did you realise we have a real dickhead in the squad? I said *a* dickhead, but there may be others.'

'Favre, Jean-Louis.'

'Hole in one. So what are we going to do with him?'

Danglard shrugged with a broad sweep of his arms. 'That's a problem for the whole wide world,' he said. 'Can we try to make improvements to him?'

'That would take at least fifty years.'

'What are you messing about with these 4s for?'

'Aha.' He opened his notebook on the page where Maryse had made her drawing. 'That's what they look like.'

Danglard glanced at the sketch and gave the pad back to Adamsberg.

'Was any offence committed? Any violence?'

'No, nothing apart from brush strokes. It won't cost anything to go have a look. Anyway, until we've

74

got the windows barred down here, all the real cases have to be handled by the Quai des Orfèvres.'

'That's no excuse for taking on nonsense. There's lots to do so as to get things set up properly.'

'This isn't nonsense, Danglard, I promise you.'

'Graffiti.'

'When did wall-daubers ever decorate stairwell doors? In three different places in Paris?'

'They could be jokers. Or the next avant-garde.'

Adamsberg shook his head slowly.

'No. There's nothing avant-garde about this. On the contrary. It's much murkier than that.'

Danglard shrugged his shoulders.

'I know what you mean,' Adamsberg said as they left the office. 'I do know.'

The photographer was coming into the court-yard and moving towards them over the builders' rubble. Adamsberg shook his hand. The name that Danglard had made him rehearse had now slipped his mind entirely. The best thing would be to copy the notes in his mind-jogger into a pocketbook so he could have it to hand at all times. He'd get on with it tomorrow, because this evening there was Camille, and Camille came ahead of Bretonneau or whatever the man's name was. Danglard came up behind his chief and said over his shoulder 'Hallo, Barteneau'.

'Hallo, Barteneau,' Adamsberg parroted, with a glance of gratitude towards his number two. 'Let's go. Avenue d'Italie. Nothing nasty today. We just need some art photos.'

From the corner of his eye Adamsberg could see Danglard putting on his jacket and tugging at the bum-flaps to make sure it sat squarely on his shoulders.

'I'll be coming with, if I may,' he mumbled.

CHAPTER 7

Joss hurried down Rue de la Gaîté at three and a half knots. He'd not stopped wondering since yesterday afternoon if he'd really heard the old bookworm aright, when he'd said 'The room's yours, Le Guern'. Yes, of course, he had heard him say that, but did the words really mean what Joss thought they ought to mean? Did they mean that Decambrais was actually prepared to rent his room to the Breton Brute? With carpets and Lizbeth and dinner and all? Of course that's what the words meant. What else could they mean? But saying that yesterday was one thing. Maybe the aristo had had a night of inner turmoil and woken up this morning firmly resolved to back out. Joss was sure that he would sidle up to him after the morning newscast and say how sorry he was, but the room had already been let – first come, first served, you know.

Yep, thought Joss, that's what was going to happen, no later than a few minutes from now. That jelly-kneed old fraud had been most relieved to learn that Joss wasn't going to blurt out the business about the lace, and that's why he'd had a sudden burst of generosity and offered his room to the old sea dog. But now he was going to take it back. That's Decambrais for you – a bore, and a louse to boot. Just like he'd always thought.

Joss unhitched his urn in high dudgeon and manhandled it on to the table at Rolaride. If there was another slur on the old bookworm in the trawl, then maybe he would not keep his mouth shut this morning. Why shouldn't he be a bigger louse than Decambrais? He rifled through the ads but didn't find anything of that kind. On the other hand the fat ivory envelope was there, with its thirty-franc fee.

'This fellow,' Joss muttered as he smoothed out the sheet, 'isn't going to stop for a good long while.'

But he could hardly grumble about it from a business point of view. The nutcase was bringing him in almost a hundred francs a day, all by himself. Joss furrowed his brow as he read:

Videbis animalia generata ex corruptione multiplicari in terra ut vermes, ranas et muscas; et si sit a causa subterranea videbis reptilia habitantia in cabernis exire ad superficiem terrae et dimittere ova sua et aliquando mori. Et si est a causa celesti, similiter volatilia.

'Bugger that,' said Joss. 'Now he's writing Italian.'

★   ★   ★

78

Joss climbed up on to his stand at 0828 and the first thing he did was to make sure Decambrais was standing at his customary doorpost. It was the first time in two years that he was keen to see him in the audience. Yes, there he was, in his grey suit, groomed to perfection, slicking back a wisp of his white hair and pretending to read his leather-bound tome. Joss cast him an evil glance, and then launched into item number one in his fine and resonant voice.

He felt he'd rushed through the newscast faster than usual in his haste to find out how Decambrais was going to eat his words. He almost bungled his closing *Everyman's History of France* as a result, and resented Decambrais all the more for it. 'French steamer,' he concluded brusquely, '300 tons, struck the rocks of Penmarch and then drifted as far as La Torche, where it sank at anchor. All lost.'

When the newscast was over Joss made himself hump his tackle back to the shop, where Damascus was just raising the steel shutters. They shook hands, and Damascus's felt unnaturally cold – as well it might, given the weather and the fact that the young man went around in nothing more than a vest. If he carried on like that he was going to catch his death.

'Decambrais is expecting you at eight this evening at the Viking,' said Damascus as he laid out the coffee cups.

'So he can't send his own messages?'

'He's got appointments all day long.'

'Maybe he has, but I'm not at his beck and call. He doesn't call all the shots just because he's a toff.'

'Why do you call him a toff?' asked Damascus with surprise.

'Come on, lad, wake up. *De* Cambrais has to be an aristocratic name, doesn't it?'

'I've no idea. Never thought about it. In any case, he's flat broke.'

'There are plenty of penniless aristocrats, you know. Actually, they're the best kind.'

'Oh, right,' said Damascus. 'I didn't know that.'

Damascus poured hot coffee into the cups and didn't seem to notice the scowl on the sea dog's face.

'Are you going to put that pullover on today or tomorrow?' Joss asked rather crossly. 'Did you know that your sister is worried sick about you?'

'I will soon, Joss, I will.'

'Don't get me wrong, lad, but while you're at it, why don't you wash your hair as well?'

Damascus raised his face in astonishment and shook his long, brown, wavy hair back over his shoulders.

'My mother used to say that a man's hair is his fortune,' Joss said. 'You could hardly claim to be looking after your assets properly, now could you?'

'Is my hair dirty, then?' the younger man asked in genuine puzzlement.

'Well, yes, it is a bit. Don't get me wrong, now.

I'm saying this for your own good, Damascus. You've got lovely hair and you should take better care of it. Doesn't your sister ever tell you?'

'Sure she does. Just that I forget.'

Damascus took hold of a bunch of hair and looked at it.

'You're right, Joss, I'll do it right away. Can you mind the store for me? Marie-Belle won't be in before ten.'

Damascus ran off, and Joss watched him bound across the square on his way to the drugstore. Poor lad, that Damascus, Joss thought with a sigh, he was too nice for his own good, and he really was one sandwich short of the full hamper. Like a lamb to the slaughter. The complete opposite of the aristo, who was all head and no heart. Why couldn't things be shared out more fairly in this bloody world?

Bertin's thunder-gong rang out at a quarter past eight in the evening. Days were now getting distinctly shorter; the square was already deep in shadow, and the pigeons had gone to roost. Joss dragged himself ungraciously to the Viking. He spied Decambrais at the back of the room, dressed in a dark suit and tie, with a white shirt that was fraying at the collar. He'd already ordered two carafes of wine. The bookworm was reading, the only person in the whole crowded bar to be doing so. He'd had all day to work up his speech, and Joss was expecting it to be nicely tied up. But Le

81

Guerns weren't easy folk to enmesh. Joss knew his way around nets and knots.

Joss slumped into the seat without even saying hallo. Decambrais filled both glasses straight away.

'Thanks for coming, Le Guern, I'd much prefer not to put the business off until tomorrow.'

Joss just nodded his head and gulped down a large dose of wine.

'Have you got them with you?' asked Decambrais.

'What?'

'Today's ads, the specials.'

'I don't lug everything around on me. They're at Damascus's place.'

'Do you remember what they said?'

Joss scratched his cheek for a minute or two.

'The fellow who keeps telling his life story was at it again, complete gobbledegook as per usual,' he said. 'Then there was another one in Italian, like there was this morning.'

'It's Latin, Le Guern.'

Joss said nothing for a moment.

'Well, I don't like it a bit. Reading out things you don't understand is not honest work. What do you think the nutter's after? Trying to get up everyone's nose?'

'Could well be. Look, would it be too much trouble to go and get the messages?'

Joss drained his glass and stood up. Things were not going as he expected. He was in a muddle, like he had been that night at sea when the instruments went haywire and he couldn't get a bearing. The rocks were supposed to be to starboard, but at dawn, there they were straight ahead, to the north. The ship had come terribly close to disaster.

He went over to get the messages and came back quickly, wondering all the while if Decambrais wasn't really to port when he thought him to starboard. He put the three ivory envelopes down on the table just as Bertin was serving the main course – veal in cream sauce with boiled potatoes – and a third carafe of wine. Joss tucked in while Decambrais read out the lunchtime message under his breath.

> Up, and to the office (having a mighty pain in my forefinger of my left hand, from a strain that it received last night in struggling *avec la femme que je* mentioned yesterday . . . My wife busy in going with her woman to a hothouse to bathe herself, after her long being within doors in the dirt, so that she now pretends to a resolution of being hereafter very clean. How long it will hold I can guess.

'I know that passage, damn it,' he said as he folded the sheet back into the envelope, 'but as through a glass darkly. Either I've read too much or else my memory is failing.'

'Sometimes the sextant does fail.'

Decambrais poured more wine and went on to the next message:

Terrae putrefactae signa sunt animalium ex putredine nascentium multiplicatio, ut sunt mures, ranae terrestres . . . serpentes ac vermes . . . praesertim si minime in illis locis nasci consuevere

'Can I keep them?'

'If they get you anywhere.'

'Nowhere for the moment. But I will track them down, Le Guern, I will. The man's playing cat and mouse with us, but one day, I'm quite sure, he'll let something out that will tell us what we want to know.'

'And what's that?

'Knowing what he's after.'

Joss shrugged. 'With your cast of mind you could never have been a crier. Because if you stop to think about everything you have to read out, well, you're finished. You can't do the newscasting because you get all clogged up. A crier has to be above all that. I've seen some right loonies come through the urn, you know. Only I never saw any who paid over the going rate. Or any who spoke Latin. Or who wrote "s" in the old way like an "f". What's that all about, I ask you.'

'He's doing it to keep under cover. In the first place it means he's not saying anything for himself, since the messages are all quotations. A clever ploy, as he's not giving himself away.'

'I don't trust guys who keep their noses that clean.'

'And in the second place he quotes passages from the distant past, whose meaning is clear to no-one but himself. That's called deep cover.'

'Mind you,' said Joss with a wave of his knife, 'I've nothing against the past. I even put a chapter from *Everyman's History of France* into the newscasts, as you well know. It goes back to my schooldays. I used to like history lessons. I didn't pay attention, but I liked them.'

Joss finished his plate, and Decambrais ordered a fourth carafe. Joss glanced at the toff. He was putting it away by the gallon, not counting all that he must have drunk while waiting for Joss to turn up. Joss could stay the pace, but even so he could feel his grip slipping. He looked hard at Decambrais. Yes, the aristo was beginning to wobble. He must have been drinking so as to summon up courage to broach the question of the room. Joss realised that he was backing off as well. As long as they kept on talking about this and that, they weren't talking about the hotel, and that was a step in the right direction.

'It was the teacher I really liked,' Joss added. 'I'd have liked it even if he'd been talking Chinese. He was the only one I missed after I got thrown out. There wasn't much milk of human kindness at Tréguier, believe you me.'

'What the hell were you doing at Tréguier? I thought you were from Le Guilvenec.'

'I was doing bugger all, and that's a fact. They'd put me in the boarding school to straighten me out.

A waste of ammo, because Tréguier threw me out two years later and sent me back to Le Guilvenec, seeing as what a bad influence I'd been on the other boys.'

'I know Tréguier,' Decambrais said off-handedly as he filled another glass.

Joss gave him a quizzical glance.

'You know Rue de la Liberté, then?'

'Certainly.'

'Well, that's where it was, the boys' boarding school.'

'Yes.'

'Just after the church.'

'Yes.'

'Are you going to say "yes" to everything?'

Decambrais looked like he was falling asleep. He shrugged his shoulders. Joss shook his head.

'You're full to the gills, Decambrais. You can't take any more.'

'Yes, I am pissed, and I do know Tréguier. The two assertions are neither incompatible nor contradictory.'

Decambrais drained his glass and motioned to Joss to replenish it.

'Bullshit,' said Joss as he acceded to the aristo's silent request. 'It's all bullshit, you just want to give me the soap. But if you think I'm going to roll over on my back just because some boozer confesses to having been to Brittany, then you're making a big mistake. I'm not a patriot, I'm a sailor. I know Bretons with brains no bigger than any foreigner's.'

'So do I.'

'Do you mean me to take that personally?'

Decambrais shook his head unconvincingly. A rather long silence ensued.

'But tell me the truth, do you really know Tréguier?' Joss asked with the persistence of a drunk.

Decambrais drained his glass and said 'Yes' once again.

'Well, I hardly know the place,' said Joss in a burst of melancholy. 'The head warder, Father Kermarec, found a way of keeping me in detention every Sunday. I think I only ever saw the town through the windows, and all I knew of it was what the other boys told me. Memory's a real bitch, because I know the name of the bastard who ran Tréguier but I can't recall the name of the history teacher who was the only one to take my side.'

'Ducouëdic.'

Joss slowly raised his head.

'What was that?'

'Ducouëdic,' Decambrais repeated. 'Your history teacher.'

Joss narrowed his eyes to a slit and leaned heavily over the table.

'That's it. Ducouëdic, Yann Ducouëdic. Hang on, Decambrais, are you tailing me? What are you after? Are you a *flic*? That's right, isn't it, Decambrais, you work for the *flics*! All these messages, they're just bullshit, aren't they? And the room, that's another piece of bullshit! Cooked up so as to steer me into your nasty little *flic*'s net!'

'Are you afraid of the police, Le Guern?'

'What's that to you?'

'Keep it to yourself, then. But I am not a policeman.'

'Pull the other one. How did you know about my Ducouëdic, then?'

'He was my father.'

Joss froze in position, with his elbows on the table and his chin jutting out. He was drunk, and he was suspended in disbelief.

'Bullshit,' he muttered after a heavy pause.

Decambrais unbuttoned his jacket and fumbled about for a while until he found the inside pocket. He pulled out his wallet and extracted an identity card which he handed to the ex-mariner. Joss looked at it this way and that, and went over name, mugshot, date and place of birth with his finger, as if checking up on his own eyes. Hervé Ducouëdic, born in Tréguier, seventy years old.

When Joss looked up, Decambrais had put his index finger over his lips. Mum's the word. Joss nodded agreement. Complications. He could see there were complications, despite having had one too many. But there was such a din in the Viking that there was no real danger of being overheard.

'So . . . what's this about "Decambrais"?'

'Crap.'

Well, hats off. Hats off to the toff. To give him

his due. Joss took the time to have another hard think.

'And so, are you or aren't you an aristocrat?'

'Am I what?'

'An aristo.'

'An aristocrat?' Decambrais put his ID card back into his wallet. 'Look here, Le Guern, if I were an aristocrat, would I be slaving away making lace for a living?'

'But you could be a ruined aristocrat.'

'Sorry to disappoint you, but I'm the first without the second. Shirtless. Down on my uppers. Cleaned out. And Breton.'

Joss leaned back in his chair, flabbergasted and bereft, like a man who has just realised his pet theory doesn't hold water.

'Be careful, Le Guern. Not a word of this to anyone, you understand?'

'Lizbeth?'

'Not even Lizbeth knows. Nobody must know.'

'So why did you tell me?'

'Tit for tat,' Decambrais explained as he emptied his glass once more. 'One good turn deserves another. Of course, if it makes you change your mind about the room, don't hesitate to say so. It would be perfectly comprehensible.'

Joss sat up to attention.

'So are you still going to take it?' Decambrais asked. 'Because there is a waiting list, you know.'

'I'll take it,' Joss blurted out.

'Well, see you tomorrow, then.' Decambrais stood up. 'And thank you for the messages.'

Joss tugged at the toff's sleeve.

'Decambrais, what's special about these messages?'

'They're sly and they're smelly. I'm pretty sure that they're dangerous, as well. As soon as I see the light, I'll let you know.'

'The beacon,' said Joss dreamily. 'As soon as you see the beacon.'

'That's right. When I see the beacon.'

CHAPTER 8

Most of the 4s had already been removed from the front doors of the three blocks, especially from the two in the eighteenth arrondissement, which inhabitants said had been marked ten and eight days ago, respectively. But as they'd been daubed with high-quality acrylic paint, blackish trace-marks were still clearly visible on the wooden door panels. On the other hand, Maryse's staircase still had several untouched examples, which Adamsberg had photographed before they were wiped. They had been done free-hand, not with a stencil, but they all displayed the same features: about three feet high, with strokes that were a good inch wide, they were all reversed, with a splay-footed downstroke and a double notch on the crossbar.

'Nice work, isn't it?' Adamsberg said to his number two, who had not said a word throughout. 'He must be very gifted. He does it in one go, as if he was writing a Chinese character. Doesn't need to make corrections or to go over it again.'

'No doubt about that,' said Danglard as he got

into the passenger seat. 'A firm and elegant hand. Very talented.'

The photographer stowed his equipment in the boot and Adamsberg drove off at a gentle pace.

'Do you need the prints urgently?' Barteneau asked.

'No, not at all,' said Adamsberg. 'Let me have them when you can."

'The day after tomorrow, then. I've got some prints to make for the Quai tonight.'

'Ah, and another thing. No need to mention this little job to the Quai. It's just a friendly excursion. All right?'

'If he's that talented,' Danglard mused, 'maybe he is a real painter.'

'But they aren't works of art, you know. I really don't think so.'

'On the other hand the whole set of 4s might just be some kind of art project. For instance, if he tackled hundreds of buildings all over Paris, he would get into the news eventually. The papers would call it a major project to take the community hostage, an "artistic intervention". Give them six months, and the man's name would be out.'

'Yes. You're probably right,' said Adamsberg.

'I'm sure he is,' the photographer chimed in.

Adamsberg suddenly recalled the name: Brateneau. No, Barteneau. Thin plus redhead plus photographer equals Barteneau. Splendid. But no way could he find the man's first name. Still, you mustn't ask for the moon, even from yourself.

'There was once a fellow in Nanteuil, where I come from,' Barteneau continued, 'who painted about a hundred dustbins in the space of a week. Bright red, with black polka dots. Then he hung them on telegraph poles. The result was the whole town looked like it had suffered an invasion of huge ladybirds sitting on giant twigs. Well, within a month, the prankster landed a job on local radio, and since then he's become the local talking head on culture.'

Adamsberg drove on quietly, finding crafty ways to get round the evening rush hour jams, and eventually they drew near to the Murder Squad HQ.

'There's something that doesn't fit,' he said when he'd stopped at a red light.

'I've got it,' said Danglard.

'What?' said Barteneau.

'The guy did not paint the doors of all the flats,' Adamsberg answered. 'He painted *all except one* of the doors. In each of the blocks. But the missed door is not in the same place in each of the blocks. Sixth floor left on Maryse's stair, third floor right at rue Poulet, and fourth floor left at rue Caulaincourt. Doesn't fit very well with "action art".'

Danglard chewed his lip, one side then the other.

'Asymmetry is what guarantees the work's status as art, not decoration,' he suggested. 'It signifies that the artist is offering us a reflection on the world and not a wallpaper design. It's the missing piece in the jigsaw, the hole in the wall, the clinamen, the throw of the dice, the perfection of imperfection.'

'That's as may be, but the dice were loaded,' Adamsberg added.

'The true artist is the master of chance.'

'But he isn't an artist,' muttered Adamsberg.

He parked on the street in front of the Brigade and pulled on the handbrake.

'All right,' said Danglard, 'what is he, then?'

Adamsberg crossed his arms on the steering wheel, looked into the far distance and thought hard.

'Could you please try not to say "I don't know", sir?'

Adamsberg smiled. 'In that case I had better keep quiet.'

Adamsberg strode home at a good pace as he really did not want to be late for Camille. He showered and then slumped into an armchair to daydream for half an hour, since Camille was usually punctual. The only thought that ruffled the surface was that he felt naked under his clothes, as he often did when he hadn't seen Camille for a while. True, being naked under clothing is the natural condition of humankind. But the logical deconstruction of Adamsberg's observation didn't worry him one bit, because the fact remained that when he was expecting Camille he felt naked under his clothes, whereas when he was working, he did not. The difference was perfectly clear and obvious to him, and to hell with logic. And deconstruction.

CHAPTER 9

On Thursday, in a state of agitated impatience, in three short return trips fitted into the gaps between his three newscasts, and with the help of the van that Damascus lent him, Joss moved his belongings to his new digs. The young man also lent his muscles on the last round, to help get the heavy stuff down six flights of stairs. But there really wasn't very much of it: a sea chest covered in black canvas with copper studs, a wall mirror with a painted panel above depicting a three-master in dock, and a heavy, hand-carved armchair made by Joss's great-great-grandfather during one of his brief sojourns at home.

Joss had had a bad night imagining ever more fearsome things to be afraid of. What with two litres of red wine inside him, Decambrais – Hervé Ducouëdic, that is – had spilled too many beans. Joss was afraid that the old fraud might wake up in a sober panic and send him packing to the ends of the earth. But nothing like that happened. Decambrais took it all in his stride. At 0830 sharp, there he was leaning on his door post, book in hand as per usual. If he had any regrets – and he probably did – or if he quaked at the thought of having placed his deepest secret in the callused hands of a stranger – and a Breton beast to boot – well, he didn't let it show. And if he had a headache, and he must have, just as Joss did, well, he didn't let that show either. He looked just as collected and concentrated as he usually did when he heard the two messages that morning which fell into the category that both of them now referred to as 'the specials'.

Joss gave them to him that evening when he'd finally settled in. Once he was at last on his own in his new room for the first time, he took off his shoes and socks, closed his eyes, relaxed his arms and stood blissfully still on the carpet. That very same moment Nicolas Le Guern, born at Locmaria in 1832, came to sit on his huge bed with its wooden posts, and said good evening.

'Good evening to you,' said Joss.

'Nice one, my lad,' the ancestor said as he leaned on his elbow on the quilt.

'Not bad, eh?' Joss replied, half opening his eyes.

'You're better off here than you were over there. Didn't I tell you newscasting had real potential?'

'You've been saying that for seven years. Is that the reason you turned up tonight?'

'Those messages,' old Le Guern drawled as he scratched his stubbly cheek, 'those screeds you call "specials", the ones you're passing on to the

97

toff, well, if I were you, I'd give them a wide berth. They don't smell right.'

'They've been paid for, old fellow, and top rate too.' Joss was putting his socks and shoes back on.

The ancient mariner shrugged. 'If I were you, I'd give them a wide berth.'

'Meaning?'

'Meaning what it means, Joss my lad.'

Decambrais, quite unaware that Nicolas Le Guern was visiting on the first floor of his house, was working away in his cubbyhole on the ground floor. He reckoned that this time one of the 'specials' had rung a bell – faintly, to be sure, but maybe it was the ring of truth.

The morning's trawl had contained what Joss called 'the next chapter from the gobbledegook guy'. That's just it, Decambrais thought: it was a quotation that followed on from the last, from the middle of some source text. The mystery scribe had avoided quoting from the beginning of it. But why? Decambrais read and reread the messages in the hope that something in these familiar yet unplaceable sentences would suddenly give away the name of their author.

Up (and with my wife, who has not been at church a month or two) . . . Now I am at a loss to know whether it be my Hares-foot which is my preservative against wind,

for I never had a fit of the Collique since
I wore it.

Decambrais sighed and put the sheet down, then
turned to the other one, the one that had rung a
bell:

Et de eis quae significant illud, est ut videas
mures et animalia quae habitant sub terra
afugere ad superficiem terrae et pati sedar, id est,
commoveri hinc inde sicut animalia ebria . . .

He had scribbled a quick and over-literal trans-
lation under it, with a question mark in the middle:
And among the things that are a sign of it, there is
that you see rats and animals that live under ground
fleeing towards the surface and suffering(?), that is to
say that they come forth from that place like drunken
animals . . .
He'd been grappling with that *sedar* for an hour,
because it was not a word of Latin. He was pretty
sure it was not a copying error, because the pedant
was in all other respects quite meticulous, and
even used ellipses to indicate omissions from the
source text. So if the pedant had written sedar, it
must be because *sedar* occurred in the middle of
a passage that was in all other respects written in
impeccable medieval Latin. Decambrais slowly
clambered up the steps of his library ladder to
fetch another dictionary, and then stopped dead
in his tracks.

Arabic. It was a word of Arabic origin.

He climbed back down in almost feverish haste and sat at his desk with his hands flat on the screed, as if to make sure it would not fly away. Arabic *and* Latin: a hybrid text. Decambrais shuffled through the papers on his desk to find all the others that referred to subterranean beasts coming to the surface, including the first Latin text that Joss had read out the previous day, and that begin in almost exactly the same way: *You will see . . .*

> You will see animals born of corruption, such as worms, frogs and flies, multiply beneath the earth, and if the reason for it is also subterranean you will see reptiles that live in the depths coming to the surface of the earth, abandoning their eggs, and sometimes dying. And if the cause is in the air, the same will happen to the birds.

The sources repeated each other, sometimes word for word. So they must be different writers dealing with the same idea, down to the seventeenth century, for sure; it was an idea being handed down from one generation to the next. Just as medieval monks handed down the precepts of the church through the ages. The source must have been related to some constituted body, to some cultured élite. But no, not to the monasteries. The texts were not remotely religious.

Decambrais had laid his head in his hand to think

ever harder when a gay song rang out through the whole house. It was Lizbeth summoning them all to dinner.

When he went down to the dining room Joss found all the inmates of the Decambrais Hotel already at their seats unfolding their napkins from their individual wooden rings, each with its distinctive mark. Joss, overcome for once by shyness, hadn't meant to join the common table on his first evening – residents weren't obliged to take dinner, as long as they signed out the day before. But he had become used to living alone, eating alone, sleeping alone, and even talking by himself, except when he went to eat at the Viking, which wasn't that often. In fourteen years of exile in Paris, he'd had three rather abbreviated affairs, but he'd never dared take any one of his girlfriends back to his room to share the mattress on the bare floor. Their places, however modest, had always been far more comfortable than his own dilapidated cabin.

Joss made a conscious effort to shake off the boorishness that seemed to be welling up from his far-distant youth, when he'd been a rough and awkward adolescent. Lizbeth smiled as she handed him his personal napkin ring. Lizbeth's smile made him want to throw himself at her in a great leap, like a drowning man straining for a rock on a dark night. She was a splendid rock to be stranded on – smooth, dark and round, and worthy of eternal gratitude. Joss was amazed at himself. He'd never known such a violent urge, save with Lizbeth, and only when she smiled. The assembled company welcomed Joss, who took a seat next to Decambrais, on his right. Lizbeth presided at the other end of the table, and busied herself with serving the meal. The other two residents were there: Castillon, from room 1, a retired blacksmith who had spent the first half of his life as a professional conjuror, performing all over Europe; and Evelyne Curie, from room 4, a tiny, timid woman under thirty with a gentle old-world face which she kept lowered over her plate. Lizbeth had given Joss his navigation chart the moment he'd moved into the hotel.

'Now listen here, sailorman,' she'd begun, as she pulled him into the bathroom for the lecture. 'Don't you go putting your foot in it here. You can push Castillon around if you like, he's got broad shoulders and he likes to think he can take a joke. He's not as tough as he looks, but he can cope. Don't worry if your watch goes missing during dinner, it's an old habit of his, he can't resist the temptation, but he always gives it back over dessert. By the way, dessert is stewed fruit on weekdays or fresh fruit in season, and semolina pudding on Sundays. No plastic food here, you can eat it all blindfold. But keep your hands off the little lady, sailorman. She's been safe here for a year and a half. She ran away from a husband who'd been thrashing her for eight years. Can you imagine, eight years of battering? Apparently, she was in love with the brute. Anyway, she finally saw the light and turned up here one fine day. But watch it, sailorman. Her bloke is scouring the city looking for her, so as to flay her alive and welcome her home. The two things don't really go together, but that's how those sort of men work, and he's on autopilot. He's up to killing her so no-one else can have her – you've knocked around, you know the scene. So, mum's the word – you've never heard of Evelyne Curie, never come across the name. We call her Eva around here, that keeps us in the clear. You got that, sailorman? Treat her nicely. She doesn't say much, she's quite jumpy, she blushes as if she was always afraid of some-thing. She's getting better bit by bit, but it's a long haul. As for me, well, you know who I am, I'm OK but I'm finished with leg-overs and all that stuff. That's about it. Go down to dinner, it's nearly time. And I'd better tell you straight away, it's two bottles per meal and not a drop more, because Decambrais has a weakness and I have to hold him back. If you want to tank up you go over to Bertin's afterwards. And breakfast is from seven to eight, suits everybody except the black-smith who's a late riser, each to his own is what I say. I've said my piece, so don't get in my way, and I'll get your ring. I've got one with a chick and one with a boat. Which would you rather have?'

'What ring?' asked Joss

'The ring for your napkin. Oh, and there's a wash every week, whites on Friday, coloureds on Tuesday.

If you don't want your smalls mixed up with the blacksmith's, there's a launderette two hundred yards down the road. If you want your stuff ironed, Marie-Belle, who comes to do the windows, will take it in for a consideration. So, which ring do you want?'

'The chick,' Joss said decisively.

Lizbeth sighed as she went downstairs. 'Why do men always try to be smart?'

Soup, veal stew, cheese and cooked pears. Castillon wittered on, Joss kept his peace and looked for his bearings, as he would in unknown waters. Little Eva ate noiselessly and raised her eyes only once, to ask Lizbeth to pass the bread. Lizbeth smiled and Joss had the impression that Eva also wanted to bury herself in Lizbeth's broad bosom. But maybe it was just him.

Decambrais said almost nothing during dinner. Lizbeth whispered to Joss, who was lending a hand with clearing the dishes, 'When he's like that it means he's working during his meal.' Indeed, as soon as the pears were finished, Decambrais got up, made his excuses and went back to his cubbyhole to work.

Light dawned in the morning, at the very moment of awakening. The name rose to his lips even before he had opened his eyes, as if the word had been eagerly waiting all night long for the sleeper to wake so it could introduce itself to him. Decambrais could hear himself saying it softly and clearly: *Avicenna.*

He got up saying it over and over so it would not

104

evaporate along with the mists of sleep. For safety, he wrote it down. *Avicenna.* Then he put alongside: *Liber canonis.* The canon of medieval medicine.

Avicenna. The great Avicenna: early eleventh century, Persian philosopher and physician, transcribed in a thousand manuscripts from East to West. Latin translations sprinkled with Arabic terms. He was on the right track now.

Decambrais hung about at the foot of the stairs with a broad smile on his face, waiting to bump into his Breton lodger. 'Sleep well, Le Guern?'

Joss could see that something was up. Decambrais had a thin, pale face that often looked like death warmed up, but this morning he looked almost ruddy, as if he'd been out in the sun too long. And he wasn't smiling his ordinary, slightly cynical and snooty smile, but simply beaming.

'I've got him, Le Guern, I've got him!'

'What?'

'Our pedant, of course! I've got him, dammit! Keep today's "specials" for me, won't you, I'm off to the library.'

'You mean downstairs in your cubbyhole?'

'No, Le Guern. I do not have every book.'

'Oh really?' said Joss, genuinely surprised at the news.

Decambrais stood there in his overcoat with his briefcase wedged between his heels taking down that morning's 'special' from Joss's dictation:

When the air varieth from his natural temperature, declining to heat and moisture, when it seemeth cloudie and dustie; when the wyndes are gross and hot; then are the Planets in disorder, and hang their poison in the sick air

He slipped the sheet into his briefcase, waited to hear the day's shipwreck story, and at five minutes to nine strode down the steps to the metro.

CHAPTER 10

That Thursday Adamsberg arrived at the office after Danglard – an event sufficiently rare for it to cause the latter to give his chief a long and meaningful glance. Adamsberg had the rumpled look of a man who's had only a few hours sleep towards dawn. He went out again straight away to have an espresso at the corner café.

It must be Camille, Danglard concluded. Camille must have come back last night. He switched on his computer in desultory fashion. He'd slept alone, as usual. With his ugly mug and his pear-shaped torso, he was damn lucky if he got to touch a woman once every two years. Danglard pulled himself back from the brink of this habitual slough of despond and its accompanying Pilsner six-pack with his usual trick of running a mental slide show of the faces of his five children. The fifth with his pale blue eyes wasn't actually his, but his wife, when she left him, let him keep the whole bunch as a job lot. That was a while back now – eight years and thirty-six days. It had taken him two years and six thousand five hundred bottles of lager to free his mind of the full-screen image of Marie's back in a green trouser suit walking down the corridor in their flat, cool as a cucumber, and slamming the front door shut behind her. Since then, the kids' gallery – twin boys, twin girls, then blue-eyes on his own – had become his place of mental safety, his refuge and comfort. In that time he must have spent thousands of hours grating carrots, washing socks, checking schoolbags, ironing T-shirts, and scrubbing the toilet bowl to a microbe-free sheen. His Stakhanovite parenting gradually subsided to a mellower if still strenuous routine, while the lager intake fell to only fourteen hundred cans a year. On bad days, though, it was supplemented by supplies of white wine. What remained was the bright sun of his relationship with the five kids, and no-one, he told himself on particularly gloomy awakenings, was ever going to take that away from him. Nobody had the slightest wish to do so, in any case.

He had tried after much patient waiting to have a woman perform the reverse operation – to come in the door frontways and walk coolly down the corridor towards him in a green trouser suit, but nothing much came of that plan. The women who came into the flat never stayed very long, and while they were there relations tended to be stormy. He couldn't aspire to a woman like Camille, he couldn't ask for the moon. Her profile was so sharp and lovely that you were torn between wanting to paint her portrait instantly and wanting to kiss her lips. He would be happy with just a woman – any woman, really. Why should he object if her middle was as broad as his own?

Danglard saw Adamsberg come back in and shut himself in his office with a silent closing of the door. He wasn't an oil painting either, but somehow he'd got the rainbow. Actually it would be truer to say that although none of Adamsberg's features was handsome in itself, their combination paradoxically made him quite a good-looking man. None of the individual traits of his face could be called balanced, harmonious or handsome; in fact, he was a hotch-potch – yet the overall impression he made was attractive, especially when he got excited. Danglard had always found this random outcome quite unfair. His own face was no worse a mishmash than Adamsberg's, but the cumulative effect was hopeless. Whereas Adamsberg, with no better cards to play, had got trumps.

Because Danglard had made himself read and think a lot since the age of two and a half, he wasn't jealous. Also because he had his mental slide show. Also because despite the chronic irritation that Adamsberg caused him, Danglard quite liked the man; he even quite liked the way he looked, with his big nose and his odd, sideways smile. He'd not hesitated for a moment when Adamsberg had asked him to join his new murder squad. Adamsberg's relaxed manner provided a much-needed counterweight to his own anxious and sometimes rather brittle hyperactivity; in fact, it calmed him down every day as much as a six-pack did.

Danglard meditated on Adamsberg's closed door. One way or another the man was going to work on those 4s and was trying not to put his number two's nose out of joint. He took his hands off the keyboard and leaned back in his chair. He was mildly worried: maybe he had been on the wrong track since yesterday evening. Come to think of it, he had seen those reversed 4s somewhere before. It had come to him in bed, as he was going to sleep, on his own. Somewhere long ago, maybe when he was still a young man, not yet a *flic*, and not in Paris. Danglard hadn't travelled much in his life, so maybe he could try to track down that memory, assuming that anything of it remained save for an almost entirely obliterated trace.

Adamsberg had actually closed his door so as to be able to call around forty Paris commissariats without feeling the shadow of his deputy's justified irritation looming over his shoulder. Danglard had plumped for a radical art operation; Adamsberg did not share that view. But to go from disagreeing with Danglard to launching inquiries over the whole metropolitan area of Paris was an illogical leap which Adamsberg preferred to perform on his own. Even this morning he hadn't been quite sure he would do it. At breakfast, apologising to Camille for bringing work home, he'd opened his notebook and stared at Maryse's sketch of the 4 as if he was playing double or quits. He asked Camille what she thought of it. 'Pretty,' she said. Before she had woken up properly, Camille's sight was so poor that she couldn't really distinguish a landscape painting from a strip cartoon. If she'd actually seen the pencil drawing, she wouldn't have called it pretty. She'd have said: 'But that's ghastly.' Adamsberg replied gently: 'No, Camille, it's not a pretty picture.' That was the moment, the word, the correction that made up his mind in a flash.

Feeling comfortably weary and agreeably woolly after his not very restful night, Adamsberg dialled the first number on his list.

He got to the end of his list by five, and he'd only once been out for a walk, at lunchtime. That was when Camille got him on his mobile, when he was munching a sandwich on a park bench.

It wasn't her style to rehearse the events of the night before. Camille used words with care and discretion, relying on her body to express feelings. It was up to you to know what they were; it wasn't easy to be sure.

Adamsberg jotted down on his pad: *woman* plus *smart* plus *desire* equals *Camille*. He broke off, and reread his note. Big words and flat words. But for all their obviousness, when applied to Camille they went into relief. He could almost see them rising like Braille from the surface of the paper. OK. Equals Camille. It was very hard for him to write the word *Love*. His ballpoint made an 'L,'

111

but out of sheer anxiety it stalled on the 'o'. Adamsberg had long been puzzled by his own reticence until he'd managed to unravel it to its core, or so he thought. He liked loving. But he didn't like what loving habitually brings in its train. Because love *leads to other things*, he thought. Staying in bed for ever or even for just a couple of days is an impossible dream. Love, hauled by a few common ideas, always *leads on to* four walls and no way out. It flares up out in the open like a grass fire but comes to rest under one roof, warming slippered feet at the stove. A man like Adamsberg could see from afar that the ineluctable train of *other things* was a ghastly trap. He shied away from its earliest symptoms, for he was as alert to its approach as an animal sensing the distant footfall of a predator. But he reckoned Camille was always a step ahead of him in flight. With her periodic leaves of absence, with her guarded emotions, and her boots always set ready in the starting blocks. But Camille played her game under better cover than he did, she did it less roughly, with more kindliness. As a result, unless you took the time to think about it for a while, you would not necessarily divine her imperious instinct for staying wild and free. And Adamsberg had to admit that he did not take enough time to think about Camille. He sometimes began to do so, but then forgot to follow through as other thoughts intervened and jostled him from one idea to another until they all fell into that kaleidoscopic pattern which presaged a moment of total mental blankness.

While hammer drills split his ears as the workmen carried on fixing the window bars, Adamsberg finished writing down the sentence in the notebook on his lap by placing a firm full stop after the L. Camille hadn't called him to gurgle mutual congratulations but to make a serious point about the 4 that he'd shown her that morning. Adamsberg got up and made his way over yet more builders' rubble into the building and Danglard's office.

'Did you find that file?' he asked, so as to open a channel.

Danglard nodded and pointed to the screen: fingerprints were scrolling down so fast that they looked like galaxies seen from the Hubble.

Adamsberg went round to the other side of the desk so as to face Danglard.

'If you had to give a figure, how many buildings in Paris would you say had been marked with the number 4?'

'Three.'

Adamsberg raised the fingers of his hands.

'Three plus nine makes twelve. If we allow for the fact that not many people apart from neurotics and idlers would bother to report this sort of thing to the police, though I suppose there are quite a few neurotic idlers around, I would put the figure at a minimum of thirty blocks already ornamented by our action artist.'

'All the same 4s? Same shape, same colour?'

'The very identical.'

'Always on a blank door?'

'We'll have to check that.'

'You mean you're going to check?'

'I guess so.'

Danglard put his hands on his knees.

'I've seen that 4 somewhere before.'

'So has Camille.'

Danglard raised an eyebrow.

'In a book lying open on a table,' Adamsberg said. 'At a friend of a friend's place.'

'What was the book about?'

'Camille doesn't know. She supposes it's a history book, because the fellow who's her friend's friend is a cleaner by day and a medievalist by night.'

'Isn't it normally the other way round?'

'What norm are you referring to?'

Danglard stretched out an arm towards the bottle of beer that was on his desk and raised it to his lips.

'So where did you see it, then?' asked Adamsberg.

'I can't remember. It was a long time ago and it was not in Paris.'

'If there are previous instances of the reversed 4, then it's not an original creation.'

'No, it's not,' Danglard concurred.

'To count as action art, it would have to be original, wouldn't it?'

'In theory, yes.'

'What are we going to do with your radical action artist, then?'

Danglard pursed his lips. 'I think we take him off the board for now.'

'And so what do we put in his place?'

'Some oddbod who's no business of ours.'

Adamsberg walked up and down and straight through the decorators' mess on the floor, getting plaster dust on his well-worn shoes.

'May I remind you, sir, that we have been transferred?,' said Danglard. 'Transferred to the Brigade Criminelle.'

'I've not forgotten that,' said Adamsberg.

'Has any offence been committed in these blocks of flats?'

'No, no offence.'

'Has there been any violence? Any threats of violence? Any intimidation of innocent parties?'

'You know very well there's been no such thing.'

'So why are we discussing the matter?'

'Because, Danglard, there is a presumption of violence.'

'In those 4s?'

'Yes. We have a silent campaign. A very serious campaign.'

Adamsberg looked at his watch.

'I've got time to take . . .'

He opened his memory-jogger then closed it quickly again.

'. . . to take Barteneau with me to see some of these places.'

While Adamsberg went to fetch the jacket he'd left all crumpled on a chair, Danglard slipped on his own, making sure it hung correctly on his frame. He might not be a handsome man, but that was no reason not to keep himself looking shipshape and Bristol fashion.

CHAPTER 11

Decambrais came home quite late and only just had time before dinner to pick up the evening 'special' that Joss had put aside for him.

[. . .] when come forth toade stooles and when fields and woods be covered in spiderwebs, when oxen ail or die in the meadow, likewise beastes in the forest; when bread doth quickly go mouldie; when new-hatched flies & worms & fleas can be seen on snow [. . .]

He folded up the sheet while Lizbeth was touring the house to call residents down to the dinner table. With a less radiant expression on his face than he'd had that morning, Decambrais put his hand on Joss's shoulder.

'We must talk,' he said. 'Tonight at the Viking. I'd like us not to be overhead.'

'Good trawling?'

'Good but deadly. The fish is too big for us to handle.'

Joss gave the old man a dubious glance.

'No, Le Guern, I'm not exaggerating. Breton's honour.'

At dinner Joss managed to get a smile out of Eva's half-hidden face by telling a partly fanciful family story, and he felt mightily pleased with himself. He helped Lizbeth clear the table, out of habit, mainly, but also as an excuse for having her company. He was just ready to set off for the Viking when she came down from her room dressed to kill in a shiny, tight-fitting black dress. She bustled past with a smile and Joss's heart sank to his boots.

Decambrais had stationed himself at the very back of the Viking, and was waiting for Joss in that over-heated and smoke-filled room with two glasses of *calva* on the table in front of him.

'Lizbeth went out in full battledress as soon the dishes were done,' Joss said as he pulled up a chair.

'Yes,' said Decambrais without the slightest surprise.

'She has a date?'

'Lizbeth goes out in a gown every night except Tuesdays and Sundays.'

'Is she seeing someone?' Joss asked anxiously.

Decambrais shook his head.

'No, she sings.'

Joss frowned.

'She's a singer,' Decambrais repeated. 'She performs. In a cabaret. Lizbeth has a voice to die for.'

'Since when, dammit?'

'Since she moved in and since I taught her the tonic sol-fa. She pulls in the crowds every night at the Saint-Ambroise. One day, Le Guern, you'll see the name of Lizbeth Galston in lights. When you do, don't forget.'

'Can't imagine I could forget. Where is this cabaret, Decambrais? Can you just go along to listen?'

'Damascus goes along every night.'

'Damascus? Damascus Viguier?'

'Who else? Didn't he tell you?'

'We have coffee together every day of the week, and he's never breathed a word about it.'

'That's only to be expected. He's in love. Not something to be shared.'

'Bloody hell! Damascus! But he's thirty years old, he is.'

'So is Lizbeth. Being overweight doesn't make her any older.'

Joss's mind wandered for a moment towards the implausible conjunction of Damascus and Lizbeth.

'Could that ever work?' he asked. 'Seeing as you're an expert on keeping an even keel.'

Decambrais smiled sceptically.

'Lizbeth hasn't been impressed by men's bodies for a very long time.'

'Damascus is a nice lad, though.'

'That's not enough.'

'What does Lizbeth want from a man?'

'Not much.'

Decambrais downed a slug of *calva*. 'Love's not the topic of tonight's seminar, Le Guern.'

'I know. Tell me about it. The big fish you've hooked.'

Decambrais's face darkened.

'Bad as that, is it?'

'I fear it is.'

Decambrais looked around the room and seemed reassured by the racket that people were making. Worse than marauding Norsemen stomping off a longboat.

'I've tracked down one of the authors,' he said. 'It's Avicenna. An eleventh-century physician from Persia.'

'Great,' said Joss, who was much more interested in Lizbeth's affairs than he was in Avicenna's.

'I've found the passage quoted, in his *Liber canonis*.'

'Great,' said Joss again. 'Tell me, Decambrais, were you a teacher, like your dad?'

'How did you guess?'

'Easy as that,' said Joss with a snap of his thumb and middle finger. 'I've knocked about a bit as well, you know.'

'Look, you might be bored by what I'm telling you, Le Guern, but you'd do well to listen properly.'

'All right, then.' Joss felt he'd been whisked back to the classroom and brought to order by Ducouëdic Senior.

'All the other authors he's quoting are people who rewrote Avicenna. They're all talking about the same thing. They're skirting around the subject

120

but not saying its name. Like vultures circling in the air before diving on their prey.'

'Circling around what?' Joss wasn't sure he was following.

'Around the subject, Le Guern, I just told you. Around the sole real subject of all the "specials". Around what they portend.'

'So what do they portend?'

A moment's pause while Bertin served two more *calvas*. Decambrais waited for the hulking barman to move away before he whispered:

'Plague.'

'What plague?'

'THE plague.'

'The great plague of yore, you mean?'

'None other. Black Death. The great affliction. The plague.'

Joss took a deep breath. Could the bookworm be off his rocker? Could he be taking Joss for a ride? Joss had no way of checking up on the *Liber canonis* stuff, so Decambrais could lead him up the garden path if he wanted to. He cast his sailor's eyes over Decambrais's face. No, he certainly did not look as if he was pulling anyone's leg.

'Are you trying to set me up, Decambrais?'

'Why should I do that?'

'Because Mr Know-All sometimes likes to score a point over Captain Dimwit. University challenge beats the intellectually challenged. But watch it, professor. If you're going to play games with me,

I can steer you out to sea as well, and leave you there without so much as a paddle.'

'Le Guern, you're a rough customer.'

'Yep,' Joss agreed.

'I guess you've beaten up a few guys in your time.'

'I've lost count.'

'Look, I'm not into competition. What would I get out of proving I'm an educated fellow?'

'Power.'

Decambrais smiled, and shrugged his shoulders.

'Could we get back to business?' he suggested.

'If you like. But why should I bother about it? For the last three months I've been reading out stuff that some guy has been copying out of the Bible. And so what? He's been paying his fees, I've been reading the messages. What's the problem?'

'The messages belong to you, legally speaking. So if I go to the police with them tomorrow morning, I'd like you to know in advance. And I would also like you to come with.'

Joss nearly choked on his *calva*.

'Police? You're off your head, Decambrais! What have the police got to do with it? This isn't a red alert, after all!'

'How do you know?'

Joss restrained himself from uttering the words that rose in his throat, because of the room. He did not want to lose that room.

'Listen, Decambrais,' he said in an effort to regain his self-control. 'According to you we're dealing with a guy who plays around copying out bits of old books about the plague. He's obviously nutty, he's got a bad case of bees in the bonnet. If we had to go the police every time a crackpot opened his mouth, well, we'd hardly have time for a drink.'

'First point,' said Decambrais as he drank half of his glass of spirits. 'The man is not adequately entertained by just copying out the extracts, because he pays you to bawl them out. He's talking to the wide world, through you, anonymously. Second point: he's getting closer. He's still on the opening passages, he hasn't yet got to the bits that contain the word "plague" or "disease" or "death". He's lingering on the doorstep, but he's not standing still. Do you get that, Le Guern? *He is moving forward.* That's what's serious. *He's moving.* But what is he moving towards?'

'Well, he's moving on towards the end of the books he's quoting, I suppose. Common sense, really. People don't begin a book at the end, do they?'

'Actually, it's several different books. I suppose you know how they end?'

'How could I, I haven't read any of the damn things!'

'In death, Le Guern. That's how they end. With tens of millions of people dying.'

'So you imagine this crackpot is going to kill half the country?'

'That's not what I said. I'm saying he's creeping

step by little step towards a ghoulish ending. It's not like he's reading us *The Arabian Nights.*'

'That's only your opinion. I think he's going round in circles. He's been boring us with his foul air and his worms and beasts for more than a month, and one way or another these messages all say the same thing. I don't call that moving forward.'

'But he *is* moving forward, Le Guern. Do you remember the other messages that sound like random extracts from somebody's diary?'

'That's my point. They're completely unrelated. It's just some fellow who eats, beds women, sleeps and so on. Hasn't got anything else to say.'

'The fellow in question is Samuel Pepys.'

'Talk about a stupid name!'

'Let me introduce you. Samuel Pepys, pronounced *Peeps,* 1633–1793. An upstanding yeoman of the city of London. And, as I'm sure you'll be pleased to hear, Secretary to the Admiralty.'

'You mean a bigwig on the Harbour Board?'

'Not exactly. But that's not the point. The point is that Pepys's diary runs from 1660 to 1669. The passages your crackpot has put into your urn all come from entries made in 1665. The year of the Great Plague of London, when seventy thousand people died. Do you see? Day by day, the "specials" are moving inexorably forward towards the date when the plague broke out. The last one is almost there. That's what I mean by *moving forward.*'

For the first time Joss felt a twinge of fear. What

the bookworm was saying made sense and seemed to fit together. But going to the police was something else.

'The *flics* will be tickled pink when we tell them a lunatic is making us read a three-hundred-year-old diary, you know. They're quite likely to think we're the lunatics.'

'Well, we won't exactly say that to the police. We'll say that there's a madman about who's making public forecasts of mass death. Then it's their problem to do something about it. At least I'll have a clear conscience.'

'They'll split their sides, even so.'

'Quite. That's why we'll not go to see any old *flic*. I know a rather special policeman who doesn't laugh at the same things as other *flics*. He's the one we should go and see.'

'You can go if you like, but count me out. Anyway, it would be a miracle if they took my word for gospel. My record isn't exactly a blank slate, Decambrais.'

'Nor is mine.'

Joss was speechless. Hats off, old man. Hats off to the toff. Not only was the bookworm a genuine Breton, like you would never have guessed, but he'd got a record too. Which was presumably why he'd changed his name.

'How long?' Joss asked plainly, refraining from asking what the charge had been, *noblesse oblige*.

'Six months,' said Decambrais.

'I got nine.'

'Inside?'

'Inside.'

'Same here.'

They were quits. A moment of heavy silence ensued.

'OK, fine,' said Decambrais. 'So you're coming with?'

Joss screwed up his face.

'But they're only words. Not sticks and stones. You know the rhyme? Words can never hurt you. If they could, we'd know about it by now.'

'But we do know, Le Guern. Rhyme isn't reason. Words have always been killers.'

'Since when?'

'Ever since someone shouted "Off with his head!" and people rushed in to do the job. Since for ever.'

'All right, you win,' said Joss. 'And what if the police close down my business?'

'Come on, Captain! Are you saying you're frightened of policemen?'

Joss pulled himself up to face this challenge.

'Now look here, Decambrais, the Le Guerns may be rough customers, but who ever said we were afraid of the police?'

'Well, there you are then.'

CHAPTER 12

'Who's the *flic* we're off to see?' Joss asked as they walked down Boulevard Arago at ten next morning.

'Someone I came across a couple of times in the course of the . . . of my . . .'

'Mishap?' Joss suggested.

'My mishap.'

'You can't have the measure of a man if you've only seen him twice.'

'You get a bird's-eye view, and the picture looked good. On first meeting I thought he was in custody himself, and that's a pretty good sign. He'll give us five minutes of his time. The worst he can do is log our call and forget it. At best he'll get interested enough to find out a few things for himself.'

'Things after the fact.'

'After the fact.'

'Why would he get interested?'

'He likes woolly stories and tracks that lead nowhere. At least, that's what one of his bosses was reproaching him for when I first ran across him.'

'Are we going to see a little fish, then?'

'Would that bother you, Captain?'

'Look, I've already told you, Decambrais. I don't give a damn about the whole business.'

'He's not small fry by any means. He's a *commissaire principal* now, and he's got his own squad. Murder Squad.'

'Murder? Well, well, he'll really lap up our quotations game, won't he?'

'How do you know?'

'And thanks to what did a woolly mind get to become *commissaire principal*?'

'He's brilliant as well as woolly, so I was given to understand. I mean, I said woolly, but I could also have said magical.'

'I won't argue over words.'

'I like arguing over words.'

'I'd noticed.'

Decambrais came to a halt in front of a tall archway entrance.

'Here we are,' he said.

Joss surveyed the front of the building.

'They could use a decorator on this place.'

Decambrais leaned back against the wall and crossed his arms.

'What's up? Are we backing out, then?'

'We have an appointment six minutes from now. He must be very busy. So we keep to time.'

Joss leaned against the wall next to Decambrais, and they waited side by side.

A man walked past with his eyes on the ground and his hands in his pockets. He sauntered into the building without seeing the pair of them standing against the wall.

'I think that's him,' Decambrais hissed.

'The swarthy little fellow? You must be joking. With that old grey jumper and crumpled jacket? Needs a haircut, too. I'm not saying he runs a market stall, but no way is that a commissaire principal!'

'I'm telling you that's him. I recognised his gait. He pitches.'

Decambrais kept his eye on his watch until the appointed hour, and then took Joss into the building, or rather, the building site.

'I remember you, Ducouëdic,' said Adamsberg as he showed the two men into his office. 'Well, to be honest, I didn't remember straight off, but I took out your file after your call and that brought you back. At the time we talked a bit about things. They weren't going too well, were they? I think I advised you to leave the profession.'

'Which is what I did,' said Decambrais, raising his voice to cover the clatter of the power drills, though Adamsberg seemed not to notice them.

'Did you find another job when you got out?'

'I took up consulting,' said Decambrais, omitting the sub-letting and lace-making sides of his life.

'Tax consulting?'

'No, personal consulting. Even Keel Counselling, that's what I call myself.'

'Oh I see,' said Adamsberg, pensively. 'And why not. Do you have many clients?'

'Can't complain.'

'What do people come to see you about?'

Joss began to wonder whether Decambrais had got the right address, or whether this odd *flic* ever bothered to do any work. There was no terminal in the room, just papers in piles on the desk, on the chairs, on the floor, all covered with notes and doodles. The *commissaire* hadn't sat down but stood leaning against the white wall with his arms to his side, and was leaning his head down so as to look at Decambrais from underneath his eyelids. Joss reckoned the *flic*'s eyes were the same colour and consistency as fucus, that brown and slippery seaweed that ties itself into knots around ships' screws. Those eyes were just as soft, just as vague and just as shiny, but they had no sparkle and no clear object. The spherical vesicles of that kind of seaweed were called floaters, and Joss reckoned the word suited Adamsberg's eyes to a T. The *commissaire*'s floaters were buried beneath a protective overhang of untidy, bushy brows. A hook nose and bony features gave the face some counterbalancing weight all the same.

'Well, mainly for love,' Decambrais went on. 'Too much, too little, or none at all, that's what they come about. Or else because it's not the kind they want, or because they just can't get hold of it because of this or that or other . . .'

'Things,' Adamsberg prompted.

'Other things,' Decambrais concurred.

'Look, Ducouëdic,' Adamsberg said as he took

off from the wall and paced around the room, 'this is a special unit here. We deal with murder. So if it's your old mishap that's the issue, if there's a sequel or if you're being bothered by it one way or another, I really can't . . .'

'No, this isn't about me,' Decambrais interrupted. 'But we've not come about a crime, either. At least, not yet.'

'Threats?'

'Maybe. Anonymous announcements. Announcements of death.'

Joss put his elbows on his knees and began to pay amused attention. The bookworm was going to have a hard time making sense of his abstruse anxieties.

'Directed at a particular individual?'

'No. Announcements of general destruction and catastrophe.'

'OK,' said Adamsberg as he continued to pace up and down. 'Are we dealing with a prophet of the Second Coming? Prophesying what? The apocalypse?'

'Bubonic plague.'

'Well, well,' said Adamsberg. He took a moment to think. 'That rather changes things. How does he announce the coming of the plague, then? By mail? By phone?'

'By means of my friend here,' Decambrais said with a gracious nod towards Joss. 'Monsieur Le Guern is by profession a town crier, the business was established by his great-great-grandfather. He gives the news broadcast for the Edgar-Quinet

– rue Delambre crossing area. He'll explain better than I can.'

Adamsberg turned his somewhat weary face to Joss.

'I'll put it in a nutshell,' said Joss. 'People who've got something to say leave messages for me and I read them out. Not very hard. All you need is a voice that carries and good timekeeping.'

'And so?'

'Every day, and two or three times a day now,' Decambrais interjected, 'Monsieur Le Guern finds he has short texts announcing the coming of the plague to read out. Each message brings us nearer to the outbreak.'

'OK,' said Adamsberg, reaching for the logbook, but so clumsily that he made it plain that the interview was nearing its end. 'Since when?'

'Since August 17,' said Joss.

Adamsberg froze in mid-movement and his eyes darted towards the ex-sailor.

'Are you sure?'

That was when Joss realised he had been wrong. Not about the date of the first 'special,' but about the *commissaire*'s eyes. A hard sharp light had switched on inside the seaweed like a tiny fire bursting forth from the gelatinous pod. So he went on and off like a beacon.

'August 17, morning trawl. Straight after dry dock.'

Adamsberg put the logbook aside and went back to pacing. August 17 was the date of the first flat-daubing, or at least of the first notification of the plague of 4s. Rue de Chaillot. Two days later, second outbreak, in Montmartre.

'And the second message?' Adamsberg asked.

'Two days later, on August 19,' Joss replied. 'Then one on August 22. Then they came thicker and faster. Almost daily since August 24, and several times a day for the last while.'

'Can I see?'

Decambrais handed him the latest sheets they'd kept. Adamsberg looked through them rapidly.

'I don't see what makes you link these with the plague.'

'I tracked down the sources,' said Decambrais. 'These messages are all quotations from old treatises about plague – there have been hundreds of them over the centuries. Our message-writer has got as far as the premonitory signs. He'll soon be at the heart of the matter. We're really very close to it. The last message, the one that came this morning,' Decambrais said as he pointed to one of the pieces of paper on the table, 'stops just short of the actual word "plague".'

Adamsberg read that morning's special:

[. . .] when many move about like shadows on a wall, when dark vapours rise like fog from the earth [. . .] when can be seen in men a great lack of self-confidence and much jealousy, hatred and licence [. . .]

'In fact, I think we'll get there tomorrow,' said Decambrais. 'That's to say tonight, for our man. Because of the *Diary*.'

'You mean those random fragments of daily life?'

'They're not random at all. The extracts are all in chronological order, from the year 1665, the year of the Great Plague of London. In a few days' time, Pepys sees his first corpse. Tomorrow, I think. Yes, tomorrow.'

Adamsberg gave a great sigh as he reshuffled the papers on his desk.

'And what do you reckon we'll see tomorrow?'

'No idea.'

'Probably nothing at all. But it really isn't nice, is it?'

'Quite so.'

'But completely imaginary.'

'I know. The last outbreak of plague in France faded away in Marseille in 1722. It's become a legend.'

Adamsberg ran his fingers through his hair (maybe that was his way of combing, Joss thought) then gathered the messages together and gave the clip back to Decambrais.

'Thank you,' he said.

'Should I go on reading them out?' Joss asked.

'Oh yes, please don't stop. And come and tell me what happens next.'

'And if nothing happens?'

'People who are that organised and bizarre nearly always end up making some kind of physical appearance, if only fleetingly. I would be interested to know what your man comes up with to conclude his campaign.'

Adamsberg showed the pair out of the building and walked slowly back to his office. The whole story was extremely unsettling. Ghastly. It had no connection at all with the 4s except the coincidence of the dates. But all the same he was inclined to go along with Ducouëdic's train of thought. Tomorrow, the diarist was going to see his first corpse on the streets of London, the first visible sign of the plague. Adamsberg took out his address book while still standing up and flicked through it to find the number of the medievalist that Camille had mentioned. That was where that she'd seen the reverse 4. He looked up at the wall clock that had just been installed: five to eleven. If the man was working as a cleaner there wasn't much chance he would be home. But a young man answered the phone. He sounded eager.

'Marc Vandoosler?'

'He's out. He's manning the front lines, big drive on floors and laundry. I can leave a message at his bunk, if you like.'

'Thank you,' said Adamsberg, somewhat taken aback.

He heard the receiver being put down, then the scrabbling sound of paper and pencil being brought to the ready.

'At your service, sir. Whom might I say?'

'*Commissaire Principal* Jean-Baptiste Adamsberg, Murder Squad.'

'Bloody hell!' The voice went serious all of a sudden. 'Is Marc in trouble?'

'Not at all. Camille Forestier gave me his number.'

'Aha. Camille,' the voice said, quite plainly. But the intonation on 'Camille' was such that Adamsberg, who was not a jealous man, nonetheless felt a jolt, or rather, surprise. Camille was connected to vast worlds and uncountably many people of whom he knew nothing and did not care to know. When he came across one of them he always got a little shock, as if he had just bumped into an undiscovered continent. But who said Camille was not a queen of many lands?

'It's about a drawing,' Adamsberg went on. 'Or rather, a design, a rather mysterious shape. Camille said she'd seen a reproduction of it in one of the books at Marc Vandoosler's place.'

'Quite possibly,' said the voice. 'But it's not going to be a very recent book.'

'Excuse me?'

'Marc's only interested in the Middle Ages,' said the voice with just a touch of disdain. 'He barely deigns to go as far as the sixteenth century. I don't suppose the Brigade Criminelle has a particular interest in medieval historiography, does it?'

'You never know.'

'OK,' said the voice. 'Can you describe the target?'

'It could help us a great deal if your friend

happened to know the meaning or signification of the design in question. Do you have a fax?'

'Yes, same number.'

'Good. I'll fax you the sketch, and if Vandoosler can tell us anything about it, we'd be most grateful if he could fax us back straight away.'

'Fine,' said the voice. 'Action stations. To the left, march.'

'Excuse me, Monsieur . . . .'

'Devernois, Lucien Devernois.'

'This is urgent. You have to believe me. Really urgent.'

'Nil desperandum, *commissaire*.'

Devernois hung up. Adamsberg put the receiver down. Very puzzling, that was. You had to admit that Devernois, even if he was a bit cheeky, was at his ease talking to the police. Maybe he'd been in the army.

Adamsberg stayed propped up against his office wall until twelve thirty, waiting for the fax machine to come to life. Then he abandoned his frustrating vigil, went out for a walk and looked for a bite to eat. Anything would do, anything that turned up in the local streets that he was beginning to learn. A sandwich, or tomatoes, or a bagel, or fruit, or a pastry, or whatever. Depending on what shops there were, on his fancy, on a whim. He dawdled on purpose round the block with a tomato in one hand and a nut-bread roll in the other. He was tempted to spend the rest of the day outside and to leave the office until tomorrow. But Vandoosler might have gone home for lunch. If he had, he could have sent a reply by now, and brought Adamsberg's lopsided paranoid construction crashing to the ground. At three he went back to his office, threw his jacket on a chair and confronted the fax machine. A sheet of thermal paper lay beneath it on the floor.

Dear *Commissaire Principal*,

The inverse 4 that you sent me is a faithful reproduction of the symbol that used to be painted in some parts of Europe on the lintels of doors and windows during an outbreak of plague. It is believed to have ancient origins, but it was absorbed into Christian culture and seen as a sign of the cross drawn without lifting the hand or stylus. It was also used as a merchants' mark and a printers' sign, but its main claim to fame is as a talisman offering protection against plague. People warded off the great affliction by drawing the inverse 4 on the doors of their houses.

Hoping this concludes your inquiry satisfactorily, I remain your devoted servant,

Marc Vandoosler

Adamsberg put one hand on his desk to steady himself and looked down at the floor with the fax hanging from his other hand. So the reverse 4 was a charm against plague. Thirty-odd blocks daubed with the sign, and a whole stack of messages in the town-crier's inbox. Tomorrow, the Londoner of 1665 was going to see his first corpse. With furrowed brow Adamsberg plodded through the decorator's rubbish and into Danglard's office.

'Danglard, your radical art fellow is behaving like a real idiot.'

Adamsberg put the fax in front of his deputy, who read it with suspicion. Then he reread it.

'Hmm. Now I remember. I saw that shape in the wrought-iron balustrade of the magistrates' court at Nancy. A historic monument, that building was. There were two 4s together, one the right way round, the other backwards way on, just like that.'

'So what do we do with your subversive installation artist, Danglard?'

'I've already told you. We put him on the back burner.'

'And then what?'

'We bring in someone else. A crackpot apostle who reckons he's saving his brothers and sisters from the plague.'

'No, he's not into saving souls. He's predicting. And he's planning. One thing after another. He's setting it all up. He could go into action tomorrow, or tonight.'

Danglard had become expert in reading Adamsberg's face. It could pass without transition from looking as cold as a rained-out bonfire to the intensity of an acetylene flame. When that happened, some still unexplained physiological process made Adamsberg's swarthy skin glow. Danglard knew from long experience that it would be pointless to contradict the man, to express any kind of doubt or to point out logical flaws in his position. All objections would just turn to steam, like drips falling on hot coals. So he preferred to keep his doubts bottled up and to save them for a less heated moment. At the same time Adamsberg's moments of intensity brought Danglard up against his own contradictions. The chief's passionate intuitions cut Danglard adrift from his rational moorings, yet he had to admit that he found it oddly relaxing to throw caution and common sense to the winds. He had no choice but to listen almost passively and to ride with his boss on a cloud of ideas for which he felt no responsibility. Adamsberg's rich and gravelly voice, his hesitations, self-repetitions and circumlocutions, which tried Danglard's patience sorely most of the time, actually contributed to the pleasure of journeys taken on the back of a woolly idea. But what Danglard had learned most of all from their long working partnership was that Adamsberg's muddled intuitions all too often landed right on target.

And so Danglard donned his jacket without demur and followed his chief out of the building and down the street, listening to his recounting of Ducouëdic's tale.

★   ★   ★

The two detectives got to Place Edgar-Quinet before six, in good time for the final newscast of the day. Adamsberg sauntered up and down, getting his bearings and absorbing the atmosphere, locating where Ducouëdic lived, noting the blue urn fastened to the tree, the sporting goods shop (he saw Le Guern dive into it with his cash box under his arm) and the Viking, which Danglard had seen straight away and entered for the duration. Adamsberg knocked on the window to attract his attention when Le Guern arrived. Listening to the evening news would not teach him anything he did not already know. But Adamsberg wanted to get as close as he could to the source of the messages.

He was surprised by the quality of Joss's voice: it was strong and pleasant to listen to, and it carried easily from one side of the square to the other. The voice itself was probably the main reason why there was a good and solid crowd gathered round the ex-sailor's little rostrum.

'One,' Joss began, fully aware of Adamsberg's presence.

> For sale, bee-keeping equipment for two hives. Two: chlorophyll comes along all by itself and trees don't brag about it. Bigheads take note.

Adamsberg was surprised. He'd not understood the second ad, but the regulars were taking it all in their stride and waiting for the next announcement.

Must have become a habit, he thought. Practice must be needed to become a proficient newscast-listener, just like for everything. Joss soldiered on, cool as a cucumber:

> Three: Looking for a soulmate, attractive if possible, but no matter if not. Four: Hélène, I'm still waiting for you. Promise never to put my hand on you ever again. Signed in despair, Bernard. Five: The silly bugger who smashed my doorbell is in for a nasty surprise. Six: 750 FZX 92, 39,000 km, new tyres and brakes, full mechanical overhaul. Seven: What's it all about then, tell me, what's it all about? Eight: High-class clothing alterations and repairs. Nine: If ever you get to go to Mars, have a nice trip but count me out. Ten: For sale, five boxes French runner beans. Eleven: I say no to human cloning. There are enough idiots on earth already. Twelve . . .

The rhythmic chant of the small ads could have lulled Adamsberg off to sleep, but he kept his eye on the crowd. Some of them jotted things down on a scrap of paper, others stood motionless, briefcase in hand and eyes on Le Guern, having a restful break after a day at the office. The newscaster glanced at the sky and announced tomorrow's weather, followed by a shipping forecast – west, increasing force 3 to 5 towards evening – that people seemed to be happy with. Whereupon the rigmarole of practical and metaphysical small ads resumed. Adamsberg woke up completely when he saw Ducouëdic growing attentive around number 16.

Seventeen. This affliction is thus present and extant in some place, and has been since the Creation, for there is nothing new under the sun, and all that is, was created

The town crier glanced at Adamsberg to indicate that the 'special' had just gone by, and carried on with his job.

Eighteen. Growing ivy up party walls is not entirely safe.

Adamsberg listened to the end of the newscast, which included the surprising item about *Louise Jenny*, a French steamer of 546 register tons, carrying wines, liqueurs, dried fruits and preserves, which capsized off Basse aux Herbes and was driven on to Pen Bras. All lost, save for the ship's dog. Mutterings of dismay and grunts of satisfaction greeted that last item; part of the crowd drifted off to the Viking straight away. The late final edition was over, the crier jumped off his box and picked it up with one hand. Adamsberg, somewhat bewildered, turned towards Danglard to see what his number two made of it all, but the latter had gone, to the Viking presumably, to finish his drink.

Adamsberg found him with his elbow on the bar, looking quite unperturbed.

'This is outstanding apple brandy,' Danglard said, pointing to his glass on the counter. 'Among the best *calva* I've ever come across.'

A hand fell on Adamsberg's shoulder from behind. Ducouëdic motioned to follow him to the table at the back of the room.

'Since you're in the area, I'd better tell you that the town crier is the one and only person in town who knows my real name. Got that? Here, my name is Decambrais.'

'Just a minute,' said Adamsberg, who wrote down the name in his memory-jogger.

Plague, Ducouëdic and *white hair* makes *Decambrais.*

'I saw you jot something down during the newscast,' Adamsberg said as he put his notebook away again.

'Ad number 10. I'm making an offer for the runner beans. You get good vegetables here, you know, at rock-bottom prices. Now, as for the "special" . . .'

'The special?'

'The message from the nutter. For the first time the plague has been referred to directly, under the transparent mask of "affliction". That was one of its names. It had many others – the malady, the infection, the contagion, the fevers . . . People tried to avoid saying its real name, out of fear. So the man continues to advance. He has almost named it, he's near to his goal.'

A diminutive young blonde with her hair done

144

in a bunch came up to Decambrais and shyly put her hand on his sleeve.

'Marie-Belle?' he asked.

She stood up on tiptoes and kissed the old man on the cheek.

'Thank you!' she said with a smile. 'I knew you'd get there in the end.'

'It was nothing, Marie-Belle,' Decambrais smiled back.

The young woman departed with a wink and left the Viking on the arm of a tall dark fellow with auburn shoulder-length hair.

'Pretty girl,' said Adamsberg. 'What did you do for her?'

'I got her brother to put on a jumper,' said Decambrais. 'And believe me, it was hard going. The next hurdle comes in November, when I have to get him to wear a jacket. I'm working on it already.'

Adamsberg gave up trying to follow the story. He reckoned he was getting into some convoluted piece of local life, which didn't interest him one bit.

'Another thing,' Decambrais added. 'You've been spotted. There were people in the square who already knew you were from the police.' Decambrais looked Adamsberg up and down. 'I cannot imagine what gave you away.'

'The town crier?'

'Possibly.'

'Doesn't matter. Might even be a good thing.'

'Is that your assistant over there?' Decambrais asked with a stab of his chin in the direction of Danglard.

'*Commissaire* Danglard.'

'Bertin the barman is currently telling him all about the rejuvenating effect of his very special home-made *calva*. At the rate your *commissaire* is lapping it up, he'll be fifteen years younger in no time at all. I'm just pointing out the facts, for your information, sir. A quite outstanding brew, in my experience, but it tends to put you out of action for the whole of the following morning, speaking conservatively.'

'Danglard is frequently out of action in the morning.'

'Oh, all right then. But all the same he ought to be told that the concoction has a stunning effect. Literally. Teaches you what it must be like to be brain-dead. To feel like a cat in an aquarium.'

'Does it hurt?'

'No, it's like being away for the day.'

Decambrais nodded and left; he thought it better not to shake the hand of a *commissaire principal* in front of so many people. Adamsberg carried on watching Danglard turn the clock back, and around eight he made him sit down at the dining table and get something solid inside.

'Why should I?' Danglard asked in bleary-eyed indignation.

'To have something inside you to bring up

146

tonight. Vomiting on an empty stomach can be painful.'

'What a good idea,' gurgled Danglard. 'Let's have dinner.'

CHAPTER 13

Adamsberg called a cab to take Danglard home from the Viking and then had himself dropped off at Camille's. From below, in the street, you could see lights on in her studio. He leaned on the bonnet of a parked car for a few minutes to rest his tired eyes on the brightly lit loft. Camille's body would soon cleanse him of the wearisome worries of the day; all those crazy notions of plot and plague would split into shreds and tatters and waft away on a breeze.

He walked up the seven flights of stairs and crept silently into the loft. Camille always left the door on the latch when she was composing so she wouldn't have to break off in the middle of a bar. She was wearing her professional headset and she kept her hands on the keyboard while giving Adamsberg a coded smile that meant she hadn't finished work. Adamsberg stood around in the meanwhile, listening to the music that leaked through the phones. Camille worked on for ten minutes before switching off the synthesiser and releasing her ears from the equipment.

'Action movie?' Adamsberg enquired.

'Sci-fi,' said Camille as she stood up. 'A TV series. I've got a contract for six episodes.'

Camille drew closer and put her arm around him.

'It's about an alien who turns up without warning,' she explained. 'He's got supernatural powers and intends to use them to do people in. No idea why. Nobody seems to be interested in the why. Wanting to do people in seems to need no more explanation than wanting a drink. He wants to do people in and that's that. What makes him special is that he doesn't sweat.'

'I've got something like that, too,' said Adamsberg. 'A science-fiction case. I'm just at the start of episode one, and I haven't yet worked out what the story is. Someone has turned up who aims to do everyone in. What makes him special is that he speaks Latin.'

In the middle of the night Camille shifted in bed and woke Adamsberg up. She had fallen asleep with her head on his midriff, and had ended up almost smothered by Adamsberg's arms and legs. He was vaguely puzzled by this. He extricated himself with infinite care to give Camille all the room she needed.

CHAPTER 14

As night fell the man slid down the little alley that led to the tumbledown house. He knew the uneven cobblestones like the back of his hand. He knocked five times on the familiar worn surface of the old wooden door.

'Is that you?'

'It's me, Narnie. Open up.'

A large, plump old woman showed him into the front room by the light of a torch, as there was no electricity in the narrow hallway. He'd offered many times to have Narnie's house fixed up but such ideas had been consistently turned down.

'One day, Arnaud,' she used to say. 'When it's your money you're offering. Mod cons don't mean much to me anyway.'

Then she would point to her feet in their coarse black moccasins and say: 'You know how old I was before they could afford to buy me a pair of shoes? I was four. Up to the age of four I went around in bare feet.'

'You've told me that before, Narnie. But right now the leak in the roof is rotting the boards in

150

the attic floor. I don't want to have you falling through the ceiling, that's all.'

'You've got your own stuff to worry about.'

The man sat down on the flowery sofa. Narnie brought in a bottle of Madeira and a plate of girdle cakes. She put it all down on the low table, and said: 'Times were, when I made your girdle cakes with the skin of the milk. But you can't get milk that has a proper skin these days. It's dead and done with. You can leave it on the sill for a week, it'll turn sour before it makes any skin. It's not milk they sell you these days, it's dishwater. So I have to use cream instead. I'm sorry, Arnaud, but I have to.'

'I know, Narnie,' Arnaud said as he poured the Madeira into the rather large glasses the old woman had laid out.

'Does it affect the taste a lot?' she asked

'No, the cakes are just as tasty, really. You shouldn't get upset about them.'

'You're right, no more of this nonsense. How far have you got?'

'Everything's ready.'

Narnie's face spread into a wide, harsh smile.

'How many doors?'

'Two hundred and fifty-three. I'm getting faster. They're really beautiful, you know. Very elegant.'

The old woman beamed with a kindlier smile.

'You've got many gifts, Arnaud my boy, and I swear by the Holy Bible that you'll come into them all.'

Arnaud smiled as well and laid his head on the old woman's broad and sagging bosom. She smelled of perfume and olive oil.

'All of them, my boy,' she repeated as she stroked his head. 'They're all going to die, every last one, and all on their own.'

'Every last one,' said Arnaud, with a tight squeeze of the old woman's hand. Then she gave a start.

'Have you got your ring, Arnaud? Where's your ring?'

'Don't worry,' he said as he sat up. 'I just put it on the other hand.'

'Show me.'

Arnaud held out his right hand with the ring on the second finger. Narnie passed her thumb over the diamond that glinted on Arnaud's palm. Then she slipped the ring off and put it on his left hand.

'Keep it on the left and never take it off again.'

'All right. No need to fuss.'

'On the left, Arnaud, and on the ring finger.'

'Sure.'

'We've been waiting and waiting for years on end. And tonight we're going to get there. I thank the Lord for letting me live to see this night. And if He has let me live so long, Arnaud, it's because He wanted me to see it. He wanted me to be there so as you could get it done.'

'That's true, Narnie.'

'Let's drink to your salvation, Arnaud.'

Narnie put her arm through Arnaud's, raised

her glass and chinked it against his. They stayed interlocked as they took several sips of Madeira without speaking.

'Now no more of this nonsense,' said Narnie. 'Is everything in place? Have you got the door code and the floor number? How many of them will there be inside?'

'He lives on his own.'

'Come on up, I'll give you the necessary, you mustn't hang around here too long. I've starved them for the last forty-eight hours, they'll be all over him, like flies on dogshit. Put your gloves on.'

Arnaud followed her to the loft ladder.

'Be careful on that thing, Narnie.'

'Mind you own business. I use it twice a day.'

Narnie climbed up to the attic which echoed with high-pitched squeals.

'Calm down, my dearies! Give me some light, Arnaud, on the left.'

Arnaud directed the torch towards a huge cage swarming with a score of rats.

'Look at that one croaking in the corner. I'll have newborns to replace her tomorrow morning at the latest.'

'Are you sure they're infected?'

'Packed to the gills, they are. You wouldn't be doubting my skill, would you now? On the eve of the great deed?'

'Of course not, Narnie. But I'd rather you let me have ten of them instead of five. To make doubly sure.'

'You can have fifteen if you want. If it helps to keep you calm.'

The old woman bent down to pick up a canvas bag lying on the attic floor beside the cage.

'Died of plague yesterday, this one did!' she said as she waved the bag in Arnaud's face. 'We'll comb the fleas from his coat, and hey presto. Light me down.'

Arnaud watched Narnie toiling in the kitchen over the dead rat.

'Do be careful. What if you get bitten?'

'I'm quite safe, as I've told you before,' said Narnie with a grunt. 'And I've got olive oil all over, from head to toe. Satisfied?'

Ten minutes later she had finished. She threw out the rat with the rubbish and handed Arnaud a fat envelope.

'Twenty-two fleas,' she said. 'That gives you plenty to spare.'

Arnaud slid the package into the inside pocket of his jacket.

'I'm off, then.'

'Open it quickly, in one go, and slip it under the door. And don't be afraid. You're in charge now.'

She held him in her arms for a moment.

'So let's get on with it. It's your move now. May the Lord watch over you. And keep an eye out for the *flics*.'

CHAPTER 15

Adamsberg went into the office around nine next day. it was a Saturday, with only a skeleton staff on duty, and no hammer drills working. Danglard was off too, presumably paying the due price for his experiment in self-rejuvenation at Bertin's bar. Adamsberg was only aware of that pleasant weariness in his thigh and back muscles which afflicted him after a night spent with Camille. The muffled echo of the night before which was lodged in his physical being would last until about 2 p.m. Then it would vanish.

He spent the morning ringing round all the stations in the metropolitan area once again. Nothing to report, they all said. Not a single suspicious death in any of the blocks that had been daubed with the 4 symbol. But three new complaints of defacement had been received, for blocks located respectively in the first, sixteenth and seventeenth arrondissements of Paris. All of the new graffiti were 4s, and all of them had that CLT signature or logo underneath. Adamsberg concluded his telephone survey with a call to an old friend at the Quai des Orfèvres.

Breuil was a likeable and complicated fellow. He took an ironical interest in art and had a passion for high-class cookery, and neither of these avocations inclined him to make peremptory judgements about his fellow men. When Adamsberg's promotion to *commissaire principal* in charge of a murder squad had ruffled feathers at headquarters, largely because of his abysmal dress sense, his apparent slackness and his incomprehensible success as a sleuth, Breuil had been one of the very few to take him as he was and to refrain from trying to bring him into line. Breuil's tolerance was all the more precious to Adamsberg because he was by no means a small fish in the big pond of the Paris police.

'So if anything untoward should happen in any of these blocks of flats,' Adamsberg summed up, 'please be so kind as to pass the message on to me. I've been on the case for several days.'

'You mean you want me to hand it over to you?'

'That's right.'

'You can rely on me,' said Breuil. 'But I wouldn't worry myself sick over it meanwhile, if I were you. Guys who work at one remove like your amateur lettering artist are rarely capable of direct action.'

'But I am making myself sick with worry. And I'm watching him.'

'Have they finished putting the bars in the windows at your new place?'

'Two windows to go.'

'Come round for a meal one of these days. My

chervil-flavoured asparagus mousse will amaze you. Even you, I mean.'

Adamsberg smiled as he hung up and went out with his hands in his trouser pockets to look for lunch. He ended up walking around beneath a dull September sky for nearly three hours, and got back to the office in mid-afternoon.

An unidentified *flic* stood to attention as he came in.

'*Brigadier* Lamarre,' the young man blurted while fiddling nervously with one of his jacket buttons and staring hard at the blank wall opposite. 'There was a call for you at 13.41. A certain Hervé Decambrais asked you to ring back at this number.' He proffered a Post-it to his chief.

Adamsberg looked the *brigadier* up and down, and tried to catch his eyes. The twiddled button gave up the ghost and fell to the ground, but Lamarre stood stock still, with arms held rigid to his trouser seams. Something about him – his height, his blond hair, his blue eyes – reminded Adamsberg of barman Bertin at the Viking.

'Are you from Normandy, *brigadier*?'

'Affirmative, sir. From Granville, sir'

'Were you in the military, Lamarre?'

'Affirmative. Enlisted as a gendarme, sir. Did the exam so as to get promotion and transfer to the capital, sir.'

'You have leave to pick up your button, you know,' said Adamsberg, 'and you've got clearance for sitting down.'

Which Lamarre then did.

'And please try to look at me. In the eye.'

Lamarre's face tautened in near-panic and his eyes remained firmly set on the paintwork.

'That was an order, *brigadier*. Please try harder.'

The young *flic* slowly rotated his head towards Adamsberg.

'Good. Stop there. Stay like that. Keep looking at my eyes. Now, *brigadier*, this is the police force. In the murder squad, more than in any other branch, you have to learn to be discreet, to be relaxed and to be humane. You're going to have to infiltrate closed groups, you're going to have to dissemble, to interrogate awkward customers, to tail them without being seen, and also to boost people's confidence, as well as getting a wet shoulder time and again. Now, the way you are now, you can be spotted a mile off. You're as plain as a pikestaff and just about as bendy. You're going to have to learn to let go, and you won't manage that overnight. So here's training exercise number one: look at other people.'

'Yes, sir.'

'Look at their eyes, not at their hairline.'

'Yes, sir.'

Adamsberg opened his memory-jogger and inscribed in it: *Viking, button* and *paintwork* make *Lamarre*.

Decambrais picked up the phone on the first ring.

'I wanted to warn you, *commissaire,* that our guy has gone over the top.'

'Meaning?'

'Best thing is for you to hear the specials from today's morning and noon newscasts. Ready?'

'Go ahead.'

'The first one is the continuation of the 1665 diary entry.'

'You mean Keeps's diary?'

'Pepys's, *commissaire.*'

> This day, much against my will, I did . . . see two or three houses marked with a red cross upon the doors and *Lord have mercy upon us* writ there – which was a sad sight to me, being the first time of that kind to my remembrance I ever saw.

'Getting worse, don't you think?'

'That's an understatement. The red cross he mentions was painted on the doors of houses where the plague had broken out, to allow illiterates to steer clear. So Pepys has just come into contact with the plague for the first time. As a matter of fact the disease had been smouldering in the poorer quarters of the city for some time already, but Pepys didn't know because he only moved about in the wealthier parts of town.'

'So what was the noon special?' Adamsberg interrupted.

'Even worse. I'll read it to you.'

'Slowly, please.'

> On *August 17* false rumours rode ahead of the affliction, Many are afeared but many kept up hope, believing the words of the illustrious physician Rainssant. But alas they hoped in vain. On *September 14* plague entered the town. It first struck the *Rousseau ward*, where corpses falling one after the other manifested its presence among us.

'Let me just add, as you haven't got the text in front of you, that there are lots of omissions marked by ellipses. Our fellow is obsessive, he can't bear to cut a part of a sentence without signalling it. Furthermore "August 17," "September 14," and "Rousseau ward" are printed in a different font. He must have altered the dates and place of the original, and the change of font must be a way of telling us that. At least, that's what I think.'

'And today is September 14, isn't it?' Adamsberg asked, since he was never very sure of the date, within a couple of days.

'Yes it is. Which means, as plainly as can be, that the nutter has just told us that plague came into Paris today, and that there is a victim. Or victims.'

'Rue Jean-Jacques Rousseau.'

'Do you think that's what he means by "Rousseau ward"?'

'I've got a daubed block in that street.'

'What's that about daubing?'

Adamsberg reckoned that Decambrais was already up to his neck in the case and so he told him about the other dimension of the madman's campaign. He was interested to note that despite his learning Decambrais seemed as unaware as Danglard of the meaning of the signs of 4. So the talisman wasn't that well known. The nutter using it must be really quite a scholar.

'Anyway,' Adamsberg said, to bring the call to a conclusion, 'do go on pursuing the case without me, it may come in useful as background for Even Keel Counselling. It'll make a nice addition to your collection of stories, and a prize item in the town crier's annals too. But I think we can now forget about any risk of a criminal act being committed. Our nutter has gone off at a tangent, he's gone completely symbolic, as my number two would say. Because nothing actually happened last night in Rue Jean-Jacques Rousseau. Nor did anything happen in any of the other blocks that have had their front doors decorated. But the painter is still painting. We'll let him go on until he stops.'

'All right then,' said Decambrais after a long pause. 'That's a relief. May I say how glad I have been to get to know you better. I hope you don't resent my having wasted your time.'

'Not at all. I set much store by wasting time.'

Adamsberg hung up and decided that his Saturday shift was now over. There was nothing in the station log that couldn't wait until Monday.

Before leaving the office he checked in his memory-jogger so he could say good night to the ramrod from Granville with suitably friendly formality.

Outside, the sun had broken through the thinning clouds and Paris once again felt like a city enjoying the tail end of summer. He took off his jacket and hung it over his shoulder and sauntered towards the Seine. He reckoned that Parisians often forget that they live on a river. The Seine, with its smell of wet laundry and its flights of squawking birds, and however sluggish and soiled its waters may be, remained one of Adamsberg's favourite city retreats.

As he wandered through side streets and alleyways, he told himself it was just as well that Danglard had stayed at home to nurse his apple hangover. He was happier to have buried the business of the 4s without any witnesses. Danglard had been right. It didn't matter whether the door-painting lunatic was a situationist crackpot or a symbolist nutter, because he was running loose in a world of his own making, and that world was not of any relevance to the work of the police. Adamsberg had lost his gamble; he didn't mind losing; and it was a relief, in any case. He didn't get uppity about winning or losing against his number two, but he was glad that he could throw in the towel all on his own. On Monday he would tell Danglard he'd been wrong and that the affair of the 4s would be filed alongside the giant lady-birds of Nanteuil. Now who had told him that story? Ah, yes, the freckle-faced photographer. And what was his name? Adamsberg just couldn't recall.

CHAPTER 16

On the Monday morning Adamsberg gave Danglard the news that the affair of the painted 4s was over. Danglard kept to his notion of proper form by keeping his lips sealed, and by the merest nod of his head signalled that he had registered the end of the case.

The following day at two fifteen in the afternoon the phone rang in the office. It was the district station in the first arrondissement, reporting that a corpse had been found at number 117, Rue Jean-Jacques Rousseau.

Adamsberg put the receiver down in slow motion as if he were afraid of waking someone up in the middle of the night. But it was the middle of the day. He wasn't trying to let anyone else sleep but to sink into oblivion without a sound. He knew he often had weird spells of withdrawal and they worried him. Spells when he would give anything to fall into a lap of nothingness, to curl up there for ever in mindless calm. But these moments when he found he'd been right without having been at all rational were not good. They plunged him into a black hole where he felt he had been burdened from birth by a poisoned gift imposed on him by a senile witch. 'Since I'm not invited to this baptism,' the Wicked Fairy had croaked (this was hardly surprising, given that Adamsberg's Pyrenean parents were as poor as church mice and had celebrated the occasion by wrapping the infant in a rug), 'since I'm not invited, I give this child a special nose, for sniffing out shit in places where other people can't see a thing.' Or something like that, anyway. In rather more stylish language, presumably, since the Wicked Fairy was supposed to be quite cultivated and not at all coarse.

Adamsberg's weird spells never lasted very long. Firstly because he had no intention of curling up under a stone or anywhere else, given that his primary requirement was to spend half the day walking and the other half standing up; and secondly because he didn't believe he had any gifts at all. What he had intuited from the start of the affair of the 4s was nothing if not logical, even if his logic was not of the same neat order as Danglard's, and notwithstanding his inability to demonstrate its delicate coherence. What had seemed self-evident to Adamsberg was that the daubings had been intended from the start as a threat, a threat that could not have been clearer if its author had written on walls: *This is me. Watch me, and watch out.* It was no less obvious that the threat had acquired substance when Ducouëdic and Le Guern had come to tell him that a prophet of plague had started a campaign the same day as the daubings had begun. It was clear that the suspect, whoever he was, had been taking perverse pleasure in a tragedy he was in the process of setting up by himself. And no less obvious that he was not going to stop halfway, and that the chronicle of a death foretold with such rigour was likely to bring a corpse in its wake. It was all perfectly logical. So logical that it scared Ducoüedic just as much as it scared him.

Adamsberg was not particularly disturbed by the madman's monstrous and complex staging of the murder nor by his high-flown language. Its very strangeness made it a rather classic case, an exemplary instance of the thankfully rather infrequent type of murderer who, motivated by immense hurt pride, raises himself to a height equal only to the depth of his own humiliation. What was more murky and very hard to understand was the use of the ancient bogey of the plague.

The report from the first arrondissement left no room for doubt. The police officers who found the body had confirmed that the corpse was black all over.

'We're off, Danglard,' the *commissaire* said as he went past his deputy's door. 'Get the emergency team together right now, there's a body. Forensics are on their way.'

On these sorts of occasions Adamsberg could move fast. Danglard had to hurry to get everyone together so as to follow the chief to the scene of the crime, without a word of explanation to guide them.

Adamsberg got the *lieutenant* and the two *brigadiers* bundled into the back seat but held his deputy back from the front door of the car with a tug of his sleeve.

'Hang on, Danglard. Let's not put the wind up these guys before we need to tell them what it's all about.'

'*Brigadier* Justin, *Brigadier* Voisenet and *Lieutenant* Kernorkian, for your information, sir.'

'It's hit the fan. The corpse is in Rue Jean-Jacques Rousseau. The building had just been daubed with backward fours.'

'Shit!'

'The victim is male, about thirty, and white.'

'Why did you say "white"?'

'Because his body is black. Black skin. I should say, blackened. So is his tongue.'

Danglard frowned deeply.

'So it is plague,' he said. 'The *Black Death*.'

'Precisely. But I don't think the man died of it.'

'What makes you think that?'

Adamsberg shrugged. 'I don't know. It seems over the top. Anyway, plague has been extinct in France for God knows how long.'

'You can infect people on purpose, though. That's not very difficult.'

'Providing you have the bacillus. You can't exactly buy it off the shelf.'

167

'Sure, but there must be plenty of it stacked away in research institutes here in Paris, places we've all heard of. The battle against bubonic diseases isn't over yet. Anyone with inside knowledge and a warped mind could go into one of those high-security labs and walk out with a test tube full of Yersinia.'

'Yer what?'

'It's the identity of the guilty party, sir. Family name *Yersinia,* given name *pestis.* Alias bacillus of the plague. Serial killer *extraordinaire.* Keeps a tally of its victims in powers of ten. Must be around seven by now, maybe eight. Motive: chastisement of the wicked.'

'Chastisement?' muttered Adamsberg. 'Are you sure?'

'It never occurred to anyone in a thousand years to doubt that the Lord Almighty sent down the plague to punish humankind for all its sins.'

'I must say I wouldn't like to bump into the Lord Almighty on a dark night. Are you making this all up, Danglard?'

'It's gospel, sir. The plague is the most obvious example of a *holy scourge.* Just think what it could do to a man's mind to strut around Paris with a tube of divine retribution in his pocket. It could blow it to smithereens. Paris, too.'

'Think a bit, Danglard. What if it's really something else? What if someone just wants us to believe there's a nutter walking around with the holy scourge in his pocket? That would be even worse. If it got out it would spread like wildfire and set off mass panic. The whole of Europe would go psychotic. It would be huge.'

Adamsberg called HQ from the car.

'This is the Brigade Criminelle, *Brigadier* Noël speaking,' said Noël, curtly.

'Look, Noël, get yourself over here and bring someone with you, someone who can handle himself properly, no, I mean, bring that woman, the brunette who doesn't say much . . .'

'*Brigadier* Hélène Froissy, sir?'

'As I was saying, could you both get in a squad car and go straight to the junction of Edgar-Quinet and Rue Delambre. Keep a low profile and make sure that a Monsieur Decambrais is at home, it's the block on the corner of Rue de la Gaîté, and wait there until the evening newscast.'

'Newscast, sir?'

'You'll know what it is when you see it. A guy on a box, just after 6 p.m. Stay there until I send a relief team, and keep your eyes peeled. Especially for the people who are there to listen to the town crier. I'll be in touch.'

Adamsberg and his four assistants clambered up the staircase to the fifth floor, where the district *commissaire* was waiting for them. On their way up they noticed that although the front doors of all the apartments had been wiped clean, they still bore clearly visible shadow-marks from the black paint.

'*Commissaire* Devillard,' Danglard whispered in

Adamsberg's ear just before they got to the top landing.

'Thanks.'

'I understand you've taken over the case?' Devillard said as he shook the detective's hand. 'I've just had Breuil on the line.'

'That's right,' said Adamsberg. 'I've been working on it since before it happened.'

'That's fine by me,' said Devillard, who looked worn out. 'I've got a really big video-store break-in to deal with, and thirty-odd torched cars on my patch. More than enough to keep me going for the week. So, you know who did this?'

'I don't know anything, Devillard.'

As they were talking, Adamsberg pulled back the front door so as to look at it from the outside. Clean as a whistle. Not the faintest shadow of paint.

'René Laurion,' Devillard read out from his note-book. 'Single man, aged thirty-two, garage mechanic. No criminal record. Body found by the cleaner. She comes in once a week, on Tuesday mornings.'

'Rotten luck for her.'

'Yes. She went hysterical, her daughter had to come and take her home.'

Devillard handed over his file of notes. Adamsberg nodded thanks. He went over to see the body, and the forensic team stood back to let him get a view. The victim was lying stark naked on his back, with his arms crossed on his chest. There were a dozen soot-black patches on his thighs, chest, one arm and face. His tongue was pulled out and was also blackened. Adamsberg knelt down.

'Is that fake?' he asked the pathologist.

'Don't play games,' the medic snapped back. 'I've not yet examined the corpse but I can tell you this guy is as dead as a dodo and has been so for some length of time. By strangulation, I'd say, because of the marks on his neck that you can see through the soot.'

'Sure,' Adamsberg said softly. 'That's not what I meant.'

He scooped up some of the black powder that had spilled on to the floor, rubbed his fingers and wiped them on his trouser leg.

'Charcoal,' he mumbled. 'He's been rubbed down with charcoal.'

'Looks like it,' said one of the forensics.

Adamsberg looked around.

'Where are his clothes?'

'Neatly folded in the bedroom. Shoes under the chair,' said Devillard.

'Any damage done? Any signs of a break-in?'

'No. Either Laurion opened the door or the murderer picked the lock very quietly. The latter seems the most likely at the moment. If we're right, it would speed things up a lot.'

'You mean, it would have to be a specialist?'

'Exactly. You don't learn how to pick locks properly at primary school. The murderer would have to be someone who'd done quite a lot of time and had used it to learn the trade. If so, he's on file. Even a single smudgy print will give him away in ten seconds flat. I couldn't wish you a better solution, *commissaire*.'

The three-man forensic team worked away quietly. One of them dealt with the body, one with the lock and one with the furniture in the room. Adamsberg made a careful tour of the premises, looking closely at the main room, the bathroom, the kitchen and the small, tidy bedroom. He'd put on gloves and mechanically opened doors and drawers in the wardrobe, the bedside table, the chest, desk and sideboard. As he was looking through the kitchen, the only room that showed some signs of muddle and life, his eyes alighted on an ivory envelope lying across a stack of letters and newspapers. It had been neatly slit open. He stood staring at it, patiently waiting for the image to click as per instructions to his memory. The image wasn't very deep down, it wouldn't take more than a minute or two. Adamsberg's incapacity to log names, titles, brands, spelling, grammar rules and everything else related to writing was counter-balanced by extraordinary powers of recall for visual material. He was a genius of the inner eye: his peculiar mind registered whole frames with all their details intact, from the shadow made by clouds to the missing button on Devillard's cuff. He could retrieve this frame too, and adjust the focus on Decambrais sitting opposite him in the station office and extracting his stack of 'specials' from an oversize, thick ivory envelope with pearl tissue lining paper. That was also what he could see in front of him on the stack of newspapers. He signalled to the photographer to take a few shots while he scrabbled through his memory-jogger to look for the name.

'Thanks, Barteneau,' he managed, just in time.

He picked up the envelope and looked inside. Empty. He went through the pile of mail pending and checked all the envelopes: all of them had been opened raggedly with a finger, and they all still had their contents inside. In the waste bin, among rubbish that was at least three days old, Adamsberg found two ripped envelopes and several crumpled sheets of paper, but none of them were the right size to have come from the thick ivory envelope. He got up and rinsed his gloves under the kitchen tap. Why had the dead man kept the empty envelope? Why hadn't he opened it quickly with his finger, the way he opened all the rest of his mail?

He went back into the main room where forensics were cleaning up.

'All right if we leave now?' asked the pathologist, unsure whether his question should be answered by Devillard or by Adamsberg.

'Off you go,' said Devillard.

Adamsberg slid the ivory envelope into a plastic sheath and gave it to one of the men in the forensic team.

'This needs to go to the lab with the rest of the stuff,' he said. 'Only it's very special. Mark it "urgent".'

He stayed on for another hour, until they came to fetch the body bag. Two of his men remained on site thereafter, to conduct interviews with all the residents.

CHAPTER 17

At five in the afternoon Adamsberg stood in front of twenty-three members of the murder squad – the full team save for Noël and Froissy, who were keeping watch at Place Edgar-Quinet, and the two officers on duty at Rue Jean-Jacques Rousseau. They were all sitting on chairs set out in rows amid the unending decorators' mess.

The *commissaire principal* had thumbtacked a large map of central Paris on to the recently decorated wall. He said nothing while he inserted red-capped drawing pins at spots listed in his notepad, at the addresses of the fourteen buildings that had had their front doors daubed with the talisman. A green pin went in at the crime scene.

'On August 17,' Adamsberg told his audience, 'some alien turned up without warning. He intended to use his powers to do people in. Let's call him CLT. CLT isn't the sort of alien who cuts people's throats just like that. No. He takes a whole month to set up his scenario, and he'd probably spent much longer than that working it out in advance. His plan is a two-pronged affair. Prong

175

A involves a specific set of residential blocks in central Paris. He goes round at night painting a number in black on the front doors of the flats.'

He switched on the projector and showed a slide of the reverse 4 on the blank wall of the incident room.

'It's a very particular version of the number 4. It's inverted left-for-right but not top-for-bottom, the downstroke is splayed at the foot and there are two little notches on the outer extension of the cross. All observed instances have these specific features. And beneath the figure, you can see a kind of signature, in three upper-case letters: CLT. Unlike the digit, the letters are graphically plain, without flourishes. Our alien puts this sign on every door in the block *bar one*. The location of the undaubed door seems to be random. The choice of the blocks to be daubed seems equally haphazard. They are located in eleven different arrondissements, some are in main thoroughfares, others in side streets. The street numbers are varied, some are odd, some are even. There's no consistency about the type of building either. Some of them are old and others new, some of them are upmarket and others are quite run-down. It looks like CLT wanted his sample to be as varied as possible. That might mean he wanted to say that he can get at anyone, that there's no way of avoiding him.'

'What about the residents?'

'I'll come on to that later,' Adamsberg said. 'The meaning of the backward 4 has been established beyond doubt. It is a sign that served long ago as a talisman to ward off the plague.'

'What plague?' someone asked.

Adamsberg immediately recognised the *brigadier*'s bushy eyebrows.

'*The* plague, *Brigadier* Favre. It doesn't come in fifty-seven varieties. Danglard, could you please say a few words about it.'

'Plague came to Europe in 1347,' Danglard began. 'In the next five years it wrought havoc right across the Continent, from Naples to Moscow, and killed around thirty million people. This dreadful chapter of human history is known as the Black Death. The name is important to remember in the case we are dealing with. Originating in –'

'I said a few words, Danglard.'

'It reappeared periodically thereafter, once every ten years or so, and cut down whole regions at a time. It didn't die out completely until the eighteenth century. – I've not said anything about the early Middle Ages, or plague today, or the Far East, sir.'

'That's fine, you've said quite enough to give us a handle on what we're dealing with. That's to say, the Black Death. It leaves you dead in five to ten days.'

This set the whole room abuzz with questions and comments. Adamsberg stood there with his hands in his pockets and his head hanging down until the hubbub died away.

Someone raised a fearful voice to ask: 'Did

the man in Rue Jean-Jacques Rousseau die of plague?'

'I'll come to that. Prong B. Also on August 17, CLT makes his first public announcement. He picks on the square at the corner of Edgar-Quinet and Rue Delambre, where some fellow has resurrected the ancient trade of town crier – rather successfully, as it happens.'

A hand went up on the right-hand side of the room.

'What's that, sir?'

'The fellow in question leaves a wooden box on a tree round the clock, and people drop in messages they want to have read out aloud, for a modest consideration, I suppose. The town crier empties out the box three times a day and stands there reading out the messages.'

'How stupid can you get,' someone opined.

'Maybe it's stupid, but it works,' Adamsberg replied. 'Selling words is no more stupid than selling flowers.'

'Or being a *flic*,' said someone on the left.

Adamsberg caught the eye of the last speaker, a short man with a beaming smile who'd already lost most of his grey hair.

'Or being a policeman,' Adamsberg echoed. 'The messages CLT put in that box are incomprehensible to the general public, or to mortals in general. They're short quotations from antiquarian books, some in French and others in Latin, and they turn up in fancy big ivory envelopes. The copy comes from a printer, the computer kind. A fellow who knows his way around old books and who lives on the square found the messages sufficiently disturbing to do some research on them.'

'Name? Profession?' asked a *brigadier* with a pencil and notepad on his lap.

Adamsberg hesitated before answering.

'Decambrais. Retired, now runs Even Keel Counselling.'

'Are they all crazy in that area?' asked another officer.

'Quite possibly,' Adamsberg replied. 'But it all depends on your angle of vision. Seen from afar, everything always looks neat and tidy. But when you get closer, and when you take the time to look at the details, you realise that everyone is more or less crazy – down in that square, or another one, or wherever. Even in this squad.'

'I don't agree, sir,' said Favre, raising his voice in protest. 'You have to have really lost it to spend your time spouting rubbish in a public place. Should get himself properly laid, that guy, that would clear his head a bit. It only costs three hundred francs a go in Rue de la Gaîté, no sweat.'

Sniggers rippled round the room. Adamsberg looked hard at each of his team in turn, and they fell silent one by one. His eyes came to rest on *Brigadier* Favre.

'Like I was saying, Favre, there are nutcases in this squad too.'

'Now hang on, sir!' Favre began as he shot from his seat, blushing from the neck up.

'Just keep your trap shut,' said Adamsberg sharply.

Favre seemed to have been hit by a heavy object. He sat down again, in a lump. Adamsberg crossed his arms and waited several seconds before saying anything.

'I've already had occasion to ask you to think, *brigadier*,' he said in a more collected voice. 'I must ask you for the second time. You have a brain somewhere in your anatomy, so please try to locate it. If you are unable to find it and use it properly, you will be requested to go perform your stunts out of my sight, and out of this squad.'

Upon which Adamsberg dropped the Favre issue and turned back to the map of Paris.

'Decambrais succeeded in decoding the meaning of the messages CLT was having read out. They all come from old plague books, or else from a diary that covers a period of plague. For the first month CLT dealt only with signs that portend an outbreak of plague. Then he speeded up and announced that the plague had entered the city last Saturday, in what he called "Rousseau ward". Three days later, that's to say, today, the first corpse turns up in a flat in a block that had been daubed with the 4s. The murder victim is a garage mechanic and a bachelor with no police record. His body was found naked and covered in black blotches.'

'The Black Death!' someone whispered. It was the same officer who had asked a worried question about the cause of death ten minutes previously. Adamsberg identified the speaker, a shy, baby-faced man with large green eyes. The woman sitting next to him stood up, looking grim and pugnacious.

'*Commissaire*, sir,' she said, 'plague is a highly contagious disease. We cannot assume that the victim did not die of it. Yet you took four officers to the scene without waiting for the path lab to report.'

Adamsberg cupped his chin in his hand. This emergency briefing was turning into his inaugural, with crossfire and intentional needling.

'Madam officer,' he said, 'plague is not transmitted by contact. It is a disease of rodents that humans only catch when they are bitten by infected fleas.'

Adamsberg's newborn medical expertise came straight from the encyclopaedia, where he'd just looked it all up.

'When I took four officers with me to the scene,' he continued, 'I already knew for sure that the victim had not died of plague.'

'And how did you know that?' the woman asked.

Danglard came to Adamsberg's rescue.

'The announcement that the plague had entered the city came in the town crier's Saturday newscast. Laurion died in the night of Monday to Tuesday, three days later. However, thc plague bacillus, once it has entered the system, takes a minimum of five days to kill its host, save in very exceptional cases.

There was thus no possibility that we were dealing with a genuine case of plague.'

'Why not? The madman could have injected the germ into his victim earlier on.'

'No. CLT is a maniac. And maniacs do not cheat. If he says Saturday, then Saturday it is.'

'Maybe so, maybe not,' the woman officer muttered as she sat down, not wholly reassured.

'The mechanic was strangled,' Adamsberg resumed. 'His body was then blackened with charcoal. That was certainly done to resemble the symptoms of plague as well as its old nickname. That means CLT does not have the bacillus. He's not a screwy lab technician with a germ jar in his duffel bag. He's acting symbolically. But it's clear he believes in his mystification and believes in it completely. The front door of the dead man was *not* daubed with a 4. May I remind you that those 4s are not threatening signs, they're *protective* talismans. Therefore the only people at risk are those living in flats whose doors have been left unpainted. CLT plans who he is going to kill, then protects all the other people living in the block by painting on their doors. Taking such outlandish pains to ensure that bystanders are not harmed proves that CLT really does believe that he is spreading a contagious disease. He is therefore not a random killer. He deals with one person and worries about protecting others who, in his view, do not deserve to suffer the scourge.'

'Do you mean to say he thinks he's spreading

the plague while he's throttling the guy?' the man on the right-hand side asked. 'If he can believe that, then we've got a real schizophrenic on our hands.'

'Not necessarily,' Adamsberg answered. 'CLT is the lord of an imaginary world which to him seems quite coherent. That's not so unusual. There are heaps of people who think they can see the future in playing cards or tea leaves. Lots of them, in the street outside, or in this room. What's the difference? Lots of other people hang an effigy of the Virgin Mary over their beds and believe that a manufactured doll costing sixty-nine francs can protect them from evil, for real. They talk to the doll, they tell it stories. What's the difference? The borderline, *brigadier*, between what you *think* is real and what *is* real is entirely subjective. It depends on your point of view, on who you are, on where you come from.'

The grey-haired baldy broke in at this point.

'But are any other people at risk? Should we assume that everyone whose front door was not daubed could end up like Laurion?'

'I fear so. We'll have extra forces stationed tonight outside every one of the fourteen unpainted doors. But we don't have a list of all the blocks that CLT visited, only of the blocks where someone has made an official complaint. There's probably a score or more of them in Paris, of which we know nothing.'

'Why not put out an appeal?' a woman officer suggested. 'So as to warn people.'

'That's a tough one. If we broadcast a public warning we could set off mass panic.'

'We only need to mention the 4s,' the balding grey-beard chipped in. 'No need to let out anything else.'

'But the rest would leak one way or another,' Adamsberg responded. 'And if it doesn't leak, CLT will be only too happy to turn on the tap. He's been stoking up psychosis from the start and this would be his golden opportunity. The town crier was a godsend, from his point of view, because if he'd sent his messages to the press, well, they'd have been thrown into the waste bin without a second thought. So he started at the bottom. But if we put him on TV tonight, he'll be getting the ride he wanted all along. Anyway, it's only a matter of days. He'll unleash a huge scare in any case fairly soon. If he goes on, if there's a second murder, if he spreads his black death a bit further, there'll be no way of avoiding a nationwide nightmare.'

'So what are you going to do about it, *commissaire*?' said a sullen Favre.

'Save lives. We're going to put out a request to the inhabitants of any block of flats where 4s have appeared to make themselves known to the local commissariat without delay.'

A warm murmur from around the whole room expressed unanimous agreement with Adamsberg's plan. He felt very weary and very much a *flic* that evening, and the two feelings were closely connected. He would have liked to say just 'Get down

184

to work and sort it out for yourselves'. But instead he had had to lay out the facts, order the issues, focus the investigation and delegate tasks. In firm order, and with some authority. An image of his earlier self flashed before him – a naked child running free on a sunny mountainside path – and he wondered what the hell he was doing in that room, playing schoolmaster to twenty-three grown-ups who followed every move he made like clock-watchers.

It came back to him. He was there because someone was strangling other people, and he was supposed to find out who it was. It was his job to stop people from doing other people in. He pulled himself together.

'Our primary objectives are, one, to protect potential victims. Two, to profile potential victims and to find out whatever way we can if there are any common factors – family, age, sex, class, occupation, anything. And three, close surveillance of Place Edgar-Quinet. Four, obviously, is to catch the killer.'

He paced quite slowly to the back of the room and then to the front twice over before saying anything more.

'What do we know about him? Actually it could be a her, we can't rule that out. But I imagine it's a male. All this bookish learning saying "look how clever I am" feels to me like macho swagger and male pride. If we get confirmation that death was caused by strangulation then we can pretty much

185

bank on it being a male. An educated man; extremely well-educated, I should say; a man of letters. Not poor, since he's got a PC and printer. Maybe he has expensive tastes – he uses fancy envelopes that don't come cheap. He's a very good draughtsman, he's a neat worker and very meticulous. Definitely an obsessive cast of mind. So he's also fearful and superstitious. Last of all, he may actually have done time. If forensics confirm that the lock was picked, we'll have to go down that track. Look for all former convicts with initials CLT. But is it a signature? Well, to sum it all up, we know next to nothing.'

'And what about the plague? Why the plague?'

'When we can answer that question, we'll have our man.'

Chairs scraped the floor as everyone got up and stretched.

'Danglard, could you work out who does what? I'm going for a walk. Back in twenty minutes.'

'Should I draft the public announcement?'

'Please, yes. You'll do it so much better than I would.'

All the evening news programmes carried the mildly worded public announcement penned by Adrien Danglard. Residents of houses or buildings that had been marked with a figure of 4 were requested to get in touch with the police without delay. The pretext given was 'to help the police with their inquiries into allegations of organised crime'.

Within half an hour of the all-channel broadcast, the Brigade switchboard was well-nigh jammed. One third of Adamsberg's team was there to field the calls. Danglard and Kernorkian had brought in supplies of snacks and drinks to last through the night, and the electricians' workbench had been converted into a temporary buffet bar. By nine thirty, fourteen additional blocks of flats with marked doors had been logged and located on the wall map with red pins. Now there were twenty-nine. A list of the addresses in chronological order of the presumed date of door-daubing was quickly drawn up, as was a list of the occupants living behind the twenty-eight doors which had been left unmarked. They made a mixed bag: the flats housed large families as well as bachelors, women as well as men, young folk, old folk and middle-aged folk. No age group, gender, category or occupation was unrepresented. It was past eleven when Danglard reported to his chief that there were two members of the force standing guard in front of every one of the unmarked doors.

Adamsberg told the officers doing overtime that they were free to go home, waited for the night roster to settle in, and then took a squad car to see what was up at Place Edgar-Quinet. The team that had relieved Noël and Froissy consisted of the greying baldilocks and the thickset woman who had almost got into a fight with him at the five o'clock briefing. They looked like they were taking it easy, chatting on a bench in the square, but they always kept one pair of eyes on the urn, hanging from a tree less than fifteen yards away. Adamsberg went over to say hallo.

'The main thing to watch for is the shape of the envelope,' he said. 'With that street lamp and a bit of luck you might just make it out.'

'We don't arrest anybody?'

'No, your job is surveillance. If you see someone who seems to fit, tail him, but don't get noticed. We've put two photographers in the stairwell of that building, they've a full-frontal view of the urn and they'll get a shot of anybody who gets close to it.'

'When do we go off?' asked the woman with a yawn.

'At three.'

Adamsberg went into the Viking and spied Decambrais at his usual table right at the back, with the town crier and five others in attendance. The *commissaire principal*'s entrance caused the general noise of conversation to falter and slow, like a rehearsal stopped by the conductor. That meant everyone at the table knew he was from the police. Decambrais decided to take the bull by the horns:

'*Commissaire Principal* Jean-Baptiste Adamsberg, allow me the pleasure of introducing to you the singer, Lizbeth Galston, to Damascus Viguier, proprietor of Rolaride, and to his sister Marie-Belle, to Castillon, recently retired from the black-smithing trade, and to our muse and madonna,

188

Madame Eva. I believe you are already acquainted with Captain Le Guern. Please join us for a glass of *calva*.'

Adamsberg waved off the kind offer and said, 'Can I have a word, Decambrais?'

Lizbeth tugged cheekily at Adamsberg's cuff. He was well acquainted with that relaxed and easy familiarity, with that way of saying, we've been through many a night down the station together. Only a prostitute who'd been hardened by countless police raids and identity checks could be so unintimidated.

'Say, officer, are you in disguise tonight? Is that costume meant to be your cover?'

'No, it's what I usually wear.'

'Pull the other one! Don't tell me *flics* are that laid back.'

'Appearances can be deceiving, Lizbeth,' Decambrais put in.

'Not always, they aren't,' Lizbeth replied. 'But this guy really is laid back. He doesn't give a tinker's fart for what other people think of him. Am I right, officer?'

'Which other people?'

'Women, for instance,' Damascus suggested with a grin. 'You've got to want to make a stunning impression on women, haven't you?'

'You're really witless, Damascus,' Lizbeth said as she turned towards him, making him blush to the roots of his hair. 'Women don't give a damn about being stunned.'

'Yeah?' Damascus frowned. 'So what do they give a damn about?'

'Nothing,' Lizbeth declared as she brought the flat of her black hand down on to the table. 'They don't need to give a damn about anything any more. Ain't that right, Eva? We don't give a damn about love, we don't give a damn about affection, and we don't give much more for a crate of green beans. You got that, then? Think about it.'

Eva said nothing and Damascus sullenly twirled his glass in his hand.

'You're not being fair,' Marie-Belle piped up in a quavering voice. 'Everybody gives a damn about love, by definition. What else is there?'

'Green beans, like I just told you.'

'You're talking nonsense, Lizbeth,' said Marie-Belle with her arms folded on her chest. She was near to tears. 'The fact that you've had lots of experience doesn't entitle you to put other people off.'

'Try it out, sweetie,' Lizbeth replied. 'I'm not stopping you.' Then she burst out laughing, gave Damascus a loud kiss on his forehead and ruffled Marie-Belle's hair.

'Cheer up, sweetie,' she said. 'You shouldn't believe everything that Big Lizzy says. Big Liz has gone a bit sour. Big Liz gets on everyone's nerves with all her talk of years in the trenches. Of course you should stand up for yourself. That's right and good. But if you do try it out, go easy, sweetie.

In my professional opinion, a small dose is all you can take.'

Adamsberg took Decambrais to the side.

'I'm sorry, *commissaire*, but I have to listen in to the chatter. It's my job to tell them how to keep an even keel, you see, so I have to keep up with the gossip.'

'He's in love, isn't he?' Adamsberg asked with the less than passionate interest of someone who has taken only a small stake in a lottery.

'You mean Damascus?'

'Yes. In love with the singer?'

'Bull's eye. So what did you want to say, *commissaire*?'

Adamsberg's voice dropped to a whisper.

'He's done it, Decambrais. A corpse in Rue Jean-Jacques Rousseau, black all over. Found this morning.'

'Black?'

'Strangled, stripped naked and blackened with charcoal.'

Decambrais's face tautened.

'I knew he would,' he said.

'Yes.'

'Was the door unmarked?'

'Yes.'

'Have you put a guard on the other doors?'

'All twenty-eight of them.'

'Sorry. I'm sure you know how to do your job.'

'I have to have those "specials", Decambrais,

everything you've got. With their envelopes, if you've kept them.'

'Follow me.'

Decambrais led Adamsberg across the square and into his cubbyhole, crammed full of books and papers. He shifted a pile so Adamsberg could sit down.

'There you are,' he said as he handed Adamsberg a swatch of sheets and envelopes. 'Useless for prints, as I'm sure you realise. Le Guern's handled them over and over, and so have I. Anyway, you've got all ten of mine on file.'

'I'll need Le Guern's too.'

'They're on file too. Le Guern was done for GBH at Le Guilvenec fourteen years ago, that's all I can tell you. Aren't we being helpful? Doing your legwork for you. No sooner do you ask than we pop up on your computer.'

'Hang on, Decambrais. Everybody in this corner of the square has been inside.'

'Some places are like that, where the wind listeth. I'll read you Sunday's special, there was only one that day:

> In the evening home to supper, and there
> to my great trouble hear that the plague is
> come into the City . . . To the office to finish
> my letters, and then home to bed – being
> troubled at the sickness . . . and how to
> put my things and estate in order, in case

it should please God to call me away –
which God dispose of to his own glory.

'Sounds like another entry from the diary of that
Englishman,' Adamsberg suggested.

'Correct.'

'Keeps?'

'Pepys, sir. Spelled P-E-P-Y-S.'

'And yesterday?'

'No specials yesterday.'

'Hmm,' said Adamsberg. 'He's slowing down.'

'I don't think he is. Here's the one from this
morning.'

The scourge is ever ready and at the
command of God who brings it down and
raises it away, as it pleaseth the Lord.

'That rather suggests that he's not letting his
guard down at all. Did you notice that "ever ready"
and "as it pleaseth the Lord"? He's blowing his
trumpet. He's taunting us.'

'He's into being the great Almighty.'

'Which means he's got an emotional age of three,
roughly.'

'But you can't use that to get at him. He's no fool.
He knows that the entirety of the Paris police is
itching to catch him, so he'll stop giving hints about
locations from now on. He needs room to move
around in. He gave the Rousseau address away so
as to be sure we'd make the connection between

the murder and the prophecy of plague, between the 4s and the "specials". But I reckon he'll get less precise from now on. Keep feeding me, Decambrais, send me each special as it comes in.'

Adamsberg went home with the 'specials' collection under his arm.

CHAPTER 18

Next morning the computer flashed up a name.

'Got him!' shouted Danglard as he waved an arm at a passing *lieutenant*.

A gaggle of detectives gathered round behind Danglard and trained their eyes on the screen. Adamsberg's deputy had spent the morning combing the data base for a 'CLT,' while others had been collating all the information they could find about the other twenty-eight flats and attempting to establish some connection between them, so far without result. Forensics had just sent in their preliminary report, which confirmed that the lock of Laurion's flat had been picked by an expert lock-picker. There were no prints in the flat apart from those of the victim and the cleaner. The charcoal that had been used to smudge the corpse had been made from apple-wood. It could not have been obtained commercially, since ready-to-use charcoal available in stores was always made from a mix of different woods. On the other hand, the ivory envelope could have been bought at any decent stationer's for three francs twenty. It had been opened with something like a paperknife. It was empty save for paper dust and one small dead insect. 'Shouldn't we get an entomologist to look at it?' someone asked. Adamsberg frowned, then gave his OK.

'Christian Laurent Taveniot,' Danglard announced as he leaned forward to read from the screen. 'Age 34, born at Villeneuve-les-Ormes. Sent down twelve years ago for GBH, did his time at Périgueux prison. Sentenced to eighteen months, with two months on top for attacking a warder.'

Danglard scrolled down, and all his assistants craned their necks to see CLT's mugshot. Low forehead, elongated features, a thick nose, close-set eyes. Danglard read out the rest of the file.

'Unemployed for twelve months after release, then got a job as a nightwatchman at a car-breaker's yard. Lives at Levallois. Married, two kids.'

Danglard looked up enquiringly at Adamsberg.

'Education?' the chief said, unconvinced.

Danglard hit the keys again.

'Put on to the practical skills track at the age of thirteen. Failed the prelim for qualifying as a roofing technician. Dropped out of education, then earned a living from betting on football and from cannibalising broken-down motorbikes, which he then resold under the counter. Until he got into this fight, where he nearly killed one of his customers by hurling a motorbike straight at him, point blank so to speak. Then clink.'

'Relatives?'

'Mother, works at a packaging plant in Périgueux.'

'Brothers and sisters?'

'One elder brother, also a nightwatchman at Levallois. That's how he got his job.'

'Not much room there for serious learning. I can't see where your Christian Laurent Taveniot found the time and the means to learn Latin.'

'Teach Yourself Books?'

'I really don't see a guy who lets off steam by throwing motorbikes around getting excited by medieval languages. He would have to have changed his style a great deal over the last ten years.'

'And so?' said Danglard, audibly disappointed.

'Two *lieutenants* had better go see. But I'm not buying it.'

Danglard put his computer on sleep and followed Adamsberg to his office.

'I've got a problem,' he declared.

'What's up?'

'I've got fleas.'

Adamsberg was taken aback. Never before had his primly unforthcoming number two confided in him on matters of personal hygiene.

'Use one can of fogger for every ten square metres in the flat. Leave it alone for two hours and air the place completely when you get back. Works like magic.'

Danglard shook his head dismally.

'I caught them at Laurion's place.'

'Who's Laurion, then?' Adamsberg asked with a smile. 'One of your suppliers?'

'Damn you, Adamsberg, Laurion's the corpse we looked at yesterday!'

'I'm sorry. The name had clean gone out of my mind.'

'Well, keep it there from now on, all right? I caught fleas from Laurion's place. They began to itch when I got back on Tuesday evening.'

'So bloody what? OK, the man wasn't as neat and tidy as he looked. Or perhaps he caught them at work. What's the fuss?'

'Good grief!' Danglard exclaimed in exasperation. 'You told the whole damn squad in your own words less than twenty-four hours ago what the fuss was about! Plague is transmitted by flea bites, damn it!'

'Ah,' said Adamsberg. He looked straight at his number two. 'I'm with you now.'

'You took your time.'

'I didn't get much sleep. Are you sure it's fleas?'

'I don't need a doctor to tell me the difference between a mosquito and a flea. I've got bites in my groin and my armpits, and they've swollen up to the size of a thumbnail. I only looked at them this morning and I've not had time to check the kids.'

At last Adamsberg grasped that Danglard was really very worried and not far short of panic.

'But what's scaring you? What's going on?'

'Laurion died of the plague and I've picked up his fleas. I've got twenty-four hours to get treatment or else I'm done for. Same for the kids.'

'Heavens above, Danglard, have you been taken in by the nutter as well? Have you forgotten that Laurion died from a *show* of the plague?'

Adamsberg went over to shut his door and pulled up a chair to sit next to his deputy.

'I know, I know. CLT is conducting a symbolic campaign, OK. But the fleas in Laurion's flat are completely real. They can't be there just by accident. In the madman's mind, they are plague fleas. And how on earth can I be sure that they are not, in actual fact, genuinely infected fleas?'

'But if they were plague-bearing fleas, why would CLT have gone to the trouble of strangling Laurion?'

'Because he wants to be the agent or angel of death himself. I'm not a coward, sir. But getting bitten by fleas released by a man with an obsession about plague is not my idea of fun.'

'Who else was there yesterday?'

'Justin, Voisenet, Kernorkian. You. The pathologist. Devillard, plus his men from the first arrondissement.

'Have you still got them?'

'What?'

'Your fleas, damn it!'

'Sure I have. Unless they've gone walkies around the station.'

Adamsberg picked up the phone and punched out the path lab number.

'Adamsberg here . . . Do you remember the insect you found inside the empty envelope? . . . Yes, that's right. Could you please get on to the entomologist, tell him it's an emergency, red alert . . . Well, so bloody what! Tell him to leave his dung-flies till later . . . Look, chum, this is red alert. We may have a case of the plague, damn it! . . . That's right! So move your butt, and tell him I'm sending him more of the same, only these ones are still alive. He'd better be careful. And tell him to keep his trap shut tight.'

He turned to Danglard as he put the phone down.

'You'd better go straight upstairs, have a shower and put everything you're wearing into a plastic bag. We'll send them off to the lab.'

'And what am I supposed to do? Sit at my computer in my birthday suit?'

'I'll go out and get you some things,' Adamsberg said as he stood up. 'You don't want to be spreading creepy-crawlies around town.'

Danglard was far too upset about his flea bites to worry very much about what clothes his boss would get him. But a vague apprehension of disaster did cross his mind.

'Hurry up. I'll get the pest control people to go over your flat, and they'd better do this place as well. And I'll tell Devillard.'

Before going out on his clothes-shopping trip, Adamsberg made a call to the medievalist-cleaner fellow. Marc Vandoosler, that was his name. By fortunate coincidence Vandoosler was having a late lunch at home.

'Do you remember the business about the 4s that I asked you about?'

'Sure,' Vandoosler answered. 'I heard your announcement on the news last night as well. And I saw this morning's papers. I understand you've found a corpse. One reporter says he saw the body being brought down and that one arm was sticking out from under the sheet. The arm had black patches.'

'Bugger,' said Adamsberg.

'Tell me, *commissaire*, was the corpse black?'

'What do you know about the plague, young man? Or do you just do numbers?'

'I'm a medievalist, *commissaire*. So yes, I know a thing or two about the plague.'

'Are there lots of people who know more than a thing or two?'

'You mean plague specialists? Well, you could safely assume that there are five real specialists in the country today. Excluding biologists, that is. I have two friends in the south of France, they're more into the medical aspects, and a colleague in Bordeaux who deals mainly with transmitting insects, and then there's a more or less demographic historian at Clermont-Ferrand.'

'What about you? What's your position in the field?'

'Centre-forward for Job-seekers United, sir.'

Five, Adamsberg thought. That's not a lot for a population of sixty million. And so far Vandoosler was the only person he'd come up with who knew the meaning of the backward 4. He was a historian, a man of letters and a plague expert, and he could undoubtedly read Latin. It would definitely be worth checking up on him.

'Tell me, Vandoosler, how long would you say the disease lasts? Give me a ballpark figure.'

'On average, three to five days' incubation, but it was sometimes as little as one to two days. Symptoms last five to seven days. More or less.'

'Treatable?'

'Only if you get it early, as soon as symptoms appear.'

'I think I'm going to need you. Would you mind if I came round?'

'Where do you mean?' asked Vandoosler suspiciously.

'Your place.'

There was a pause.

'OK,' said Vandoosler.

The man wasn't keen. But lots of people weren't keen to have a *flic* call round. A reluctance that was virtually universal, in fact. So the pause didn't necessarily mean that Vandoosler was CLT.

'In two hours' time,' Adamsberg proposed.

He hung up and set off for the big department store at Place d'Italie. He reckoned Danglard must be European size 48 or 50, since he was six inches taller and maybe sixty pounds heavier than Adamsberg was. He needed something that would go round his waist. Adamsberg harvested a pair of socks, a pair of jeans, and a big black T-shirt in a trice (he'd heard it said that whites and stripes make you look fatter, so black presumably did the opposite). No point getting a jacket, it was a mild day and beer kept Danglard warm in any case.

The naked *commissaire* was waiting in the shower room with a towel round his waist. Adamsberg gave him his new clothes.

'I'll have your rags taken straight off to the lab,' he said as he picked up the big bin bag where Danglard had put his clothes. 'Don't panic. You've got two days of incubation still to go, you've got time on your side. We'll have the lab results well before then. I've said this is red alert, so they'll do the tests straight away.'

'Thanks,' Danglard muttered as he unwrapped the T-shirt and the jeans. 'Bloody hell, do you expect me to wear that?'

'Wait and see. It'll suit you like a dream.'

'I'll look like a banana!'

'Do I look like a banana?'

Danglard held his tongue and dipped down further into the shopping bag.

'You forgot underpants.'

'Sorry, I did forget. But it's not the end of the world. Go easy on the beer until you get home tonight.'

'Very likely.'

'Did you phone the school? To check the kids?'

'Of course I did.'

'Now, show me those bites.'

Danglard raised an arm. There were three size-able swellings under the armpit.

'No doubt about it,' Adamsberg admitted. 'Those are flea bites.'

'Aren't you scared of catching the same thing?' Danglard asked as Adamsberg pulled the bin bag around looking for the tie-string.

'No, I'm not. I don't get scared very often. I'll wait till I'm dead to get scared, that way it won't mess up life too much. To tell the truth, the only time I was really scared was when I slid down that glacier all on my own, on my back. The slope was almost vertical. What scared me most, apart from the sheer drop, were all those bloody big-eyed does standing round and staring at me as if to say: "You poor fool, you'll never make it." I pay a lot of attention to what does and deer tell me with their eyes, but that's another story. I'll tell it to you when you're not as stressed out as you are today.'

'That's a nice idea.'

'I'm off to see that historian-cum-cleaner fellow, Marc Vandoosler. He lives in Rue Chasle, just round the corner. Look him up and see if we've got anything on him. And forward any calls from the lab to my mobile number.'

CHAPTER 19

When Adamsberg got to Rue Chasle he found a tall and narrow tumbledown town house which despite being in the heart of Paris had miraculously escaped demolition. It was set back from the street behind a wasteland of long grass, and the country touch warmed Adamsberg's heart. When he knocked, the door opened to reveal an old man with a twinkling smile who looked as though he still found life fun, unlike Decambrais. He had a wooden stirring spoon in his hand and used it to show Adamsberg in.

'Take a seat in the refectory, if you please.'

It was a large room lit by three tall mullion windows, and furnished with a long wooden table. A man in a shirt and tie was treating it with beeswax, rubbing it in with a professional circular twirl of the cheesecloth.

'Lucien Devernois's the name,' the young man said clearly and firmly as he put down the cheesecloth and thrust out his hand in greeting. 'Marc will be ready in a minute.'

'Sorry for the disturbance,' the old man said.

'It's polishing hour by the duty roster. Can't mess about with the roster, can you now?'

Adamsberg refrained from comment and sat down on one of the wooden benches. The old man took the place opposite ex officio and beamed as if in anticipation of something really enjoyable.

'So, Adamsberg,' he began gleefully. 'We've forgotten old mates, have we? Not even a hallo and how's the wife? No respect for niceties, as per usual?'

Adamsberg was struck dumb. He stared hard at the face and scoured the deepest recesses of his visual memory. It couldn't have been any time recently, no, it must be from long ago. It was going to take at least ten minutes to trawl through his memory bank. The cheesecloth man, Devernois, was slowing down with his polishing and looking at one then the other of the two seated men.

'I can see you're the same as ever,' the old man went on with a broad smile. 'Hasn't stopped your irresistible rise from *brigadier* to *commissaire principal*. Have to admit you've scored some famous victories, though. The Carreron case, the Somme affair, the Valandry tip, they were real feathers in your cap. Not to mention more recent bull's-eyes, like the Nermord case, the wolf-man murders, and the Vinteuil affair. My heartiest congratulations, *commissaire principal*. I've been keeping my eagle eye on your exploits, as you can see.'

'Why?' Adamsberg asked defensively.

'Because I always wondered whether they'd keep you on or kill you off. You really don't fit the job, seeing as you look like a dandelion in the grass on court number one and you behave as if nothing ever ruffled you or mattered very much. As far as the hierarchy was concerned, you were as handy as a ping-pong ball on a pool table. No way of potting you. Yes, I really did wonder whether they would let you stay on. You slipped through the net, and I'm glad for that. I wasn't so lucky. I got caught and then got the sack.'

'Armand Vandoosler,' Adamsberg muttered as he divined beneath the old man's skin the face of that forceful, witty, selfish and self-indulgent detective he'd last seen twenty-three years before.

'Got it in one.'

'Down south,' Adamsberg went on.

'Yeah. The girl that vanished. You got that one tied up in two ticks, *brigadier*. We trapped the man at the harbour in Nice.'

'And we had a celebration dinner in a quayside restaurant.'

'Octopus.'

'Octopus it was.'

'I'll grant us a glass of wine,' said Vandoosler as he stood up. 'This calls for lubrication.'

'So Marc's your son, then?' Adamsberg asked as he nodded his agreement to a glass.

'He's my nephew and my godson. He lets me live in the eaves, because he's a kind boy. I have to warn you, Adamsberg, that I'm just as bloody-minded as I used to be. More bloody-minded, I should say. Have you grown less laid back?'

'I don't know.'

'Back then there were heaps of things you didn't know and that didn't seem to worry you. So what have you come to discover in this place that you don't know?'

'A murderer.'

'What's the connection between that and my nephew?'

'Plague.'

Vandoosler Senior nodded. He grabbed a broomstick and knocked twice on the ceiling, adding to the many dents already clearly visible in the plaster at that position.

'There are four of us here,' the elder Vandoosler explained, 'and we live on top of each other. One knock for St Matthew, three knocks for St Luke, present and outstanding with cheesecloth in hand, and four knocks for me. Seven knocks is red alert for all the apostles.'

Vandoosler glanced at Adamsberg while he put away the broomstick intercom.

'You're just the same, aren't you? Butter wouldn't melt in your mouth.'

Adamsberg smiled silently, and Marc came down into the refectory. He went round the table, shook the *commissaire*'s hand, and gave his uncle a dark look.

'I see you've taken command of operations,' he said.

'Sorry about that, Marc. But we ate octopus together twenty-three years ago.'

'A lot of bonding goes on in the trenches,' Lucien mumbled as he folded away his duster.

Adamsberg looked carefully at Vandoosler Minor, the plague man. Slim, tense, straight black hair, and something Sioux about his features. He wore black all over, save for a rather gaudy belt and silver rings on his fingers. Adamsberg noticed that his footwear was rather like Camille's – heavy black boots with buckles.

'If you want to talk privately,' he said, 'I fear we may have to go elsewhere.'

'I'm fine here,' Adamsberg replied.

'I understand you have a problem with plague, *commissaire*.'

'A problem with a plague expert, to be more precise.'

'The man who's been painting those 4s?'

'Yes.'

'Connected to yesterday's murder?'

'What's your view?'

'In my view, yes.'

'Because?'

'Because of the black skin. But the backward 4 is supposed to protect you from the disease, not bring it on.'

'And so?'

'So I suppose your murder victim was not protected.'

'Quite right. Do you believe in the power of the talisman?'

'No.'

Adamsberg's eyes met Vandoosler's. He seemed sincere and slightly irritated.

'Nor do I believe in amulets, rings, turquoises, emeralds or rubies. Or in the hundreds of other nostrums that were invented to ward off plague. All of them far more costly than a figure of 4, obviously.'

'People wore rings?'

'Those who could afford them. Rich folk died much less of plague than the poor because their better made houses were less attractive to rats than paupers' hovels. Most of the dead were the poor. And that lent credibility to the idea of jewels. Poor people didn't wear rubies and so they died. The top model was diamond, it was the ultimate antidote: "A diamond worn on the left hand is reputed to counter all kinds of becomings." Which is why a wealthy man would give his beloved a diamond to plight his troth, so as to save her from the scourge. The habit's stayed with us, but nobody has the faintest idea any more why we buy diamond rings. Nor does anyone remember what the backward 4 really means.'

'The murderer remembers. Where did he dig it up?'

'In some book,' Marc Vandoosler said dismissively. 'Look, if you tell me what the problem is maybe I could help solve it for you.'

'First, I have to ask you where you were Monday last around 2 a.m.'

'Is that the time of the murder?'

'Approximately, yes.'

Forensics had made it 1.30 a.m. but Adamsberg liked to be vague. Vandoosler pushed his black hair behind his ears.

'Why me?' he asked.

'I'm sorry, Vandoosler. Not many people know what these 4s mean. Not many at all.'

'It's perfectly logical, Marc,' Vandoosler the Elder butted in. 'It's trade.'

Marc squirmed with irritation. Then he got up, took the broom handle, and knocked once.

'Calling St Matthew,' said the Elder.

They waited in silence, trying not to hear the clatter that Lucien was making as he attended to the washing up so as not to eavesdrop on the interview.

A minute later a tall, fair young man came into the refectory. His shoulders were so broad that they barely got through the doorway. He was wearing nothing apart from rough canvas trousers held at the waist by a piece of string.

'There was a call?' he asked in a baritone.

'Mathias,' Marc said, 'what the hell was I doing Monday last at 2 a.m.? It's important so nobody breathe.'

Mathias concentrated hard, crossing his blond eyebrows.

'You came home late with ironing to do around 10 p.m. Lucien gave you something to eat and then went up to his room with Elodie.'

'Emilie,' said Lucien by way of correction. 'It's

really terrible the way you can't get that name to stick in your thick skull.'

'Then we played two rounds of cards with the Elder,' Marc continued. 'He bagged three hundred and twenty francs, and then went up to bed. You started with Mme Boulain's ironing, then you did Mme Druyet's. At 1 a.m., when you were putting the board away, you suddenly remembered you had two pairs of sheets to deliver in the morning. I gave you a hand and we did them together on the refectory table. I used the old iron. We finished folding around 2.30 a.m. and wrapped them up in two packages. As we went up to bed we saw the Elder going down to take a piss.'

Mathias looked at Adamsberg as if to say, how's that? Lucien butted in from his station at the sink:

'He's a prehistorian so he's good on detail. You can trust him.'

'Can I go now?' asked Mathias. 'I'm in the middle of a reconstitution.'

'Sure, and thanks for the help,' said Marc.

'Reconstitution?' Adamsberg queried.

'He's sticking shards of palaeolithic flint back together in the basement,' Vandoosler Junior explained.

Adamsberg nodded without trying to understand. What he realised nonetheless was that it would take more than the odd interrogation to get the hang of this household and its inhabitants. A whole seminar would hardly suffice and he didn't have time for that.

'Obviously Mathias might be lying,' Marc said. 'But if you want to cross-check, you could try asking each of us separately what colour the sheets were. He can't have invented the date because I picked up the laundry that morning from Mme Toussaint at 22 Avenue de Choisy and you can check that out with her. I washed and dried it during the day and we ironed it in the evening. I returned it to Mme Toussaint the next day. One pair of light blue bed sheets with a shell motif, and another flesh-coloured pair with grey turn-downs.'

Adamsberg nodded. The housekeeping alibi was rock solid. The fellow knew what he was talking about as far as linen was concerned.

'OK,' he said. 'I'll put you in the picture.'

Adamsberg was a slow talker and it took him all of twenty-five minutes to tell the tale of the 4s, the town crier, and the Tuesday murder. Vandoosler Senior and Junior listened intently. Marc kept on nodding his head as if he was checking off each paragraph of Adamsberg's account. He gave his verdict as soon as Adamsberg finished talking.

'OK, so what you've got on your hands is a would-be plague-monger. But he also likes playing saviour. That means he thinks he's in full control. Has happened, but the vast majority of them were fantasies.'

'Sorry?' said Adamsberg as he opened his pad to start taking notes. Marc explained.

'Every outbreak of plague caused such fear and

panic that people invented culprits they could actually get at, that's to say, culprits other than God, comets and miasma. They looked for *plaguemongers*. They would accuse bods of spreading the disease on purpose by smearing unguents or oils or potions on doorbells, handles, railings and so forth. Any poor yokel who leaned his hand on a wall when this sort of panic was abroad most likely got lynched. He would be denounced as a "spreader" or "greaser," as they called people who were supposed to sow the seeds of the disease. Nobody stopped to ask why anyone should want to do that kind of a job. But it's perfectly obvious that we're dealing with just such a person in the present case. On the other hand he's not casting his plague seeds just anywhere, is he? He's taking aim at a particular individual and acting as a saviour for all the rest. He's God, so he can use God's curse for his own purposes. It's up to God to decide whose turn it is.'

'We've been looking for a link between all the people in the line of fire. We haven't come up with anything yet.'

'If there's a plague-monger at work, then there ought to be a hand tool too. Did you find any smears on the unmarked doors? Or on the keyholes?'

'We haven't been looking for that. But why would he need a hand tool if he kills by strangling?'

'Well, I suppose that in his own mind he doesn't think he's a murderer. If he was aware of his own murderous intent he wouldn't have needed to set up all these theatricals. He's using the scourge as a screen. The plague is like a convenient fog in between the victim and the murderer. He can't see himself killing. It's the plague that does it for him.'

'Which accounts for the ads he has the town crier read out.'

'That's right. The plague scare is a wind-up but its aim is to make the disease the one and only cause of what happens next. So he obviously needs a tool as well.'

'Those fleas?' Adamsberg suggested. 'My deputy got bitten by fleas at the dead man's flat yesterday.'

'Good Lord, did you say fleas? Are you telling me there were fleas in the flat?'

Marc jumped up and strode around the room with his hands clenched in his trouser pockets.

'What kind of fleas? Cat fleas?'

'I don't know. I'm having Danglard's clothes looked at by the path lab.'

'If they're cat fleas or dog fleas, no need to worry,' Marc said as he paced up and down. 'They aren't carriers. But if we've got rat fleas, if the fellow has really infected rat fleas and then released them, then we've bloody well got a disaster on our hands.'

'Are they really dangerous?'

Marc looked at Adamsberg as if he'd just been asked whether sharks had sharp teeth.

'Let me call the lab,' he added.

Adamsberg went to one side to make the call.

Marc signalled to Lucien to stop making so much noise putting away the dishes.

'Yes, that's right,' Adamsberg said into his mobile phone. 'You've got the results? . . . What was that you said? . . . Spell that for me, for God's sake.'

Adamsberg traced N, then O on his pad but found it hard to get the rest down. Marc grabbed the pencil from his hand and finished the word for him: *Nosopsyllus fasciatus*. Then he added a question mark. Adamsberg confirmed that was right.

'Thank you, I've got the word now,' he told the entomologist at the other end.

Marc scribbled 'carriers of the bacillus?' on the pad.

'Get them taken down to the bacteriology department,' Adamsberg said into the phone. 'Test them for plague. Tell the lads to put their skates on. I've already got one man bitten. And for God's sake don't go and lose the bloody things in the lab . . . Yes, same number, any time, day or night.'

Adamsberg folded up his phone and put it back in his pocket.

'There were two fleas in my deputy's clothing. They were not ordinary human fleas. They were –'

'*Nosopsyllus fasciatus*, rat fleas,' Marc said.

'There was a dead specimen in the envelope we found in the victim's mail. Same kind.'

'So that's how he spreads them.'

'Looks like it,' Adamsberg agreed as he too began to pace around the refectory table. 'He slits open the envelope and lets the fleas out in the flat. But I don't believe those bloody insects really are infected. I think it's all part of his symbolic game.'

'He's taking the game pretty close to a reality show, though, with his genuine rat fleas. They're not easy things to get hold of.'

'I think it's another wind-up. That's why he killed the victim himself. He knows his fleas won't do any harm.'

'How can you be so sure? You'd better have every single flea in Laurion's flat caught and bagged.'

'And how am I supposed to do that?'

'The easiest way is to take a couple of guinea pigs into the flat, and let them poke around on their own for five minutes or so. They'll pick up any fleas that happen to be there. Then you pop them straight back into a plastic bag and rush them over to the lab. Then you have pest control come and do the flat over from top to bottom. Don't let the guinea pigs stay in the flat for very long because once the fleas have had their bite they usually hop off and look for another snack. You have to get the beasts while they're still having lunch.'

'OK, thanks,' Adamsberg said as he scribbled notes on the recommended procedure. 'You've been very helpful, Vandoosler.'

'A couple of other points before you go,' Marc said as he was showing Adamsberg out. 'Your plague-monger is not quite on top of his subject, you know. There are some gaps in his knowledge of the field.'

'You mean he's making mistakes?'

'Yes.'

'About what?'

'Charcoal. Black Death. It's just an image, as well as a bad case of mistranslation. The Latin term *pestis atra* means "terrible plague," not literally "black" plague. Victims' bodies never did go black. Sure, there could be nasty dark bluey-black blotches here and there, or just about. But the black idea came quite late in the history of the plague. It's a folk thing, a popular misapprehension. Everybody thinks the plague turns you black, but it's not true. So when your man smudged his victim's corpse with charcoal, he was making a big mistake. A bloody great howler, if I may say so.'

'Ah,' said Adamsberg.

Lucien came past on his way out. 'Keep a cool head, *commissaire*,' he advised. 'Marc has a blinkered vision of things, which is only to be expected from a medievalist. He often can't see the wood for the trees.'

'And what's the name of the wood, then?'

'Violence, *commissaire*. Human violence.'

Marc smiled and stood aside to let Lucien get out of the front door.

'What does your friend do for a living, then?' Adamsberg asked.

'His principal avocation is to get up everyone's nose, but that doesn't pay the rent. He does it not-for-profit, gratis and for free. His secondary activity is modern and contemporary history, with a particular interest in the First World War. We have big fights between periods.'

'Ah, I see. And what was the other thing you wanted to tell me?'

'Am I right in thinking you're looking for someone whose initials are CLT?'

'It looks like a serious lead.'

'Drop it. CLT is just an acronym. It used to be called the electuary of the three adverbs.'

'Excuse me?'

'Almost every treatise of the plague told you that the very best way to ward off the disease was to say *cito longe fugeas et tarde redeas*. Word for word, "Go away fast and for a long time, and come back slowly". To put it another way, "Scram right now and take your time about coming back". That's what was meant by the "remedy of the three adverbs" – fast, long, late. Latin original: *cito, longe, tarde,* which makes CLT.'

'Can you write that down for me?' Adamsberg held out his notepad for the historian to use.

Marc scribbled down a couple of lines.

'CLT is a piece of advice that your murderer is giving the people that he's protecting with those

4s,' said Marc as he handed the pad back to the *commissaire*.

'I'd much rather they were initials,' Adamsberg confessed.

'That's comprehensible. Can you keep me up to date, please? About the fleas?'

'Are you that interested in the case?'

'That's not the point,' Marc said with a smile. 'But you might have a *Nosopsyllus* on you right now. Which means I might have one too. As might other members of this establishment.'

'I see.'

'Here's another remedy for plague: shower, soap and scrub. SSS.'

On his way out Adamsberg bumped into the blond giant and stopped to ask him a single question.

'One pair was beige,' Mathias replied, 'with grey turn-downs, and the other pair was blue, with a seashell pattern.'

Adamsberg left the house by way of the fallow garden, feeling punch-drunk. There were people around who knew a horrendous number of things. People who had paid attention at school, to begin with, and had then gone on storing up truckloads of facts for the rest of their lives. Facts about other worlds. There were people who devoted their lives to learning about mongers and mixtures and fleas and adverbs and Latin and Greek. And it seemed obvious that he'd glimpsed only a sliver of the huge heap of knowledge that Marc Vandoosler had stuffed into his head. It didn't seem to make it any easier for the young man to get on in life. All the same, in the very particular circumstances they were in, facts were going to make a big difference now. A vital difference.

CHAPTER 20

When Adamsberg got back to his office he found several new faxed reports from the lab and he read them straight away. The only fingerprints on the 'specials' were the town crier's and Decambrais's, and they were easily identifiable on all of the sheets.

'It's hardly likely our plague-monger would have been careless enough to touch the messages with bare hands,' said Adamsberg.

'Why does he use such expensive stationery?' asked Danglard.

'A sense of ceremony. In his mind, all his acts are of utmost importance, so he can't possibly put them in common or garden envelopes. He wants them to look distinguished and superior, because all his acts are deeds of exquisite refinement. Not the sort of thing plain folk like you or me might be able to perform, Danglard. You wouldn't expect a top chef to serve a soufflé in a plastic cup, would you. Same thing here. The envelope fits the crime. Both are superior.'

'Le Guern's and Ducouëdic's prints,' Danglard

said as he put the faxes back on the desk. 'Two jailbirds.'

'Yes. But they didn't do a lot of time. Nine months and six months.'

'That's quite enough to make useful acquaintances.' Danglard scratched his armpit energetically. 'Anyway, lock-picking can be learned when you get out. What were they in for?'

'Le Guern was sent down for grievous bodily harm and attempted manslaughter.'

Danglard whistled. 'That's quite something. Why didn't he get longer?'

'Mitigating circs. The shipowner he took apart hadn't done proper maintenance on Le Guern's trawler, and so it sank. Two crew drowned. Le Guern was crazy with grief when he came off the rescue helicopter and he went horizontal.'

'Did the owner get done too?'

'No. He got off scot-free, and so did the port authority cats who'd been paid off, or so Le Guern said in the box. They passed the word along and got Joss blackballed in every fishing port in Brittany. He never sailed again. So he landed on the platform at Montparnasse fourteen years ago, as lean as a string bean.'

'So he has got a reason for being angry with the whole wide world.'

'Sure, and he's got a temper, and he can lash out. But as far as we know René Laurion never went near a harbour master's office.'

'Maybe Le Guern's displacing. That's happened

before. Choosing to kill people in lieu. The crier is surely in the best position to send messages to himself. What's more, since we've been watching the square – and Le Guern knew we were from the start – there haven't been any more "specials".'

'He wasn't the only one to know the police were around. At 9 p.m. in the Viking, they'd all smelled a rat.'

'If the murderer isn't a local, how would he have known?'

'He'd already done the deed, so he must have realised the police would be moving in. And he must have seen through the plain-clothes officers sitting on the bench in the square.'

'So surveillance is pointless, then?'

'We're doing it as a matter of principle. And for another reason.'

'So tell me, what brought Decambrais-Ducouëdic down?'

'Attempted rape of a minor at the school where he taught. He was hounded by every newspaper in the land. He was nearly lynched, at the age of fifty-two. He needed police protection until the trial.'

'Ah yes, I remember, the Ducouëdic affair. Some poor girl who was attacked in the lavatory. You really wouldn't think he was like that, would you, when you look at him now.'

'You've forgotten his side of the story, Danglard. Three twelve-year-old boys had been beating up the girl during lunch break when there was no-one around. Ducouëdic came across the fight, laid into the lads really hard, and carried the girl out of the lavatory in his arms. Half the girl's clothes had been torn off in the fight, so there was teacher running down the corridor with a half-naked girl screaming her head off in his arms. That's what all the kids in the school saw. The three boys told a different story: Ducouëdic had been raping the girl, they intervened, so the teacher hit them hard and then ran off with the girl. It was their word against his. Ducouëdic lost. His girlfriend dropped him on the spot, the teachers turned the other way. In the absence of certainty. You know, Danglard, doubt is a void, and doubt goes on and on. That's why he's taken the name of Decambrais. Ducouëdic died at the age of fifty-two.'

'How old would those schoolboys be now? Thirty-two, thirty-three, roughly? Roughly Laurion's age?'

'Laurion went to school in Périgueux. Ducouëdic taught at Vannes. That's a long way away.'

'But he could be displacing as well, using substitutes for his real enemies.'

'Him as well?'

'But it's perfectly comprehensible. There are heaps of old men who detest everyone under thirty-five.'

'Don't remind me.'

'We've got to dig deeper into these two men. Decambrais is well placed to be the message-sender and he's obviously capable of writing the "specials". After all, he's the one who decoded them. Supposedly because a single Arabic word led him to Avicenna. He'd have to be a genius to have worked that one out from scratch!'

'We have to get to the bottom of those two in any case. I'm convinced that the killer comes to the newscasts. We've agreed that he must have started his campaign that way because he had precious little alternative. But I also reckon he's been familiar with the urn for a good while, at close quarters. What looks to us like a loopy mode of communication must have seemed to the killer to be the obvious way of talking to the world. I mean, look at the size of the audience: using the town crier has become part of normal life round there. I know I'm on the right track. I'm sure he comes to listen to his own "specials". He's there at the newscasts. I'll swear to that.'

'I can't see why you're so sure,' Danglard objected. 'He'd be putting himself at risk.'

'You can't see why, and I don't mind, because I know he's there, he's one of the people in the crowd. That's why we're not taking the watch off the square.'

Adamsberg got up and they both went to the incident room, where the chief stood with his back to the Paris wall map. All eyes were on them, but Adamsberg realised that the object of interest and attention was not himself but Danglard in his outsize sleeveless black T-shirt. He raised his arm, and eyes swivelled left.

'The premises will be evacuated at 1800, for pest control. When you all get home, you will shower immediately, body-wash and hair-wash obligatory, and you will place all your clothes, repeat all your clothes without exception, in the washing machine. Set water temperature to very hot, and run a full wash cycle. Objective: to kill any fleas you may have picked up.'

Smiles and grumbles.

'That was not a suggestion but an order,' Adamsberg said. 'It applies without exception to everyone in this team but most especially to the three officers who came with me to Laurion's flat. Now, has anybody been bitten since yesterday?'

A hand rose timidly. Kernorkian. The others stared at him, apprehensively.

'*Lieutenant* Kernorkian.'

'Now don't worry too much, *lieutenant*. You're not alone. *Commissaire* Danglard got bitten yesterday too.'

'My shirt will be wrecked if I put it through a hot wash,' someone piped up.

'Well, put it in the incinerator instead. That's your only alternative. If you're thinking of disobeying orders, let me emphasise that you would be running the risk of catching the plague. I repeat: a risk, not a certainty. I am personally convinced that the fleas in Laurion's flat are perfectly healthy and just another part of the set-up. Nonetheless, my order stands, and the hygienic measures required are not optional. Fleas bite mostly at night, which is why I insist you get on with personal hygiene the moment you get home. Second: after scrub-down and putting on the washing machine, you must all use the foggers which you can pick up from the changing rooms on your way out. OK. Now for tomorrow. Noël and Voisenet, your job is to check out the alibis of these four academics who know a lot about plague and are therefore provisionally suspect. And you,' said Adamsberg to the smiling face with thinning grey hair above it . . .

'*Lieutenant* Mercadet,' the man said as he half stood up in order to bow.

'Mercadet. Your job is to check out the ironing story with Mme Toussaint in Avenue de Choisy.'

Adamsberg gave out two slips of paper which were handed along the rows to Mercadet and to Noël. Then he pointed straight at the quaking green-eyed baby-face and then at the ramrod from the Channel coast.

'*Brigadier* Lamarre,' the pikestaff said as he stood up to attention.

'*Brigadier* Estalère,' said baby-face.

'Your job is to check the unmarked doors in all twenty-nine of the affected buildings. I want you to find any trace you can of an oily or greasy substance – skin cream, dripping, anything like that – on the keyhole, bell push, or doorknob. Take proper precautions and wear gloves at all times. Now, who's been working on the twenty-nine residents of the unmarked flats?'

Noël, Danglard, Justin and Froissy each raised a finger.

'What's come up? By way of connections?'

'Negative so far,' Justin said. 'Statistical analysis of the sample has produced no significant result.'

'Statements from the other residents in Rue Jean-Jacques Rousseau?'

'Useless. Nobody saw an intruder. Neighbours heard nothing.'

'The door code?'

'That's an easy one. The five numbers have completely worn away from over use. So given that you know which keys to punch, you've got only 120 combinations to try out, and that takes less than ten minutes.'

'Who took statements from the residents of the other twenty-eight buildings? Did anyone get a glimpse of the phantom painter?'

The big woman officer with the rock-hewn face held her hand up forthrightly.

'*Lieutenant* Retancourt,' she said. 'Nobody saw the dauber. He works at night, obviously, and his brush makes no sound. With all the practice he's had, he gets the job done in no more than half an hour.'

'Door codes?'

'We found traces of plasticine on several of the keypads, sir. The murderer slaps the stuff on the whole set of keys and then peels it back. It shows you which keys have been used because greasy fingermarks show up on plasticine.'

'That's trade,' Justin said. 'Means he's been inside.'

'But it's child's play,' said Noël. 'Anyone could think it up for himself.'

Adamsberg looked at the wall clock.

'Ten to,' he said. 'Time to evacuate the premises.'

The biologist rang at 3 a.m. and woke Adamsberg up.

'No bacilli,' a sleep-deprived male voice said. 'Result negative. Negative re fleas from clothing, negative re insect in envelope, negative re twelve specimens brought direct from the flat. Fine healthy fleas, sir. They're as clean as a pig's whistle.'

Adamsberg was aware of a feeling of relief.

'And they're all rat fleas, are they?'

'Rat fleas every one, sir. Five male, ten female.'

'Wonderful. Keep them safe under lock and key.'

'But they're already dead, *commissaire*.'

'Forget about the funeral announcement, would you. Keep them in a jar.'

Adamsberg sat up in bed, switched on the light, and rubbed his head. Then he called Danglard and Vandoosler with the news from the lab. Then he dialled all twenty-six other members of the team, the police pathologist who'd been in the flat, and Devillard. Not a single one grumbled about being woken up in the middle of the night. Adamsberg's head was swimming with all these *lieutenants* and *brigadiers* and he was afraid his telephone book wasn't up to date. He'd not had time to keep up his memory-jogger either. Or to call Camille to find out when they could get together again. The plague-monger was eating up his life. He wasn't going to get much sleep for a while.

At half past seven in the morning he got a call on his mobile as he was walking to the office from his flat in the fourth arrondissement.

'*Commissaire Principal* Adamsberg?' The caller was out of breath. 'This is *Brigadier* Gardon, on the night roster. We've got two corpses. They were lying in the street, in the twelfth arrondissement, one in Rue de Rottembourg and another not far away on Boulevard Soult. Both laid out stark naked on the roadway, both bodies smudged with charcoal. Both male.'

CHAPTER 21

By noon the two bodies had been bagged and taken off to the mortuary and the police cordons at the crime scenes had been taken down. The outdoor staging of the murders destroyed any chance of keeping the story under wraps. It was bound to break on the eight o'clock television news, and it could hardly fail to make the front page in the morning papers. No way of withholding the victims' identities either. The link between their home addresses in Rue Poulet and Avenue de Tourville and the unmarked doors on the two blocks that had been daubed with backwards 4s would be made in a trice. Two males, aged thirty-one and thirty-six respectively. One married with kids, the other living with a partner. Three-quarters of the murder squad were out on the job, looking for witnesses to the dumping of the bodies, or going through the blocks of flats where the victims had lived, or interviewing relatives and trying to find any kind of connection between these men and René Laurion. All the others were at their keyboards, logging the details and writing up.

Adamsberg stood leaning against the wall of his office, near the window with its brand new iron bars, vaguely aware of normal life flowing past down the street. He was trying to get a grip on what was now a vast skein of leads and all the stuff that came *after the fact.* The tangled ball had got too big for a single brain, at any rate for his brain. He couldn't get a grip on it, and he felt it was about to crush him. There were the 'specials' with their weird contents, there was local trivia down at the square, then the louche backgrounds of Le Guern and Ducouëdic; there was the mysterious topography of the door-daubing, the question of who the murdered men really were, and who their relatives, their neighbours and their friends might be; there was the charcoal business, and the fleas, and the envelopes, and results from the path lab and the autopsy reports and the hypothetical psychology of the culprit. A thousand strands that tied him in knots, a spiderweb of deception that stopped him standing up and seeing the lie of the land. He was drowning in a sea of detail. For the first time he wondered whether Danglard and his computer wouldn't get the better of his woolly mind all on its own in a howling storm.

One night, two stiffs. Two at a go. Their front doors had been under guard. So the killer must have made them go somewhere else to get killed. It was an elementary diversion, no more subtle than the Germans flying their troops across the

Maginot line in 1940 because the land routes were cut off by the army. The *lieutenants* on duty in Rue de Rottembourg outside the flat of Jean Viard saw the man go out around 8.30 p.m. It wouldn't have been right to make a man miss his date, now would it? In any case, Viard didn't give a damn for 'all that bloody 4 nonsense,' as he said to the man on duty. The other victim, François Clerc, went out around ten – for a walk, so he'd said. He was feeling claustrophobic with two *flics* outside the door, it was a lovely evening, he felt like a drink in a bar. What's wrong with that? You can't tell a man he's not to have a pint, now can you? Both men had been strangled to death, like Laurion. About an hour between the two murders. Serial slaughter. The bodies had then been moved, presumably in the same vehicle, and probably stripped and charcoaled in it together. Then dumped on the highway with all their belongings, near the outer edge of the city. This time the plague-monger hadn't taken the risk of being seen. Instead of stopping to lay out the limbs in a spread-eagle position, he'd pushed the dead men out the back of a van or a hatchback and left them in the road as they fell. Adamsberg imagined the killer being agitated about having had to skimp on the final ritual touches. Laurion had been arranged to look like a crucifixion, and that could not have been by chance. Anyway, the deed had been done in the dark of night, and there were no witnesses to be found for love or money. At 4 a.m. on a weekday, despite its millions of inhabitants, Paris can be as deserted as a Pyrenean village. Just because it's the capital city doesn't make any difference. Down time is down time on Boulevard Soult just as it is on the Tourmalet.

The only new fact to emerge so far was that all the victims were males over thirty. It was a pretty weak kind of common denominator but that was all there was. In other respects the victims could hardly be more different. Jean Viard hadn't been a slacker in a bad neighbourhood school like Laurion. He came from a pampered background, worked in computers and was married to a lawyer. François Clerc had started lower down, he'd grown into a large and broad-shouldered fellow, and he worked as a delivery man for one of the major French wine distributors.

Adamsberg called the pathologist without shifting from his buttress position. The man was in the middle of examining Viard. Adamsberg looked at his memory-jogger while waiting for the medic to come to the phone. He got the name just in time.

'Hallo, Romain, Adamsberg calling. Sorry for the interruption. Can you confirm death by strangulation?'

'No doubt about it. The killer used a sturdy line, probably a length of plastic-coated wire. There's a fairly obvious trauma in the lower rear area of the cranium. It might have been made by a slip-knot or a garrotte. The killer would only have to pull it to the right, not very much strength needed.

Incidentally, he's improved his technique now he's gone wholesale. Both victims got a good whiff of high-strength tear gas. By the time they got their wits back they must have been in the noose already. It's a quick and fail-safe way of doing things.'

'Did Laurion have any bites on his body – flea bites, I mean?'

'Good Lord, I forgot to put that in the autopsy report. It hardly seemed relevant at the time. But yes, he had fairly recent flea bites in the groin. There are some on Viard as well, on the inside of his right thigh and on his neck, but those are less recent. I've not had time to look at the third man yet.'

'Do fleas bite corpses?'

'No, Adamsberg, they would never do that. They would leave any host as soon as it began to lose heat.'

'Thanks, Romain. Please test for the bacillus, same as for Laurion. You never know.'

Adamsberg snapped his mobile back into his pocket and pressed his fingers to his eyelids. So he'd been wrong. The plague-monger didn't open his flea bag at the same time as he got the rope round his victim's neck. There must have been a time lag between his releasing the insects and his strangling because the fleas had had time to bite a warm body. Quite a substantial lag in the case of Viard, since the pathologist said the bites on his body were not recent ones.

He paced around the room with his hands clasped behind his back. The madman had a method that seemed truly insane: first, he slipped into the building, slit his flea-laden envelope open, pushed it under the door and went away again. Then he came back some time later with a lump of apple-wood charcoal in his pocket, picked the lock and strangled his victim. A two-stroke murder machine. One, fleas; two, neck. And that's leaving the diabolical distribution of the 4s and the 'specials' out of the count. Adamsberg felt he was losing it ever more completely. The leads crossed over, the way ahead was lost in fog, and this ritual killer seemed to grow ever more distant, ever more alien. On the spur of the moment he dialled Camille's number and half an hour later he was on her bed, naked beneath his clothes, and shortly after, naked without his clothes. Camille lay on top of him and he closed his eyes. A minute later he'd completely forgotten that he had twenty-seven men combing streets and servers under his command.

One hundred and fifty minutes later he was on his way back to Place Edgar-Quinet in far better spirits and with that slightly wobbly feeling in his upper legs giving him a sense of warmth and safety.

'I was going to call you, *commissaire*,' said Decambrais as he came out of his front door to greet him. 'There weren't any yesterday, but one came today.'

'Nobody was seen putting it in the urn,' Adamsberg pointed out.

'It came by post. He's switched tactics. He's not taking the risk of dropping it in in person any more. He puts it in the post.'

'Addressed to whom?'

'To Joss Le Guern, at this address.'

'So he knows the town crier's name?'

'Lots of people know the name.'

Adamsberg followed Decambrais into his cubby-hole and opened the outsize envelope.

> To my great trouble hear that the plague is come into the City, in two parishes together. They said [. . .] that both had been found with tokens that could not be denied or mistaken.

'Did Le Guern read it out?'

'Yes, at the noon newscast. You did say we should carry on.'

'This message is much clearer, now that our man has started killing. What sort of audience reaction did Le Guern get?'

'Murmurs in the crowd, questions and a lot of talk afterwards at the Viking. I think there was a journalist in the bar. He was firing off questions at Joss and other people. I don't know how he got on to us.'

'Gossip points the way, Decambrais. Can't be helped. The latest specials, the public warning and the corpse have set tongues wagging. It had to happen. Our plague-monger might even have cranked it up by putting out a press release, just to be sure that he's got ignition.'

'Yes, he could have done just that.'

'Yesterday's postmark,' Adamsberg said as he turned the envelope over. 'Mailed from the first arrondissement.'

'Two deaths foretold.'

Adamsberg looked Decambrais straight in the eye. 'That's already history, I'm afraid. You'll hear all about it on the evening news. Two men dumped in the road like sacks of potatoes. In their birthday suits, and charcoaled.'

'Two at a go!' Decambrais muttered. He pursed his lips, puckering his ageing skin with a thousand wrinkles.

'In your opinion, Decambrais, do plague victims turn black before they die?'

The former teacher furrowed his brow.

'*Commissaire*, I'm no expert on the plague, and I'm not a medical historian. That's why it took me so long to work out where those "specials" were coming from. But I can tell you that physicians of the period don't mention discoloration of the skin. They say plenty about pustules, blotches, buboes, lumps – "the tokens", they were called – but not about people turning black. The black business is a part of folk culture, and it's far less ancient than the great plague epidemics. All due to semantic drift, if you know what I mean.'

'Sure.'

'It didn't matter because the mistake got entrenched, and now everyone knows that "Black Death" means bubonic plague. But the phrase itself is probably critical for our killer, because words spread havoc. He's trying to impress, trying to make a big impact, and it doesn't matter if what he uses for that purpose is true or false. "Black Death" hits people like a bullet.'

Adamsberg took a pew at the Viking, which wasn't too noisy at that hour, and asked the big barman, Bertin, to bring him a black coffee. He had a good view of the whole square from where he was sitting. Danglard rang him fifteen minutes later.

'I'm at the Viking.'

'Go easy on the calva,' Danglard advised, 'it is rather peculiar. It empties your brain in no time at all.'

'My brain's empty as it is. I'm all at sea. I think he's bust my compass and turned my head inside out. He's won. He's beaten me hollow.'

'You mean Bertin and his apple brandy?'

'No, the plague-monger. Our man CLT. By the way, Danglard, drop those initials.'

'You mean drop Christian Laurent Taveniot?'

'Leave that man alone, Danglard. CLT is the electuary of the three adverbs.'

Adamsberg got out his pad and turned it to the page where Marc Vandoosler had scribbled his notes. He was waiting for Danglard to respond, but there was just silence on the line. Danglard couldn't cope either. He was losing it. Drowning.

'*Cito, longe, tarde*,' Adamsberg recited. "Scram now and take your time coming back."'

'Shit,' Danglard hissed after a long pause. 'Why didn't I remember that?'

'Because he's addled our minds, yours included. He's running rings round us.'

'*Cito, longe fugeas et tarde redeas*. Same thing as LHM.'

'What's LHM?'

'Short for "The Lord Have Mercy on Us All". You come across it in all the old books about the plague. Who put you on to CLT, anyway?'

'Marc Vandoosler.'

'I've got a whole file on him for you.'

'You can drop that too. He's out of the picture.'

'Did you know his uncle was a *flic* and got sacked just before retirement?'

'Yep. I've supped with the man. Octopus.'

'Oh, I see. Did you know the nephew, Marc, got mixed up in a case?'

'An actionable case?'

'Yes, but as part of the action. He's a bright lad.'

'I'd realised that.'

'I was calling to report on the other four plague specialists. Their alibis are watertight. Beyond all reasonable doubt. They're completely in the clear.'

'So we've drawn a blank there too.'

'Yes, sir. Nobody else in the picture at all.'

'I can't even see the bloody picture any more. I'm blind as a bat on a beach.'

Danglard could have gloated over the demise of Adamsberg's intuitive method. But to his own surprise he found he was dismayed, and he tried to put some spine back into his boss.

'Now come on, sir,' he said sharply. 'You must have sniffed something. Just a little something.'

'Just a little something,' Adamsberg parroted. And after a pause, 'It still smells the same, you know.'

'And what does it smell of? Tell me.'

Adamsberg looked right round the square. People were beginning to gather in little knots, others were stumbling out of the bar, all were getting ready for Joss's late final newscast. People standing under the big plane tree on the other side were laying bets on whether that day's crew would be 'all saved' or 'lost at sea'.

'I know he's here,' Adamsberg said.

'Here where?'

'Right here. The killer is on the square.'

Adamsberg had got rid of his television and his habit was to drop in to the Irish pub on the corner when he needed to watch the news, despite the loud music and the reek of Guinness. Enid, the barmaid he'd known for ages, let him use the portable set she kept switched on under the counter. So he breasted the swing doors of the Waters of Liffey at 7:55 p.m. and took his place behind the bar. The pub's name seemed about right, as he felt he'd been drinking deeply of oblivion all day long. While Enid put a monstrous baked potato with bacon filling on his plate – where did Irish pubs get such outsize spuds? a mystery worth investigating when he had the time, that's to say when his brain wasn't entirely consumed by a plague-monger – Adamsberg listened in to the eight o'clock news. It was nearly as disastrous as he had feared.

The anchorman announced that three men had been murdered in Paris, late Monday and late Wednesday night. The circumstances were a cause of considerable concern. All the victims lived in buildings that had had their doors painted with 4s, about which the police had put out a public warning two days previously. The police had made no comment about the significance of the signs but their meaning was now known thanks to a brief communiqué sent to Agence France-Presse by the painter himself. The message was to be regarded with extreme circumspection and a hoax could not be ruled out. The anonymous informant claimed that the three men had died of plague and declared that he had been trying to warn Parisians of the scourge through numerous messages read out to passers-by at the Edgar-Quinet–Rue Delambre crossing. The claim suggested strongly that the informant was mentally unbalanced. Although the bodies did show external symptoms of the Black Death, the Paris police had stated that they were certain beyond the shadow of a doubt that death had been caused by strangulation, and the three unfortunate men were the victims of a vicious serial killer. Adamsberg heard his own name mentioned.

Next came shots of doors that had been daubed, with a pedantic commentary, then interviews with neighbours and a clip of the square, before a live cut to the office of the Chief Superintendent in person. Superintendent Brézillon solemnly declared that all persons at risk were under tight protection, that the plague story was nothing but a fantasy in the mind of the man they were now looking for with all available resources, and that the black blotches on the bodies were nothing more than charcoal smudges. But instead of closing the item after these sensible reassurances, the anchorman went on to introduce some truly horrifying excerpts from an old documentary about the Black Death in France.

Adamsberg went back to his seat in the bar and began mechanically to demolish the vast tuber on his plate. He didn't really notice what he was eating.

At the Viking, Bertin turned up the volume on the television set, put back the time of serving mains, and also delayed his evening thunder-roll. Joss was in the thick of it, fielding questions as best he could, with Decambrais behaving impeccably as his cool-headed deputy. Damascus didn't really know what he could usefully do, but because he realised that a tense and complicated situation had arisen he stood like a centurion at Joss's left side. Marie-Belle burst into tears and Damascus was in dismay.

'Lord have mercy! Has plague come back?' she shouted out in the middle of the item. Nobody else dared say it so plainly but that was what everyone felt and feared.

'Didn't you hear, Marie-Belle?' boomed Lizbeth over the din. 'These guys did not die of plague, they were strangled to death. Didn't you hear what the man said? You should pay more attention, missy!'

'How do you know the boys in blue aren't pulling the wool over our eyes?' said a man at the bar. 'You don't think they would actually tell us on the TV news if there was an outbreak of plague, do you? They never let all their cats out of the bag, do they now. Like all the stuff they put in cows and corn nowadays. They don't shout the formula from the rooftops, do they?'

'Yeah, and meanwhile, what do we do? We go on eating the corn.'

'Not me. I won't eat sweetcorn any more,' said a woman's voice.

'You never have,' her husband butted in. 'You don't like it.'

'I bet it's another cock-up,' said another man at the bar. 'The idiots in white coats probably forgot to close the fridge door and let the bloody germs blow away on the wind. You know that plague of algae in the Med? Do you know how that got there?'

'Yeah,' someone said. 'And there's no way you can put it back in the bottle. Same as for maize and beef.'

'Three down already! Do you realise what that means? And how are they going to stop it from spreading? I bet they haven't got a bloody clue.'

'You can say that again,' said a young fellow leaning on the end of the bar.

'Lordy, Lordy!' Lizbeth's voice rang out above the hubbub. 'The geezers got it in the neck! They weren't ill, they were throttled to death!'

'But!' said a man wagging his finger like a schoolmaster. 'They died because their doors weren't protected by a 4! It was because they didn't have the talisman! Isn't that what they told us on the news? Or was I dreaming? Do you get it? Or don't you?'

'OK, but if that's how it is, then it's not a germ that got out of a lab. It must be a guy who's spreading it on purpose.'

'No, you haven't got it,' the pedagogue said. 'It's an acccidental release from a top secret biowarfare establishment. And there's a guy who knows about it going round trying to save people. He's doing his best.'

'Look, that doesn't add up. How come he leaves some people off his list? How come he's only done a couple of dozen blocks in the whole of Paris?'

'Give us a break! The guy's not God Almighty! He's only got one pair of hands. Go paint some 4s yourself if you're shitting in your pants.'

'Lordy, Lordy!' Lizbeth hollered at the top of her voice.

'Lizbeth, please, what's the matter?' Damascus asked quietly, without anyone noticing.

'Give up, Lizbeth,' Decambrais advised as he took the mountainous singer by the arm. 'They've all gone mad. Maybe the night will bring wiser counsel. Let's get on with dinner. Be so good as to round up the residents.'

Lizbeth calmed down and gathered in her flock while Decambrais went to the back of the room to ring Adamsberg on his mobile.

'*Commissaire*, it's hit the fan down here. They're all going mad.'

'Same here. I'm in a pub, and they're off their rockers. A scare story at prime time sends the whole country psychotic.'

'What are you going to do?'

'Keep on saying that the three men were strangled. And keep on and on until the cows come home. What are people saying at your end?'

'Lizbeth wasn't born yesterday, so she's keeping her head. Le Guern's not making too much of a fuss, as he doesn't want to damage his business. Anyway, he's been through worse at sea. I think Bertin's quite alarmed. Damascus doesn't know what's hit him and Marie-Belle is hysterical. Everyone else is stampeding down the usual path to the cliff – they're keeping us in the dark, they're pulling the wool, and haven't you noticed what funny weather we've been having. *When the air*

247

varieth from his natural temperature, when the wyndes are gross and hot; then are the Planets in disorder, and hang their poison in the sick air.'

'You've got your work cut out, Mr Even Keel Counselling.'

'You too, *commissaire principal.*'

'I can't see what's cut out and what's not right now.'

'What's your next step?

'Sleep, Decambrais. I'm going to bed to sleep.'

CHAPTER 22

By 8 a.m. on Friday Adamsberg had twelve extra officers helping to man the fifteen additional phone lines he'd had put it to cope with the flood of calls that local stations were transferring night and day. Thousands of Parisians were demanding to know whether or not the police had told the whole truth about the black deaths, whether they should take any special precautions, and if so, how. The commissioner of police had given strict orders to all local stations to log all such calls and to deal with them individually. Unconsoled hysterics could be a major factor in spreading havoc.

The morning papers were not likely to be much help in staunching the rising tide of fear. Adamsberg laid them all out on the table and glanced through. For the most part they just printed what had been said on television, plus their own ha'p'orth of commentary, with more photos. Several of them had also put the backwards 4 on the front page. Some of them hyped it up but others tried to keep a low key in their accounts of the affair. All of them covered themselves by reproducing substantial

parts of Chief Superintendent Brézillon's statement. All of them also printed the last two 'specials'.
Adamsberg reread them trying to imagine what it
would be like to see them for the first time in the
present context, that is to say, with three corpses
attached:

> The scourge is ever ready and at the
> command of God who brings it down and
> raises it away, as it pleaseth the Lord.

> To my great trouble hear that the plague
> is come into the City, in two parishes
> together. They said [. . .] that both had
> been found with tokens that could not be
> denied or mistaken.

Those two paragraphs were quite enough to sway
the gullible, and that made 18 per cent of the population, since 18 per cent had fallen for the Y2K
scare. Adamsberg was surprised by the amount of
attention to the case in the press, and just as surprised by the speed with which the story had flared
up, even though he'd worried that it might happen
that way from the moment the first body was
found. An obsolete affliction buried beneath the
dust of ages was hatching anew and rising up to
strike again with almost as much vigour as it ever
had had.
Adamsberg glanced at the wall clock since he
was due to hold a press conference at nine, by

order of the Super. He didn't like orders and he didn't like conferences but he was aware that circumstances required him to put up with both for the moment. The line he had to take was to head off panic by showing the marks of strangulation on the photographs of the victims and by demonstrating the vacuousness of the rumours going round. The police doctor who'd done the autopsy came along to back him up, and in the absence of any more killings or a particularly terrifying 'special,' he reckoned he could keep things under control. He could hear the swelling crowd of journalists outside his door and the rising tone of their jabber.

At the same hour Joss was drumming out his shipping forecast to a rather larger crowd than usual and was about to come on to the 'special' that had arrived in the morning post. The Super's orders were crystal clear: carry on reading, don't cut the only line we have to the plague-thrower. There was a slightly apprehensive silence as Joss announced ad number 20:

A direction concerning the plague or pestilence for poor or rich. Containing a description of the same with its symptoms and effects, and instructions concerning preservatives and antidotes dot dot dot. He shall know himself afflicted by said plague who hath lumps in the groin, commonly clept

251

buboes, hath the fevers and or is afflicted by fainting, sickness of mind and other kinds of folly, and also blains that are also called tokens that may be blue or green or black and grow ever larger. He who would fain ward off such affliction should attend to placing on his door the talisman of the four-pointed cross, for it will most surely keep the pestilence from his house.

Joss had barely finished stumbling through this long description when Decambrais picked up the phone to relay it to Adamsberg.

'It's full steam ahead from now on,' he said. 'Our killer has finished setting the stage. He's describing the disease as if it really had broken out. I would guess the text he's quoting is early seventeenth century.'

'Repeat the last sentence, would you? Slowly, please.'

'Have you got people with you? I can hear noises.'

'Only about sixty yapping reporters, Decambrais. How about the square?'

'A bigger audience than usual. Almost a crowd. Lots of new faces.'

'Try to remember the regulars. Write me a list of people who've been attending for a while. Scour your memory. Make it as full as you can.'

'You don't get the same people at all three newscasts.'

'Do your best, Decambrais. Ask the other pillars

252

of the local establishment to help you. The barman, the sports-shop fellow, his sister, the singer, the town crier, anybody who knows anything.'

'You really think he's here?'

'Yes, I do. That's where he started, that's where he'll stay. Everyone has his own hole, Decambrais. So, read me that last bit again.'

> He who would fain ward off such affliction should attend to placing on his door the talisman of the four-pointed cross, for it will most surely keep the pestilence from his house.

'He's appealing to people to start painting 4s on their own front doors. Then we really won't see the wood for the trees.'

'That's right. I said early seventeenth, but I suspect that this is actually the first instance of him fabricating a passage for his own ends. It sounds genuine but I think it's a pastiche. There's something wrong with the language in that last part.'

'For instance?'

'That "four-pointed cross". I've never seen that before. The writer clearly means us to understand a figure of four, he wants that to be crystal clear, but I think he's made up the whole thing.'

'If the passage was sent to a wire service the same time it was sent to Le Guern, then we're going to be submerged.'

'One moment, Adamsberg, I can hear the wreck coming.'

Two minutes passed before Decambrais came back on the line.

'So what happened?'

'All saved,' Decambrais answered. 'What were you betting on?'

'All saved.'

'So we got something right.'

As Joss was getting off his soapbox in the square to go and have his cup of coffee with Damascus, Adamsberg was walking into the conference room at the Brigade and stepping up on to the low rostrum that Danglard had set up. The police doctor was there already, the slide cassette was loaded and the projector plugged in. He turned to face the horde of reporters and their bristling microphones.

'Your questions, please.'

The press conference took ninety minutes and went rather well. Adamsberg answered the queries point by point and kept it all in low key. He reckoned he dealt with all the doubts the press had about the three black deaths. But halfway through he caught Danglard's eye and guessed from the tautened jaw that something was up. Squad members started trickling discreetly out of the room by the back. As soon as the conference was over Danglard followed Adamsberg into his office and shut the door behind him.

'There's a body been found in Avenue de Suffren,' he announced. 'Stuffed underneath a pick-up, alongside a heap of clothes. Only noticed when the driver pulled out at 9.15 a.m..'

'Bloody hell.' Adamsberg collapsed into his seat. 'Male? Thirty-something?'

'No, female, twenty-something.'

'That's our one lead done for. Did she live in one of these bloody daubed blocks?'

'Number fourteen on our list. Rue du Temple. It was daubed with 4s two weeks ago, but the victim's door was untouched. Second floor right.'

'What's the info?'

'Name, Marianne Bardou. Bachelor girl, parents live in Corrèze, weekend lover in Mantes, and another boyfriend for nights out in Paris. A salesgirl in a high-class deli in Rue du Bac. A pretty woman, kept herself fit, belonged to several gym clubs.'

'I don't suppose she came across Laurion or Viard or Clerc on the rowing machines?'

'I would have told you that straight off.'

'Was she out last night? Did she say anything to the man on duty?'

'We don't know yet. Voisenet and Estalère have gone to her flat. Mordent and Retancourt are at the scene and are waiting for you to get there.'

'I can't remember who's who, Danglard.'

'They're squad members, sir. Men and women.'

'And the girl, was she strangled? Was she naked? And charcoaled?'

255

'Same as the others.'

'Any sexual aggression?'

'Apparently not.'

'Avenue de Suffren is a canny choice of locale. One of the emptiest spots in Paris at night. You could dump forty corpses there without any worry. But why do you reckon she was left under a pick-up truck?'

'I've been thinking about that. He must have dumped her quite early in the evening and not wanted the body discovered before dawn. Perhaps because the dead carts used to come round at dawn during the plague. Perhaps to ensure that the morning newscast would go out before the body was found. Was there a special to announce the death this morning?'

'No, there wasn't. Today's message told us how not to get the plague. And guess how?'

'Fours?'

'That's right, fours. Do-it-yourself fours. Be a big boy and paint your own front door.'

'So the killer's too busy killing, do you reckon? No time for artwork now. So he's delegating.'

'I don't think that's quite it,' said Adamsberg. He got up and slipped on his jacket. 'It's so as to blind us. Imagine just 10 per cent of the population following the order and putting the talisman on the front door. We'll never know which are genuine and which are fake. It's an easy shape to make, and it's been spread over all the front pages. All you have to do is copy it.'

'A handwriting expert could soon sort the real ones from the fakes.'

'No, not soon he wouldn't. Not when you've got five thousand 4s painted by five thousand different hands. And that's certainly an underestimate. What's 18 per cent of two million?'

'Why the 18 per cent?'

'Because that's how many anxious, gullible and superstitious people live among us. The people who are afraid of an eclipse, who panic at the end of a millennium, who are scared by prophecies and believe that Doom is Nigh. The 18 per cent who admit to these things in surveys, at all events. So how many does that make it, Danglard?'

'Three hundred and sixty thousand – in central Paris, that is.'

'So that's roughly how many 4s we can expect to have to deal with. If it becomes a real scare we'll be completely snowed under. If we can't sort the real 4s from the fake we won't be able to identify the unmarked doors either, will we? So we won't be able to provide any security at all. The killer will have the city to himself, because there won't be a *flic* standing in front of the flat he wants to get into. He'll be able to paint away in the middle of the day when the main doors aren't even locked. No more door-code busting! We aren't going to arrest every one of the thousands of people who'll be painting their doors at the same time. Danglard, do you understand what he's doing? He's manipulating public opinion because it suits him to do so, and because he needs to do so in order to get the *flics* off his back. He's sharp, Danglard. He's got a very smart practical mind.'

'Smart? He didn't need to paint his bloody 4s. He didn't need to single out his victims for us. The trap was entirely of his own making.'

'He wanted to get us to think plague.'

'But he could have done that by putting a red cross on the door after the murder.'

'True enough. But his plague is targeted, not random. He picks his victims, then does his best to protect bystanders from contagion. That's also joined-up practical thinking.'

'Joined up inside a completely loopy mind. He could have murdered people without setting up any of this bloody antique scourge nonsense.'

'But it's not *him* who wants to kill. He wants people to be killed. He wants to be the agent directing where the curse will strike, but not the curse itself. That must be a hugely meaningful difference for our killer. In his own mind, he's not responsible.'

'Good Lord, but why does it have to be an outbreak of plague? It's grotesque! Where's this man coming from? The loony bin? Or has he crawled out of a grave?'

'Danglard, I've said this before. When we can understand where our man's coming from, we'll have him. But yes, of course the plague's a grotesque idea. All the same, don't underestimate the old

258

bogey, the plague's got life in it yet. You'd be surprised how many people are still bewitched. OK, so it's an outdated old bogey all tattered and torn, but nobody thinks it looks remotely funny. The scare may be grotesque, but we have to handle it with care.'

Adamsberg got in the car. On the way to Avenue de Suffren he called the entomologist to ask him to go over to the last victim's flat in Rue du Temple with a guinea pig. *Nosopsyllus fasciatus* had been found in the flats of Viard and Clerc – fourteen in the former, nine in the latter – plus some more in the clothing that the plague-monger had dumped alongside them. All healthy fleas. All released from a large ivory envelope slit open with a paperknife. Then he rang the AFP wire service. Anyone receiving an envelope of that description should contact the police immediately. And please get a picture of the envelope on to the lunchtime television news.

Adamsberg was deeply saddened by the sight of the naked woman. She was disfigured by strangulation and almost entirely black from charcoal and truck dirt; the small heap of clothes beside her looked quite pathetic. Rubbernecks were now being kept at bay behind a cordon but hundreds of passers-by had already seen the sight. Not a chance of keeping this out of the limelight. Adamsberg thrust his hands into his trouser pockets in a gesture of despair. His intuitions were

259

deserting him. He couldn't get a fix on the plague-monger, couldn't see where he was going. Whereas the killer was deadly effective. He announced his moves openly, he was master of the media and, despite a massive police operation that was supposed to have him cornered, he killed where and when he pleased. There were now four victims that Adamsberg had failed to protect even though he'd been on the alert well ahead of the murders. When was it he'd first sniffed what was in the air? When Maryse, the woman with kids on the verge of a breakdown, had come back to see him a second time. He remembered precisely when he'd started worrying. But he couldn't recall exactly when he'd begun to lose the thread, the point at which he'd got lost in a fog of detail and sank in a sea of facts.

He stayed to see Marianne Bardou bagged and loaded on to the hearse. He gave a few curt orders and lent an inattentive ear to officers reporting back from Rue du Temple. The woman hadn't gone out for the evening, she simply didn't go home from work. He sent two *lieutenants* off to see her boss, though he'd didn't expect to get much out of that, and walked back to the Brigade. He walked for over an hour and then cut off towards Montparnasse. If only he could summon up the memory of the exact moment when he lost the thread of this case.

He walked down Rue de la Gaîté and sauntered into the Viking. He ordered a sandwich and took a seat at the table by the window which was always empty because you had to bend low when approaching it to avoid banging your head on the fake longboat prow sticking out of the wall. He'd not had more than two bites when Bertin stood up and gave a sudden blow to a brass plate over the bar, setting off a great thunder-roll. Adamsberg was taken aback. There was a great flutter of pigeonry in the square as all the birds flew off, whereas customers flocked into the restaurant part of the bar. Le Guern was among them, and Adamsberg caught his eye. Without a question, the town crier came and sat down opposite the *commissaire*.

'You're down in the dumps, *commissaire*.'

'I am pretty down, Le Guern. Is it really obvious?'

'Yeah. Lost at sea?'

'Could not put it better myself.'

'That happened to me three times in all. We went round and round in the fog, just missing one disaster after another. On two occasions it was the equipment that had gone wrong. But once, it was my fault. I'd misread the sextant after a sleepless night. When you're overtired you can easily get it wrong, you can make a really bad howler. And you don't ever get away with that.'

Adamsberg sat up straight and Joss saw in those seaweed eyes the same flame he'd seen come alight when he first encountered Adamsberg at the Brigade.

'Say that again, Le Guern. In the same words.'
'You mean about the sextant?'
'Yes.'
'Well, OK, it was the sextant. You get it wrong, you make a howler, you don't get away with it, ever.'

Adamsberg stayed stock still, staring hard at a fixed point on the café table, with an arm stretched out as if to silence the town crier. Joss didn't dare open his mouth as he watched Adamsberg's clenched fist slowly compress the remnants of a sandwich.

'I've got it, Le Guern. I know when I lost the thread, when I stopped being able to see the fellow.'

'What fellow?'

'The plague-monger. I stopped being able to see him, I lost my bearings. But now I know *when* that happened.'

'Does it matter?'

'It matters as much as being able to go back to get a proper reading on your sextant and start over from where you were before you got lost.'

'In that case, *commissaire*, it matters.'

'I must go,' said Adamsberg as he put money down on the table.

'Watch out for the longboat!' Joss warned him. 'You could brain yourself.'

'I'm not that tall. Was there a "special" this morning?'

'You would have been told if there had been.'

As Adamsberg stepped out on to the street, Joss asked, 'Are you off to find your bearing?'

'That's right, Captain.'

'Do you really know how to find it?'

Adamsberg pointed a finger to his forehead, and off he went.

It was when he heard about the howler. When Marc Vandoosler had explained the howler. That's when he lost the thread. As he walked along the street, Adamsberg tried to reconstruct the exact words Vandoosler had used. He scanned the recent images in his memory and tried turning up the sound. Vandoosler leaning on the doorpost, Vandoosler with his clunky trouser belt, Vandoosler gesticulating, Vandoosler with his slender hand and his silver rings, one two three silver rings. That's right, they were on to the charcoal. *When your bod smudged his victim's corpse with charcoal, he was making a big mistake. A bloody great howler, if I may say so.*

Adamsberg gave a great sigh of relief. He sat on the first bench he could find, wrote Marc Vandoosler's remembered words in his notebook and munched through the rest of his sandwich. He still had no idea what course to set, but at least he now knew where he was starting from. Where his sextant had let him down. He also reckoned that from now on the mist might lift. He felt a sharp pang of gratitude for sailorman Joss Le Guern.

He wandered peacefully back to the office, though he could not keep his eyes from being accosted by headlines at every newsvendor's kiosk on his route. This evening, or maybe tomorrow. If the plague-monger sends his vicious *direction concerning the pestilence* to the AFP. And when the fourth murder gets out. Could happen this evening, could happen tomorrow. That's when the plague of gossip and rumour would run amok, and no press conference in the world would hold it back. The monger had mongered, and won hands down.

Could be tonight, could be tomorrow.

CHAPTER 23

'Is that you?'

'It's me, Narnie. Open up,' he said insistently.

As soon as he was inside he buried himself in the old woman's bosom, twisting gently from side to side.

'It's working, Narnie. It's working!'

'They're falling like flies. Like flies!'

'They wriggle and then die, Narnie. Do you remember how in the old days the sick went crazy, tore off their clothes and ran into the river to drown themselves? Bashed their brains out on brick walls?'

'Come on in,' the old woman said as she tugged him by the hand. 'Let's not stay here in the dark.'

Narnie led the way to the lounge by the light of her torch.

'Settle down, I've made you some girdle cakes. Have a glass of Madeira.'

'In the old days there were so many affected they got thrown out of windows on to the street like piles of rubbish. That was sad, wasn't it, Narnie? Parents, brothers, sisters, all thrown out with the rubbish.'

'They're not your brothers or sisters. They're wild animals who don't deserve to breathe the same air as you do. Later, when it's over, you'll recuperate. It's your turn now.'

Arnaud smiled. 'You know they go dizzy and collapse within a few days?'

'The scourge of God will strike them down where'er they may hide. Where'er they flee they'll not be saved. I think they've realised.'

'Sure they've twigged, and they're scared, Narnie. Their turn now,' Arnaud added as he emptied his glass.

'Now no more of this nonsense. You've come for the necessary?'

'I need lots of it. I'll be out and about from now on, Narnie. I'll be moving around.'

'The necessary was all right, wasn't it, my boy?'

The old woman moved between the cages in the attic amid squealing and scratching.

'Now, now, my dearies,' she mumbled, 'are we going to stop making such a fuss? Doesn't Narnie give you enough to eat?'

She picked up a small, tightly sealed bag which she handed to Arnaud.

'Here you are. Give me a surprise.'

Arnaud went down the ladder ahead of Narnie to save her from a fall, and he felt deeply moved by the bag with the dead rat in it that he held well away from his body. Narnie was a fantastic ratter, the best in the world. He would never have managed it all without her. He was in charge, of course, he thought as he twiddled the ring on his finger, and that was now plain to see. All the same, he would have wasted ten years of his life if Narnie hadn't been around to help. He needed all the life he had, and he needed it now.

Arnaud left the tumbledown house in the black of night. In his pockets were secreted five envelopes full of wriggling *Nosopsyllus fasciatus*, full to the brim with the power of death. He mumbled to himself as he picked his way down the dark alley. Ingluvies. Median stylet of the oral apparatus. Proboscis, probe, insertion. Arnaud loved fleas and Narnie was the only person he could talk to about the vast universe of their anatomy. Not cat fleas, though. They were out of the question. Frivolous, ineffective insects which he held in utter contempt. As did Narnie.

CHAPTER 24

Everyone in the squad who could do over-time had been asked to stay on throughout Saturday and, save for three members with insuperable domestic problems, the team with the twelve extra officers was at full strength at the start of the weekend. Adamsberg had been at his desk since 7 a.m., sifting through the pile of papers in his in-box. He cast a dreary eye over the latest lab reports and then got down to the morning news-papers. Actually, he tried to keep the word 'in-box' out of his mind. It rhymed with cell blocks, door-locks, stocks. 'In-tray' wasn't a lot better but it had a less gloomy assonance, struck a less burdensome chord. You could stray with a tray. Imagine a surf-board or a sleigh. Whereas 'in-box' felt like a ton of rocks.

He put to one side the recent forensic reports which only confirmed what was known or sup-posed already: Marianne Bardou had not been raped; her boss had stated she had changed in the back room for an evening in town but hadn't said where she was going. The boss's alibi was watertight; Marianne's two lovers, idem. Death by strangulation had occurred around 10 p.m. Like Viard and Clerc she'd also had a whiff of tear gas. Bacillus test, negative. Zero flea bites found on the corpse, and the same for François Clerc. But nine *Nosopsyllus fasciatus* had been found in Bardou's flat, bacillus negative. Type of charcoal used – apple wood. No trace of grease or oily substance found on any of the doors.

It was 7.30 a.m. and phones began ringing all over the building. Adamsberg had put his own line on divert and was relying on his mobile to keep in touch. He turned to the pile of morning papers. The front page facing him did not bode well. He had warned Brézillon after news of the fourth 'black death' had gone out on television on Friday evening: if the plague-monger had sent the press his 'instructions concerning preservatives and antidotes,' then the police would no longer be able to offer protection to potential victims.

'What about the envelopes?' Brézillon queried. 'We've highlighted that aspect so far.'

'He could change stationery. Not to mention the jokers and score-settlers who'll be slipping dozens of the things under their best friends' doors.'

'And the fleas? Shouldn't we ask anyone who gets bitten by a flea to report to a commissariat, for their own safety?'

'Fleas don't always bite straight away,' Adamsberg told the Chief Superintendent. 'Clerc and Bardou had no bites at all. If we do what you're suggesting, sir, we'll have thousands of panicky walk-ins fussing about bites that turn out to be just human fleas or cat fleas or dog fleas. That way we'd probably miss all the real targets.'

'And help set off mass psychosis too,' Brézillon added glumly.

'The media are doing their best to get that going in any case,' Adamsberg replied. 'We can't do a thing about it.'

'You do something about it all the same,' was Brézillon's final command.

Adamsberg had hung up aware that his recent promotion to the Brigade Criminelle was in the balance, with the plague-monger tipping the scales the wrong way. He wouldn't be especially upset if he lost this job and got transferred somewhere else. But what he would really hate would be to lose the thread of it again, just when he'd remembered when it was that it had all gone haywire.

He spread the papers out and then closed his door so as to muffle the staccato medley of the telephones that were keeping the entire team busy in the conference room.

The plague-monger's *direction concerning the plague or pestilence for poor or rich* was the lead item in all the papers. Plus photos of the latest victim and background pieces on plague with scary headlines:

COULD BE PLAGUE, COULD BE KILLER
DIVINE SCOURGE IS NUMBER ONE SUSPECT

POLICE SAY MURDER, OTHERS MALADY
FOURTH SUSPICIOUS DEATH IN PARIS

And so on and so forth.

There were articles that tackled and tried to pick holes in the official statement that four cases of death by strangulation were being investigated. Most of the papers rehearsed the facts that Adamsberg had provided at the press conference, but only to question their reliability and to muddy the issue with guesswork. The press seemed altogether less cautious than on Friday. Seasoned reporters and normally unflappable commentators were clearly haunted by the blackened corpses. As if, after lying dormant for three hundred years and more, a headless horseman had galloped out of his hollow and on to the streets of Paris. Despite the fact that the blacking of the bodies was nothing more than an ignorant blunder. A *bloody great howler*, as Marc had said. But it could still send the city howling mad.

Adamsberg looked for the scissors and began to cut out an article that struck him as more disturbing than all the others. Before he had finished, an officer – Justin, probably – knocked and came in. He sounded out of breath.

'Sir, masses of 4s have been found in the area around Place Edgar-Quinet. It goes from Montparnasse to Avenue du Maine and it's spreading along Boulevard Raspail. Apparently, two or three hundred separate blocks of flats affected, about a thousand doors done. Favre and Estalère are out on a recce. Estalère doesn't want to pair with Favre any more, he says Favre gets on his tits, what do I do about it, sir?'

'Change the detail and pair up with Favre yourself.'

'He gets on my tits too, sir.'

'*Brigadier* . . .'

'*Lieutenant* Voisenet,' Voisenet corrected.

'Look here, we've not got time for Favre's tits, your tits or anyone else's tits!'

'I'm aware of that, sir. We'll handle that one later.'

'Precisely.'

'Carry on with the patrols, sir?'

'Might as well try to drain the Channel with a chamber pot. And we've got spring tides coming. Take a look at that,' Adamsberg said as he shoved the morning papers under Voisenet's nose. 'The plague-monger's instructions are right up front: paint your own 4s to keep the scourge at bay.'

'I've seen it, sir. It's a disaster. We'll never be able to cope. We haven't a clue who needs protection, apart from the first twenty-nine.'

'There's only twenty-five of them now, Voisenet. Has anyone called about envelopes?'

'Over a hundred calls, sir, to this office alone. We can't keep up.'

Adamsberg sighed.

'Tell them to come here with their envelopes. And have every one of the things tested. There could be a genuine one among them.'

'Carry on with the patrols, sir?'

'Yes. Try to get an idea of how big this is. Do some sampling.'

'At least we didn't have a murder overnight, sir. Our twenty-five were all bright-eyed and bushy-tailed for breakfast.'

'I know, Voisenet.'

Adamsberg finished cutting out the article which had struck him as particularly well-informed and firmly put. It was the last straw, or rather, all that was needed to light the whole haystack. A veritable incendiary device.

DISEASE NUMBER 9

The police authorities have assured us in the statement put out by Chief Superintendent Pierre Brézillon that four suspicious deaths that have occurred in Paris over the last seven days were murders committed by the same serial killer. The victims are alleged to have died from strangulation, and the detective in charge of the investigation, *Commissaire Principal* Jean-Baptiste Adamsberg, has provided journalists with persuasive photographs of the alleged neck wounds. It is, however, common know-ledge that an anonymous informant has claimed that these deaths were actually caused by bubonic plague and that an epidemic of this terrible scourge of yesteryear is upon us.

The official position is open to serious question. It is rarely recalled that the last outbreak of plague in Paris took place only eighty years ago, in 1920. This third bubonic pandemic began in China in 1894, ravaged the Indian subcontinent, where it killed a million people, and made its way to all the major European ports – Lisbon, London, Oporto, Hamburg and Barcelona. It reached Paris on a river barge from Le Havre which cleaned out its hold near Levallois. In Paris as elsewhere in Europe, this outbreak did not spread very far and died out within a few years. Nonetheless, 96 people were infected, most of them in the working-class districts to the north and east of the city. Nearly all the victims were indigents and rag pickers living in unsanitary hovels. Even so, the contagion spread into the city centre where it killed 20 people.

The French authorities successfully covered up the outbreak. The press was not allowed to know the true nature of a quite unusual vaccination campaign carried out in vulnerable areas. The Public Health Department and the Police Authority agreed in an exchange of confidential notes that total secrecy had to be maintained, and they referred to the outbreak only under the codename of 'Disease Number 9'. As the Chief Medical Officer wrote in 1920: *A number of cases of disease number 9 have been reported at*

Saint-Ouen, Clichy, Levallois-Perret, and in the nineteenth and twentieth arrondissements [. . .] May I stress that this note is entirely confidential and that unnecessary public alarm must be avoided at all costs. This leaked document allowed *L'Humanité* to reveal the true story in its issue of 3 December 1920. *The upper chamber spent yesterday's session debating disease number 9. What is disease number 9? By 3.30 p.m. we had our answer. Senator Gaudin de Villaine let it drop that he was talking about bubonic plague . . .*

We hesitate to accuse police spokesmen of falsifying information so as to hide the true state of affairs. But it has happened before, as we trust this note has demonstrated. It would not be the first time that the truth has been sacrificed to expediency by those who rule over us. The authorities have long known how to be economical with the facts.

This devastating clipping trailed from Adamsberg's fingers as he put his arm down and plunged into thought. Plague in Paris in 1920. First time he'd heard of it. He dialled Vandoosler.

'I've just seen the papers,' Vandoosler said before Adamsberg got a word in. 'We're heading over the edge.'

'At full speed,' Adamsberg agreed. 'Is it true, that story about the 1920 plague, or is it bullshit?'

'It's twenty-four carat. Ninety-six cases, thirty-four of them fatal. Rag pickers from the shanties and a few people in the city centre. Particularly nasty in Clichy, where whole families went down. Their kids used to collect dead rats from the rubbish tips.'

'Why didn't it get worse?'

'Vaccination and prevention. But the main reason seems to be that rats had acquired much higher resistance to the disease. You could call it the death rattle of European plague. Even so, it didn't peter out in Corsica until 1945.'

'And is the stuff about the cover-up true as well? And "disease number 9"?'

'I'm sorry, *commissaire*, but it's all true. You can't deny it, I'm afraid.'

Adamsberg hung up and paced around the room. Something about the 1920 epidemic had clicked in his mind with a noise that sounded like the spinning of a dial that opens a secret passage. Adamsberg had found the starting point. Now he reckoned he had the courage to go through the secret door and down that dark and musty staircase – the back stairs of History. His mobile phone rang and he got an earful of Brézillon ranting on about the morning papers.

'What's all this rubbish about a police cover-up?' the Super screamed. 'What's all this utter crap about plague in 1920? Influenza epidemic, sure! But plague? Get a rebuttal out to the press this minute, Adamsberg. No discussion.'

'I'm afraid I can't do that, sir. It's all true.'

'Are you trying to take the piss, Adamsberg? Or are you looking forward to spending more time mowing your Pyrenean lawn?'

'I'm not trying anything, sir. There was an outbreak of plague, it happened in 1920, there were ninety-six cases and thirty-four deaths, and the police and the government tried to keep it hush-hush.'

'Put yourself in their shoes, Adamsberg!'

'I am in their shoes, sir.'

A moment's silence. Then Brézillon slammed the receiver down.

Justin or perhaps Voisenet came in the door. Voisenet, most likely.

'Going up like a volcano, sir. People are calling from all over the place. The whole of Paris knows all about it. People are panicking and painting 4s on anything flat. Don't know which way to turn, sir.'

'Don't turn any way. Let it go.'

'If you say so, sir.'

The mobile phone rang again and Adamsberg went back to his wall-prop position. Would it be the Ministry of the Interior? Or the state prosecutor? When all about him were losing their cool, Adamsberg found it easier to keep his head. Ever since he'd got his bearings back, his tenseness had slackened off by degrees.

It was Decambrais on the line. Only he wasn't ringing to say he'd read the papers and that we were about to fall off a cliff. Decambrais was still focusing on the 'specials' that he was the first to see, before they got to the AFP. The plague-monger was still giving the town crier a modest head start, maybe because he felt he owed it to the man who'd given him his first audience, or maybe to say thank you for not having grumbled about it.

'This morning's "special",' Decambrais said. 'A tricky one. It's long, so get pencil and paper first.'

'I've got both.'

> Threescore years and ten had passed since the last lash of that fearsome scourge and men went freely about their business when dot dot dot, there came into port dot dot dot, a ship laden with cotton and other merchandise. Dot dot dot.

'*Commissaire*, I'm giving you the suspension points out loud so you can write down the text as it is written.'

'I understand. Go on, please. Slowly.'

> But the licence given to voyagers to enter the city with their baggage and their mixing with the inhabitants soon had dire effects. For as early as dot dot dot *messire* dot dot dot who were physicians went to warn the aldermen of the city that having been called on the morning of dot dot dot to the side of an ailing sailor, Eissalene by name, they judged him to be sick with the Contagion.

'Is that it?'

'No, there's a curious epilogue about the aldermen's state of mind that's going to make your boss's day.'
'I'm all ears.'

The aldermen were fearful on receiving such counsel. As if they had already foreseen the misfortunes and dangers which they would soon endure, they fell into a slough of despond which spoke outwardly of the anguish in their souls. Verily, we should not be surprised that fear of the pestilence and its first steps in the city threw their minds into a frenzy, for the Holy Writ doth tell us that of the three plagues that the Lord threatened to visit on His People the Pestilence is the harshest and least forgiving.

'I doubt the Super has fallen into a slough of despond,' Adamsberg remarked. 'He's more inclined to throw other people into a pile of shit.'
'I know what you mean. I've been through it myself, in a different context. A fall guy has to be found. Are you nervous about keeping your job?'
'We'll see about that. What does today's broadcast say to you, Decambrais?'
'It says that it's long. It's long because it has two purposes. One, to make public fear seem justified by showing that the authorities were right to be scared. Two, to forecast more killings. And to forecast them precisely. I've got an inkling what's going

on here, Adamsberg, but I have to go and check. I'm not a specialist.'

'How's Le Guern's audience doing?'

'Bigger than yesterday evening. It's getting hard to find standing room in the square at the news-cast hour.'

'The captain should start charging admission. Then at least someone would be doing well out of all this.'

'Careful, *commissaire*. I must warn you not to make that kind of joke. The Le Guerns may be rough customers, sir, but they've never stolen a farthing.'

'Are you sure of that?'

'Well, Joss's deceased great-great-grandfather is adamant about it. He comes to pay a call every now and again. It's not like he's dropping in every afternoon, but it is a fairly regular event.'

'Decambrais, did you paint the 4 shape on your front door this morning?'

'Are you trying to rub me up the wrong way, *commissaire*? I've taken my stand against morbid superstition. I'll fight it on the beaches, I'll fight it in the streets, I'll never surrender! I, Ducoüedic, Hervé, Breton by birth and obstinate by nature, will stick my finger in the dyke until my dying day! Alongside Le Guern. And Lizbeth. You are cordially invited to join the resistance.'

'I'll think about it.'

Decambrais was in full spate.

'Superstition is the rotten fruit of human

stupidity! Stupidity is the seedbed of disinformation! And the sole product of disinformation is disaster! Superstition is the greatest pestilence mankind has ever known and it has killed more people than all plagues put together! *Commissaire,* please do try to catch the plague-monger before you're sacked. I don't know whether he's aware of what he is doing, but he is wronging the population of Paris by driving it back down to the very lowest basement of human nature.'

Adamsberg hung up with a pensive smile on his face. 'Aware of what he is doing.' Decambrais had put his finger on the thread that had been teasing Adamsberg's mind since the previous evening. He was just beginning to see where that thread might lead. With his transcription of the last 'special' in front of him, Adamsberg rang Vandoosler again while Justin, or maybe Voisenet, came into the office and used sign language to tell him that the total number of buildings affected by the plague of do-it-yourself 4s had just gone over the seven hundred mark. Adamsberg acknowledged the information with a measured blink. At the current rate of progress the figure would be in four digits by the evening.

'Vandoosler? Adamsberg here again. I want to read you this morning's special, have you got time? It'll take a moment or two.'

'Go ahead.'

Marc listened carefully to the *commissaire*'s calm voice relating how disaster was about to enter the city in the person of a young man called Eissalène.

'What does it mean, then?' Adamsberg asked when he'd finished reading, as if he was consulting a human dictionary. It didn't occur to him that a solution to the mystery of the latest message wouldn't be instantly forthcoming from the truck-loads of knowledge that Marc Vandoosler had stacked up in his brain.

'Marseille.' Marc's answer was loud and clear. 'The plague is going to hit Marseille.'

Adamsberg was expecting some kind of diversionary tactic, since the plague-monger's message alluded to a fresh outbreak, but he hadn't imagined it would be outside of Paris.

'Are you quite sure of that, young man?'

'Sure as sure can be. The message refers to the *Grand Saint-Antoine*, a ship out of Syria and Cyprus that docked off Marseille, at the Fortress of If – you know, the island of Monte Cristo – on 25 May 1720, carrying a cargo of infected silk and with half its crew already dead. The names omitted from the message are those of two physicians, Peissonel and his son of the same name, who raised the alarm. The passage he's quoting is pretty well known, as is the epidemic. It carried off almost half the population of Marseille.'

'Now that boy, Eissalène, the one the physicians went to see, do you know where they saw him?'

'Place Linche, called place de Lenche nowadays, just back of the north quay in the Vieux-Port. The primary seat of the contagion was in Rue de l'Escale, but the street disappeared long ago.'

'Could you conceivably have got any of that wrong?'

'No, sir, there's not a shadow of a doubt. It is Marseille. I can send you a xerox of the original passage if you want some supporting evidence.'

'No need, Vandoosler. Thank you very much.'

Adamsberg felt shattered by this turn of events. He left his office and went to see Danglard in the conference room where alongside thirty other officers he was trying to cope with telephone callers and to track the path and intensity of the hurricane of mumbo-jumbo. The room reeked of stale beer and even more of human sweat.

Danglard put down the phone and jotted a number on his pad. 'Soon there won't be a can of paint left in the whole of Paris,' he muttered. He raised his dripping brow and looked at Adamsberg.

'Marseille,' said the *commissaire* as he stuck the transcription of the special in front of his number two. 'The plague-monger's on the move. We're going on a trip, Danglard.'

'Good Lord! The docking of the good ship *Grand Saint-Antoine*!'

'You're familiar with the passage, then?'

'You said Marseille, so it rings old bells. But I'm not sure I would have twigged without that clue.'

'Is it better known than all the other texts the plague-monger has pilfered?'

'Oh yes, definitely. The Marseille outbreak was the last epidemic in France, and dreadful it was too.'

'Not quite the last,' Adamsberg said as he handed his deputy the article on 'Disease Number 9'. 'Read that and you'll understand why by this evening there won't be a man or woman alive in Paris who'll believe a word the police say.'

Danglard read the piece and nodded agreement.

'It's a disaster,' he said.

'Please don't use that word, Danglard, I beg you. Get me the Super in Marseille, in the Vieux-Port station.'

It took Danglard barely a second to consult his mental filing cabinet of all the police chiefs, super-intendents and *commissaires* in the land (he also knew the names of every county, town and borough by heart).

'His name is Masséna. His predecessor was a complete thug who got himself relegated for suggesting that Arab immigrants should be beaten to pulp, and then acting on it. Masséna got promoted in his place. He's a reliable and decent fellow.'

'That's just as well,' Adamsberg said. 'Because we're going to have to team up with him.'

At five past six Adamsberg took up position on Place Edgar-Quinet in time to hear the late final news-cast but it taught him nothing new. Ever since the monger had been obliged to use ordinary mail instead of the urn to get his messages to the town crier, he'd lost his freedom to vary between morning, lunchtime and evening newscasts. Adamsberg was aware of that. What he'd come for was to get a good look at the people milling round Le Guern's soapbox. There were far more of them than there had been earlier that week and many of them had to crane their necks to glimpse the face of the 'Crier' who was now famous for being the mouthpiece of the contagion. The two officers who kept the square under twenty-four-hour watch were also on hand to give Joss Le Guern protection if the crowd should turn nasty during a newscast.

Adamsberg was propping up a tree quite near the soapbox and Decambrais was giving him the rundown on the regulars who were there. He'd drawn up a neat list of about forty names, set out in three columns, for the 'very regular,' the 'fairly regular' and the 'occasional,' with a fourth column for physical features 'after the fact' as Le Guern might have said. He'd used red underlining for the people who laid bets on the outcomes of shipwrecks in the Atlantic approaches as retold every day in *Everyman's History of France*; blue underlining for people who shot off to work as soon as the newscast was over; yellow for the idlers who hung around chatting in the square or drifted into the Viking; and purple for locals whose attendance was affected by street market hours. Decambrais used the list to point out the faces corresponding to the names that Adamsberg needed to memorise.

285

Carmella, three-master flying the Austrian flag, 405 register tons, in ballast out of Brest for Cardiff, ran aground on Gazck-ar-Vilers. Fourteen crew on board. All saved.

That was the end of the news, and Joss jumped off his box.

'Now look around quickly,' Decambrais said. 'Anyone who looks surprised or mystified or is frowning or scowling is a novice.'

'Newcomers, right?'

'Exactly. Anyone who's chatting, nodding, talking with his hands is a regular.'

Decambrais went to help Lizbeth top and tail the beans they'd got cheap by the bushel, and the *commissaire* went over to the Viking, slid under the protruding prow and sat down at the table he'd come to think of as his. The shipwreck gamblers were standing at the bar and money was changing hands noisily. Bertin kept the book to ensure there would be no cheating. People assumed that the barman's divinely distinguished ancestry gave him a safe and unbribable pair of hands.

Adamsberg ordered a black coffee and studied Marie-Belle's face in profile. She was sitting at the next table and penning a letter with the appearance of effort. She had fine features and would have been a real beauty if her lips had been more firmly shaped. She had thick, wavy hair down to her shoulders, like her brother, only hers was blonde – and clean. She looked up, smiled at Adamsberg, and went back to writing. The woman called Eva was sitting next to her and trying to help Marie-Belle get the job done. Eva wasn't so pretty, probably because she was less able to be open. Her smooth-skinned, serious face, with dark bags under the eyes, seemed to Adamsberg to come straight out of a nineteenth-century oak-panelled drawing room.

'Is that all right? Do you think he'll understand?' Marie-Belle asked Eva.

'It's fine. But a bit short.'

'Should I mention the weather?'

'You could.'

Marie-Belle leaned over her screed once more, gripping her pen very tightly.

'There's a double "c" in "succumb",' Eva said.

'Are you sure?'

'I think so. Let me try.'

Eva wrote the word out a couple of times on scrap paper, then furrowed her brow in perplexity.

'I'm not sure any more. I'm getting in a muddle.'

Marie-Belle looked up and turned toward Adamsberg.

'*Commissaire*,' she said shyly, 'can you tell us if "succumb" has one "c" or two?'

It was the first time in his life that Adamsberg had been asked to give a ruling on how to spell a word. He had no idea.

'In the sentence "However, Damascus has not succumbed to the flu",' Marie-Belle added.

'The context doesn't make any difference,' Eva whispered with her head still bent over the scrap.

Adamsberg explained that he didn't know a thing about spelling. Marie-Belle seemed quite dismayed by the news.

'But you're a police officer,' she countered.

'But that's the way it is, Marie-Belle.'

'I have to go,' Eva said as she lightly stroked Marie-Belle's wrist. 'I promised Damascus I would help him cash up.'

'Thanks for standing in for me, you're very kind. Because what with this letter to do, I'm not going to get away in time.'

'The pleasure's mine,' said Eva. 'It keeps my mind off other things.'

She slipped away, and Marie-Belle immediately turned to Adamsberg.

'*Commissaire*, should I say anything about this . . . this affliction? Or is that something I should keep quiet about?'

Adamsberg shook his head slowly and firmly.

'Young lady, the affliction, as you call it, does not exist.'

'But the signs on the doors? And all those black bodies?'

Adamsberg shook his head side to side once again.

'A murderer, Marie-Belle, is quite sufficient to be getting on with. But plague there is not. Not the tiniest bit.'

'Should I believe you?'

'Blindly.'

Marie-Belle smiled again and suddenly became more relaxed.

'I fear Eva has fallen for Damascus,' she said with furrowed brow, as if Adamsberg, now he'd solved her problem about mentioning the plague, was going to straighten out all the other tangled bits of life. 'The even-keel counsellor says it's fine and good, that she's waking up to life at last, and that we have to let her go her own way. But this time, for once, I don't see things the same way he does.'

'Because?'

'Because Damascus is in love with big Lizzy, that's why.'

'You aren't fond of Lizbeth, I gather?'

Marie-Belle made a sour face, and then controlled herself.

'She's a good soul,' she said, 'but she makes a lot of noise. She frightens me a bit too. But the main thing is that in this place, Lizbeth is untouchable. My counsellor says she's like a tree that gives shelter to hundreds of different birds. That's all right by me, but she makes a hell of a noise about it. And then Lizzy's pretty much a law unto herself. Blokes lie down in front of her. No two ways, I suppose, seeing what she's been through.'

'Are you jealous by any chance?' Adamsberg enquired with a smile.

'My therapist says I am, but I don't feel it that way at all. What worries me is that Damascus spends all his evenings down there. I have to admit that when you've heard her sing you can't help being under her spell. Damascus is completely bewitched and he doesn't even notice Eva because she doesn't make a sound. Obviously, Eva is much more boring, but that's only to be expected seeing what she's gone through.'

Marie-Belle stared at Adamsberg with an inquisitorial eye intended to winkle out whatever he might know about Eva. Nothing, clearly.

'Her husband beat her black and blue for years,' she explained, since she couldn't resist telling the story. 'She ran away but he's after her and wants to do her in. Can you imagine? How come the police don't kill her husband first? Nobody's allowed to know Eva's real name, that's an order from the counsellor, and woe betide anyone who sticks his nose into the business. The counsellor knows the name but he's got a right to, since he has to keep us all on an even keel.'

Adamsberg drifted along with the conversation but he kept one eye on what was going on outside in the square. Things were running down for the night, and Le Guern was just putting his blue urn back on the plane tree. The clangour of phones that had gone on ringing in his ears long after he'd left the office was finally fading away. The less serious the conversation, the more he felt at ease. He'd had his fill of high-powered head-to-heads.

'OK,' said Marie-Belle turning round properly to face him. 'It's good for a woman like Eva. After what she went through she used to take fright every time she saw a man's shadow. It's waking her up. The woman, I mean. Damascus lets her know that some guys are not as bad as the animal who used to hit her. And I say it's a good thing as well, because a woman can't do without a guy. Like a horse and carriage. One without the other isn't a lot of use. Lizbeth doesn't agree, she says love is a joke and all it does is keep people in business. She even says love's complete crap. It's as bad as that.'

'She was a prostitute, wasn't she?' Adamsberg asked.

'Good Lord, no!' said Marie-Belle. 'Whatever made you say that?'

Adamsberg wished he hadn't said it. Marie-Belle's innocence was way beyond his expectation, and all the more refreshing for it.

'It must be your job,' Marie-Belle diagnosed. 'It distorts everything.'

'I fear so.'

'But what about you? Do you believe in love? I reckon I've got the right to ask lots of people because down here Lizbeth's opinions rule the roost.'

Adamsberg didn't answer. Marie-Belle shook her head.

'Seeing as what you have to put up with, it's only natural. But my counsellor is in favour of love, whether it's crap or not. He says it's better to have a good crap than to soil your underpants sitting still. You can see it with Eva. She's perked up since she started helping Damascus with the

291

till every evening. Only trouble is that Damascus is head over heels about Lizbeth.'

'Yes,' Adamsberg replied, rather enjoying the way things had come full circle. Every time they went round he would have less to contribute, and the more the plague-monger and the hundreds of doors being painted with 4s in the same instant would seep out of his head.

'And Lizbeth is not in love with Damascus. So there's no two ways, Eva's going to get hurt, then Damascus is going to get hurt, and Lizbeth is . . . well, I don't know, actually.'

Marie-Belle tried to think of alternative pairings that might make everyone happy.

'Tell me, Marie-Belle, do you have anyone?'

The young woman blushed and drummed her fingers on the letter she'd just written.

'I've got all the men in my life I can cope with, seeing as I've got two brothers.'

'Is that your brother you're writing to now?'

'Yes, he's the youngest of us three. He lives at Romorantin and he likes to get news from Paris. I write every week and I phone too. I'd like him to come up but he says the city scares him. He's like Damascus, he's not too smart. Actually, he's not even as smart as Damascus. I have to tell him what to do all the time, even with girls. He's a good-looking lad, though, with very blond hair. But he won't lift a finger if I haven't told him which one, when, and where. So I'll just have to look after them until they both get married. I've got my work cut out for a long while yet, specially if Damascus goes on gaping at Lizbeth for years and for nothing. Who else is going to be there with a shoulder to cry on when it hits him? But the counsellor says I'm not obliged to look after him.'

'He's quite right.'

'But he looks after people, doesn't he? He's got customers in that cubbyhole of his all day long. And they're not throwing their money down the drain! He doesn't talk bullshit. All the same, I can't let go of my two brothers.'

'That doesn't stop you having a man in your life.'

'Yes it does. Seeing as I've got my job to do and my hands tied at Rolaride, I don't get to meet many blokes anyway. I haven't seen Mr Right around here. The counsellor tells me I should look further afield.'

The café clock struck half past seven and Marie-Belle jumped. She hastened to fold up the letter, put it in an envelope, stick on a stamp and shove it in her handbag.

''Scuse me, *commissaire*, I have to rush. Damascus is expecting me.'

She bustled away. Bertin came to clear the table.

'Quite a chatterbox, that girl,' the barman said, almost as an apology. 'You have to take what she says about Lizbeth with a pinch of salt. Marie-Belle is jealous and she's afraid of having her brother swept off. It's only natural. Lizbeth comes from somewhere else, and you can't expect everyone to understand. Will you be staying for dinner?'

'No, thank you. I've got things to do.'

'Hey, *commissaire*,' Bertin said as he showed Adamsberg to the door. 'Are we supposed to paint our doors, you know, with that thing, that 4?'

'I've been told you're a descendant of Thor,' Adamsberg said turning round to face the hulking restaurateur. 'Or is that just silly gossip I've picked up on the square?'

Bertin drew himself up to full height and stuck his great chin forward.

'No, it's not silly gossip. My mother was a Toutin and through her the blood of thunder runs in my veins.'

'Well, in that case, don't paint a 4 on your door, Bertin. Otherwise your glorious ancestors will disown you and give you a kick up the backside to boot.'

Bertin pushed the door closed behind the *commissaire* but did not lower his proud chin. He had seen the light. No way was any 4 going to disfigure the door of the Viking.

Thirty minutes later Lizbeth had gathered all the regulars for dinner at the table of Decambrais's hotel. Decambrais clinked his wine glass with a knife to call everyone to order. It was a vulgar thing to do, in his view, but sometimes it had to be done. Castillon recognised the call to order and fell in almost instantly.

'It is not my custom to instruct my guests on how they should behave.' (Decambrais much preferred to call them guests, rather than tenants, lessees or customers.) 'Your room is your castle and you may do as you please in it. However, given the very special circumstances of the present moment, I must insist that none of you yield an inch to the current wave of collective lunacy, and that you all refrain from painting signs or talismans of any kind on your doors. It would bring dishonour on this house. But if any of you wish nonetheless to seek the protection of the 4, I shall not prevent you, for we live in a free country and it is not for me to restrain your liberty. On the other hand, if you do wish to do so, I would ask you to exercise your rights elsewhere, outside of this establishment, for as long as it takes for everyone to snap out of the hallucination which this plague-monger is trying to drag us into. I would like to hope that no-one present is tempted by this option.'

He looked at each of his dinner guests in turn, sitting in complete silence around the long table. Decambrais could see that Eva was hesitating on the brink, that Castillon wasn't entirely at ease despite the brave and smiling face he was putting on, that Joss didn't give two hoots and that Lizbeth was fuming at the mere idea of anyone sticking a four anywhere near her.

'That's agreed then,' said Joss, who was getting hungry. 'Approved *nem. con.*'

'All the same, if you hadn't read out all those letters from the devil . . .' Eva began.

'I'm not afraid of the old bogey, Eva dearest,' Joss cut in. 'I'm scared of rollers and breakers, I'll admit to that, because they can really harm you. But you know what you can do with devils and 4s and all that rubbish? Wipe them off with your hanky and stuff it up your sleeve. Breton's honour.'

'That settles it,' said Castillon, visibly bolstered by Joss's words.

'That settles it,' Eva echoed in a mumble.

Lizbeth said nothing and got on with doling out generous helpings of soup.

CHAPTER 25

Adamsberg was hoping that Sunday would pour some water on the flames, as France doesn't go in for weekend papers. The final estimate on Saturday evening had depressed but not surprised him – between four and five thousand blocks in central Paris daubed with mostly amateur 4s. On the other hand, on a Sunday almost everyone has time to get out the brush and paint tin, so maybe Saturday's figure would be vastly exceeded by the end of the day. The weather would be the decisive factor. If Sunday September 22 turned out fine and sunny, people would get out into the country and drop the whole story for a few hours. But if it was a miserable day, they would feel low, and their first victims would be front doors.

As soon as he woke up, before even lifting a leg, Adamsberg looked at the window pane. It was raining outside. He folded his arm over his eyes and confirmed his intention of not setting foot inside the office for the day. The weekend staff knew how to get hold of him if, in spite of re-inforced security at the twenty-five original blocks, the plague-monger had struck again.

He took a shower, dressed and lay down again fully clothed. He was just waiting, looking at the ceiling, letting his mind drift. He stood up at nine thirty reckoning he had one piece of good news: the death-monger had not struck on Saturday night.

He went down to the river bank of Ile Saint-Louis to keep the rendezvous he'd made on Saturday with Ferez, the forensic psychiatrist. Adamsberg didn't like the idea of talking to him perched on a chair in his office, so he'd got clearance to hold the meeting outdoors, by running water. Ferez wasn't accustomed to humouring the whims of his patients, but Adamsberg wasn't a patient, and the mass emotions provoked by the 4-dauber had intrigued him from the start.

Ferez could be seen from afar. He was a very tall man stooping slightly under a broad, grey umbrella, with a square face, a high forehead and a fringe of white hair around his bald pate. Adamsberg had met him a couple of years back at a dinner party – he couldn't remember at whose place. Ferez had seemed impassive yet sensitive, he had exuded quiet contentment, and maintained his distance from others without losing the ability to focus on them intently. As a result he had modified Adamsberg's somewhat stereotyped notion of what psychiatrists were like. The policeman had thus fallen into the habit of consulting Ferez whenever his own surmises about how other people worked ran up against his lack of medical expertise.

Adamsberg didn't own an umbrella so he was soaking wet when he got to the meeting point. Ferez knew only what the media had told him about the killer and his obsessions, so he listened intently with his eyes on Adamsberg's face while the detective filled him in with the rest of the story. Ferez maintained his professional blank face while listening, but his clear steady gaze didn't waver from the speaker's lips.

'What I think,' Adamsberg said as he wrapped up his forty-five-minute briefing which the psychiatrist had not once interrupted, 'is that we must try to elucidate why the killer is using the plague. The plague isn't exactly ordinary or topical or knocking around in everyone's mind, like . . .'

He stopped to try to find a suitable example.

'Like a front-page issue, or a talking-point such as . . .'

He stopped again. He sometimes found it difficult to find the right words to express something specific. Ferez wasn't making the slightest effort to prompt him.

'Such as the Y2K scare, or Star Wars.'

'Yes,' Ferez agreed.

'Or standard fantasies about vampires, the second coming, or sun spots. Any of those things, Ferez, would be transparent covers for a killer who was trying to dissociate himself from his acts. When I say transparent, I mean generally comprehensible, in today's context. If the killer claimed he was the Fifth Horseman of the Apocalypse, the

Messenger of the Sun, or an envoy from outer space, then everyone would know straight away that we'd got a crackpot or a loony cult follower on our hands. Do you follow?'

'Carry on, Adamsberg. Would you like to stand under my umbrella?'

'Thanks, no, the rain will soon stop. Our plague-monger isn't even living in the twentieth century. He's a throwback. My deputy calls him "grotesque". And he is like a gargoyle, because he's completely out of touch. Spreading bubonic plague in modern Paris is like saying dinosaurs have arrived in the Jardin des Plantes. Our monger just isn't with it. He's out on his own. Am I making sense?'

'Carry on,' Ferez said again.

'On the other hand, even though it's as dead as a dodo, plague can still reawaken ancient fears that are far less fuzzy than you might think. But that's beside the point. The point I'm trying to make is that our man is out of sync, that he's hit on an incomprehensible cover that no-one, but no-one else could have dreamed up. What we have to tackle is precisely the *eccentricity* of the idea. I'm not saying there's nobody working away on the plague, as a historical issue, I mean. But Ferez, please tell me if I'm wrong: however fixated a fellow might be on his research topic, it can't get so deep down inside as to turn him into a serial killer.'

'True. Intellectual pursuits are always outside the primitive psyche, especially if the pursuit's

300

been taken up in adult life. They're activities of the mind, not psychological drives.'

'Not even if the activity becomes a frenzy, a passion?'

'Not even.'

'So I can rule out intellectual motivation, and I can rule out mere coincidence. We're not looking for a chap who woke up one fine day and said, hey, let's have a go with the scourge of the Lord, that'll make a terrific impact. Nor are we looking for a fraud or a prankster. No way. Our man hasn't got enough separation to play practical jokes. He believes profoundly in the whole thing. He paints the 4s with love and care, he's completely absorbed by the thing. His recourse to the pestilence is instinctive, it's got no basis in conscious life, in his education or his culture. He doesn't give a damn whether people understand what he's up to or not. Because *he* knows what he's up to. He's using plague because he has to. – And that's where I've got to, Ferez.'

'Good,' said Ferez patiently.

'So if our monger is in the same place, then the plague is inside him, deep down inside. That means it comes from . . .'

'Family business,' Ferez filled in.

'Precisely. Do you agree?'

'No doubt about it, Adamsberg. Because there's no alternative.'

'Good,' said Adamsberg, relieved to have the psychiatrist's support and to have got over the worst of his vocabulary problems.

'To begin with, I imagined that maybe our man had caught plague in childhood, in some distant land, and that it had been his blight, his trauma, or whatever you call it. But I wasn't happy with that.'

'And so?'

'So I scratched my head and tried to work out how anyone's childhood could be deeply affected by a tragedy that ended in the early eighteenth century. I came to the logical conclusion that our plague-monger is 260 years old. But I wasn't happy with it.'

'Not bad. Would make a fascinating client.'

'Then I learned that plague had hit Paris in 1920. In *our* century. And two decades into it. Did you know that?'

'No,' Ferez conceded. 'Frankly, I did not.'

'Ninety-six cases, thirty-four fatalities, mostly in poverty-stricken areas on the edge of town. And Ferez, I reckon our man's forebears were in the eye of the storm, that some of them must have died, maybe his great-grandparents. And the story became part and parcel of the family saga.'

'Some of us psychiatrists call that a family phantom.'

'Great. The phantom must have got stuck, and that's how the plague got into the child's mind. The story of how the great-grandparents died must have been reinforced by constant repetition down the generations. And in that boy's mind – I think it must be a boy – plague was a fact of life, it became part of his . . .'

'Part of his inner world.'

'That's right. It's a natural thing for him, not something from past history, like it is for us. I should find our monger's surname among the descendants of the thirty-four families mortally affected by the 1920 outbreak.'

Adamsberg stopped walking, crossed his arms and looked up at the psychiatrist.

'You're very good at this, Adamsberg,' Ferez said with a smile. 'And you're on the right track. All you need to add is some brutal upset which made a large enough wound for the plague to get inside. Phantoms nestle in fissures and cracks.'

'Of course.'

'But I fear I'm going to put a spanner in your works. I wouldn't go looking for your monger among the descendants of the families that died. I'd look for him in a family that was *spared*. That gives you thousands of candidates, not just thirty-four.'

'Why the spared?'

'Because your man is using plague as an instrument of power.'

'And so?'

'He wouldn't do that if his family had been *victims* of the plague. He would hate the scourge.'

'I thought I'd made a mistake somewhere down the line,' said Adamsberg as he began to stride forward again with his hands clasped behind him.

'That's not a mistake, Adamsberg, it's just a nut you put on upside down. If your man is using plague as a power tool, then it must have given power to his forebears once upon a time. Some apparent miracle must have saved them from the fate of all the neighbours. The survivors might have had to pay a heavy price for the miracle. People slip only too easily from hating the lucky ones to suspecting them of having a secret force on their side and then to accusing them of being agents of the disease. It's the same old story, I'm sure you've come across it before. I wouldn't be surprised if our monger's ancestors had fingers pointed at them, then got threatened and blackballed, and were forced to leave the original area for fear of getting torn to shreds by the neighbours.'

'Good Lord!' Adamsberg said, kicking a clump of grass at the foot of a tree. 'You're right!'

'I may be.'

'You most certainly are. The family saga is the miracle of survival followed by persecution and social isolation. The story is the escape from the plague and, on top of that, mastery of the disease. They turned what was held against them into a source of pride.'

'People often do just that. If you tell a man he's dumb, he'll answer back that he's proud not to be too smart. It's a normal mechanism of defence. Irrespective of what you're being accused of.'

'The phantom in that man's mind was hearing over and over that "our" family was different from others, that "we" could control an affliction sent down by God.'

'But don't forget, Adamsberg – your monger must have had a broken home, or else lost his father or his mother, at all events he felt abandoned, and immensely fragile. That's the most likely explanation for the boy clinging on to the violent side of the family's sole claim to glory as his only source of power. Probably rehashed over and over by a grandfather. Inheritances of this kind often skip a generation.'

'All that's not going to help find the man's ID,' said Adamsberg, who'd gone round in a circle and was berating the same clump of grass again. 'Hundreds of thousands of people didn't die of the plague.'

'I'm sorry.'

'Never mind, Ferez. You've really helped.'

CHAPTER 26

Adamsberg went up Boulevard Saint-michel on the side that was just beginning to be warmed by the sun. He'd taken off his jacket and was drying it off as he walked. He wasn't trying to find ways round Ferez's arguments, he knew the psychiatrist was right. That put the plague-monger out of reach, just when he thought he'd nearly got him cornered. All that was left was Place Edgar-Quinet, which was where he was heading. He kept coming back to the conclusion that someone on the square had great-grandparents who'd been rag pickers in 1920. Actually on the square, or else a constant visitor, despite the danger. But what did the monger have to be frightened of, in fact? He felt he was in command, and he'd proved that he was, at a time in his life when he'd needed to show his strength. Twenty-eight *flics* weren't going to scare a guy who could lay on the scourge of the Lord and lay it off with a flip of his wrist. Twenty-eight *flics* were no more threat to him than twenty-eight bird droppings.

The whole story to date could only boost the plague-monger's pride and self-confidence. Parisians had obeyed his command and were painting the talisman on their doors. Twenty-eight *flics* hadn't been able to stop the killing. Four down, and Adamsberg hadn't the faintest idea how to prevent the next murder. Except by stationing himself at this crossing and keeping his eyes open. But what was he looking for? He didn't rightly know. But at least it would let him dry off his jacket and his wet trouser legs.

He was just stepping on to the square when Bertin's thunder-roll rang out. Now he'd got the hang of the routine, he hastened into the Viking to enjoy a hot lunch and to join Decambrais, Lizbeth, Le Guern and melancholy Eva round a table with a few other people he didn't yet know. Conversation stuck doggedly to any topic other than the plague-monger, as if an order to avoid the subject had been given, obviously by Decambrais. On the other hand, Adamsberg could eavesdrop on other tables where the topic was clearly not taboo, and he picked up a number of declarations in support of the press attacks on the police. Those photos of neck wounds, they were obviously faked, do they think we're blind, or stupid, or what? That's as may be, someone riposted, but how do you account for the victims having time to get undressed and to pile their clothes up neatly before they died? How did they get themselves stuck under a truck, eh? You can explain that, can you? You think that looks like plague, do you? Looks more like murder to me, chum! Good thinking, Adamsberg said to himself, and he craned round to get a glimpse of a firm and intelligent female face on top of an extremely large bust tightly encased in a flowery top. Look, her decidedly weakened opponent said, I didn't say this was simple. You're not with it at all, someone else butted in – a desiccated fellow with a falsetto voice. It's both together. They did die of plague, but as the mystery man doesn't want it to be hushed up, he goes round to haul them out of their flats, and he undresses them so everyone can see what it's all about and not be kept in the dark. He's not a faker. He's trying to help. Come off it, the woman replied, if that were the case he'd only have to come clean. I've never trusted mystery men or fellows who don't say who they are. He's hiding because he can't come out in the open, said the falsetto, spinning his laborious theory as he spoke. He's a lab technician, and this technician, he knows they let the plague out when they bust a test tube, or something. He can't come out with it because the lab's under orders to hush it up to prevent panic. Politicians don't like the people panicking, they only like the people when they keep quiet. So mum's the word. But the technician, he's trying to tell people, without breaking cover. Whatever for? the woman riposted. Afraid of losing his job, is he? If that's all that's stopping him from coming clean, then let me tell you this, André: your saviour is a despicable little man.

Adamsberg moved away from the table when coffee was being served so as to take a call on his mobile from one of his *lieutenants*, Mordent. Current estimate of buildings daubed, six thousand. No, no new murders reported, they had a breathing space on that front. But on the other front, they were being run into the ground. Couldn't they now stop responding to panic callers? Because on top of all that, there were only six of them on Sunday duty at the Brigade. Of course, Adamsberg answered. Good, Mordent responded, that's a relief. The *commissaire*, for his part, was relieved that things were really beginning to move in Marseille as well. The more the merrier. Masséna had asked Adamsberg to come down south.

Adamsberg shut himself in the WC and sat on the lid to call Masséna.

'It's started, *commissaire*. As soon as local radio broadcast your nutter's message and journalists started explaining, it's just piling in.'

'He's not *my* nutter, Masséna,' Adamsberg replied rather curtly. 'He's yours too from now on. Share and share alike.'

Masséna paused while sizing up who he was dealing with.

'All right, fair shares. *Our* crackpot has put his finger on a sore point down here. The Marseille plague may be long gone but it doesn't take much to bring it to life again. The Archbishop of Marseille still holds a Mass every June to thank the Lord for ending the epidemic. We've still got streets named after Chevalier Roze and Bishop Belsunce, and statues of them too. Those names haven't dropped off the map, because down here people don't have a drainpipe in the place of memory.'

'Who are these fellows?' Adamsberg asked calmly.

Masséna had a short fuse and it had probably been lit in advance by the traditional mistrust that Marseillais have for Parisians. Adamsberg didn't give a damn because he wasn't from Paris, and anyway he wouldn't have given a damn if he were. Where you came from didn't make any difference. But Masséna was all bluster, really; it wouldn't take Adamsberg more than ten minutes to get behind the façade.

'These fellows, as you call them, *commissaire principal*, slaved away day and night to help people during the great contagion of 1720, when cartloads of local officials, bigwigs, medics and priests took to their heels. They were heroes, damn it!'

'It's perfectly all right to be afraid of death, Masséna. You weren't there.'

'Look here, it's not our job to rewrite the history books. I am simply explaining that in Marseille when you touch the *Grand Saint-Antoine* it's like you'd hit a live wire.'

'Are you telling me that everyone in your town knows who Roze and Belsain are?'

'Belsunce, *commissaire*.'

'Belsunce.'

'No, I'm not saying that,' Masséna conceded.

'Not everyone knows. But the plague, the fact that the city was wiped out, the containment wall around the whole of Provence – everyone around here is aware of the history. The plague is permanently lodged somewhere in people's heads here in Provence.'

'Looks like the same is true up here too, Masséna. We've got to ten thousand buildings daubed with 4s. All we can hope is that shops run out of paint.'

'Well, here, just this morning, I counted about two hundred in the area around the Vieux-Port. Work out how many that makes for the whole city! Bloody hell, Adamsberg, have people gone completely crazy?'

'They're doing it for protection, Masséna. If you counted up all the people who go around with a brass bracelet, or a rabbit's foot, or a St Christopher, or Lourdes water, or who knock on wood – and I'll leave out the crucifixes – you would tot up forty million just in France, easy as pie.'

Masséna sighed.

'As long as they're doing it themselves,' Adamsberg continued, 'it's no big deal. But is there anything at all that looks to you like it might be authentic? A 4 painted by the plague-monger himself?'

'That's a hard one, Adamsberg. People are copying the sign. It's true that lots of them forget to thicken the downstroke at the bottom, and others put one notch instead of two on the crossbar. But about 50 per cent of them do it carefully. Their signs look bloody close to the original. How do you expect me to get it right?'

'Any envelopes reported?'

'No.'

'Have you recorded any blocks where all doors are marked save for one?'

'There are some of those, *commissaire*. But there are also heaps of people who are keeping their heads and wouldn't think of painting on their own front doors. There's also a contingent of faint-hearts who draw a tiny little 4 at the bottom of the door. That way they can have the talisman and not have it at the same time, or not have it and be protected none-theless, take your pick. I can't go over every door in the city with a magnifying glass, can I? Would you?'

'It's a tidal wave up here, Masséna, it's what everyone's doing by way of weekend redecoration. We aren't even checking any more.'

'Not at all?'

'Almost. I'm keeping an eye on a thousand square feet, out of one thousand million square feet in central Paris. All I'm keeping under surveillance is the patch where I hope to see the monger – but he could be prowling round the Vieux-Port even as I speak.'

'Have you got a description? Any idea what he looks like?'

'No. Nobody's seen him. I don't even know if it's a man.'

'So what are you looking out for on your patch, Adamsberg? An ectoplasm?'

'An impression. I'll call you back tonight, Masséna. Keep it up.'

Someone had been violently rattling the handle of the WC door for a while. Adamsberg exited calmly, slipping past an exceedingly impatient beer drinker in need of urgent relief.

Adamsberg asked the barman if he could leave his jacket to dry out on a chair-back while he went for a walk in the square. Ever since the *commissaire* had bolstered Bertin's courage in his hour of need and thereby saved him from general ridicule and from the irrecoverable loss of divine authority over his customers, the barman considered himself to be in Adamsberg's eternal debt. So he gave his hundredfold permission, insisted that he would watch over the wet jacket with maternal solicitude, and pressed the *commissaire* to please borrow a green oilskin before he ventured into the wind and the shower that Joss had forecast at his midday performance. Which Adamsberg accepted, so as not to risk offending the proud scion of Thor.

He idled away the whole afternoon on the square, alternating between coffees in the Viking, plodding around and making calls. By evening, he learned, the Paris total would hit fifteen thousand, and Marseille was having a spectacular start and was well on the way to four thousand already. Adamsberg was ceasing to care, inflating his already considerable capacity for indifference so as to resist the rising tide. He wouldn't have raised an eyebrow if he were told there were two million 4s. He was going slack right through, closing himself down. Except for his eyes. They were the only parts of his body still alive.

He took up his position for the evening newscast by the plane tree, standing sloppily with his arms at his sides, swallowed up by Bertin's oilskin which was several sizes too big for him. Le Guern's Sunday timetable ran later than the weekday schedule, and he didn't set up his soapbox on the paving until almost 7 p.m. Adamsberg wasn't expecting anything from this newscast, since there was no mail delivery on Sundays. But he was beginning to recognise faces in the crowd that was gathering around Joss's rostrum. He got out the list Decambrais had drawn up and checked off his new acquaintances as they rolled up. At two minutes to seven Decambrais emerged on to his doorstep, Lizbeth elbowed her way through the crowd to her usual place, Damascus appeared in front of Rolaride wearing a sweater and leaned against the steel shutters that hadn't been raised that day.

Joss launched himself energetically into the newscast, projecting his resonant voice to the four corners of the square. Adamsberg enjoyed listening to the harmless small ads in pale sunlight. An entire afternoon spent doing bugger all except letting body and mind wind down had helped him recover from the dense discussion with Ferez. He had reached the level of animation of a sponge bobbing about on a stormy sea. It was a state he sometimes sought specifically.

And at the close of the newscast, as Joss was announcing the wreck of the day, he jumped, as if a pebble had just hit the sponge hard. The bump almost hurt physically, leaving Adamsberg nonplussed and alert. He could not tell where it had come from. It was necessarily a picture that had hit him while he'd been drowsing with his shoulder leaning on the trunk of the plane – a fleeting frame, a split-second flash of a visual detail of some kind.

Adamsberg straightened up and scanned the whole scene in search of the lost image, trying to recover the sense of shock. Then he went back to leaning on the tree positioned exactly as he had been at the moment of impact. His field of vision ranged from Decambrais's hotel to Damascus's shop, bridging Rue du Montparnasse and incorporating about a quarter of Joss's audience, seen face on. Adamsberg pursed his lips. That made quite a large area and quite a lot of people – and they were already drifting off in all directions. Five minutes went by. Joss had already packed up his box and the square had emptied. All gone. Adamsberg closed his eyes and lifted his head towards the sky as if light falling on his eyelids would make the image return to him, ethereally. But the picture had dropped back to the bottom of the well like a moody, unlisted asteroid, maybe because it was irritated that Adamsberg hadn't paid more attention to it during its brief flight through the light of his eye. It would probably be months before that shooting star would deign to crop up again.

Adamsberg left the square in a state of dismay. He was convinced he'd just missed his one and only chance.

When he got home and started to undress he realised that he'd still got Bertin's green oilskin on and had left his old black jacket drying on a chair-back beneath the Viking prow. Did that prove that he too had started believing the barman could exercise divine protection? It meant more probably that he was letting everything go to pot.

CHAPTER 27

C amille clambered up the four narrow flights that led to Adamsberg's flat. As she crossed the third floor landing she noticed that the resident of the left-hand flat had daubed a huge black 4 on his door. She and Jean-Baptiste had agreed to spend this night together, but she wasn't to turn up before ten because of the hectic timetable the plague-monger had imposed on the squad.

The kitten was a bloody nuisance. It had been following her down the street for ages. Camille had stopped to stroke it, then left it, then tried to lose it, but the kitten kept on catching her up in jerky leaps and bounds, and stayed glued to her heels. Camille had crossed to the other side of the square to put an end to the stalking. She'd left it outside when she'd gone in to have dinner but found the thing still on the landing when she came out again. The kitten bravely resumed its unwavering pursuit of her. Fed up with the effort of keeping the cat at bay, Camille picked the beast up and stuck it on her shoulder when she got to Adamsberg's staircase door. It was just a ball of white and grey fluff weighing no more than a globe of foam, with two round blue dots for eyes.

At five past ten Camille went through the front door that Adamsberg almost never locked, and found the lounge and the kitchen deserted. The dish rack showed that he'd done the washing-up and Camille guessed that Adamsberg had dropped off to sleep while waiting for her to turn up. She would get into bed without waking him up – she knew how much the first hours of sleep mattered during a stressful case – and lay her head on his belly for the night. She put down her backpack, took off her jacket, settled the kitten on the sofa and tiptoed into the bedroom.

In the unlit bedroom Jean-Baptiste was not sleeping. It took Camille a moment to work out what she was seeing – a tanned, naked back among white sheets, moving about on top of a girl.

A flash of pain hit her forehead like a metal shard driving right between her eyes. For a split second the intensity of the flash made her believe she would stay blind for the rest of her life. Her knees gave way and she sank on to the cabin trunk that served various functions and which this night had served as the place to put the girl's clothes. The two bodies, unaware of her silent presence, carried on jiggling about. Camille was stunned by the sight. She watched Jean-Baptiste do things with his hands and lips, things that she recognised, each and every one. The red-hot bit drilling a hole in the middle of her head forced her to screw up her eyes. It was a violent sight and an ordinary sight, it was deeply wounding and utterly trivial. Camille looked down.

Don't cry, Camille.

She left off looking at the bodies in bed and stared hard at a spot on the floor.

Beat it, Camille. Scram right now, and take your time about coming back.

Cito, longe, tarde.

Camille tried to move but realised that her legs wouldn't support her. She lowered her gaze further and concentrated hard on the toes of her boots. On her black leather boots. On their squared-off toes. On their side buckles. On the dirt in their creases. On the corners of their heels, worn smooth from walking.

Carry on, Camille, carry on looking at your feet.

I am.

It was a stroke of luck that she still had her shoes on. If she were barefoot and defenceless, she could not have got up to go any place at all. Most likely she would have stayed nailed to the trunk with a drill bit in her head. A masonry bit, for sure, not a woodworking bit. Look at your boots since you've got them on. Look hard, Camille. Now run.

But it was too soon. Her legs were still no stiffer than flags on a windless day. Don't look up, Camille, don't look.

Of course she knew. It had always been like that.

There had always been other women, lots of other women, for longer or shorter periods, depending on how tough the girl was, since Adamsberg always screwed up his affairs, let them fall apart. Of course there'd always been other women, other fish in the sea, other Loreleis beckoning from the river bank. 'They get to me,' Jean-Baptiste used to say laconically. Sure, Camille knew all about it, she knew what was going on when Jean-Baptiste went into eclipse, when he disappeared behind a curtain, she knew what the fuss was about in the far distance. On one occasion she'd turned her back and given up. She had managed to forget Jean-Baptiste Adamsberg, his overpopulated river bank, his world of whispers and upsets that came just too close to her. She'd stayed away for years, and given Adamsberg the kind of grand burial that great love requires.

Until he'd crossed her path by chance once more last summer. Though she'd blocked up the river, by some convoluted process the headwaters still ran as strong as ever. She'd put one foot back in while keeping the other on dry land, she'd done the splits trying to hold a balance between freedom's embrace and that of Jean-Baptiste. Until tonight when that unforeseen collision had stuck that thing between her eyes. All because of a diary mistake. Jean-Baptiste had never been very careful about dates.

The long stare at her boots had given some consistency back to her legs. Things were going quiet on the bed. Camille stood up very carefully and made her way round the trunk. She was just slipping out of the door when the girl sat up and screamed. Camille heard the ruffling of bedclothes and bodies in panic, of Jean-Baptiste jumping to the floor and calling out her name.

Scram, Camille.

I'm doing what I can. Camille grabbed her bomber jacket and her backpack, then saw the lost kitten on the sofa and grabbed that too. The girl was talking, asking questions. Scram right now. Camille clattered down the stairs, ran out into the street and kept running for a long while. She stopped when she was out of breath and found herself in a deserted square around a locked garden. She climbed over the railings and hunched up on a park bench, cuddling her knees. The thing in her head began to slacken off.

A young man with dyed hair sat down beside her.

'Not too happy tonight, are we?' he said softly.

He kissed her on the temple and walked off without a sound.

CHAPTER 28

It was past midnight but Danglard was still awake when he heard a timid knock at his door. He was in his vest, in front of a television he wasn't watching, with a beer in his hand, going over and over the notes he'd made on the plague-monger and his prey. It could not be random. The killer chose his victims, there had to be some kind of a connection between them. He'd interviewed the relatives for hours on end in the pursuit of some point of intersection, and now he was going over his notes trying to find that elusive link.

Danglard's day-time dress sense gave way in the evening to inherited working-class attire – off duty, Danglard, like his father before him, slouched around shirtless, unshaven and in heavy cord trousers. The five kids were asleep, so he slid noiselessly down the long corridor of his flat to answer the door himself. He expected to see Adamsberg, but clapped eyes on Queen Matilda's girl standing bolt upright on the landing, breathing heavily, with some sort of kitten in the crook of her arm.

'Have I woken you up, Adrien?' Camille asked.

Danglard shook his head and motioned her to follow him without making a noise. Camille didn't even stop to wonder whether Danglard had a girl or anything like that in the flat, and flopped down exhausted on the worn settee. In the light Danglard could see she'd been crying. He switched off the television without saying a word, opened a bottle of beer and pushed it towards Camille. She downed half of it in one gulp.

'I'm in a bad way, Adrien,' she blurted out as she put the bottle down.

'Is it Adamsberg?'

'Yes. We got it wrong.'

Camille drank the rest of her beer. Danglard knew what it was like. When you've been crying you need to replace all the lost liquid. He leaned over the arm of his chair, took another bottle from the still nearly intact six-pack, uncapped it and pushed it towards Camille across the shiny top of the coffee table between them, as if he was moving a pawn and hoping to take a piece.

Camille made a broad gesture with her arm, and explained.

'There are fields of different kinds, Adrien. Your own field, which you dig by yourself; and other people's fields, which you can visit. There's lots to see – clover, rape, flax, wheat. Then there are fallow patches and nettles as well. I keep away from the nettles, Adrien, I don't try to uproot them. They're not mine, you see, no more than anything else.'

Camille put down her hand and smiled.

323

'But all of a sudden you make a mistake, you put your foot in the wrong place. And you get stung, without meaning to.'

'Does it itch?'

'It's OK, it'll stop soon.'

She picked up the second bottle and took a few sips, slower now. Danglard was watching her. She looked a lot like her mother Queen Matilda, she had the same square jaw, the same slender neck, the same slightly hooked nose. But Camille had a very fair complexion and her lips were still very childlike, quite different from Matilda's wide, imperial smile. They said nothing for a minute or two. Camille emptied the second bottle.

'Do you love him?' asked Danglard.

Camille propped her elbows on her knees and gazed intently at the little green bottle standing on the coffee table.

'Major hazard,' she said quietly, shaking her head.

'You know, Camille, the day when God made Adamsberg, He'd not slept at all well the night before.'

Camille looked up.

'Really? No, I didn't know that.'

'Well, it's true. Not only had He had a bad night, He'd run out of stuff. So like an idiot He popped down to ask the Other Guy if he could borrow some gear.'

'You mean . . . the Guy down below?'

'Himself. So the Other Guy seized a golden

opportunity and lent Him loads of gear. And God, who still hadn't recovered from His night on the tiles, didn't get the mixture right either. That's the primal soup He made Adamsberg from. Not your usual working day.'

'Nobody told me that before.'

'You can check it in all the right books,' Danglard said with a smile.

'And what then? What did God give Jean-Baptiste?'

'He gave him intuition, gentleness, beauty and ease.'

'And what did the Devil give him?'

'Indifference, gentleness, beauty and ease.'

'Bugger.'

'Quite. But it was never discovered what proportions the absent-minded Lord used for His concoction. It remains a major theological mystery down to this day.'

'I don't want to be involved in the argument, Adrien.'

'That's only to be expected, Camille. It's a well-known fact that when God created you, He'd just woken from seventeen hours' sleep, and was consequently in tip-top shape. He spent a whole blessed day shaping you with His skilled hands.'

Camille smiled.

'And what about you, Adrien? How was God feeling when he made you?'

'He'd spent the whole evening boozing with his mates, Raphael, Michael and Gabriel. They got right pickled. It's not such a well-known story.'

'The result could have been great.'

'No, it gave the Lord the DTs. That's why I've got this fuzzy, jellywobble look.'

'There's a reason for everything.'

'Yep. Things aren't that complicated, really.'

'I'm going out for a walk, Adrien.'

'Are you sure?'

'Have you got a better idea?'

'Drop him.'

'I don't like dropping people. It makes dents in them.'

'You're right. I've been dropped, once.'

Camille nodded.

'You have to help me. Call me tomorrow when he's got into the office. Then I can go round and collect my stuff.'

Camille grabbed a third bottle and downed a good part of its liquid contents.

'Where are you off to?' Danglard asked.

'No idea. Where is there room for me?'

Danglard pointed to his own forehead.

'Yes indeed,' Camille said with a smile, 'but you're an old sage, my friend, and I'm quite devoid of wisdom. Adrien?'

'Yes?'

'What can I do with that?'

Camille pointed to a fur ball on the settee. It was actually a kitten.

'It's been trailing me all evening. I suppose it

wanted to help. It's tiny, but wise and very proud. I can't take it with me, it's too delicate.'

'Do you want me to look after that cat?'

Danglard picked it up by the scruff, looked at it, and put it down in alarm.

'I would rather give houseroom to you,' said Danglard. 'He'll miss you.'

'The kitten will miss me?'

'Adamsberg will miss you.'

Camille finished her third beer and put the bottle back down without a sound.

'No, he won't. He's not delicate.'

Danglard didn't try to sway Camille. It's not a bad idea to take a trip after an accident. He'd keep her cat, it would be a souvenir, as soft and cute as Camille herself, though obviously less spectacular.

'Where are you going to sleep?'

Camille shrugged.

'Here,' Danglard decided. 'I'll make up the sofa bed.'

'Please don't bother, Adrien. I'll lie out on the settee, with my boots on.'

'Whatever for? You'll be uncomfortable.'

'That doesn't matter. From now on I shall always sleep in my boots.'

'That's not very hygienic,' said Danglard.

'Better to be upstanding than hygienic.'

'You know, Camille, fine words never did mend broken bones.'

'Yes, sure, I know. It's just the stupid bit of me that makes me spout sometimes. Or trickle.'

'Spouting words fine or foul won't give you what you need, my dear. Nor even a Shakespearean soliloquy.'

'What will, Adrien?' said Camille as she began to undo her laces.

'Thinking with your head.'

'OK. I'll go and get one.'

Camille lay down on her back on the settee with her eyes open. Danglard went to the bathroom and came back with a towel and a bowl of cold water.

'Dab your eyes, it'll help the swelling go down.'

'Adrien, did God have any soup left when He'd finished making Jean-Baptiste?'

'A bit.'

'What did He do with it?'

'A few bits and pieces, tricksy things like leather soles. They're great to wear, but they slip on slopes and skid as soon as it gets wet. Mankind has only solved this ancient conundrum in recent years with rubber stick-ons.'

'Can't we stick rubber soles on Jean-Baptiste?'

'To stop him slipping away? No, can't do that.'

'What else did He make, Adrien?'

'He didn't have much soup left, you know.'

'What else?'

'Skittles.'

'There you are, you see. Skittles are really clever.'

Camille dropped off and Danglard stayed up for another half an hour to take off the cold compress and switch off the lights. He looked at the girl in the half-light. He'd give a year's beer just to be able to stroke her every time Adamsberg forgot to give her a kiss. He picked up the kitten, brought it up to his face and stared in its eyes.

'Accidents are bloody stupid,' he told the cat. 'Really stupid. You and me, kid, we're going to have to get along together for a while. We'll wait for her to come back, if she does. Won't we, Woolly?'

Before going to bed Danglard hovered over the phone, wondering whether he should let Adamsberg know. Whether to rat on Camille, or to rat on Adamsberg. He pondered for a good while as he stood at this sombre fork in his path.

As Adamsberg put his clothes on in a rush to go after Camille, the girl didn't stop firing worried questions at him – how long had he known her, why had he never mentioned her, did he sleep with her, did he love her, what was he thinking of, why was he running after her, when would he come back, why didn't he stay, she didn't like to be left on her own. It made Adamsberg dizzy and he didn't know how to answer a single one of the questions. He left the girl in the flat, confident that she'd still be there when he got back, and left the unopened parcel of questions for later. Camille was much the greater of his worries, because Camille didn't mind being on her own. She minded it so little that the slightest bump could have her setting off on one of her treks.

Adamsberg strode at a good pace in Bertin's

billowing oilskin with its cold and draughty arms. He knew Camille. She was going to take off, pretty damn quick too. When Camille wanted a change of scenery, she was as hard to pin down as a bird on helium, as hard to catch as her mother Queen Matilda was when she launched herself on to the high seas. Camille would go and potter about in her own far yonder once she'd had enough all of a sudden of the here and now with its twisting paths all awkwardly tangled up with each other. Right now she was probably lacing up her boots, packing her keyboard, shutting her toolbox. Camille relied a great deal on that toolbox to sort her out in life, much more than she relied on him, because she didn't trust him that much, and quite right too.

Adamsberg came round the corner into her street and looked up at her loft. Lights out. He sat on the bonnet of a parked car to catch his breath and crossed his hands on his waist. Camille hadn't gone back to her place and she would probably take off without looking over her shoulder. That's the way it was when Camille went walkabout. Who knows when he would see her again? In five years, in ten years, or never. You couldn't tell.

He walked miserably back home. It wouldn't have happened if his time and his mind hadn't been consumed by the plague-monger. He collapsed on to his bed, weary and speechless, while the girl picked up the skein of her worried questions.

'Stop it, please,' he said.

'It's not my fault!' she protested.

'It's my fault,' said Adamsberg as he closed his eyes. 'But you either stop it or you get out.'

'You don't care either way?'

'It makes no difference to me. Nothing makes any difference.'

CHAPTER 29

Danglard was quite worried when he went into Adamsberg's office at 9 a.m., despite knowing that, at bottom, nothing would ever alter the *commissaire principal*'s eternally roving eye, owing to his extremely limited contact with reality. And there indeed sat Adamsberg at his desk, leafing through a heap of morning papers with fairly disastrous front-page headlines, but seeming quite unaffected by them, his face as calm as it ever was, with maybe just a slightly more distant look in the eye.

'Eighteen thousand blocks now daubed,' Danglard said as he put a memo on the chief's desk.

'That's fine, Danglard.'

Danglard stood there, speechless.

'I almost caught the man, yesterday, on the square,' Adamsberg said in a rather muted voice.

'The plague-monger?' queried Danglard in surprise.

'The monger himself. But he slipped away. Everything's slipping out of my hands, Danglard,' he added as he looked up at his deputy and met his eyes.

'Did you see something?'

'No. That's the point. I didn't see anything.'

'You didn't see anything? So how can you say you almost nabbed him, then?'

'Because I felt it.'

'Felt what?'

'I don't know, Danglard.'

Danglard gave up. It seemed wiser to leave Adamsberg on his own when he was wandering in such dark waters, walking out behind the tide with his feet squelching in the mud up to his ankles. With the shameful feeling of being a spy in his own squad Danglard slipped away to the courtyard entrance to ring Camille.

'Coast clear,' he whispered into his mobile. 'He's down here, he's got a pile of work as high as the Eiffel Tower.'

'Thanks, Adrien. Goodbye.'

'Goodbye, Camille.'

Danglard hung up in sadness, went back to his desk, mechanically switched on the computer which gave its usual welcome jingle, too jolly by half for the officer's glum thoughts. Computers are bloody stupid, they can't adapt to circumstances. Ninety minutes later he saw Adamsberg passing by, walking quite briskly. Danglard rang Camille's number again to warn her of a probable home call. But she had already set sail.

Adamsberg encountered a closed door once again but this time he didn't hesitate. He got out his pass key and undid the lock. A single glance was enough to tell him that Camille had flown the nest. The keyboard was gone, so was the plumbing kit and the backpack. The bed was made, the fridge was empty and the power switched off at the mains. Adamsberg sat down on a chair to survey the abandoned nest and to try to think. He surveyed plenty but no thought came. He was torn from his torpor forty-five minutes later by the beeping of his mobile phone.

'Masséna just called,' Danglard told him. 'They've got a body in Marseille.'

'That's fine,' Adamsberg opined, just as he had earlier on. 'I'll be going down. Get me a seat on the first plane.'

Around two, when Adamsberg was about to leave the Brigade in turmoil, he put his bag down next to Danglard's desk.

'I'm off,' he said.

'Yes,' said Danglard.

'I'm leaving you in charge.'

'Yes.'

Adamsberg was looking for his words and his eyes lighted on Danglard's feet, half-hiding a round wicker basket with a tiny but similarly circular kitten sleeping in it.

'What's that, Danglard?'

'It's a cat.'

'You're bringing moggies into the office, are you?

Don't you think we've got enough mess on our hands already?'

'I can't leave it at home. It's too little, it pees everywhere and doesn't yet quite know how to feed itself.'

'Danglard, you told me you did not want a pet.'

'Well, there's what you say, and there's what you do.'

Danglard was curt, somewhat hostile, and keeping his eyes on his monitor. Adamsberg recognised it for what it was, the unspoken disapproval he had to put up with from his deputy now and again. He looked down at the basket and the picture came back to him in clear focus. Camille leaving, seen from behind, with a bomber jacket over one arm and a white and grey kitten in the other. He hadn't given it a thought as he chased after her.

'She gave it to you, didn't she, Danglard?'

'Yes,' came the reply from a face still glued to the computer screen.

'What's its name?'

'Woolly.'

Adamsberg drew up a chair and sat down with his elbows on his knees.

'She's gone walkabout,' he said.

'Yes,' Danglard said again. This time he turned round and stared at Adamsberg's weary, washed out face.

'Did she tell you where she was going?'

'No.'

There was a brief silence.

'There was a minor collision,' Adamsberg said.
'I know.'

Adamsberg ran both his hands through his hair, slowly, over and over again, as if he was trying to push his skull back into place. Then he got up and left the building without another word.

CHAPTER 30

Masséna met his opposite number at Marignane Airport and took him straight to the morgue where the body was being kept. Adamsberg wanted to have a look, as Masséna couldn't tell whether this was the serial killer or a copycat case.

'He was found naked in his flat,' Masséna explained. 'The locks had been picked by a professional. Very neat work. Despite two hefty brand new bolts.'

'Child's play,' said Adamsberg. 'Was there a police guard on the landing?'

'I've got four thousand blocks to look after, *commissaire*!'

'Yes. A stroke of genius. It took him just a few days to demolish police protection. ID of the victim?'

'Sylvain Jules Marmot, age thirty-three. Works as a fitter down at the repair yards.'

'Ship repair?' Adamsberg queried. 'Any connection with Brittany?'

'How did you know?'

'I don't know. I'm wondering.'

'When he was seventeen he had a job at

Concarneau. That's where he trained as a fitter. But he dropped it all of a sudden and headed for Paris, where he survived as a jobbing carpenter.'

'Was he living on his own down here?'

'Yes. His girlfriend is a married woman.'

'That's why the plague-monger killed him at his own flat. He does his research properly. He leaves nothing to chance, Masséna.'

'That's as may be, but there's not a single common factor linking Marmot and your four victims, *commissaire*. Apart from his life in Paris between the ages of twenty and twenty-seven. Don't worry about the interviews, *commissaire*, I've sent the whole file up to your squad.'

'That's where it happened. In Paris.'

'Where what happened?'

'The crossover. The five of them must have come across each other, got to know each other, one way or another.'

'No, *commissaire*, I think the monger is taking us for a ride. He's trying to make us believe that there's a meaning to all these murders, to put us off the scent. It wasn't difficult to find out that Marmot lived on his own. All his neighbours know. Down here, people gossip all the time, there's not much you can keep hidden.'

'Did he get the usual dose of tear gas?'

'A fair old squirt in the eyes. We'll test a sample against the Paris stuff, just to see if he brought it with or bought fresh in Marseille. That might give us a start.'

'Don't kid yourself, Masséna. Our man is a genius, that's for sure. He worked it all out in advance – every hinge and joint, all the cogs and wheels, like an engineer. And he knows exactly what the machine is supposed to do. I wouldn't be surprised if the fellow turned out to be a scientist.'

'A scientist? I thought you'd said he was a man of letters.'

'He could be both.'

'A scientist and a crackpot?'

'He's been living with a phantom since 1920.'

'Good Lord, *commissaire*, do you mean to say we're looking for an eighty-year old?'

Adamsberg smiled. Masséna was much more amiable in the flesh than on the phone. Maybe too amiable. He couldn't speak without waving his arms around, taking Adamsberg by the wrist, clapping him on the shoulder, slapping him on the back, or, in the car, pawing his leg.

'I'd see him more as a man in his twenties or thirties.'

'That's not an age range, friend! That's the whole damn field!'

'But you can't rule out an octogenarian, either. The murder method requires minimal strength. It's choke and go. He uses some kind of self-locking noose – could be a jumbo clip, or a nylon tie, the sort you use for keeping big bunches of electrical cables together. Something you can't beat, something a child could handle.'

Masséna found a shaded parking slot some way

from the entrance to the morgue. It was still high summer in Marseille and people were going around in shirtsleeves or keeping cool in the shade, sitting on their stoops, peeling vegetables in their lap. Whereas in Paris Bertin must be wondering how to cope with the showers without his green oilskin.

The sheet was drawn back from the corpse and Adamsberg inspected it with care. The charcoal smudges were much the same in extent and location as on the Paris bodies – over most of the abdomen, and also on the arms, the upper legs and the tongue. Adamsberg rubbed a finger on a smudge and then on his trouser leg.

'We've sent it off to the lab,' Masséna said.

'Any bites?'

'Two, here,' said Masséna as he pointed to the groin.

'At the flat?'

'We picked up seven fleas, the way you told us, *commissaire*. That's a neat trick, the guinea pig. The insects have also gone to the lab.'

'Ivory envelope?'

'Yes, in the bin. I don't understand why the man didn't report it.'

'He was frightened, Masséna.'

'Quite.'

'Frightened of the *flics*. More frightened of *flics* than of the killer. He thought he could fight it on his own, that's why he had two extra bolts put on his door. What about his clothes?'

340

'Higgledy-piggledy, all over the bedroom. Marmot was a messy bugger. When you live alone, who cares anyway?'

'That's odd. The monger is a tidy undresser.'

'But he didn't have to undress him, my friend! Marmot was asleep in bed in the altogether. Most people do, down here. Because of the climate.'

'Can I see the flat?'

Adamsberg stepped through the archway of a dilapidated and undistinguished red-washed block not far from the Vieux-Port.

'He didn't have to bother about doorcodes, I see.'

'Must have been out of order for quite a while,' said Masséna.

Masséna had brought along a high-voltage portable searchlamp because the time switch on the stairwell lights had stopped working too. In the torch beam, Adamsberg looked carefully at the flat doors on each landing.

'Well?' asked Masséna as they got to the top floor.

'Well, you've had a visit. From the monger. Not a shadow of doubt about it. The form of the strokes, the speed of execution, the command of the shape, the placing of the notches on the crossbar – it's him all over. You could even say he took his time over this one. Not much risk of being caught at it in a block like this, is there?'

'Well, seeing the state the block is in,' Masséna

explained, 'if you came across a fellow painting a door, you wouldn't give a damn, you might even think it was a step in the right direction. Anyway, with hundreds of other people painting the same sign at the same time, what risk was he running? Zero. Shall we go for a walk, my friend?'

Adamsberg looked at him in amazement. He'd never come across another policeman who liked going for walks the way he did.

'I've got a wee dinghy moored in a *calanque*. Let's head out to sea for a bit. Helps to think, doesn't it? It's one of my habits.'

Half an hour later Adamsberg was on board the *Edmond Dantès,* a motor launch with an even keel. He'd taken his shirt and vest off and was sitting aforeships with his eyes closed in the mild breeze. Masséna had also stripped to the waist and was manning the rudder at the aft. Neither man was wracking his brain for ideas.

'Are you going back tonight?'

'Tomorrow, early,' said Adamsberg. 'I want to nose around the harbour.'

'Oh yes. You can pick up ideas in the Vieux-Port too.'

Adamsberg had switched off his mobile phone during the boat ride so when he got back to land he checked his voicemail. Chief Superintendent Brézillon, deeply worried about the tornado of 4s in Paris, to rap his knuckles; Danglard, to give him the latest tally; Decambrais, to dictate the latest 'special', just in on Monday morning:

> It elected to reside in the first days in the damp, low-lying and filthy quarters. At first it made slow progress. It even seemed to disappear. But not many a month had passed before it took courage and set forth, slowly at first, through busy and comfortable streets until it shewed itself brazenly in every quarter, spreading its mortal poison. It is everywhere.

Adamsberg wrote the message down in his pad then reread it slowly to Marc Vandoosler's voice-mail machine. He fiddled with his mobile, irrationally trying to find another message that might have got lost in the pile but there was nothing to find. Camille, please.

Adamsberg had a real beanfeast with Masséna that evening, and they parted with hearty hugs and promises of renewing the pleasure. He then sauntered along the southern side of the Vieux-Port, beneath the floodlit tower of Notre-Dame-de-la-Garde. He studied the shadows of each boat in turn, noting that their precise outlines, down to the detail of the toprigging, were reflected in black on the water. He knelt down and dropped a pebble in the harbour. It made the reflection shimmer and shake like a man in fever. Tiny slivers of moonlight caught the edges of each ripple. Adamsberg froze with the flat of his hand on the ground. The monger was nigh. He was there.

He raised his head and turned it cautiously to take a good look at the night-time strollers who were making the most of the last heat of the day. Couples and a few knots of youngsters. No solitary male. Adamsberg, still on his knees, scanned the quay yard by yard. No, he wasn't on the dockside. He was near but not there. With barely a muscle moving Adamsberg threw another equally tiny pebble into the still, dark water. The shadow shimmered, and once again a moonbeam put a twinkle into the wavelet's leading edge. That's where he was. On water. On shining water. In the twinkling that came and went. Adamsberg steadied himself in his squatting position, with both his hands on the ground and his eyes firmly fixed on the water line of the white-hulled boat. The monger was in the twinkling light. Adamsberg hung on, stock still. Like a lichen breaking free from a submarine cliff, the picture that he'd lost the day before on the square in Paris began its gradual ascent towards the surface. Adamsberg was barely breathing. His eyes were closed. It was in the sparkle. The picture *was* the sparkle.

Then it popped right up, whole and entire. The flash he'd felt right at the end of Joss's newscast. Someone had budged, and something had twinkled. A short, sharp sparkle. Not a photo flash, no, definitely not; nor would it have been a lighter. It was a much tinier, whiter sparkle, like the twinkling of the ripples in moonlight, only even more fleeting. It had moved in a sweeping, downward direction, as if a hand had held a shooting star.

Adamsberg stood up and took a deep breath. He'd got it. Someone attending the newscast had been wearing a real sparkler. It was the monger's twinkle and it came from his talismanic ring. He'd been there, on the square, protected by his diamond ring.

Next morning in the departure lounge at Marignane airport, he got Vandoosler's reply.

'I spent all night trying to find your bloody gobbet,' Marc said. 'The text you gave me was in modernised French – it was rewritten in the nineteenth century.'

'So?' asked Adamsberg, who had not lost any of his trust in Vandoosler's repository of knowledge.

'Troyes. Written in 1517, originally.'

'*Trois?*'

'No, not three, *commissaire*. The city of Troyes. Your monger is taking you on a tour.'

Adamsberg rang Masséna straight away.

'Good news, Masséna, you can relax. The monger's dropped you.'

'What's going on, my friend?'

'He's off to Troyes, you know, where the bubbly comes from.'

'Poor guy.'

'The monger?'

'No, you.'

'I've got to go, Masséna, that's my flight they're calling.'

'We'll meet again, my friend, we'll meet again.'

Adamsberg rang Danglard just before he got on the plane and passed on the news. He should get in touch straight away with the town that was now under threat.

'Is he going to have us traipse round the whole country?'

'Danglard, the plague-monger wears a diamond ring.'

'Is it a woman, then?'

'Could be. Perhaps. I don't know.'

Adamsberg switched off his mobile phone for the flight. As soon as he was in the arrivals hall at Orly airport he reconnected and scoured his voicemail. No new messages. He stuck the phone back in his pocket and stiffened his upper lip.

CHAPTER 31

While the city of Troyes geared up to face the onslaught, Adamsberg lost no time in getting back to the Brigade and then directly on to Place Edgar-Quinet. Decambrais bore down upon him with a large envelope in his hand.

'Did your consultant unravel yesterday's "special"?' he asked.

'Troyes, epidemic of 1517.'

Decambrais stroked his cheek, as if he was checking up on his shave.

'The monger has discovered the joy of travel,' he said. 'If he goes round all the places which ever had an outbreak of plague, then he'll be at it for the next thirty years! All over Europe, too. There's barely more than a couple of Hungarian villages and a part of Flanders that he won't have to visit. He's really screwing things up.'

'He's making them simpler. He's going after his targets.'

Decambrais gave the *commissaire principal* a quizzical look.

'I don't think he's travelling around for the fun

of it,' Adamsberg explained. 'His targets have moved. So he's going after them.'

'His targets?'

Adamsberg pursued his train of though without answering Decambrais's question directly.

'If they've moved off in different directions, that means the business happened some time back. There was a gang, or a group, and a crime. The monger is picking them off one by one by bringing the scourge of the Lord down upon them. I'm sure the killings aren't random. He knows what he's aiming at and he's had his victims marked out for years. They've probably understood that they're not far down the line. They probably know who the monger is.'

'No, they can't know that, *commissaire*. Otherwise they'd ask for police protection.'

'No, Decambrais. Because of the crime. It would be like confessing. The guy in Marseille had understood, because he'd put two extra bolts on his door.'

'But what crime, for heaven's sake?'

'How the hell should I know? There was some awful mess. This is the comeback. You make a mess, you get fleas.'

'But if that's the answer, then your data base would have come up with it ages ago.'

'There are two of them. All the victims, male and female, are of the same generation, and lived in Paris. That's why I say it was a gang or a group.'

He put out his hand and Decambrais gave him

the big ivory envelope. Adamsberg pulled out that morning's missive:

> This epidemic stopped abruptly in August 1630 and every [. . .] was overjoyed; unfortunately the interruption was but short-lived. It was the sinister foreboding of a resurgence so horrible that from October 1631 to around the end of 1632 [. . .]

'Where are we up to on the sign-painting?' Decambrais asked as Adamsberg punched out Vandoosler's number. 'The papers say eighteen thousand buildings in Paris, four thousand in Marseille.'

'That was yesterday. Today it's twenty-two thousand, conservatively speaking.'

'How dreadful.'

'Vandoosler? Adamsberg here. Can I read you this morning's missive? Are you ready?'

Decambrais's face expressed a degree of superciliousness and mild jealousy as he watched the *commissaire principal* read the 'special' into his mobile phone.

'He'll do some research and call back,' Adamsberg said as he snapped the phone shut.

'Your consultant, he's very good, isn't he?'

'Very,' Adamsberg confirmed with a smile.

'If he can find the town on the basis of that snippet alone, hats off, I say. That would be more than good, that would be second sight. Or a give-away.

All you'd need to do would be to set your police dogs on him.'

'We did that ages ago, Decambrais. The fellow is completely out of the picture. First, he had a snow-white laundry alibi for the time of the first murder. Second, I've had him tailed every night ever since. He sleeps at home and goes out in the morning to do the cleaning.'

'The cleaning?' Decambrais queried.

'He's a cleaning lady, sorry, cleaning man.'

'And an expert on the plague?'

'You're a lace-maker, aren't you?'

Decambrais paused awkwardly.

'He won't find it.'

'He will.'

The old man slicked back his white hair, adjusted his navy-blue tie, and retreated to his ill-lit cubbyhole study, where he knew no rival.

Bertin's thunder-roll swept across the square. People made their way though the drizzle to the Viking, skirting pigeons taking off in the opposite direction.

'Please forgive me, Bertin,' Adamsberg said. 'I took your oilskin all the way to Marseille.'

'Your jacket is dry. Madame Bertin gave it a press.'

Bertin hauled out from under the counter a neat, square paper parcel and put it in the *commissaire*'s hands. The denim jacket had never looked so smart since the day it had been bought.

'Hey, Mr Barman, are you sucking up to *flics*

these days? He takes a bloody liberty and you just roll over and ask for more!'

The mighty restaurateur turned towards the speaker, a man with an evil grin on his face who was stuffing his paper napkin between his collar and his ox-like neck prior to eating.

The scion of Thor came out from behind the counter, made a straight line towards the man's table, casting chairs right and left as he went, until he got right up to him, seized him by the shirt front, and pushed him back hard. The man started objecting in the language of screams, so Bertin gave him two good slaps in the face, lifted him up and ejected him bodily into the street.

'Don't bother to come back, there's no room at the Viking for shit-piles like you!'

'You've no right, Bertin!' The man was making great efforts to get himself off the ground. 'You're a public house! You've no right to filter your customers!'

'I choose my *flics* and I choose my men,' Bertin said as he slammed the door shut. Then he brushed his fair hair back into place with his hand, and with determination and dignity resumed his duty station behind the bar.

Adamsberg was about to slip under the longboat on the right.

'Are you lunching here?' asked Bertin.

'I'm having lunch and settling in until the newscast.'

Bertin nodded agreement. He didn't like *flics*

more than anyone else did, but that table had been allocated to Adamsberg in perp.

'I can't see what you're going to find on that square,' the barman said as he sponged the table clean. 'It wouldn't be half dreary without Joss.'

'Precisely,' said Adamsberg. 'I'm waiting for the town crier.'

'Fine. That gives you five hours to kill, but I guess every man has his method.'

Adamsberg laid his mobile beside his plate and looked at it dreamily. Camille, for heaven's sake, ring. He picked it up, turned it round, put it back. Then he flicked it at one end and the phone spun round like a roulette wheel. Will she, won't she, who cares anyway. But ring me. Who gives a damn.

Marc Vandoosler called in mid-afternoon.

'Not exactly a piece of cake,' he said, sounding like a man who'd spent all day looking for a needle in a haystack.

Adamsberg didn't doubt that he'd found it and waited to hear the answer.

'Châtellerault,' Vandoosler continued. 'A text written long after the facts.'

Adamsberg relayed the news to Danglard.

'Châtellerault,' Danglard logged. 'Superintendents Levelet and Bourrelot. I'll alert them.'

'Any 4s in Troyes?'

'Not yet. The newspapers can't crack this one the way they could with the Marseille message. I must leave you, sir. Woolly is doing dreadful things in wet plaster.'

Adamsberg hung up and only realised after a minute's reflection that his deputy had been talking about a cat. For the fifth time that day he looked his mobile phone straight in the eye and spoke to it man to man.

'Ring,' he pleaded softly. 'Get a move on. It was a bump, there'll be other bumps. It was none of your business, and what difference does it make to you anyway. They're my bumps, they're my affairs. Leave them to me. Ring.'

'Does that gizmo do voice recognition as well?' Bertin asked as he served the main course. 'Does it ring back on its own?'

'No,' said Adamsberg, 'it doesn't.'

'They don't always do what they're supposed to, do they?'

'No.'

Adamsberg spent the afternoon at the Viking, his vigil disturbed only by Castillon and then Marie-Belle, who distracted him with thirty minutes' chatter that went round full circle. He stationed himself for the newscast five minutes ahead of time just as Decambrais, Lizbeth, Damascus, Bertin and Castillon got into position, as well as melancholy Eva, half hiding behind one of those cylindrical bill-boards known as *colonnes Morris*. The audience was as large as ever and packed up close to Joss's soapbox.

Adamsberg abandoned his plane tree so as to get as close as possible to the crier. He trained his eyes on one then the next of the regulars, going over their hands one by one, alert for the slightest movement that might reveal the faintest glint. Joss got through eighteen small ads without Adamsberg seeing anything at all. During the shipping forecast, someone wiped a brow, and Adamsberg spotted it in a flash. The sparkle.

He was astounded and retreated to his plane tree. He propped himself against it and stood there for a long moment, unsure of himself, in doubt.

Then he slowly extricated the mobile phone from his freshly pressed jacket pocket.

'Danglard,' he mumbled, 'get yourself down here PDQ with two men. At the double, *commissaire*. I've got the monger.'

'Who is it?' Danglard was already on his feet and beckoning Noël and Voisenet to come with him.

'Damascus.'

A few minutes later the squad car screeched to a halt at Place Edgar-Quinet, three men tumbled out and went straight over to Adamsberg, who was waiting for them by the plane tree. It caused quite a stir among the idlers still standing round and chatting, especially because the largest of the three *flics* was holding a white and grey kitten in his hand.

'He's still here,' Adamsberg said in a loud whisper. 'He's doing the till with Marie-Belle and Eva. Don't touch the women, just get the bloke.

Watch out, he could be dangerous, he's a great hulk of a man, so check your weapons are working. If it gets rough, please, no damage. Noël, you're coming with me. There's a second door on the side street, the one the crier uses. Danglard, Justin, take that position.'

'Voisenet,' Voisenet corrected.

'Guard that exit,' Adamsberg repeated as he pulled himself upright from his leaning post.

'Wagons roll.'

When four *flics* brought Damascus out in hand-cuffs and bundled him straight into the squad car, the entire local community was struck dumb with disbelief. Eva ran to the car which zoomed off in front of her eyes as she stood there with her head in her hands. Marie-Belle collapsed in tears on Decambrais's shoulder.

'He's crazy,' Decambrais said as he hugged the girl. 'He's gone completely crazy.'

Even Bertin, who had followed the whole show through the window of the Viking, felt his veneration for *Commissaire Principal* Adamsberg coming under serious threat.

'Damascus,' he muttered. 'They're off their heads.'

Within five minutes the whole square had crammed into the Viking and begun a heated debate in an uproar not far short of a riot.

CHAPTER 32

Damascus for his part was as calm as could be, his face unclouded by the slightest sign of worry or doubt. He'd not resisted arrest, he'd not resisted the ride in the car to the station, he'd not said a word nor even altered the steady expression on his wide-open face. He was the quietest detainee Adamsberg had ever eyeballed in the interview room.

Danglard perched on the corner of the desk, Adamsberg crossed his arms and propped himself up against the wall, Noël and Voisenet stood to attention, guarding the exits. Favre was stationed at a corner desk ready to type up the statement. Damascus sat easily in a chair with his long hair thrown back over his shoulders and his handcuffed wrists in his lap, waiting for it all to begin.

Danglard slipped out to put Woolly back in his basket and to ask Mordent and Mercadet to fetch food and drinks for everyone, as well as a pint of milk, please, if they would be so kind.

'For the customer?' Mordent asked.

'For the kitten,' Danglard said under his breath. 'If you could fill his bowl, that would be very kind of you. I'm going to be busy all evening, maybe through the night.'

Mordent said he could be counted on for that, and Danglard went back to his desk-corner perch.

Adamsberg was taking off the handcuffs, a measure Danglard considered premature, seeing as there was still one unbarred window in the building and they had no clue how the man would behave. But despite that he wasn't really worried. What worried him much more was to have a man charged with being the plague-monger without the slightest evidence. Damascus's peaceable manner made it absolutely obvious it wasn't him, anyway. They were looking for a man of great learning and intellect. Damascus was a simple fellow, almost a simpleton. A guy like that whose main concern in life was keeping fit could not possibly have sent such complicated messages to the town crier. Danglard wondered if the chief had even thought about that before rushing in to make this implausible arrest. Full of foreboding, he sucked on his teeth. In his view Adamsberg was heading for a fall.

Adamsberg had already been on to the magistrate's office and had got a search warrant for Damascus's shop and for his dwelling, in Rue de la Convention. Six men had left fifteen minutes earlier to go over them with a toothcomb.

'Damascus Viguier,' Adamsberg began with the man's dog-eared ID card in front of him. 'You stand accused of the murder of five individuals.'

'Why, sir?'

'Because that is what you are accused of,' Adamsberg repeated.

'Oh, I see. You're saying that I killed people?'

'Five people,' said Adamsberg as he laid out photographs of the victims on the table for Damascus to see, and gave each one his and her proper name.

'I haven't killed anyone,' Damascus said with his eyes on the photos. 'Can I go now?' he added immediately, and stood up.

'No. You are helping us with our inquiries. You may make one phone call.'

Damascus gave Adamsberg a look of incredulous surprise.

'But I can use the phone whenever I want,' he said.

'These five people,' Adamsberg said as he pointed to the photos in turn, 'were all throttled to death within the last week. Four were killed in Paris, one in Marseille.'

'Fine,' Damascus said as he sat down again.

'Damascus Viguier, do you recognise them?'

'Sure I do.'

'Where did you last see them?'

'In the papers.'

Danglard got up and went out, leaving the door open so he could still hear how this very sticky interview was proceeding.

'Show me your hands, Damascus.' Adamsberg put the photos away. 'No, not like that. The other way up.'

Damascus did what was asked without demur and held out his long-fingered hands, palm uppermost. Adamsberg grabbed his left hand.

'Is that a diamond, Damascus?'

'Yes.'

'Why do you wear it on the palm side?'

'So as not to damage it when I'm repairing skateboards.'

'Is it worth a lot?'

'Sixty-two thousand francs.'

'Where did you get it? Or did you inherit it?'

'It was in lieu of cash for a bike I sold, an R1000 7, nearly new. The buyer paid me with the ring.'

'It's not very common for a man to wear a diamond ring.'

'I do. Since I've got it on.'

Danglard appeared in the doorway and beckoned Adamsberg to join him out of earshot of the others.

'The search team have just called in,' Danglard whispered. 'Clean as a whistle. No charcoal, no flea-breeding, no rats dead or alive, no books. At home or in the shop. Except for a couple of paperback novels.'

Adamsberg massaged the back of his neck.

'Drop him, sir,' Danglard said insistently. 'You're heading for a bad fall. This man is not the plaguemonger, sir.'

'Yes, he is, Danglard.'

'You can't build a case on a diamond ring, that's ridiculous.'

'Men do not wear diamonds, Danglard. But this guy wears one on his left ring finger and turns it in to hide it.'

'To protect it from scratching, sir.'

'That's rubbish, diamonds don't scratch. Diamonds are the prime protectors against plague. He's had it in the family since 1920. He's lying, Danglard. Don't forget he handles the town crier's urn three times a day.'

'The man hasn't read a book in his life, for heaven's sake!' Danglard was almost angry.

'How do you know?'

'Can you see that fellow doing Latin? You must be joking!'

'As I haven't come across people who do do Latin, Danglard, I don't labour under your preconceived notions.'

'What about Marseille? How did he get to Marseille? He's in Rolaride, morning, noon and night.'

'Not on Sundays, he isn't, and he doesn't reopen till two on a Monday afternoon. After the Sunday evening newscast he had plenty of time to catch the 8.20 p.m. train. And to be back in Paris by ten on Monday morning.'

Danglard shrugged his shoulders, almost beside himself, and went off to consult his computer. If Adamsberg wanted to take a fall, well, he could bloody well jump all on his own.

The *lieutenants* had brought in pizzas and Adamsberg had them served in their cardboard bases on the interview-room table. Damascus wolfed down his, looking pleased. Adamsberg waited for everyone to finish eating, stacked the empty boxes by the waste-paper bin, closed the door and resumed the interrogation.

Danglard knocked half an hour later. His anger seemed to have subsided to some degree. He told Adamsberg with his eyes he should come out and follow him.

'Damascus Viguier does not exist,' he whispered. 'No ID has ever been issued in that name. The papers he's using are fake.'

'So you see, *commissaire*. He is lying. Send his fingerprints off for matching, I'm sure he's been inside. We've been saying it again and again: the guy who opened Laurion's front door and the flat in Marseille is a professional.'

'The fingerprint data base is down. Didn't I tell you that bloody data base has been playing up all week?'

'So get down to Central Records at the double. Ring me from there.'

'Good Lord, everybody at Edgar-Quinet is using an alias.'

'Decambrais says that there are places like that. Where the wind listeth.'

'Is your name Viguier or is it not?' Adamsberg asked as he resumed his position propping up the wall.

'It's my trading name.'

361

'But it's on your ID card, young man. Forgery and dissimulation.'

'A friend made it for me. I prefer it that way.'

'Because?'

'Because I do not like my father's name. It speaks too loud.'

'Speak it, all the same.'

For the first time Damascus kept his mouth tight shut. Finally:

'I do not like the name. My name is Damascus.'

'OK, so we'll have to be patient. We'll wait until we find out your real name,' said Adamsberg.

The *commissaire principal* went out for a walk, leaving his officers to keep an eye on Damascus. It's often quite easy to spot when a fellow is lying and when he is telling the truth. Damascus was telling the truth when he said he hadn't killed anybody. Adamsberg could hear the ring of truth in his voice, he could read it on his lips, he could see it on the man's brow. But he was no less certain that he had the plague-monger. No suspect had ever cut him into two irreconcilable halves like that before. He called the men who were still searching the shop and the flat. Zilch. Adamsberg got back to the office an hour later, read through the fax that Danglard had sent in, and transcribed it on his notepad. It hardly surprised him to see that Damascus had dropped off sitting up and was sleeping the deep sleep of a man with a clear conscience.

'He's been asleep for three-quarters of an hour,' said Noël.

Adamsberg put a hand on his shoulder.

'Wake up, Arnaud Damascus Heller-Deville. I'm going to tell you your story.'

Damascus opened his eyes, then shut them again.

'I've heard it before.'

'Is your father Heller-Deville, the aircraft manufacturer?'

'He was. He smashed himself to pieces in his private plane two years ago, thank the Lord. May his soul not rest in peace.'

'Why not?'

'No reason,' said Damascus, his lips beginning to quiver. 'You've no right to interrogate me about it. Ask me about anything else. Anything at all.'

Adamsberg thought back to what Ferez had said and let the matter drop.

'You were sentenced to five years, you did your time at Fleury prison, and you came out two and half years ago,' Adamsberg said with his eye on his notes. 'For manslaughter. Your girlfriend went out an upstairs window.'

'She jumped out.'

'That's what you kept on saying like a speak-your-weight machine during the trial. Your neighbours told a different story. They'd heard you scrapping like cats for weeks. They'd been on the point of calling the police several times. What was the quarrel about, Damascus?'

'She was off her head. She shouted all the time. She jumped.'

'You're not in court, Damascus, and you can't ever be tried again. So you can change the tape.'

'No.'

'Did you shove her?'

'No.'

'Heller-Deville, did you or did you not kill four men and a woman last week? Did you strangle them?'

'No.'

'Are you good with locks?'

'I learned.'

'Had those four blokes and the girl done you any wrong? Did you do them in? Like you did for your girlfriend?'

'No.'

'What did your father do?'

'Make money.'

'What did your father do to your mother?'

Damascus clammed up again.

The telephone rang, the magistrate was on the line.

'Has he said anything?' the magistrate asked.

'No, he's shutting his mouth.'

'Any prospect of getting it to open?'

'Nope.'

'House search?'

'Nix.'

'Get a move on, Adamsberg.'

'No. I want to keep the man in custody, sir.'

'No way, *commissaire*. You have no grounds at all for a charge. Get him to talk or get him out.'

'Viguier is not his real name and he's carrying a fake ID. We're dealing with a Mr Arnaud Damascus Heller-Deville who got five years for manslaughter. Will that do by way of grounds for custody?'

'No, it weakens the case further. I remember the Heller-Deville business very well, Adamsberg. He went down because the jury was swayed by the neighbours' statements in the witness box. But the defence made just as good sense as the case for the prosecution. I won't have a man lumbered with plague-mongering just because he went down for five years.'

'The doors were picked by a professional.'

'Look, you've got any number of jailbirds knocking round your square, if I'm not very much mistaken. Ducouëdic and Le Guern have got just as much form as Heller-Deville. All his probation reports are first-rate.'

Justice Ardet was a decisive man as well as a sensitive and cautious magistrate but these uncommon virtues were not what Adamsberg needed this evening.

'If we release this suspect,' Adamsberg said, 'I will not answer for the consequences. He will either commit another murder, or give us the slip for good.'

'No custody order,' the magistrate hammered. 'Produce some evidence by seven thirty tomorrow evening, Adamsberg. And I said evidence, not guess-work. Hard evidence. Like a confession. Good night, *commissaire*.'

Adamsberg hung up and said nothing for a long while. Nobody dared interrupt the *commissaire*'s silence. He leaned on the wall, then paced around the room with his head down and arms folded. Danglard noticed the strange glow beginning to suffuse Adamsberg's cheeks and brow, the light of his concentrated thought. But however hard he concentrated he would never find the right angle to crack Arnaud Damascus Heller-Deville. Because Damascus may have murdered his girlfriend and he may be carrying fake ID, but Damascus was not the monger. He would eat his hat if that blank-eyed lad knew Latin. Adamsberg left the room to make a call and came back in.

'Damascus,' he began again as he sat on a chair and drew it closer to the suspect. 'Damascus, you've been spreading the plague. You've been slipping messages into Joss's urn for a month and more. You've been breeding rat fleas and releasing them underneath the front doors of your victims. These fleas are carriers of bubonic plague, they're infected, and they bite. The corpses have fatal flea-bites all over them, and they've turned black. They died of plague, the whole lot of them died of the plague.'

'Yes,' said Damascus. 'That was in the papers.'

'You're the one who's been painting black 4s on people's doors. You're the one who's been spreading the fleas. You're the murderer.'

'No.'

'There's one thing you've got to understand, Damascus. The fleas you lug around make no distinction between your body and any other. You've got them on you. You don't change your clothes very often and you're not very clean.'

'I washed my hair last week,' Damascus protested.

Once again Adamsberg felt unnerved by the candid look in the young man's eyes. It was the same innocent look that his sister Marie-Belle had. Almost simple-minded.

'These plague fleas are crawling all over you. But you're safe, aren't you, as you've got the diamond. So the fleas can't do you any harm. But what if you didn't have the ring, Damascus?'

Damascus clenched his hand to hide the stone.

'If you're not involved in all this, what difference would it make? Because in that case you wouldn't have any fleas. Do you get me?'

Adamsberg left a pause and kept his eyes trained on the twitches on the young man's face.

'Give me the ring, Damascus.'

Damascus did not move.

'Just for ten minutes, Damascus. I'll give it back, promise.'

Adamsberg stretched out his hand and waited.

'The ring, Damascus. Take it off.'

Damascus didn't budge and everyone else in the room stood stock still too. Danglard could see the young man's muscles tensing. Something was beginning to give.

'Give it here,' Adamsberg repeated, with his hand still out. 'What are you scared of?'

'I can't take it off. It's a solemn vow. The girl who jumped. It was her ring.'

'I'll give it back to you. Come on, take it off.'

'No,' said Damascus, and he sat on his left hand.

Adamsberg got up and walked around.

'You're scared, Damascus. You know that you'll be bitten as soon as the ring is off your finger, you know that this time they'll pass the disease on to you. And that you'll die like the others.'

'No. It was a vow.'

No goal, Danglard thought, with shoulders slumped. A good try, but no goal. The diamond story couldn't drive that far. A hopeless angle.

'OK, take your clothes off.'

'What?'

'Undress, down to the altogether. Danglard, get a bin bag.'

A man Adamsberg couldn't tell from Adam popped his head round the door.

'Martin,' he said by way of self-introduction. 'Entomology department. You called, sir.'

'I'll be with you in a minute, Martin. Damascus, take your clothes off.'

'In front of all these people?'

'What's the problem? Noël, Voisenet, Favre, leave the room please. Apparently he's shy.'

'Why should I strip?' Damascus asked angrily.

'I want your clothes and I want to see your body. So bloody well get undressed!'

Damascus scowled as he carried out the order reluctantly.

'Put it all in the bag,' said Adamsberg.

When Damascus had finished and was wearing nothing but his diamond ring, Adamsberg knotted the drawstring and took the bag out to Martin.

'Rush job. Test for those . . .'

'*Nosopsyllus fasciatus.*'

'Exactly.'

'For tonight?'

'Tonight, as soon as you can.'

Adamsberg went back into the interview room where Damascus was standing with his chin on his chest.

Adamsberg lifted one of his arms then the other.

'Stand with your feet eighteen inches apart.'

Adamsberg stretched the skin around the groin to the left then to the right.

'Sit down, that's over. I'll get you a towel.'

He went to get a green bath towel from the washroom and threw it to Damascus, who caught it in the air.

'Aren't you cold?'

Damascus shook his head.

'You've got bites, young man. Flea bites. Two in your right armpit, one in your groin on the left-hand side, and three on the right. Nothing to worry about, you've got your ring.'

Damascus carried on looking at his feet as he stood there wrapped in the towel.

'What have you got to say about that?'

'There are fleas in the shop.'

'Human fleas, you mean?'

'Yes. The back room isn't very clean.'

'They're rat fleas, and you know that full well. We'll wait a little while, an hour or so, and then we'll know. Martin will ring back. He's a tremendous expert. One look at a rat flea and he'll tell you its name and date of birth. You can get some sleep if you want. I'll get you some bedclothes.'

He took Damascus by the arm and led him to the cell. The young man remained calm, but he had lost his bewildered indifference. He'd become worried and tense.

'It's a brand new cell,' Adamsberg said as he handed him two blankets. 'And the bedclothes are clean.'

Damascus lay down without a word and Adamsberg shut the door on him. He wandered back to his office feeling uneasy. He'd got the monger, he'd been proved right, but it left him with a bad feeling. All the same, the man had slaughtered five people in seven days. Adamsberg forced himself to remember, to recall the victims' faces, and the woman stuffed under a truck.

Nobody said anything for the next hour as they waited, and Danglard didn't dare express a view. You couldn't rely on there being plague fleas on Damascus's clothes. Adamsberg doodled on a pad in his lap. His face was looking drawn. It was one thirty in the morning. Martin rang at ten past two.

'Two *Nosopsyllus fasciatus*,' he announced gravely. 'Both living specimens.'

'Thanks, Martin. Incredibly valuable items. Don't let the little lasses hop away, because they'd take the entire prosecution case with them.'

'Lads, sir,' the entomologist countered. 'They're males.'

'Sorry, Martin, I didn't mean to cause offence. Send the clothes back here, could you, so the suspect can get dressed again.'

Five minutes later Justice Anglet, who'd been woken up with the new information, gave his consent for the police to remand Damascus in custody.

'You were right, sir.' Danglard's eyes were bleary and he could hardly lift his sagging body from the chair. 'You were right,' he conceded, 'but only by a whisker.'

'Whiskers can be tougher than you think. You just have to pull on them gently and persistently.'

'May I point out, sir, that Damascus has not confessed.'

'But he will. He knows the game's up. He's not stupid.'

'I can't agree with that.'

'No he's not, Danglard. He's only pretending to be dim. But since he's very clever he's extremely good at it.'

'I'll eat my hat if that lad reads Latin,' Danglard said as he left the room.

'*Bon appétit*, my friend.'

Danglard switched off his computer, picked up

the basket and its sleeping woolly ball, put it under his arm, said goodbye to the night staff. In the hallway he came across Adamsberg hauling a camp bed and blanket out of the locker room.

'Hell,' he said, 'are you going to bed down here?'

'In case he sings.'

Danglard made no comment and went on his way. What comment could he make, anyway? He knew Adamsberg wasn't keen on going back to his flat where the wreck of his collision was still smouldering. He'd be over it by tomorrow. Adamsberg could bounce back with incredible speed.

Adamsberg set up the camp bed and folded the blanket to make a pillow. He had the monger a few feet away. The fourmonger, the scary letter-monger, the rat-flea-monger, the plague-monger, the monger who choked and charcoaled his victims. The charcoal was his final touch. And his only great *howler*.

He took off his jacket and his trousers and put his mobile phone on the chair. Ring, for heaven's sake.

CHAPTER 33

The main bell rang in the dark of night, repeatedly, insistently, urgently. *Brigadier* Estalère unbolted the side door and found before him a man in a great sweat wearing a hastily buttoned two-piece suit and a tieless shirt revealing a chestful of thick black hair.

'Let me in, quick,' the man said as he barged in to the shelter of the Brigade Criminelle. 'I want to make a statement. About the killer, the plague-man.'

Estalère didn't dare alert the *commissaire principal* so he woke up his deputy Danglard.

'Bloody hell, Estalère,' said Danglard into the phone by his bed. 'Why did you call me? Rouse Adamsberg, he's napping in his office.'

'That's just it, *commissaire*. I'm afraid of getting a row from the chief if it's not important.'

'And you're not so frightened of me, is that it?'

'Yes, sir.'

'You're wrong. You've been working for Adamsberg for six weeks now. In all that time, have you once heard him shout or scream?'

'No, sir.'

'Well, you can stay on for the next thirty years and you still won't hear him let rip. But you're about to get the wrong side of my tongue, young man. Fucking well wake the man up. Anyway, he doesn't need much sleep. And I do.'

'Got that, sir.'

'Wait a minute. What does the guy want?'

'He's in a blue funk, he thinks the killer is going to kill him.'

'We decided ages ago to stop looking after scaredy-cats. Ten a penny all over Paris. Chuck him out and leave Adamsberg alone.'

'He says he's a special case, sir.'

'Chickenhearts always think they're special cases. If they didn't they wouldn't panic.'

'No, sir, but he says he's just been bitten by fleas.'

'When?' Danglard sat up in bed.

'Just now.'

'OK, Estalère. Wake him up. I'll come over too.'

Adamsberg splashed cold water on his face and chest, told Estalère to get him a black coffee (the dispenser had at last been installed, less than twenty-four hours ago) and shoved the camp bed to the back of his office.

'Bring him in, *brigadier*.'

'*Brigadier* Estalère,' *brigadier* Estalère added.

Adamsberg nodded and took out his memory-jogger. With the monger locked up in a cell, he might have time to get to grips with his nameless horde of a squad. He entered: *baby face, green eyes,*

374

scaredy-cat adds up to *Estalère.* Which prompted him to add: *entomology* plus *fleas* plus *Adam's apple* equals *Martin.*

'What's his name?'

'Roubaud, forename Kevin,' the *brigadier* supplied.

'How old?'

'Around thirty,' Estalère guessed.

'Got a flea bite in the night, is that the story?'

'Yes, sir, and he's doing it in his pants.'

'As he should be.'

Estalère showed Kevin Roubaud to Adamsberg's office while balancing a cup of sugarless black coffee in his left hand. Adamsberg took no sugar. Unlike his chief, Estalère liked personal quirks, he liked remembering them, and he liked showing that he remembered them.

'I didn't put any sugar in, *commissaire*,' he said as he put the coffee on the desk and Roubaud into a chair.

'Thanks, Estalère.'

The customer sat there in a sweat and a fuss, running his fingers back and forth through the mat of hair on his chest. You could smell his sweat and his sweat smelled of booze.

'Never previously had fleas?' Adamsberg queried.

'Never.'

'Are you sure the bites are fresh tonight?'

'I was bitten less than two hours ago, it was the bite that woke me up. That's why I rushed round here to let you know.'

'Are there any 4s on the doors of your stair, Mr Roubaud?'

'Two of them. The janitor put one on her window, in felt pen, and so did the guy on the fifth floor left.'

'Then it isn't the killer. And these aren't his fleas. You can go back to bed.'

'Are you joking?' Roubaud raised his voice. 'I demand police protection.'

'The monger daubs every door on a stair save for one before he lets out his fleas,' Adamsberg said insistently and slowly. 'Your fleas are of a different kind. Did anyone come to stay in the past few days? Did anyone drop in with a pet?'

'Yes.' The man's face fell. 'A friend of mine came by the day before yesterday. With his dog.'

'So there you are. Go home, Mr Roubaud, and get back to sleep. We're all going to nap for the next hour or two, it'll do us all good.'

'No, I don't want to.'

'If you're that worried,' Adamsberg said as he stood up, 'call in pest control and be done with it.'

'That won't be any use. The killer has got his finger on me, and he's going to get me, fleas or no. I demand police protection.'

Adamsberg went round behind his desk, moved back to lean on his wall and took a better look at Kevin Roubaud. Thirty-ish, a bruiser and a worrier. There was something shifty about the look in his big, dark, slightly bulging eyes.

'All right,' said Adamsberg. 'Let's say he's fingered

you. There's not a single 4 worth the name on your staircase, but you know he's got you on his list.'

'It's the fleas,' Roubaud grunted. 'It was in the papers. All the targets had fleas.'

'And your friend's dog?'

'No, that's not what it was.'

'How come you're so sure?'

Adamsberg's tone of voice had softened and Roubaud noticed. He pulled himself together and sat up straighter.

'It was in the papers,' he repeated.

'No, Roubaud, that's not the reason. There's something else.'

Danglard had just come in, at five past six in the morning, and Adamsberg motioned him to join in. Danglard walked across the room without a word and sat down at the workstation.

'Fuck that,' said Roubaud with renewed self-confidence. 'I'm under threat, a nutter's trying to kill me, and it's me the police want to mess around with?'

'What's your line, Roubaud?'

'I sell flooring materials in a furniture store behind Gare de l'Est.'

'Married?'

'Divorced, two years ago.'

'Children?'

'Two.'

'Do they stay with you?'

'With their mother. I have access rights at the weekend.'

'Do you eat out? Or in the flat? Can you cook?'

'It varies,' Roubaud said, rather nonplussed. 'Sometimes I heat up a plate of soup and a frozen dinner. Sometimes I go down to the café. Proper restaurants are too expensive.'

'Do you like music?'

'Yes,' said Roubaud, now quite at sea.

'Have you got a hi-fi and a telly?'

'Yes.'

'Do you watch soccer?'

'Yes, obviously.'

'Do you follow it?'

'I'm quite keen, yes.'

'Did you watch the Nantes–Bordeaux?'

'Yes.'

'Pretty cool playing, wasn't it?' said Adamsberg, who'd not watched the match.

'Well, up to a point,' Roubaud said with a pained expression on his face. 'They took it easy and it ended in a nil-nil draw. You could see it coming in the first half.'

'Did you the watch the news bulletin at half-time?'

'Sure,' Roubaud answered without thinking.

'So,' Adamsberg said as he sat down opposite, 'you know we brought in the plague-monger last night.'

'So they said,' the man muttered uneasily.

'In that case, what's making you so scared?'

Roubaud bit his lip.

'What are you frightened of, Mr Roubaud?' Adamsberg repeated.

His voice was unsteady when he answered.

'I don't think you've got the right man.'

'Oh, really? We can spot killers, can we?'

Roubaud almost swallowed his lip and massaged his chest hair again.

'So you're giving me the second degree, when I'm the one at risk?' he repeated. 'I should have known. As soon as you go to the *flics* you get jumped on, that's the only thing they know how to do. I should have sorted it on my own. You try to help the law, and that's all the thanks you get.'

'But you are going to help us, Roubaud, you're going to help us a great deal.'

'Is that right, *commissaire*? You're kidding yourself right and proper.'

'Come off it, Roubaud. You know you're not smart enough to play the clever guy.'

'You think?'

'Yes, I do. But if you don't want to help us with our inquiries, then off you go, Roubaud. Back home, back to bed. And if you try to give us the slip, we'll give you an escort. All the way to the morgue.'

'Since when do *flics* tell me where I have to go?'

'Since you got up my nose. Off you go, Roubaud. You're a free man. Scram.'

He did not move.

'You're scared, aren't you? You're scared he'll get you in the neck with a nylon tie, like he got the others. You know there's no defence. You know he'll catch up with you, in Lyon, Nice, Berlin, wherever. You are the target. And *you know why*.'

379

Adamsberg opened his desk drawer and got out the photographs of the five victims to date.

'You know you'll be number six, don't you? You know all of them, that's why you're shitting yourself.'

'Fuck off,' said Roubaud, turning his head to the side.

'Then push off. Get the hell out.'

Two minutes passed in silence.

'All right,' said Roubaud.

'You know these people?'

'Yes and no.'

'Explain.'

'It's like, I met them all a long while back, one evening, it must have been seven or eight years ago. We had a drink.'

'I see. You all had a drink together, and that's why someone's knocking you off one by one.'

Roubaud was sweating heavily and the whole room reeked of his body odour.

'Do you want some coffee?' Adamsberg asked.

'Thanks.'

'Something to eat?'

'Thanks.'

'Danglard, tell Estalère to get some food and coffee.'

'And some fags,' Roubaud added.

'So tell me,' Adamsberg continued as Roubaud restored himself with sweet milky coffee. 'How many of you were there?'

'Seven,' Roubaud mumbled. 'We met in a bar, honest.'

Adamsberg glanced at the man's big black eyes and reckoned there was a sliver of truth in that 'honest'.

'What were you doing?'

'Nothing.'

'Roubaud, I've got the monger in a cell. If you like, I'll bung you in too, leave you there and close my eyes. End of story. In a half an hour from now you're a dead man.'

'It's like, we pushed a guy around.'

'What for?'

'It was a long time ago. We were being paid to make the guy sing, that's all. He'd nicked a heap of stuff and he was supposed to give it back. We pushed him around, that was the deal.'

'What deal?'

'Like, we had a contract. No big deal.'

'Where did you "push him around"?'

'In a gym. We'd been given the address, the guy's name and the bar where we were supposed to rendezvous. Because we'd never met.'

'None of you knew each other beforehand?'

'Nope. There was seven of us, and none of us knew any of the others. He'd got hold of us separately. Clever bugger.'

'Where did he get hold of you?'

Roubaud shrugged his shoulders.

'Places where you find blokes who'll do a bit of rough stuff for bread. No great shakes. He picked me up in a shithole in the red-light district. I got out of that kind of stuff years ago, honest. I mean that, *commissaire*.'

'Who picked you up?'

'I dunno, it was all done in writing. One of the girls passed on a letter. Classy paper, it was. I fell for it.'

'Who wrote the letter?'

'Honest, I never found out who was behind the deal. He was too smart for that, the bugger. In case we asked for more cash.'

'So the seven of you got together and went off to nab the guy.'

'Yep.'

'When?'

'It was 17 March, a Thursday.'

'So you took him down to the gym. Then?'

'I told you already, bloody hell,' said Roubaud, twisting around on his chair. 'We roughed him up.'

'Did it work? Did he split what he was supposed to split?'

'Yep. He made a phone call in the end. He spilled all the beans.'

'What was it about? Loot? Shit?'

'I wasn't in on that, guvnor. But it must have been what the big man wanted, because we never heard from him again.'

'Did it pay well?'

'Sure.'

'Roughed him up, did we? And the guy split nice

and easy? Or was it more like, you gave him the third degree?'

'No. We thumped him.'

'And am I supposed to believe that the guy you roughed up is making you all pay for it eight years down the road?'

'That's what I think.'

'For bumps and bruises? You're pulling the wool, Roubaud. Go home.'

'It's the truth,' Roubaud said, and gripped the side bars of his chair. 'Fucking hell, why should we have tortured them? They were chickens, they were shitting themselves as soon as they clapped eyes on us.'

'You said "they"?'

Roubaud bit his lower lip again.

'There was more than one, wasn't there? Get a move on, Roubaud, things are speeding up.'

'There was a girl as well,' Roubaud grunted. 'We had no choice. When we went to get the guy, he had his girl with him, and so what? We took the pair of them down to the gym.'

'Did the girl get pushed about as well?'

'A bit. It wasn't me, honest.'

'You're lying. Get out of this office, I don't want to set eyes on you again. Run away to what's at the end of your road, Kevin Roubaud, it's no skin off my nose.'

'It wasn't me,' Roubaud hissed, 'I swear. I'm not an animal. A bit of a rough customer when someone winds me up, but I'm not like the others.

I was just having a bit of a giggle, I was the back-up man.'

'I believe you,' said Adamsberg, who didn't believe a word of it. 'What made you giggle?'

'Well, what they were doing.'

'Spit it out, Roubaud, you've got five minutes, then I'm throwing you out of here.'

Roubaud took a deep, noisy breath.

'They stripped him,' he went on, speaking almost in a whisper. 'Then they poured kerosene on his . . .'

'Genitals?' Adamsberg prompted.

Roubaud nodded. Drips of sweat were forming on his brow and trickling down to his chest.

'They got their lighters, they went round and round, closer and closer to his . . . to his thing. The guy, he was screaming his head off, he was scared to death that his thing was going to go up in smoke.'

'So that's "pushing around",' Adamsberg muttered. 'And then?'

'Then they flung him on his front on the gym table and tacked him.'

'Tacked him?'

'Sure. It's what's called a poster job. They stuck drawing pins in him all over, then stuck a club up his, up his, his arse.'

'Tremendous,' Adamsberg said between clenched teeth. 'And the girl? Don't tell me you left her alone.'

'I didn't do it! I was just the back-up man. Only, I had a giggle.'

'Are you still giggling now?'

Roubaud lowered his head. He was still holding on tight to his chair.

'The girl,' Adamsberg repeated.

'Gang-raped, five guys, took it in turns. She started bleeding. When it was over she was out cold. I even thought we'd done something stupid and that she'd died. Actually, she'd gone off her rocker, she didn't know who anyone was any more.'

'Five guys? I thought there were seven of you.'

'I did not touch her.'

'And number six? He didn't either?'

'Number six was a girl. Her,' Roubaud said, pointing to the photograph of Marianne Bardou on the desk. 'She and one of the guys was an item. We didn't want any birds but she was hitched and so we let her come along.'

'And what did she do?'

'She was the one who poured the kerosene. She was having the time of her life.'

'Real good fun.'

'Yes,' said Roubaud.

'What next?'

'When the guy had made his phone call, all covered in sick, we threw them out stark naked with all their gear, and we all went off to get sloshed.'

'Nothing wrong with a pint after a hard day's night, right?' Adamsberg said.

'Honest, sir, it really pissed me off. I've kept well

away ever since, and I never clapped eyes on any of them ever again. I got the dough in the mail, as agreed, and that was the end of that.'

'Until this week.'

'Yep.'

'When you recognised the murder victims.'

'Only that one, and that one, and the woman,' said Roubaud, pointing to the photos of Viard, Clerc and Bardou. 'I only saw them that one time.'

'Did it click straight away?'

'Only when the woman got done in. I recognised her because she had loads of moles on her face. So then I looked at the other mugshots and the penny dropped.'

'That he's come back, you mean?'

'Yes.'

'Do you know why he waited so long?'

'No, no idea.'

'Because he did five years inside straight after. His girlfriend, the lass you drove out of her mind, threw herself out of an upstairs window four weeks later. Put that in your pipe and smoke it, Roubaud. That's if you haven't choked yourself to death on your own crap already.'

Adamsberg got up and opened the windows to get some fresh air in his lungs and to get rid of the smell of sweat and horror. He leaned for a while on the railing, looking down on people walking in the street, people who hadn't heard the story he'd been listening to. Seven fifteen. The monger was still asleep.

'Since he's in custody, what are you afraid of?'

'Because he's not the one,' Roubaud hissed. 'You're barking up the wrong tree. The beanstalk we roughed up was a real pushover. A doormat, if you know what I mean. A patsy and a nerd who couldn't swat a fly to save his life. But the bloke you put on telly is a big brawny fellow. No relation, believe you me.'

'Are you sure?'

'Sure I'm sure. Our guy had a face like a bird, I can see it clearly. He's still out there, and he's waiting for me. I've told you everything now, so I want protection. Honest, I didn't do anything, I was just the . . .'

'Back-up man, sure. We know that already. Don't you think that five years inside might change a man, though? Especially if he's got one thing on his mind, and one thing only: to get his own back. Don't you think you can build your own body? Not the same as the brain, is it? You've stayed as thick as you ever were. But maybe he worked on himself and ended up with those biceps.'

'Why should he do that?'

'To wipe the slate clean, to survive without shame, and to get you for good.'

Adamsberg went over to the cupboard, took out a plastic bag, withdrew an ivory envelope from it and waved it in front of Roubaud's nose.

'Seen that before?'

Roubaud furrowed his brow.

'Yes. There was one lying on the ground when

I left the flat to come here. There wasn't anything in it, it was empty, it had already been opened.'

'That's him then, that's the monger. It's the envelope he used to get his fleas on to you.'

Roubaud hugged himself.

'Are you frightened of the plague?'

'Not really,' Roubaud answered. 'I don't swallow it. I think it's nonsense, it's eyewash, it's meant to lead us up the garden path. I think he's a choker.'

'And you're right to think that. Are you sure the envelope was not lying there yesterday?'

'Sure I'm sure.'

Adamsberg stroked his cheek pensively.

'Come and look at him,' he said as he stepped towards the door.

Roubaud hesitated.

'Not such a giggle now, is it? Those were the days! Come on, he's not dangerous, the animal's in a cage.'

Adamsberg dragged Roubaud to Damascus's cell. He was still sleeping soundly, his head resting easily on the blanket.

'Now look at him properly', Adamsberg said. 'Take your time. Don't forget you last saw him eight years ago, and he wasn't in very good shape at the time.'

Roubaud stared through the bars, in a state close to fascination.

'And so?'

'Could be,' Roubaud said. 'The mouth, could be. But I'd need to see his eyes.'

When Adamsberg unlocked the cell door Roubaud's eyes filled with alarm.

'You prefer the door closed? Or do you want me to lock you two in together so you can have a good giggle for old times' sake?'

'Cut the crap,' Roubaud said darkly. 'He could be dangerous.'

'And you're not? In your time you were bloody dangerous too.'

Adamsberg shut himself in the cell with Damascus and Roubaud looked on as if watching a lion-tamer stepping into the ring. The *commissaire* shook Damascus by the shoulder.

'Wake up, Damascus, you've got visitors.'

Damascus sat up with a groan and looked in bewilderment at the walls of his cell. Then it came back to him, and he threw his hair back over his shoulders.

'What's up?' he asked. 'Can I go?'

'Stand up. There's a fellow wants to get a good look at you. An old acquaintance of yours.'

Obedient as ever, Damascus did as asked and stood up with his blanket wrapped around him. Adamsberg watched each man in turn. Damascus seemed to narrow his face, slightly. Roubaud gave a wide-eyed stare, then moved away.

'So?' Adamsberg enquired once they were back in his office. 'Can you see it now?'

'Could be,' said Roubaud, far from confidently. 'But if it is him, he's doubled his weight.'

'Face?'

'Could be. He didn't have long hair.'

'You're covering yourself, aren't you? Because you're scared.'

Roubaud nodded.

'You could be right, of course,' Adamsberg put in. 'The avenger is probably not a lone wolf. I'll keep you here until we can see our way through a bit better.'

'Thanks,' said Roubaud.

'Tell me who the next target is.'

'Me, sod it.'

'I know that. But the one after? There were seven, minus five who are dead already makes two, minus you leaves one. Who's left?'

'He had an ugly mug and was as thin as a rake. I reckon he was the nastiest one in the bunch. The one who did the thing with the club.'

'Name?'

'We didn't give our names or our first names. On a job like that nobody takes risks.'

'Age?'

'Same as everyone else. Twenty-something.'

'Parisian?'

'I suppose so.'

Adamsberg put Roubaud in a cell but did not lock it. Then he put his head through the bars of Damascus's cell and gave him back his clothes.

'The magistrate's given clearance for us to put you on remand.'

'All right,' the placid young man replied from the bench seat.

'Can you read Latin, Damascus?'

'No.'

'Isn't there anything you want to tell me? About the fleas, for example?'

'No.'

'Or about six guys who gave you third degree one Thursday, on a seventeenth of March? Nothing to tell me? Or about a girl who had a real giggle?'

Damascus remained silent, wringing his hands in his lap, with his right thumb touching the diamond ring.

'What did they rob you of, Damascus? Apart from your girl, your body and your honour? What were they after?'

Damascus didn't move an inch.

'All right. I'll send you some breakfast. Get dressed.'

Adamsberg drew Danglard to one side.

'That shitbag Roubaud won't give a positive ID,' Danglard said. 'Leaves you up the creek.'

'Danglard, Damascus has an accomplice who's still out there. The fleas were put under Roubaud's door when Damascus was already here. Someone took over the message system, too, as soon as he was arrested. And he did it on the trot, without bothering to paint 4s for protection.'

'An accomplice would account for why he's so

cool and collected. He's got someone to carry on the job, and he's relying on him.'

'Send some of our men down to interview his sister, and Eva, and all the regulars in the square, to find out who his friends are. I especially want a list of all the phone calls he's made for the last two months. From the shop and from the flat.'

'Aren't you coming with?'

'My *persona*'s not very *grata* down there right now. I'm Judas. They'll open up more if they're talking to officers they've not met before.'

'Got that,' said Danglard. 'We could have taken years to find the link. Guys who didn't even know each other joining up in a dive one dark night. We're dead lucky Roubaud took fright.'

'He had good reason, Danglard.'

Adamsberg got out his mobile phone and looked it straight in the eye. He pleaded with it silently for so long – to ring, to jump, to do anything at all – that he ended up mistaking the phone for a vision of Camille herself. So he talked to it and told it his life's story, as if Camille could hear him, no trouble. But as Bertin had so rightly remarked, those gizmos don't always do all they're supposed to. Camille failed to arise from the keypad like a genie from a bottle. Who cares anyway. He put the phone on the floor, very gently so as not to bruise it, and lay down to sleep for an hour and a half.

Danglard woke him with the record of all

Damascus's telephone activity. The interviews at Place Edgar-Quinet hadn't produced much by way of results. Eva clammed up totally, Marie-Belle sobbed as soon as anyone said anything, Decambrais was in a mood, Lizbeth let rip, and Bertin, as if reverting to the ancient tongue of the Northmen, would utter only monosyllables. The sum total was: Damascus virtually never left the square, he spent every evening at the Saint-Ambroise listening to Lizbeth and talking to nobody, he had no known friends and he spent Sundays with his sister.

Adamsberg went through the call list looking for repeat numbers. If there was an accomplice, Damascus had to be in touch with him or her: the synchronisation of the 4s, the fleas and the murders was too complex and too tight to brook any other explanation. But Damascus used the telephone remarkably rarely. There were calls from the flat to the shop, that was probably Marie-Belle calling Damascus. The shop phone was hardly used, and there were only a handful of repeat numbers. Adamsberg checked up on the four numbers that appeared more than once on the list – all of them to bona fide suppliers of skateboards, bearings and helmets. He pushed the sheets to one side of his desktop.

Damascus wasn't stupid. Damascus was a genius who'd learned how to look blank. Something else he'd picked up in prison, and gone on practising after. He'd been planning this for seven years. So if he had an accomplice he wasn't going to risk giving the game away by calling him up from his own phone. Adamsberg got on to the phone company's fourteenth arrondisssement branch to request a listing of calls made from the public telephone in Rue de la Gaîté. Twenty minutes later the info arrived in the form of a fax. Mobile phones had made a huge dent in the use of public telephones, so the list he had to go through wasn't enormously long. He found only eleven repeat numbers.

'I'll unscramble them for you if you like,' Danglard offered.

'That one first,' said Adamsberg, pointing to a number. 'That one, it's an out-of-town number, somewhere in the north-east suburbs, department of Hauts-de-Seine.'

'Any reason?' Danglard asked as he went off to his computer to look it up in the reverse directory.

'Northern edge of the city, that's our baby. Any luck and it'll land us in Clichy.'

'Wouldn't it be wiser to eliminate the others?'

'They're not going to fly away.'

Danglard hit a few keys and waited in silence.

'It's Clichy,' he reported.

'Bull's-eye. Heart of the 1920 outbreak. It's in his family, it's his phantom. That's where he used to live, I'll bet you. Come on, man, give me the name and address.'

'Clémentine Courbet, 22, rue Hauptoul.'

'Look her up.'

As Danglard got himself into the central ID data

base Adamsberg strode up and down, trying not to step on the kitten, who was playing with a loose thread trailing from his trouser ankle.

'Clémentine Courbet, maiden name Journot, born Clichy, married Jean Courbet.'

'Anything else?'

'Drop it, sir. She's eighty-six, damn it, she's an old lady. Let it go.'

Adamsberg pursed his lips.

'She gave birth to a daughter, in Clichy, in 1942,' Danglard continued, following routine. 'Name of Roseline.'

'Click on Roseline Courbet.'

Adamsberg picked up Woolly and stuck it back in its basket. It jumped out again.

'Roseline, maiden name Courbet, married name Heller-Deville, forename Antoine.'

Danglard looked up mutely at Adamsberg.

'Did they have a son? Arnaud?'

'Arnaud Damascus,' Danglard read off the screen.

'It's his granny,' said Adamsberg. 'He calls Granny on the QT from the phone box down the road. What about Granny's parents, Danglard?'

'They died, sir. We're not going to take this all the way back to the Norman Conquest, are we?'

'Names, please.'

A few quick taps on the keys.

'Emile Journot and Célestine Davelle, born in Clichy, Cité Hauptoul.'

'So there they are. The plague-beaters. Damascus's grandma was six years old during the epidemic.'

He picked up Danglard's extension and dialled Vandoosler.

'Marc Vandoosler? Adamsberg here.'

'One moment, *commissaire*, let me switch off the iron.'

'Cité Hauptoul, in Clichy, does that ring a bell?'

'It was the epicentre of the outbreak. A rag pickers' shanty. Is there a special that mentions it?'

'No, we've got an address.'

'The shanty was bulldozed years ago and they built back-to-backs over it. Narrow streets, small houses, for the poor.'

'Thank you, Vandoosler.'

Adamsberg put the receiver down slowly.

'Two *lieutenants*, Danglard. We're getting over there. Fast.'

'You want four men? To pick up an old lady?'

'Four men, Danglard. On the way we'll stop by the magistrate's to get a search warrant.'

'When do we get lunch?'

'On the hoof.'

CHAPTER 34

They made their way over ancient cobbles and down a rubbish-strewn alley to a dilapidated house with a ramshackle clapboard lean-to on one side. Rain plashed on the tiles. It hadn't been much of a summer, and September was no better.

'Fireplace,' said Adamsberg, pointing to the chimney. 'Wood. Apple tree.'

He knocked on the door and it was opened by a tall, fat old lady with a creased and heavy face and her hair done up in a flower-printed head-scarf. Without saying a word she turned her dark eyes on each of the policemen in turn. Then she removed the drooping cigarette from between her lips.

'*Flics*,' she said.

It was not a question but a diagnosis.

'The *flics*,' Adamsberg confirmed as he went inside. 'Clémentine Courbet, I presume?'

'Herself,' answered Clémentine.

The old woman showed them into the lounge and pummelled the cushions before she let them sit on the sofa.

'So they have lasses in the force these days, do they?' she said with a sneer for *Lieutenant* Hélène Froissy. 'Can't say I think much of that. There's too many fellows playing around with guns already, that's what I say. No need for girls to go and play with them. Ain't you got nothing better to do, miss?'

Clémentine's accent seemed to come from long ago, from the days when life was spent toiling in the fields.

She huffed and puffed as she went to the kitchen and brought back a tray of glasses and a plate of girdle cakes.

'The trouble is, people never have enough imagination, that's what I say.' She put the tray on a low table covered with a lace doily, next to the flowery sofa. 'Can I interest you in some Madeira and girdle cakes made with the skin of the milk?'

Adamsberg looked at her with surprise, finding something attractive in that strong, battered face. Kernorkian made it plain that he wouldn't say no to the cakes, since his system had made light work of the sandwich he'd bolted down in the car.

'There's a good boy,' said Clémentine. 'But you can't get the skin of the milk any more. The milk you get these days is just dishwater. So I have to make do with cream. I'm sorry, but I have to.'

Clémentine filled the five glasses, took a sip of Madeira, and looked at the party.

'Now no more of this nonsense,' she said as she lit another cigarette. 'What's this all about?'

'Arnaud Damascus Heller-Deville,' Adamsberg began as he reached out for one of the girdle cakes.

'I beg your pardon, but it's Arnaud Damascus Viguier. He prefers it that way. The name of Heller-Deville is not uttered under this roof. If you can't help yourself, go say it somewhere else.'

'Is he your grandson?'

'Whoa there, pretty face, what you do take me for? A donkey?' said Clémentine, jutting her chin towards Adamsberg. 'If you didn't know that you wouldn't have come here, would you? How do you like my cakes? Tasty? Or not?'

'Tasty,' Adamsberg asserted.

'Very tasty,' Danglard insisted, and quite sincerely too. To tell the truth, he'd not had such delicious girdle cakes in forty years, and the sensation filled him with joy.

The old woman had not sat down all this time.

'Now no more of this nonsense,' she said once more, sizing up the policemen. 'Give me a few minutes to take off my apron, switch off the gas and tell the neighbour, and I'm all yours.'

'Clémentine Courbet,' said Adamsberg, 'I have here a search warrant. We will first search the premises.'

'What's your name, then?'

'Commissaire Principal Jean-Baptiste Adamsberg.'

'Mr Jean-Baptiste Adamsberg, I'm not in the habit of endangering the lives of people who done me no wrong, *flics* included. The rats are in the attic,' she said, pointing to the ceiling. 'Three hundred and twenty-two of them, plus ten cadavers crawling with ravenous fleas, what I don't recommend approaching, or I'll not answer for your life. If you want to poke around up there, you'll have to call in pest control. There's no great mystery. That's where I breed 'em, and the side room is where you'll find Arnaud's machine, what he types his messages on. With the envelopes. Anything else you want to clap eyes on?'

'The book collection.'

'Attic as well. But you have to get past the rats first. Four hundred volumes, quite something, ain't it?'

'All about the plague?'

'What else?'

'Clémentine,' Adamsberg asked gently as he took another cake, 'wouldn't you like to sit down?'

Clémentine lowered her large frame into a flowery armchair and crossed her arms.

'Why are you telling us all this? Why aren't you denying it?'

'What, the plaguey stuff?'

'I mean, the five murders.'

'Murder my arse,' said Clémentine. 'They're the murderers, every one of them.'

'Yes, murderers and torturers,' Adamsberg agreed.

'They can drop dead. The more of 'em drop dead, the more Arnaud comes back to life. They took everything off him, they drove him right to the bottom of the pile. Arnaud's got to come back to life. And he can't do that as long as that dogshit stays on the face of the earth.'

'But dogshit doesn't just wipe itself off the face of the earth, Clémentine.'

'Wouldn't it be wonderful if it did? But dogshit spreads worse than nettles.'

'You had to give it a hand, didn't you, Clémentine?'

'A big hand.'

'Why plague?'

'The Journots are lords of the plague,' Clémentine announced curtly. 'You can't mess with a Journot, and that's that.'

'Or else?'

'Or else the Journots will put the plague on you. They are lords of the great affliction.'

'Clémentine, why are you telling us all this?'

'Instead of what?'

'Instead of keeping you mouth shut.'

'You found me, didn't you? And the lad's inside since yesterday. So no more of this nonsense, I say, let's get on with it and be done. What difference does it make?'

'It makes all the difference in the world.'

'No, it doesn't,' said Clémentine with a steely smile. 'Job's done. You get it, *commissaire*? Done. The enemy is within the walls. The next three will die in the coming week no matter what, whether I stay here or go somewhere else. It's too late now. The job's done. All eight will die.'

'Eight?'

'The six animals, the girl sadist and the man

behind it. By my reckoning that comes to eight. Do you know all about it or don't you?'

'Damascus hasn't said anything.'

'Only to be expected. He couldn't say anything until he was sure the job was over. That's what we'd agreed, in case either of us got nabbed. How did you find him?'

'The diamond was what gave him away.'

'He hides it.'

'I saw it.'

'Aha,' said Clémentine. 'You've got the gen, have you, all the gen about the scourge of God? We never reckoned on that.'

'I tried to learn fast.'

'But not fast enough. The job's done. The enemy is within the walls.'

'You mean the fleas?'

'Dead right. They've already got them in their clothes. They've already caught it.'

'Who are *they*, Clémentine?'

'Go find out for yourself. You think I'll let you save them? It's what was waiting for them, and it's got them. They shouldn't have done down a Journot. They demolished him, *commissaire*, they took him to pieces, him and his girl, the one who jumped out the window, poor kid.'

Adamsberg nodded.

'Clémentine, was it you who persuaded Arnaud to take revenge?'

'We talked about it almost every day when he was in clink. He's his great-grandfather's heir, and he inherited the ring. Arnaud had to raise his head high again, like Emile, during the outbreak.'

'Aren't you scared of prison? For yourself, for Arnaud?'

'Prison?' Clémentine slapped her thigh and guffawed. 'You must be joking, *commissaire*. Hold your horses, Arnaud and me, we ain't killed nobody.'

'So who did, then?'

'The fleas.'

'Releasing infected fleas is like aiming a gun and pulling the trigger.'

'Hold your horses, they didn't have to bite. It's the scourge of God, it falleth where it listeth. If anyone done murder, it's God. You ain't aiming to arrest God, are you?'

Adamsberg took a long look at Clémentine's face, which showed the same calm confidence as her grandson's. He suddenly understood where Damascus's imperturbable tranquillity came from. Both he and his grandmother felt profoundly unguilty of the five murders they'd just committed and of the three they still had in train.

'No more nonsense,' Clémentine said. 'Now I've told you all that, do you want me to stay here or come with you?'

'I'm going to ask you to come with us, Clémentine Courbet,' said Adamsberg as he stood up. 'To make a statement. You are helping us with our inquiries.'

'Suits me down to the ground,' said Clémentine, also rising. 'That way I'll get to see the boy.'

While Clémentine cleared the table, put out the fire and switched off the mains, Kernorkian made it clear to Adamsberg that he was definitely not keen on searching the attic.

'*Brigadier*, the fleas are not infected. Good Lord, where do you think that old lady could have got hold of rats infected with bubonic plague? She's dreaming, Kernorkian, it's all in her head.'

'That's not what she says,' Kernorkian retorted glumly.

'She handles them every day. And she's not got the plague.'

'The Journots have protection, sir.'

'The Journots have got a phantom, and the phantom won't do you any harm, young man. You have my word. He only attacks people who have done a Journot grave harm.'

'A family avenger, like?'

'Exactly. Take a sample of the charcoal too and send it off for analysis, rush job.'

When they got her back to the station the old lady caused quite a stir. She had brought a big tin full of girdle cakes which she waved gaily at Damascus when she stopped in front of his cell. Damascus smiled.

'Nothing to worry about, Arnaud,' she said without even trying to lower her voice. 'Job's done. They've got them all, the whole lot of them.'

Damascus smiled even wider, took the tin that his granny was holding through the bars of his cell door, and went back with it to sit quietly on his bench.

'Set up the cell next to Damascus's for her,' Adamsberg instructed. 'Get a mattress from the locker room and make it all as comfortable as you can. She's eighty-six years old. Clémentine,' he said as he turned back to the old lady, 'no more nonsense now. Do you want to give your statement right away, or are you feeling too tired?'

'Right away,' she said determinedly.

Around six in the evening Adamsberg went out for a walk with his head buzzing with all that Clémentine Courbet née Journot had told him. He'd listened to her for two and a half hours, then he'd put the old lady up against the young man. Their certainty that the last three torturers would be dead very soon didn't waver for an instant throughout the interviews. Not even when Adamsberg proved that the time lag between the release of the fleas and the deaths of the victims was too short, much too short, for the deaths to have been caused by plaguy fleas. *The scourge is ever ready and at the command of God who brings it down and raises it away, as it pleaseth the Lord,* Clémentine kept repeating, quoting word for word the 'special' of 19 September. Nor even when Adamsberg showed them the negative lab test results which proved that the fleas were utterly harmless. Nor even when he showed them photographs of the choke marks on the victims' necks. The faith they had in their insects was utterly unshakeable – and just as steady was their firm belief that three more men would soon die, one in Paris, one in Troyes, and the third in Châtellerault.

He wandered round the streets for more than an hour and came to halt outside the walls of the Santé prison. Up top a prisoner had put his foot out through the bars. There was always someone twiddling his toes through the bars over Boulevard Arago. Not a hand, but a foot. Unshod, bare. Some guy like himself who only wanted to go for a walk outside. He looked up at that foot, and then thought of Clémentine's and then of Damascus's, twirling in the sky. He didn't think they were completely mad, save down that dark passageway where their phantom led them. But the foot went suddenly back inside the prison bars, which reminded Adamsberg forcibly that there was a third member of the team still out there, getting ready to complete the job under way, be it in Paris, in Troyes or in Châtellerault.

CHAPTER 35

Adamsberg cut off towards Montparnasse and made his way to place Edgar-Quinet. There were fifteen minutes to go before Bertin's evening thunder-roll.

He swung through the door of the Viking, wondering if the burly barman was going to lift him up by his shirt front, like he'd done to yesterday's awkward customer. But Bertin didn't budge as Adamsberg sidled under the longboat prow and sat down at his usual table. He didn't budge, but he didn't say hallo either, and went out as soon as Adamsberg had sat down. The *commissaire* was aware that it wouldn't take more than two minutes for everyone in the neighbourhood to know that the *flic* who nabbed Damascus was in the café, and he would soon have a posse on top of him. Maybe that's what he'd come for. It was even possible that the Decambrais crowd would move their dinner to the Viking this evening. He laid his mobile phone on the table and waited.

They came five minutes later. An angry mob, led by Decambrais, with Lizbeth, Castillon, Le Guern, Eva and several others in the tail. Le Guern alone

407

seemed unbothered. Upsetting news had ceased upsetting him long ago.

'Sit down,' Adamsberg ordered, raising his head and facing up to the hostile eyes bearing down on him. 'Where's the girl?' he asked, as he couldn't see Marie-Belle anywhere.

'She's ill,' Eva said flatly. 'She's in bed. Because of you.'

'You sit down as well, Eva,' Adamsberg said.

The young woman had undergone a transformation. Adamsberg saw unimagined depths of hatred in her face, which had lost its old-world look of elegant melancholy. Yesterday she made you feel sorry for her. Tonight she gave you the shivers.

Decambrais broke the silence. 'Let Damascus go, *commissaire*. You're up the garden path, you've put your foot in the compost. Damascus is a gentle soul and a kind heart. He hasn't killed anyone, ever.'

Adamsberg held his counsel and went to the toilets to call Danglard on his mobile. Put two men on Marie-Belle's door, Rue de la Convention. Then he went back to his seat at table, opposite the aged bookworm who returned his stare with haughty pride.

'Give me five minutes, Decambrais,' he said, splaying the fingers of his raised hand. 'I'll tell you a story. And I don't give a damn whether you like it or not, I'll tell it all the same. And when I tell stories, I go at my own speed and I do it in my own words. I've been known to put my deputy to sleep.'

Decambrais jutted his chin and kept his mouth shut.

'In 1918,' Adamsberg began, 'Emile Journot, a rag picker by trade, came back from the Great War in one piece.'

'Fuck that,' Lizbeth said.

'Shut up, Lizbeth, he's telling a story. Give him a break.'

'Four years in the trenches and not a scratch to show for it. In other words, a miracle. In 1915, the rag picker saved his CO's life by going out into no man's land and carrying him back to the trench. Before he was evacuated to the rear, the CO expressed his gratitude by giving Private Journot his ring.'

'*Commissaire*,' Lizbeth butted in, 'we've not come to listen to bedtime stories about the good old days. Don't pull the wool over our eyes. We've come to talk about Damascus.'

Adamsberg looked at Lizbeth. She had gone pale. It was the first time he'd seen a black person go pale. Her complexion had gone grey.

'But Lizbeth, Damascus's story is an old story about bygone days. Let me go on. It turned out Private Journot hadn't been over the top for nothing. The captain's ring had a diamond on it the size of a pea. All through the war Emile Journot kept the ring on his finger, but he caked the diamond with mud and turned it into his palm, so he wouldn't get it stolen. He was demobbed in '18, he went back to his hovel in Clichy, but he didn't

409

sell the ring. In Emile Journot's mind the ring had been his salvation, and so it was sacred. Two years later, plague broke out in the shanty and swept away a whole street. But the Journots – Emile, his wife and their six-year-old daughter Clémentine – weren't affected. People said things under their breath, then came out with accusations. A doctor working in the shanty told Emile that diamonds protect you from the scourge.'

'Is that nonsense true?' Bertin asked from behind the bar.

'It's true in books,' Decambrais said. 'Get on with it, Adamsberg. It's slow going.'

'I warned you. If you want news of Damascus, you'll have to go slow with me right to the end.'

'News is news,' Joss reflected. 'Can be old, can be new, can be fast, can be slow. But news is still news.'

'Thank you, Le Guern. Emile Journot was thereupon accused of being in control of the plague, maybe of spreading it on purpose.'

'We don't give a fuck for your Emile,' said Lizbeth.

'Lizbeth, our Emile is Damascus's great-grandfather,' Adamsberg retorted rather sharply. 'The family could have got lynched, so they scarpered from the Hauptoul shanty under cover of darkness. The little girl rode piggyback as the father strode across the waste tips where plague-infected black rats lay dying. The diamond kept them safe. They took refuge at a cousin's place in Montreuil and didn't go back to Clichy until the whole awful business was over. But now they had standing in the neighbourhood. Before, they were hated and scorned; now they're treated as heroes, as leaders, as the lords of the plague. Their miraculous story gave them status in the rag pickers' world, it became their badge of office. Emile started taking the ring and all the plague stuff completely seriously. When he died, his daughter Clémentine inherited his ring, his status and all his notions about plague. She married and brought up her own daughter, Roseline, to believe in the Journots' special force. And that daughter married Heller-Deville.'

'You're getting further and further away from the point,' Lizbeth muttered.

'I'm getting nearer,' Adamsberg retorted.

'Heller-Deville? You mean the aircraft manufacturer?' Decambrais asked stiffly.

'That's what he became later on. At this point in time he was a lad of twenty-three brimming with ambition, brains and brutality, and he wanted to have the whole world for breakfast. And he's the father of Damascus.'

'Damascus's name is Viguier,' Bertin said.

'No, it's not. Damascus's real name is Heller-Deville. He was brought up by a father who was a bruiser and a mother forever breaking down in tears. Heller-Deville beat his wife around and used his fists on his son; and he left them, more or less completely, when the boy was seven years old.'

411

Adamsberg looked at Eva, who suddenly put her head down to hide her face.

'What about the girl?' asked Lizbeth, who was beginning to get interested.

'They didn't say anything about Marie-Belle. She was born long after Damascus. He ran away to Clichy to stay with his grandma Clémentine whenever he could. She comforted the boy, gave him back his self-confidence, and propped him up with oft-told tales about his glorious Journot side. What with his father's rough handling and then his disappearance, Damascus leaned completely on his famous Journot side, which turned into his sole source of strength. Granny solemnly gave him the diamond ring when he reached the age of ten, the ring that was supposed to give him lordship over the scourge of God. What was at the start just a toy soldier for the boy got deep inside him and grew into a fantastic, but still make-believe tool of vengeance. Over the years, scrabbling through the second-hand bookstalls in the flea markets at Saint-Ouen and Clignancourt, Granny built up an impressive collection of books about the plague – about the 1920 outbreak, her own plague so to speak, and also about all the other epidemics, which fed into and swelled the family legend. It's not hard to see how that happened. Damascus grew up and had no trouble consoling himself on his own with all those ghastly accounts of the Black Death. They didn't scare him; quite the opposite. He'd got the diamond that belonged to Emile the Great, the war hero and the master of the plague. The stories comforted him, they were like a natural way of overcoming the damage done to him in childhood. They were his lifebuoy. Do you all follow?'

'I still can't see the connection,' Bertin said. 'It doesn't prove anything.'

'So Damascus turned eighteen. He was a weakling – a scrawny, lopsided weed. He did physics, probably to compete with his father. But he was also a great reader, as well as being a classicist, a plague expert, and an outstanding and wide-ranging scientist to boot. And he had a phantom in his head. He beavered away at his studies, specialising in aeronautics. At the age of twenty-four he invented a device for manufacturing superlightweight honeycomb steel alloys which makes them a hundred times less likely to fail – I didn't really understand all the details, but that's roughly it. Don't ask me why, but the special steel was something that aircraft companies would have given their eye teeth to lay hands on.'

'You mean to say that Damascus invented something?' Joss exclaimed in amazement. 'At the age of twenty-four?'

'Absolutely. And he wanted a handsome reward for it. But someone decided the boy wouldn't get his reward. He would just take the invention off Damascus, and let the nerd go tell the marines. That someone hired a hit squad, six wild animals who humiliated Damascus, gave him the third degree and raped his girlfriend. Damascus spilled the beans there and then: and at a stroke he lost his dignity, his love and his invention. As well as his chance of glory. A month later his girlfriend threw herself out of an upstairs window. The case of Arnaud Heller-Deville came to trial just short of eight years ago. He was found guilty of defenestrating the young woman, and he copped five years. He didn't get any remission, and wasn't released until just over two years ago.'

'Why didn't Damascus say anything during the trial? Why did he let himself get flung into clink?'

'Because if the police had been able to identify the animals, Damascus would have lost his freedom of action. No price was too high for the chance of avenging himself. At the time he wasn't up to the fight. But five years on it was a different story altogether. The weedy nerd had put on forty pounds of muscle in prison, he'd dropped metallurgy for good, and the only thing he could see in front of him was revenge. Prison is very conducive to seeing things in front of you. In fact, it's just about the only thing you can do when you're inside: see things in front of you. So he came out, with eight people to kill – the six animals, the girl who was with them, and the man behind the deed. Granny Clémentine had spent those five years patiently tracking them down, using information Damascus gave her. Now they were ready. To carry out the murders Damascus obviously had recourse to the family force. What else was there? Five went down this last week, there are three still to go.'

'That cannot be right,' said Decambrais.

'Damascus and his grandmother have admitted everything,' said Adamsberg, looking the old man in the eye. 'Seven years in the planning. The rats, the fleas and the old books are at Granny's place. She still lives at Clichy. So are the ivory envelopes. And the printer. Everything.'

Decambrais shook his head.

'Damascus cannot be a killer,' he repeated. 'Or else I hang up my Even Keel Counsellor's apron for good.'

'Go ahead, I'm starting a collection. Danglard has already eaten his hat. Look, Decambrais, Damascus has confessed. He's confessed to the whole thing. He's told us everything except the names of the last three targets, he just can't wait to see them drop dead.'

'Did he confess to having killed the victims himself? With his own hands?'

'No,' Adamsberg conceded. 'He said the plaguy fleas had killed them.'

'If the story is true, I'll not hold it against him,' said Lizbeth.

'Decambrais, go and see him if you feel like it, and meet his "Narnie" in the next-door cell. He'll confirm everything I've just told you. Go on, Decambrais. Go and hear him in his own words.'

A heavy silence settled over the table. Bertin had forgotten to put out his dinner-call. Suddenly realising it was already eight twenty-five, he slapped his fist against the big brass disc and set off a growling wave of thunder which brought the ghoulish story of Arnaud Damascus Heller-Deville's good old days to a fittingly sombre full stop.

By half past nine the news had been more or less digested, bit by lumpy bit, and Adamsberg was hanging round on the square with Decambrais, who'd calmed down after his meal.

'That's the way it is, Decambrais,' said Adamsberg. 'Can't do anything about it. I don't like it, either.'

'There's something not quite right about it,' said Decambrais.

'That's true. There's something not quite right. The charcoal.'

'Ah, so you knew?'

'It's a *bloody great howler* for an expert on the plague,' Adamsberg said under his breath. 'Nor am I sure, Decambrais, that the three pending targets are going to escape the chop.'

'Damascus and Clémentine have been locked up.'

'Notwithstanding.'

CHAPTER 36

Adamsberg left the square around ten with the feeling he'd missed a link, and he knew which link it was. He would rather have seen Marie-Belle in the crowd.

Family business was what Ferez had called it.

Marie-Belle's absence had made a hole in the mob at the Viking. He had to talk to her. She'd been the only note of discord in the marriage of Damascus and his 'Narnie'. When Adamsberg had uttered the girl's name, Damascus had wanted to say something, but old Clémentine had turned on him furiously and ordered him to forget that 'slag's spawn'. The old woman then muttered something under her breath; he thought he could make out something like 'that blowsy hag at Romorantin'. Damascus looked pretty upset and tried to change the subject, with an intense and plaintive look at Adamsberg that seemed to be saying, please don't bother about my sister. Which was precisely why he was bothering about her.

He got to Rue de la Convention well before eleven. He spotted two of his men slumping in an unmarked squad car not far from the main door. The light was on up top, on the fourth floor. So he could ring Marie-Belle without fear of waking her from her sleep. But Lizbeth had said she was ill. He dallied. Marie-Belle cut his mind in two just as Damascus and Clémentine had, one half softened by their claims of innocence, the other half hardened by his determination to get the plague-monger, however many people he was.

He looked up at the building. A typical late nineteenth-century residential block, quite grand, with a dressed stone façade and caryatids holding up the balconies. The flat had six full windows on to the street. Heller-Deville had made a lot of money, a real pile. Adamsberg wondered why Damascus, if he needed to work at all, hadn't opened a luxury boutique instead of slaving away in the ill-lit, cluttered, ground-floor hole that he called Rolaride.

While he was standing out of the light trying to make up his mind, Adamsberg saw the side door open. Marie-Belle emerged from it on the arm of a quite short man, and accompanied him a little way down the deserted street. She was talking to him, or rather, expostulating, remonstrating. Must be a lover, thought Adamsberg. A lovers' tiff, about Damascus. He tailed them, slowly. He could see them clearly by the light of the street lamps. Two heads of fine blond hair. The man turned round to answer back, giving sight of his face. A quite good-looking lad, though rather blank, no eyebrows, a bit fragile. Marie-Belle gripped his forearm tightly, then kissed him on both cheeks and moved away.

Adamsberg watched her close the door behind her while the young man went off down the street. No, that wasn't her lover. Lovers don't kiss on the cheek, not quickly like that. So it was someone else, maybe a friend. Adamsberg tracked the silhouette until it shrank down the long street, then he crossed over to go up to Marie-Belle's flat. She hadn't been ill. She had had an appointment to keep. With who knows who.

With her brother.

Adamsberg stood stock still with his hand on the side door. Her brother. Your little brother. Same hair, same invisible eyebrows, same thin smile. He was Marie-Belle in poor focus, a fuzzy version of his sister. The younger brother from Romorantin who was so scared of the big city. But up in town all the same. It suddenly flashed into Adamsberg's mind that he'd not picked up a single number in Romorantin, in the department of Loir-et-Cher, on the listing of Damascus's telephone calls from the flat. Whereas Marie-Belle was supposed to call the young man on a regular basis. The boy was supposed to be not too bright, the boy was supposed to want to keep in touch.

But the boy was in Paris. The third descendant of the Journot clan.

Adamsberg sprinted down Rue de la Convention. It was a long street, and he could see Heller-Deville from afar. When he was thirty yards behind the young man, Adamsberg slowed down and maintained his distance, keeping in the shadows. The boy kept looking out at the road, as if he was hoping to hail a cab. Adamsberg took shelter in a doorway to call for a car. He put the phone back in his pocket, then took it out again and looked at it. The gizmo's dead eye told him that Camille wouldn't call. Five years, ten years, maybe for ever. Heigh-ho. Who cares anyway.

He put his thoughts away and carried on tailing Heller-Deville.

It was Heller-Deville Junior, the second man, the man who was going to complete the plague job now that big brother and Granny were in clink. Neither Damascus nor Clémentine doubted for a moment that their baton had been picked up. That was the family saga in all its force. The Journots knew how to work together and mess-ups were out of the question. They were lords not martyrs. And they would wash the damage done to them in the blood of the plague. Marie-Belle had just appointed the youngest of the tribe to the vacant leadership role. Damascus had killed five; he would kill three.

Must avoid losing him, must avoid scaring him. It was hard to keep tailing him because he kept turning round – and so did Adamsberg, because he was afraid that if a taxi did come cruising past, he wouldn't be able to flag it down without raising the alarm. An off-white four-door driving gently with its lights dipped appeared in the distance, and Adamsberg identified it immediately as one of his squad cars. It came up alongside him and Adamsberg signalled discreetly to the driver, without turning his head, to slow down.

Four minutes later Heller-Deville came out on to the roundabout at Félix-Faure, where he flagged down a cab which then drew up beside him. Adamsberg was thirty yards behind him. He jumped into the off-white squad car.

'Follow that cab,' he blurted out as he closed the door without making it clunk.

'I'd already got that,' replied *Lieutenant* Violette Retancourt, the hulking great woman who'd harried him at the first emergency meeting of the team.

Green-eyed Estalère was sitting next to her.

'Retancourt,' said the woman.

'Estalère,' said baby-face.

'Tail him gently, there's no margin for near misses, Retancourt. I want that man like I want a million dollars.'

'Who is he?'

'The second man, a fourth-generation Journot and a lordling of the plague. He's the one who's gearing up to chastise a brute in Troyes, an animal in Châtellerault and Kevin Roubaud in Paris, as soon as we let him out.'

'They're human excrement. I won't shed no tears.'

'*Lieutenant*, we can't sit around playing cards until they get it in the neck,' said Adamsberg.

421

'Why not?' Retancourt riposted.

'No way are those men going to get out from under, believe you me. If I'm not very much mistaken, the Journot–Heller-Deville clan work on a ladder principle, beginning with the least of the crimes, and going up a step in horror with each of their murders. It seems to me they started the series by knocking off one of the less wicked members of the gang, and they're going to finish with the top man and the worst bugger of the whole bunch. Bit by bit, you see, the animals began to twig – Sylvain Marmot fitted extra bolts, Kevin Roubaud came to us – that their former victim had returned to haunt them. The last three know what's in store and they're frightened to death. It makes vengeance doubly sweet. Left here, Retancourt.'

'I saw.'

'Logically, the last in line should be the man behind the extortion. Must be a physicist working in aeronautics, it has to be, otherwise how would he have understood the value of the thing Damascus worked out. There can't be a whole heap of aeronautical engineers in Troyes and Châtellerault. I've put Danglard on to that. I reckon we've got a chance of finding that one.'

'We could just let the man lead us to him.'

'That's a big risk, Retancourt, as dicey as playing chicken. If we've got any other way of doing it, I would prefer to use it.'

'Where's he taking us now? We're going due north.'

'To his place, it'll be a rented room or a hotel. He's been given his orders, and now he'll have a sleep. It'll be all quiet until the sun rises. He's not going to take that cab all the way to Troyes or Châtellerault. All we really need tonight is his address. But he'll be on the road at first light. He has to work fast.'

'What about his sister?'

'We know where she is, and we're keeping an eye on her. Damascus filled her in on all the details so she could pass them on to baby bro if anything went wrong. What they're set on, *lieutenant*, is finishing the job. Nothing else matters to them. Finish the job. Because no Journot has ever been defeated since 1914, and no Journot may be defeated, ever.'

Estalère whistled through his teeth.

'Well, that teaches me one thing for sure. I'm not a Journot, and that's that.'

'Nor am I,' said Adamsberg.

'We're not far off the railway station,' Retancourt said. 'What if he hops on a train tonight?'

'It's too late. And he hasn't even got his bag.'

'He could travel light.'

'What about the black paint, detective? And locksmithing tools? The envelopes for the fleas? The tear gas? The nylon tie? The charcoal? He can't have all that in his back pocket, can he?'

'Do you mean that the younger brother also knows how to pick locks?'

'Definitely. Unless his trick is to entice his

423

victims out of their flats, as was done for Viard and Clerc.'

'That wouldn't be easy if the targets were on their guard,' said Estalère. 'Which they are, according to you, sir.'

'But what about the sister?' Retancourt said again. 'It's much easier for a girl to get a man to come out of doors. Is she pretty?'

'Yes. But I think Marie-Belle's role is to keep in touch and to pass things on. I'm not sure she knows everything. She's very naive and a great chatterbox, and I guess Damascus is careful with her, or else tries to shelter her.'

'So this is all a man's game, like?' Retancourt said rather roughly. 'Superman's game, I should say.'

'That's the point. Brake, *lieutenant*, and switch your lights off.'

The taxi had just dropped the young man on a deserted stretch of Quai de Jemmapes, which runs alongside the Saint-Martin Canal.

'This must be the unbusiest street in the whole city,' Adamsberg muttered.

'He's waiting for the taxi to drive off before he goes home,' Retancourt observed. 'He's a canny little superman. I reckon he didn't even give his full address. He'll walk the last yards.'

'Trail him with the lights off, *lieutenant*' said Adamsberg as he saw the young man starting to walk away. 'Follow him. Stop.'

'Shit, sir. I saw that,' said Retancourt.

Estalère gave his colleague Violette Retancourt

a horrified glance. For heaven's sake, you just could not say 'shit' to a *commissaire principal*.

'Sorry, sir, couldn't help it,' she muttered. 'It's because I saw. I've got very good night vision. The guy's stopped moving. He's waiting by the canal. What's he getting up to? Has he nodded off, or what?'

Adamsberg studied the lie of the land, leaning forward from the rear seat, looking over both his *lieutenants'* shoulders.

'I'm going. I'll get as near as I can, behind that billboard.'

'The one with the coffee-cup poster? And *To Die For*? Doesn't exactly cheer you up, does it?'

'You *do* have night vision, *lieutenant*.'

'When I need it. I can also tell you there's a pile of gravel round the billboard, and you're going to make a noise when you tread on it. Superman's lighting a fag. I think he's expecting a visitor.'

'Or else he's just enjoying the night air and having a think. Get forty yards behind me, at ten o'clock and two o'clock.'

Adamsberg got out of the car without making a sound and made his way towards the slender silhouette beside the canal bank. At minus thirty yards he took off his shoes, tiptoed across the gravel patch and hid right behind *To Die For*. In this almost entirely unlit area you could hardly make out the water. Adamsberg looked up and saw that the three nearest street lamps were broken; the glass had been smashed. Maybe the guy was not really enjoying the night air. He threw his cigarette butt into the canal, then cracked the joints of his fingers by pulling them out, one hand then the other, and all the while keeping an eye on the canalside street to his left. Adamsberg looked in the same direction. A tall, slender, uncertain shadow was moving towards them in the far distance. A man, an old man, looking where he was putting his feet. Journot number four? An uncle? A great-uncle?

The old man came nearer in the dark and then came to a halt. He was hesitating.

'Is that you?' he asked.

By way of reply he got a straight right to the jaw and a savage left to the gut, which brought him down like a pack of cards.

Adamsberg ran across the ground between his hideout and the canalside as the young man tipped the KO over the parapet. He heard Adamsberg running, and in a flash he took to his heels.

'Estalère! Get him!' Adamsberg yelled before taking a running jump into the water where he found the old man floating face down, giving no sign of life. It took Adamsberg only a few strokes to haul him to the embankment where Estalère was waiting to help him up.

'Damn you, Estalère!' Adamsberg bawled. 'Get the guy! You have to get that guy!'

'Retancourt's doing that,' the *lieutenant* explained, as if to say he'd let a whole pack of dogs off the leash.

He gave Adamsberg a hand up, and helped him drag the old man's heavy, slippery body out of the water.

'Mouth-to-mouth,' Adamsberg ordered, and ran off down the canalside street.

He could see the young man's silhouette speeding away in the distance, as swift as a doe. Retancourt's broad shadow came clip-clopping behind, with about as much purchase on him as a panzer trying to down a seagull. But the gap between the broader shadow and the slighter one began to narrow. She seemed to be closing in on her prey. Adamsberg slacked off, quite stupefied by what he could see. Twenty jogs later and he heard a crash, then a thump, then a cry of pain. Nobody was running any more.

'Retancourt?' he called out.

'Take it easy, sir,' came the contralto response. 'I've got him nice and comfortable, like.'

Shortly after Adamsberg came upon *Lieutenant* Retancourt sitting comfortably, as she said, on the runaway's chest, with her considerable weight compressing his entire upper ribcage. The young man could hardly breathe and was twisting this way and that in a futile attempt to get out from under the human bombshell that had fallen on top of him. Retancourt hadn't even bothered to get her pistol out of its holster.

'You're a good runner, *lieutenant*. I wouldn't have bet on you catching him.'

'Because I've got a fat behind?'

'No, not at all,' Adamsberg lied.

'You're wrong. Because it does slow me down.'

'Not so it matters.'

'Let's say, I've got lots of energy,' Retancourt answered. 'I can switch it to whatever's needed.'

'For instance?'

'For instance, right now, I'm concentrating on being heavy.'

'Have you got a torch? Mine's washed out.'

Retancourt handed him her torch lamp and Adamsberg used it to get a view of his arrestee's face. Then he handcuffed him to Retancourt. To a tree trunk, that is.

'Young man, last in the Journot line, this is where the vengeance comes to a stop, here, on Quai de Jemmapes.'

The lad looked up at him with bewilderment and hatred in his eyes.

'You've got the wrong man,' he said with a scowl. 'The old fellow hit out at me, I was just acting in self-defence.'

'I was right behind you. You punched him in the face.'

'Because he had a gun! He said, "Is that you?" and pulled a gun simultaneously! I hit him. I've no idea what the old geezer was after! Please, couldn't you tell your lady officer to get off? I'm suffocating.'

'Sit on his legs, Retancourt.'

Adamsberg searched him, looking for his ID card. He found his wallet in the inside pocket of his jacket, and emptied it on to the ground in the beam of the torch.

'Let me go!' the young man yelled. 'He attacked me!'

'Shut up. I've had just about enough of that.'

'It's a case of mistaken identity! I've never heard of any Journots!'

Adamsberg furrowed his brow as he read the ID by the light of the torch.

'And you're not called Heller-Deville either?' he said in surprise.

'No, I'm not! You can see you've got it wrong. The old fellow was trying to kill me!'

'Get him up, Retancourt,' Adamsberg said. 'Put him in the car.'

Adamsberg stood up in his dripping clothes reeking of dirty canal water, and went over to Estalère with a worried look on his face. The lad was called Antoine Hurfin, born at Vétigny in the department of Loir-et-Cher. Could he be just one of Marie-Belle's friends from down there? Set upon by an old man?

Estalère seemed to have resuscitated the old fellow, whom he'd propped up into a sitting position and was keeping upright by the shoulders.

'Estalère,' Adamsberg asked as he strode up, 'why did you not run when I told you to?'

'I'm sorry, sir, I took a liberty. Retancourt can run three times faster than I can. The guy was already out of my reach, and I thought she was the only chance we had of getting him.'

'Isn't it odd that her parents called her Violette.'

'You know, sir, a baby isn't very big, you can't imagine it developing into an armoured half-track. As well as a nice person.'

'Really?'

'When you get to know her, sir.'

'How is he?'

'He's breathing, but the water had already got into his lungs. He's still in a pretty bad way, he's exhausted, there might be heart trouble. I've called in first aid, was that right, sir?'

Adamsberg knelt down and shone the torch on the face of the man leaning on Estalère.

'Bloody hell. Decambrais.'

Adamsberg cupped his chin and waggled it gently back and forth.

'Decambrais, wake up, it's Adamsberg. Open your eyes, old fellow.'

Decambrais appeared to stir, then to struggle, and then lifted an eyelid.

'It was not Damascus,' he blurted out almost inaudibly. 'The charcoal.'

The ambulance braked to a halt alongside and two men clambered out with a stretcher.

'Where are you taking him?' asked Adamsberg.

'To hospital, Saint-Louis, A & E,' said one of the stretcher-bearers who was lifting the old man on to the canvas.

Adamsberg watched Decambrais being installed on the stretcher and carried off to the waiting ambulance. He got his mobile phone out, and then shook his head.

'Mobile drowned,' he said to Estalère. 'Give me yours.'

It struck Adamsberg that if Camille now wanted to ring him, she wouldn't be able to. Mobile drowned. But who cares anyway, because Camille didn't want to ring. Fine. So don't ring. Be on your way, Camille. Be on your way.

Adamsberg rang the Hotel Decambrais and got Eva on the line, as she was still up.

'Eva, get Lizbeth for me, it's urgent.'

'Lizbeth is on stage,' Eva replied curtly. 'She's singing.'

'Well, give me the cabaret's number, then.'

'You cannot disturb Lizbeth when she's per-forming.'

'That was an order, Eva.'

Adamsberg waited for a moment, wondering if he wasn't turning just a little bit into a *flic*. He appreciated that Eva had a pressing need to punish the whole world, but this really was not the right time.

It took him ten minutes to get Lizbeth on the line.

'I was going to give up, *commissaire*. If you're ringing to tell me you're about to release Damascus, I'll hear you out. Otherwise you're wasting your time.'

'I'm ringing to say Decambrais has been assaulted. He's on his way to A & E at Saint-Louis . . . No,

Lizbeth, I think he'll pull through . . . No, it was a young man . . . I don't know, we'll be asking him that very soon. Look, be so kind as to put his things in a bag, and don't forget he'll want a couple of books, and go down to see him. He's going to need you.'

'It's all your fault. Why did you make him come out there?'

'Out where, Lizbeth?'

'Where you said when you rang him. Haven't you got enough guys in the police already? Decambrais's not in the reserve, you know.'

'But I did not ring him, Lizbeth.'

'It was one of your officers,' Lizbeth declared. 'He was calling for you. I'm not crazy, it was me who took down the message with the meeting place.'

'Quai de Jemmapes?'

'Opposite number 57, at 11.30 p.m.'

Adamsberg nodded his head in the dark.

'Lizbeth, Decambrais must not leave his room, not by an inch, not for any reason whatever, no matter who says he's calling.'

'So it wasn't your call, right?'

'No, it wasn't, Lizbeth. Stay with him. I'll send you a relief officer.'

Adamsberg hung up and then called the squad.

'*Brigadier* Gardon here,' said the voice at the other end.

'Gardon, send a man down to Saint-Louis A & E, to stand guard on the ward where Hervé

Ducouëdic is staying. And another two to relieve the team watching Marie-Belle's flat in Rue de la Convention. No, no change, just keep close watch on the building. When she goes out in the morning, bring her in to me.'

'Remand in custody, sir?'

'No, just to help with inquiries. How's the old lady getting on?'

'She had some kind of a discussion with her grandson, through the bars of his cell. Now she's gone to sleep.'

'What kind of a discussion, Gardon?'

'It was a game, actually, sir. Like charades. We used to call it Chinese portraits. You ask questions like "If he was a colour, what colour would he be?," "If he was an animal, what animal would he be?," "If he was a noise," and so on. You have to guess the person being hidden behind the answers. It's dead hard, sir.'

'Doesn't look like they're worried about the future, does it?'

'No, sir, no change on that. The old lady actually cheered the station up a bit. Heller-Deville is a decent fellow too, he shared his girdle cakes with us. Usually Narnie makes them with the skin of the milk, but seeing as you can't –'

'Don't tell me, Gardon. She uses cream. Have we got the lab results for Clémentine's charcoal?'

'An hour ago. I'm sorry sir, it's no go. Not a trace of apple wood. It's ash, elm and acacia, mixed stuff you can get from any firewood supplier.'

'That's a bugger.'

'I know, sir.'

Adamsberg began to shiver in his sticky wet clothes as he went back to the car. Estalère was at the wheel, Retancourt was in the back hand-cuffed to the prisoner. He leaned through the side window.

'Estalère, was it you who picked up my shoes?' he asked. 'I can't see them anywhere.'

'No, sir, I haven't seen them.'

'Well, I'm not going to fuss about that,' said Adamsberg as he got into the front seat. 'We can't spend all night looking for them.'

Estalère drove off. The young man in the back had stopped protesting, as if the imposing mass of Retancourt had depressed his spirits.

'Drop me off at my place,' said Adamsberg. 'Tell the night roster to start interviewing this Antoine Hurfin Heller-Deville Journot or whatever his name is.'

'Hurfin,' growled the back-seat passenger. 'Antoine Hurfin.'

'Run an ID check, go through his flat, check his alibis, the whole works. I'm going to concentrate on this bloody charcoal.'

'Where, sir?'

'In bed.'

Adamsberg lay down in the dark and closed his eyes. Through his fatigue and the whirl of the day's events, he saw three things outstanding, or standing out. Clémentine's cakes, his drowned mobile and the charcoal. He put the girdle cakes out of his mind, they weren't relevant to the investigation, even if they were the flourish that kept the monger and his forebear in a state of mental calm. His waterlogged mobile kept coming back to him, like flotsam on the rising tide, like a lost hope, like one of those wrecks that Joss Le Guern put into his *Everyman's History of France*.

The good ship *Adamsberg Mobilphone*, long-life battery, under ballast out of Rue Delambre, struck the bank of the Saint-Martin Canal and sank at her mooring. All crew lost. Female passenger, Camille Forestier, unaccounted for.

OK, don't ring, Camille. Off you go. Who cares anyway.

That left the charcoal.

That's where they were at. Almost back at the beginning.

Damascus was a real expert on the plague and he'd made a *bloody great howler*. The two statements were mutually contradictory. Either Damascus knew next to nothing about bubonic plague and he'd been making a widespread and popular mistake by smearing his victims with charcoal. Or else Damascus knew what he was about, in which case he would never have dared make such a blunder. A fellow like Damascus couldn't have done that. Not a guy who had such religious respect for historic documents that he indicated explicitly every omission he made. Damascus didn't have to put in those *points of suspension* that made the town crier's job so much harder. That was the key to it all: those *dot dot dots* set down to blind us and also to signal an unflinching scholarly respect for originals. The respect of a historian of the plague. Who doesn't mess around with the words of an Authority, who doesn't blend them to suit as if they were plain birdfeed. Who honours and respects Authority, who treats it with reverence, like a true believer who would not think of taking the Lord's name in vain. Someone who uses dot dot dots like that wouldn't go and smear bodies with charcoal, he wouldn't commit a bloody great howler. It would be an offence and an insult to the scourge of the Lord in the hands of a worshipper. If you think you're the lord of a cult then you are necessarily a follower. Damascus made use of the Journot force. He was the last man alive who would mock it.

Adamsberg got up and wandered around his two-room flat. Damascus had not fiddled his historical sources. Damascus had put in those points of suspension. Ergo, Damascus had not charcoaled the corpses.

Ergo, Damascus was not the murderer. The charcoal distinctly obscured the strangulation marks. The smearing was the final flourish, after death, and it hadn't been done by Damascus. No charcoaling, no strangling. Nor had he undressed them. Nor had he forced the doors.

Adamsberg stood by his telephone. All that Damascus had done was to carry out what he believed in. He was a lord of the plague, he'd sent in the letters, he'd painted the 4s, he'd released plague fleas. Messages forewarning of a recurrence of a real plague which would relieve the man of his burden. Messages that set off a mass panic, re-inforcing his belief that he had got his lordship back. Messages spreading confusion, leaving him with his hands free to act. The 4s to reduce the amount of damage he thought he was doing and salving the conscience of a phantom killer beset with scruples. A lord doesn't make mistakes about who his victims are. The 4s were necessary to check the insects' appetites, to keep the aim on target, to avoid collateral damage. No way was Damascus going to slaughter a whole block of flats for the sake of killing one of its inhabitants. For a Journot, that kind of clumsiness would have been simply unforgivable.

That's what Damascus had done. He'd believed in what he'd done. He'd unleashed his force on the people who had destroyed him so he could be born again. He'd released harmless fleas under five front doors. Clémentine had 'finished the job' by letting out fleas under the doors of the three remaining thugs. The victimless crimes of the self-mystified plague-monger added up to no more than that.

But someone was doing real murder behind

Damascus's back. Someone who'd donned the cloak of his phantom and was standing in for him, but for real. Somebody with a practical cast of mind who didn't believe a word of the plague story and who didn't know the first thing about the disease. Someone who believed that people who died of bubonic plague turned black. Someone who could make a *bloody great howler*. Someone who was pushing Damascus into the hole he'd dug for himself, driving him inexorably into the pit. The operation looked simple enough. Damascus thought he was dealing out death, and the other man was committing murder on his behalf. The case against Damascus was overwhelming, it slotted together like a Meccano set – what with the rat fleas, the charcoal and everything else in between, the evidence alone would get him sent down for his natural life. Who would have the courage to base a counter-case on a mere handful of dot dot dots? You might as well ask a twig to stop a tidal wave. No juror was going to hang his decision on those points of suspension.

Decambrais had twigged. He'd tripped on the contradiction between the monger's meticulous erudition and the crass mistake of his finishing touch. He'd tripped on the charcoal and he was about to deduce the only possible explanation: *there were two of them*. A monger and a murderer. And Decambrais talked too much down at the Viking, after dinner. The murderer had realised that. He'd seen what his howler was leading to. Only a matter of hours before the old schoolteacher would work it all out in his head and then go blab to the *flics*. It was staring him in the face: the old man had to be made to keep his mouth shut. No time for subtlety. So what was left? A nasty accident, falling in water, one of life's shitty turns.

Hurfin. He must have hated Damascus badly enough to want to bring him down. Who'd got close to Marie-Belle just so as to pump the dim sister for information. His face was weak and lifeless, it made him look easy to push around, but underneath he was fearless and decisive, and could chuck an old man in a lake without a second thought. A quick and brutal killer. But if that's what he was, why hadn't he dealt with Damascus directly in the first place? Why kill five others beforehand?

Adamsberg went over to the window, leaned his forehead on the pane, and looked down on the street in darkness.

What if he got a new mobile but kept the old number?

He went through the pockets of his sopping-wet jacket, got out the gizmo and took it apart to let its inner organs dry out. You never know.

But what if the killer just *could not* kill Damascus? Because he would get lumbered with the crime straight away? The way a penniless husband is automatically fingered if his wealthy wife gets done in? That had to mean that Hurfin was Damascus's husband. The penniless husband of an heiress called Damascus.

Or the heir. To the Heller-Deville millions.

439

Adamsberg called the squad on his land line.

'What's he coughed up?' he asked.

'He's sticking to the old man attacking him and legitimate self-defence. He's a tough bugger. Very tough.'

'Keep on at him. Is that Gardon on the line?'

'*Lieutenant* Mordent, sir.'

'He's our man, Mordent. He strangled the four blokes and the girl.'

'That's not what he's saying, sir.'

'But it's what he did. Has he got an alibi?'

'At home, sir, at Romorantin.'

'Take it to pieces, Mordent. Get right to the bottom of the Romorantin story. Look for the link between Hurfin and Heller-Deville's money pile. Hang on a minute, *lieutenant*. Remind me of his first name.'

'Antoine.'

'Old man Heller-Deville was called Antoine. Wake up Danglard, get him down to Romorantin at the double. He's got to start poking around down there at first light. Danglard knows all there is to know about how families function, especially when they don't. Tell him to find out whether Antoine Hurfin isn't one of Heller-Deville's sons. Illegitimate. Or paternity denied.'

'Why should he do that, sir?'

'Because that's who he is, *lieutenant.*'

When he woke up Adamsberg cast his eye on his gutted mobile phone, all undressed and dry. He used his home phone to ring the twenty-four hour answering service for nuisance callers of all kinds, and asked for a replacement handset on his old washed-out number.

'Can't do that, sir,' a weary female voice replied.

'You can. The electronic bit has dried out. All I have to do is put it into another handset.'

'Sorry, sir, we can't do that. It's not a piece of laundry, it's an electronic chip which cannot be –'

'Enough of this nonsense, miss. I need a new handset with my old number on it.'

'Why don't you want to have a new number?'

'Because I'm expecting an urgent call within the next ten to fifteen years.' Then he added, 'Brigade criminelle'.

'Oh, I see,' said the voice, clearly impressed. 'I'll have it brought over within the next hour.'

He hung up, hoping his phone chip would turn out less soggy than Damascus's ineffectual plot.

CHAPTER 37

Danglard called when Adamsberg was just finishing getting dressed. He'd put on a pair of trousers and a T-shirt that were almost identical to what he'd been wearing the day before. Adamsberg was well on the way to developing a uniform wardrobe that allowed no room for selection or for doubt, so he wouldn't ever have to bother his head about matching or even choosing what to wear. On the other hand he hadn't managed to track down an equivalent pair of shoes in the back of the cupboard. All he'd got were hiking boots, not suitable for clumping around the streets of Paris, so he ended up putting on a pair of leather sandals, which he wore without socks.

'I'm down at Romorantin,' said Danglard, 'and I'm half asleep.'

'You can sleep for a week when you've finished going through the place. We're nearly there, Danglard, we're almost touching the wire. Don't let the Hurfin trail go cold.'

'I've finished with Hurfin. I'm going to have a nap, and then get on the road back to Paris.'

'Later. Have a triple espresso and carry on.'

'I've carried on and I've come to the end of it. All I had to do was interview the mother, she's completely open about the fact that Antoine Hurfin is Heller-Deville's son, eight years younger than Damascus, paternity denied. Heller-Deville has –'

'Lifestyle, Danglard? Rolling in it?'

'No, sir, very modest, down-at-heel. Antoine works at a locksmith's and he has a room over the shop. Heller-Deville has –'

'Perfect. Get in the car, you can tell me the rest when you get here. Did you get anywhere with the scientist thug?'

'He finally popped up on screen late last night. It's Châtellerault. Messelet Fabricators, a huge plant out in the industrial park. World's largest suppliers to the aircraft industry.'

'That's a big fish you've caught, Danglard. Does Messelet actually own the firm?'

'Yes, the owner's called Rodolphe Messelet, he's got degrees in mechanical engineering, a university chair and his own research lab, as well as being CEO and sole proprietor of nine industrial patents.'

'One of them for unshatterable superlight steel?

'Shatterproof, sir. Among others. That patent was granted seven years and seven months ago.'

'That's him, Danglard. He's the one who set up the chamber of horrors and the theft.'

'Of course it is. He's also a provincial bigwig

443

and a famous captain of French industry. Friends in high places, sir.'

'They'll dry their tears.'

'I doubt if the Ministry will back us up, sir. Too much money at stake, not to mention national interest.'

'We don't have to ask permission, Danglard, nor even let Brézillon know ahead of time. Leak it to the media and they'll have the animal buried under his own shit within forty-eight hours. He'll have no option but to drive into a large tree. We'll scrape him off the courthouse floor later on.'

'Perfect,' said Danglard. 'Now, as I was saying, Madame Hurfin –'

'Later, Danglard. Her son's expecting me.'

The night officers had left their report lying in Adamsberg's in-tray. Antoine Hurfin, age twenty-three, place of birth Vétigny, residing at Romorantin, department of Loir-et-Cher, had stuck obstinately to his original story and had phoned a solicitor who'd advised him off the cuff to keep his mouth shut. Since when Antoine Hurfin hadn't said a word.

Adamsberg went and stood at the door of Antoine's cell. The youngster was sitting on the bunk. He was clenching his teeth; dozens of tiny muscles were twitching all over his bony face; and he kept on cracking the joints of his slender fingers.

'Antoine,' Adamsberg said, 'you are the son of Antoine. You are a Heller-Deville without anything

444

to show for it. You've not got the name, you've not got a father, you've not got the dough. But you probably got all the thrashings and misery you could take. You're a rough customer, too. You thumped your big brother Damascus, the lucky boy who got the name. Your half-brother. Who got pushed around as much as you did, in case you weren't aware of it. Same father, same bruiser.'

Hurfin did not respond, save for giving Adamsberg a look revealing vulnerability and profound hatred at the same time.

'Your solicitor told you to keep your mouth shut and you're following his orders. You're obedient and self-controlled, Antoine. That's odd, in a murderer. If I came into your cell, I don't know if you'd knock me over and slit my throat, or curl up in a ball in the corner. Or do both. I don't even know if you're aware of what you've done. You're all action, and I don't know what's on your mind. Whereas Damascus is all mind, and no action. You're both destructive, but you do it with your hands and he does it in his head. Are you listening to me, Antoine?'

The lad shivered but didn't move an inch.

Adamsberg let go of the bars of the door and moved away, feeling as upset by the twitching, tortured face of Antoine as he had been by Damascus's imperturbable blankness. What a wonderful father you must have been, Mr Heller-Deville.

Clémentine and Damascus were at the other end

of the cell block. They'd begun a game of poker, sliding the cards to each other on the floor, through the gap under the bottom bars. Since they didn't have any chips they used girdle cakes for stakes.

'Did you get any sleep, Clémentine?' Adamsberg enquired as he unlocked the door.

'Can't grumble,' the old lady replied. 'Not like my own bed, but a change is as good as a rest, that's what I say. When can we go home, me and the boy?'

'*Lieutenant* Froissy will take you to the wash-room and give you a towel. Where did you get hold of the playing cards?'

'Your *brigadier* Gardon lent them to us. We had a fine time down here last night.'

'Damascus,' Adamsberg said. 'Get ready. It'll be your turn next.'

'My turn for what?'

'To wash.'

Hélène Froissy took the old lady down the corridor and Adamsberg moved on to Kevin Roubaud.

'You're getting out, Roubaud, so get up. You're being transferred.'

'I'm quite OK here,' said Roubaud.

'You'll be back,' said Adamsberg as he opened the cell door wide. 'You're going to be charged with grievous bodily harm and on suspicion of rape.'

'Bloody hell,' said Roubaud, 'I was just the back-up man.'

'But you weren't very backward about coming up front, were you? You were number six on the list. That means you were one of the nastiest in the bunch.'

'Fucking hell, I came in of my own accord, didn't I? Helping the police with inquiries, don't I get something off for that?

'Bugger off. I don't fix sentences.'

Two officers came to take Roubaud away. Adamsberg looked at his memory-jogger. *Acne* plus *jutting* plus *solicitude* equals *Maurel*.

'Maurel, who took over outside Marie-Belle's?' he asked, with an eye on the wall clock.

'Noël and Lamarre, sir.'

'What are they playing at? It's nine thirty.'

'Maybe she doesn't want to go out. She's not opened Rolaride since her brother got nabbed.'

'I'll get over there,' Adamsberg said. 'Since Hurfin won't sing, Marie-Belle will have to tell me what he dragged out of her.'

'You're going just like that, sir?'

'Just like what?'

'I mean, in your sandals, sir. Would you like to borrow some shoes?'

Adamsberg looked down at his toes, poking out through worn leather straps and wondered what was wrong with them.

'What's the problem, Maurel?' He was genuinely puzzled.

'I don't know, sir,' said the *lieutenant*, back-pedalling as fast as he could. 'You're the boss.'

'Ah, I see,' said Adamsberg. 'Not dressed properly? Is that it, Maurel?'

The *lieutenant* didn't dare answer.

'I've not got time to go buy a pair of shoes' said Adamsberg with a shrug. 'And Clémentine is just a tiny bit more important than my appearance, don't you think?'

'Certainly, sir.'

'Make sure she has everything she needs. I'm going to get the sister, and will be back shortly.'

'Do you think she'll say anything?'

'I expect so. Marie-Belle loves telling her life story.'

As he went out the main gate a special delivery man handed him a parcel which he opened in the street. It contained his new handset, which he stuck on a car roof while he looked for the contract note with terms and conditions *after the fact*. The chip was good. They'd managed to transfer the old number to the new phone. Great. He put the gizmo in his inside pocket and walked on, with his hand on his chest as if he was warming the handset through the denim and resuscitating the conversation he'd been having with the phone.

He spotted Noël and Lamarre on duty in the street when he got to Rue de la Convention. The shorter of the two was Noël. *Big ears* plus *crew cut* plus *bomber jacket* make *Noël*. The pikestaff was Lamarre, the fellow from Granville who'd trained as a gendarme. Both men glanced at the *commissaire*'s feet.

'Yes, I know, Lamarre, I'll get a pair later. I'm going up,' he said, nodding towards the fourth floor. 'You can stand down.'

Adamsberg crossed the opulent hallway and went up the red-carpeted staircase. Before he even got to the landing he could make out the envelope tacked to Marie-Belle's front door. He slowed down in dismay and walked up the last few steps to put his hand finally on the white rectangle of paper inscribed with his name: *To Jean-Baptiste Adamsberg*.

Flown the nest. Marie-Belle had slipped out under the noses of his officers of the watch. She'd scarpered. Scarpered without taking care of Damascus. Adamsberg frowned as he looked at the envelope. Damascus's sister had abandoned the theatre at the height of the battle.

The sister of Damascus *and* of Antoine.

Adamsberg slumped down and sat on the top step with the envelope in his lap. The time switch on the stair light ran out. Antoine hadn't dragged info out of Marie-Belle, Marie-Belle had given it to him. To my brother the strangler. To my obedient brother. Murder by order of big sister, Marie-Belle Hurfin. He rang Danglard in the dark.

'I'm in the back of the car,' said Danglard. 'Trying to sleep.'

'Danglard, did Heller-Deville have another illegitimate child, by the Romorantin woman? A daughter, by any chance?'

'That's what I was trying to tell you. Marie-Belle

Hurfin is two years older than Antoine. She's Damascus's half-sister. She'd never met him before she turned up in Paris twelve months ago and tracked him down.'

Adamsberg nodded to himself.

'Is that a nuisance?'

'Yes. I was after the killer's mind. Now I've got it.'

Adamsberg shut the phone, stood up to switch the stair light back on and propped himself against the flat door to open the letter.

Dear *Commissaire*,

This letter is not intended to make your life easier. You thought I was an idiot, and I don't take that lightly. But since I looked like an idiot, naturally I can't hold it against you. I'm writing about Antoine. I want this letter to be read out at his trial, because Antoine is not responsible for his acts. I pulled all the strings from start to finish and I asked him to commit murder. I told him why, who, how, where and when. Antoine has no responsibility, he was obeying the orders I gave him, just like he always did. It's not his fault, he's not to blame for any of it. I want that said at his trial and I trust I can rely on you to do that. I'm rushing because I've not got much time left. You were a bit stupid to call Lizbeth down to the hospital to look after

450

the old codger. Because you'd never know it, but Lizbeth sometimes needs a shoulder to cry on. *My* shoulder. So she rang me straight away to tell me about Decambrais's accident.

So we didn't manage to kill the codger and Antoine got nabbed. It won't take you long to twig who the father was, specially as my mother has never tried to hide the fact, and you'll be round here in two ticks. Two of your blokes are outside already, in the car. The game's up and I'm off. Don't waste your time looking for me. I've got heaps of cash that I siphoned out of that idiot Damascus's bank account, and I wasn't born yesterday. I've got an African robe that Lizbeth lent me for a fancy-dress party, your blokes won't even notice who's inside, so I'm laughing. Give up, OK?

I'll jot down some details so you cotton on properly that Antoine's not responsible for anything. He hates Damascus as much as I do, but he couldn't change a light bulb without the instruction manual. When he was a kid the only thing he ever learned to do, apart from listening to Mother and getting thrashed by Father, was how to throttle chickens and rabbits to vent his anger. Naturally, he hasn't changed. Our father may have been top man in the aeronautical industry, but his main claim to

451

fame is as world-champion heavyweight bastard. You have to get that straight. He spent his time getting girls pregnant and using his fists. He had a son, legal like, and he stuffed his mouth with the whole silver teaset. I mean that nutter Damascus, in case you hadn't noticed. Antoine and me were his dark secret, the skeleton he kept in the country closet, and he always refused to give us legal recognition. It would damage his standing, so he said. But he wasn't so careful when it came to the back of his hand. Me and my brother and my mother got knocked about a fair bit, I can tell you. I didn't give a damn as I'd already decided to kill him one day, but he got there first and blew himself to bits. As for bread, he kept Mummy on war rations, just enough to keep going, because he was afraid what the neighbours might say if they saw us rolling in it. He was a bastard, a beast and a coward, nothing more, nothing less.

When he kicked the bucket, me and Antoine got together and said, don't see why we shouldn't have a slice of the dough, seeing as we weren't even allowed to have the name. We had a right to it, we were his kids, weren't we? Right, but we had to prove it first. Naturally, we knew we couldn't do it with DNA because the bastard had blown himself up over the Atlantic. But we could make a case with Damascus, who was getting the whole pile to himself. Only we reckoned Damascus wouldn't agree to a DNA test because he stood to lose two-thirds of a fortune. Unless he got fond of us, naturally. Or took a fancy to his sister. That's a game I know how to play. Obviously we thought about killing him straight off, but I told Antoine it was out of the question. When we turned up to claim the inheritance, who would become suspects number 1 and 2? Him and me, naturally.

I came up to Paris with a simple plan – to tell him I was his half-sister, to cry poverty, and get taken in. Damascus fell for it in two days flat, hook, line and sinker. He took me to his bosom, then he started weeping, and when he found out he had a brother, you could have washed the floor. The stupid twit would have eaten out of my hand. The DNA plan was going to work like a dream for Antoine and me. Once I'd got my hands on two-thirds of the pile, I was going to drop Damascus Birdbrain like a hot potato. I don't like guys who thump their hairy chests but burst into tears when someone treads on a ladybird. I didn't realise Damascus was barking mad until later on. As he was eating out of my hand and needed someone to lean on, he told me all about his crazy scheme, about his revenge, his plague, his fleas, the whole bang shoot. I knew the stuff inside out, he spent hours going over the details with me. The names of the guys he'd tracked down, where they lived, the whole lot. I never believed his stupid fleas were going to kill anyone. So naturally I changed strategy. Put yourself in my shoes. Why should we settle for two-thirds when we could get the lot? Damascus had the name, and that meant a heap of a lot. We had zilch. The best of it was that Damascus didn't want to touch a penny of his father's loot, he said it was filthy money, that it had ghosts. By the way, I don't think he had a whale of a time as a kid, either.

On with the story. All we had to do was to let Damascus get on with his scheme, and we'd shadow him, doing his murders for him. If we carried through, brother Damascus would go down for life, no remission. After the eight deaths I'd have put the police on to him, just by fluttering me eyelashes, I know how to play that game. Then since he eats out of my hand I'd have got power of attorney for all his loot, I mean, me and Antoine would have got our hands on it in a trice, so we'd have put things back the right way round. Antoine only had to do what I told him and do the killing, the role suited him, because he likes to obey, and he likes to kill. I've not got the right build and it's not to my taste. I gave him a hand to get two of the guys to come out when the police were crawling all over – that was Viard and Clerc – and he throttled them both. That's why I'm telling you it's not Antoine's fault. He did what I told him, he's not up to doing anything else. If I asked him to go fetch a pail of water from Mars, off he'd go, without a murmur. It's not his fault. If you could have him looked after, in some intensive care place, if you see what I mean, that would be fairer, because he's not responsible. What he's got between the ears is just cotton wool.

Damascus saw that people were dying, and he didn't want to know more than that. He was convinced it was the effect of his 'Journot force,' that's all he wanted to know. Poor idiot! I'd have hoodwinked him right through to the end if you hadn't turned up. He'd better get care as well, in something intensive.

As for me, I'm OK. I'm never short of ideas, I've got no cares for the future, so don't worry your head about me. It wouldn't do any harm if Damascus could send some of his filthy money to Mum. But don't forget about Antoine, specially. I'm relying on you. Give Lizbeth a hug from me, and another one for Eva, the poor wreck. And a kiss on

the cheek for you, *commissaire*. You fucked it all up for us, but it was a classy act. With no hard feelings from
    Marie-Belle

Adamsberg folded up the letter and sat down in the dark, resting his mouth on his knuckles, for a good long while.

Back at the station he opened Damascus's cell door and silently beckoned him to follow him into his office. Damascus took a chair, sat down, threw his hair back over his shoulders, and stared at the *commissaire*, patiently and intently. Adamsberg remained silent as he handed Marie-Belle's letter to her half-brother.

'Is it to me?' the young man asked.

'It's to me. Read it.'

It hit Damascus hard. When he'd finished, his head was in his hands, the letter was trailing on the floor and tears were dripping into his lap. There was a lot to swallow at one go: being hated by your brother, being hated by your sister and finding out that the Journot force was just bullshit. Adamsberg stayed seated behind the desk, and carried on waiting in complete silence.

'So the fleas weren't carrying anything at all?' Damascus finally whispered, with his head still facing the floor.

'Nothing at all.'

Damascus fell silent for another while, gripping his knees like a man who'd drunk something ghastly and was trying hard to keep it down. Adamsberg could almost see the real world hitting Damascus – as if a huge, heavy lump had crashed into his skull and burst open the balloon of his imaginary world, spilling its paltry contents all around. He wondered if the man would ever be able to drag himself out of the office after having the sky fall in on his head like that.

'No plague?' he mumbled, barely able to articulate.

'No plague.'

'They didn't die of plague?'

'No. They were throttled by your half-brother, Antoine Hurfin.'

He slumped forward, squeezing his knees even tighter.

'Throttled and smeared,' Adamsberg went on. 'Weren't you at all surprised by the neck wounds and the charcoal?'

'Yes, I was.'

'So?'

'I thought the police had cooked that up to keep the plague under wraps so as to avoid mass panic. You're telling me that's not so?'

'Precisely. Antoine was tailing you, and killed them after you'd left.'

Damascus looked at his hand and stroked his diamond.

'And Marie-Belle was pulling the strings?'

'Yes.'

Another pause. Another collapse.

At this point Danglard came in and Adamsberg

pointed him to the letter lying on the floor at Damascus's feet. Danglard picked it up, read it and nodded solemnly. Adamsberg scribbled a few words on a scrap of paper which he handed to his deputy.

Emergency call to Dr Ferez, for Damascus. Get Interpol on to Marie-Belle. No real chance, she's too smart.

'So Marie-Belle didn't like me?' Damascus whispered.

'No.'

'I thought she loved me.'

'So did I. Everyone did. That's what put us off the scent.'

'Did she love Antoine?'

'Yes. A bit.'

Damascus hunched himself up.

'Why didn't she ask me for the money? I'd have given her the lot.'

'They didn't dream they would get it that way.'

'I don't want to touch it, in any case.'

'But you're going to, Damascus. You're going to hire a top barrister for your half-brother.'

'Yes,' said Damascus, still hugging himself.

'You should look after their mother, too. She's not got anything to live on.'

'Yes. The "blowsy hag from Romorantin". That's what they called her at home. I didn't know what it meant, I'd no idea who she was.'

Damascus looked up suddenly.

'You won't tell her, will you? You won't tell her!'

'Tell who? Their mother?'

'Narnie. You won't tell her that her fleas weren't . . . weren't . . .'

Adamsberg didn't try to help him along. Damascus had to find the words himself, and say them over and over again.

'Weren't . . . carriers?' Damascus managed to say in the end. 'It would kill her.'

'I'm not a killer. Nor are you. Think about it, young man, think hard about that.'

'What are they going to do to me?'

'You didn't kill anybody. All you have to answer for is a score or more of flea bites and a big scare.'

'So?'

'I don't think they'll press charges. You can go home today. Now.'

Damascus shuffled to his feet like a man with backache, keeping his fist clenched on his diamond ring. Adamsberg watched him leave, then shadowed him to see how his first contact with the real world outside would go. But Damascus went off down the corridor to his open cell, got into his bunk and curled up. In his own cell Antoine Hurfin was curled up just the same, but facing the other way. What a wonderful father you must have been, Mr Heller-Deville.

Adamsberg opened Clémentine's cell. She was smoking and playing patience.

'So?' she said with a glance at the *commissaire*.

'You getting anywhere? All that hustle and bustle down the corridor, but nobody tells me what's going on.'

'You can go now, Clémentine. We'll give you a lift back to Clichy.'

'Not a moment too soon.'

Clémentine put her stub out on the floor and put on her cardigan, which she buttoned up with care.

'Those sandals are nice,' she said appreciatively. 'They look well on your plates.'

'Thank you.'

'Hey, *commissaire*, now we've got acquainted, you can tell me, can't you, if the last three of the animals have kicked the bucket or not. What with all these comings and goings I've not kept up with the news.'

'They all died of plague, Clémentine. Kevin Roubaud was the first to cop it.'

Clémentine smiled.

'Then number seven, I've forgotten his name, and lastly Rodolphe Messelet, barely an hour ago. Keeled over like a ninepin.'

'Warms the cockles of me heart, that does.' Clémentine grinned. 'Things do turn out right in the end. Only thing is, it can take a long time.'

'Clémentine, remind me of the name of number seven, it's plain slipped my mind.'

'It ain't likely to slip mine in a month of Sundays. Henri Tomé, he lives in Rue de Grenelle. The worst scoundrel on God's earth.'

'That's it, thanks.'

'What about the boy?'

'He's gone back to sleep.'

'Of course he has, he's bound to be tired what with all of you harassing him. Tell him he's expected for Sunday lunch, as usual.'

'He'll be there.'

'Well, *commissaire*, I reckon we've said all there is to say.' The old lady gave him her sturdy hand to shake. 'I'll write a note for your Gardon to thank him for the playing cards, and a word for the other man, the tall, podgy fellow who's losing his hair, the sharp dresser.'

'Danglard?'

'Yes, he's a man of good taste, he'd like to have my girdle cake recipe. He didn't actually say as much, but I knew what he meant. Looked like it mattered quite a lot to him.'

'That could be so.'

'He knows what the good things in life are,' Clémentine said with a knowing nod of her head. ''Scuse me, I'll go out first.'

Adamsberg took Clémentine Courbet back to the main door and gave a wave to Ferez who was on his way in.

'Is that him?' asked Ferez, pointing to the cell where Hurfin lay doubled up.

'He's the murderer. Big family business, Ferez. He'll probably spend the rest of his days in a lunatic asylum.'

'We don't call them "lunatic" any more, Adamsberg.'

Adamsberg gestured to Damascus.

'But that one must be let out, and he's not up to it. It really would be a good turn, Ferez, a good turn indeed, if you could give him some help and keep an eye on him. Return to real world. A huge jump for him, from the tenth floor, very painful.'

'He's the fellow with the phantom?'

'The very one.'

While Ferez tried to get Damascus to unwind, Adamsberg sent two officers off to find Henri Tomé and he set the press on to Rodolphe Messelet. Then he called Decambrais, who was going to be discharged that afternoon, as well as Lizbeth and Bertin, to alert them to the need to give Damascus a gentle let-down. He ended up with a call to Masséna and one to Vandoosler, whom he told about the outcome of the great howler.

'I can't hear you properly, Vandoosler.'

'Lucien's emptying the shopping trolley on to the refectory table. Makes a hell of a racket.'

On the other hand Adamsberg could hear Lucien's loud voice declaiming in the fine acoustics of the dining room:

'Among all the fruits of the earth we often fail to recognise the amazing potential of the vegetable marrow.'

He hung up thinking that Lucien's point would make a good item in the town crier's newscast. A clear and healthy message, with a good rhythm and no baggage, a million miles from those sinister but now fading echoes of the plague. He put his

462

mobile back on the desk, in the middle, and looked at it for a minute. Danglard came in bearing a manila file and followed his *commissaire*'s eyes. He too stared at the small plastic object.

'Anything wrong with your handset, sir?'

'Nothing wrong,' Adamsberg said. 'It hasn't rung.'

Danglard put the file labelled 'Romorantin' in the in-tray and went out without another word. Adamsberg put the file in front of him, lay down on it with his head in the crook of his arm and dropped off.

CHAPTER 38

At seven thirty in the evening Adamsberg set an unhurried foot on Place Edgar-Quinet, feeling less weighed down than he'd felt for two long weeks. Lighter and also emptier. He entered Hotel Decambrais and went up to the door of the cubbyhole with its sign saying 'Even Keel Counselling'. Decambrais, still pale but sitting up much straighter now, was at his job, lending his ear to a fat red-faced fellow in a stew.

'Well, well,' the old man said as he looked first at Adamsberg and then at his footwear. 'A messenger from the gods. Hermes, I presume? Bearing tidings of what?'

'Tidings of peace and goodwill, Decambrais.'

'Give me a few moments, *commissaire*. I have a client with me.'

Adamsberg drifted down the corridor where snippets of the counselling session reached his ears.

'It's bust for good, it really is,' the fat fellow was saying.

'You've patched it up before,' Decambrais replied.

'Bust.'

Ten minutes later Decambrais showed Adamsberg in and sat him down in an armchair still warm from the previous occupant.

'What was that about? A piece of furniture? A limb?'

'An affair. Twenty-seven break-ups and twenty-six patchings-up with the same woman, it's a record, at least among my clients. We call him Break-and-Mend.'

'And what advice do you give him?'

'None at all. I try to understand what people want and to help them to do it. That's what counselling is, *commissaire*. If a client wants to break up, I help him to break up. If he comes back in the morning wanting to start over, I help him start over. And you, *commissaire*, what is your problem?'

'I don't know. And if I did, who cares anyway.'

'In that case I can't help you.'

'No. Nobody can. That's how it's always been.'

A smile flickered on the old man's face as he leaned back in his chair.

'Was I wrong about Damascus?'

'No. You're a good counsellor.'

'He could not kill *for real*, that's what I knew for sure. Because he did not want it *for real*.'

'Have you seen him?'

'He went into Rolaride about an hour ago. But he hasn't pulled up the shutters.'

'Did he listen to the town crier?'

'He missed the newscast, *commissaire*. The late final is at six ten on weekdays.'

465

'Sorry. I'm not too hot on times and dates.'

'That's nothing to worry about.'

'Sometimes it is. I've fixed Damascus up with a doctor.'

'You did well. He's taken a great fall off a cloud and down to earth. That can't be much fun. Up there, things don't break. That's why he lived there.'

'Lizbeth?'

'She went in to see him as soon as he got back.'

'Ah.'

'Eva's going to find this hard.'

'Naturally,' said Adamsberg.

An angel passed. Adamsberg moved around in the armchair so as to face the old man straight on.

'You see, Ducouëdic, Damascus did five years' prison for a crime that never happened. Today he's been released for crimes he only thought he committed. Marie-Belle is on the run for carnage that she ordered. Antoine will be sentenced for murders he didn't choose.'

'Guilt versus the appearance of guilt,' Decambrais muttered. 'Does the issue interest you?'

'Yes.' Adamsberg's eyes met Decambrais's. 'It's the only issue.'

Decambrais held Adamsberg's stare for a few minutes, and then nodded his head.

'I did not lay a finger on that girl, Adamsberg. The three schoolboys were on top of her in the lavatory. I lashed out with all I had, picked her up and got out. It was evidence from witnesses who saw me rush out that got me cornered.'

Adamsberg batted his eyelids by way of agreement.

'Is that what you thought at the time?' asked Decambrais.

'Yes.'

'Well, you'd make a good counsellor too, then. I'd already become virtually impotent. Did you think that too at the time?'

'No.'

'And now, I don't mind at all,' Decambrais said as he crossed his arms on his chest. 'Almost not at all.'

At that moment the Norseman's thunder rolled out across the square.

'*Calva,*' said Decambrais with his little finger in the air. 'Hot dish. Not to be sniffed at.'

At the Viking Bertin was serving a free round in honour of Damascus, who was leaning his weary head on Lizbeth's shoulder. Le Guern got up and came over to shake Adamsberg's hand.

'The breach has been mended,' Joss opined. "Specials' have stopped. Ads for fresh veg have taken over.'

'Among all the fruits of the earth,' Adamsberg said, 'we often fail to recognise the amazing potential of the vegetable marrow.'

'True enough,' Joss said pensively. 'I've seen marrows grow from nothing to the size of rugby balls in two nights.'

467

Adamsberg slipped into the group as it was starting to tuck in. Lizbeth pulled up a chair for him and gave him a smile. He was overcome with the desire to hug her, but her bosom was already occupied by Damascus.

'He'll fall asleep in my arms,' she said, pointing to the young man.

'That's only to be expected, Lizbeth. He'll sleep for ages.'

With a ceremonial flourish Bertin brought an extra plate and put it in front of the *commissaire*. Not to be sniffed at.

Danglard swung through The Viking's door as they were all having dessert. He leaned on the bar, put Woolly down at his feet, and beckoned discreetly to Adamsberg.

'I can't stay long. The kids are expecting me home.'

'Did it all go OK with Hurfin?' Adamsberg asked.

'No. Ferez went to see him. Gave him a tranquilliser. He took it and is now resting.'

'Fine. The sum total is, everyone's going to get some shut-eye tonight.'

Danglard ordered a glass of wine from Bertin.

'Aren't you going to get some sleep too?' he asked.

'I don't know. Maybe I'll go for a walk.'

Danglard downed half his glass and looked at Woolly, who'd perched on his shoe.

'She's getting bigger, isn't she?' Adamsberg said.

'Yes.'

Danglard finished his glass and quietly put it back down on the bar.

'Lisbon,' he said as he slid a scrap of paper along the counter. 'Hotel São Jorge. Room 302.'

'Marie-Belle?'

'Camille.'

Adamsberg felt his body tense up as if he'd been shoved in the back. He crossed his arms tightly and leaned on to the counter.

'How do you know that, Danglard?'

'I put a tail on her,' he said as he leaned down to snatch up the kitten, or else to hide his eyes. 'Right from the start. Like a rotter. She must never know.'

'A police tail?'

'It was Villeneuve, he's retired, used to be attached to the fifth arrondissement.'

Adamsberg stood stock still with his eyes on the scrap.

'There'll be other collisions,' he said.

'I know.'

'And anyway . . .'

'I know. Anyway.'

Adamsberg carried on staring at the address, then put out his hand and clenched the scrap of paper in his fist.

'Thank you, Danglard.'

Danglard settled the kitten under his arm and left the Viking with a wave of his hand, from behind.

'He works with you, does he?' asked Bertin.

'A messenger. From the gods.'

When it was pitch dark on the square Adamsberg propped himself up against his leaning tree, opened his notebook and tore out a page. He thought, then wrote down *Camille*. He paused for a moment and then wrote down *I*.

You can begin a sentence like that, he thought. Not a bad way to begin.

Ten minutes later, seeing as the rest of the sentence just would not come, he put a full stop after *I* and folded the sheet around a five-franc coin.

Then he slowly went over and dropped his wish into the blue urn that belonged to Joss Le Guern.